And Then There Were Four

Celestial Series Book One

Lillith Carrie

Lillith Carrie Publishing

To the people who believed that I could accomplish my dream of being an author. Thank you.
But a huge thank you to my amazing editor, Aimee.
If it wasn't for you putting up with all of my crazy ideas, none of this would be possible.

Love always,
Lillith Carrie

Departing the Past

It had been ten years since I made my way back to Idaho.

My parents separated when I was five, and my mom tried so hard to stay around so I was close to my father growing up—but it didn't work. After five years of being too close to my father, my mom upped and moved us clear across the states to Savannah, Georgia.

My mother, having been a southern belle all her life, loved the sweetness of Georgia and everything it had to offer. In fact, the only reason she was with my father was because they had met in college, and before graduation, she got pregnant with me.

That was why he married her—or kept her around, at least.

Mom doesn't talk about it often, and even though I get the occasional birthday gift or deposit of money in my account; I don't hear from him. He always kept me at arm's length, which broke my heart at first, but eventually I grew to accept it.

After some time, he got married to my step-mother, who had four strapping godsons and a hatred for me I would never understand. The one and only time my father came to see me was at my high school graduation, and he brought her. We will just say that she was a Stepford wife in the making, and if looks could kill–I'd be dead.

"Ivy! If you don't come on, you're going to miss your plane!" Mother hollered from downstairs, causing me to sigh.

I had finished my first two years of my adult life at the local community college until I was able to get the prerequisites done for the university I wanted. However, out of the five that I applied for, my least favorite was the only one to accept me.

And that one just happened to be located in Idaho–where my father was.

I knew the university had been the best for a degree in Agriculture, but I didn't want to be close to my dad. Part of me was still hurt that he had chosen my step-mother and her godsons over me.

I am his daughter–his blood.

Yet, it didn't seem to be enough.

Grabbing my suitcases, I pulled them toward the door as I slung my backpack over my shoulder, giving my room one last look around. It was bittersweet leaving, but if I was ever going to accomplish my dreams, I had to take some risks.

Heading downstairs, my eyes landed upon my mother, who stood by the doorway smiling at me. I knew that there was a lot I could say to help change my mind about going, but this was important to her.

My mother would never admit to me she was sick, but after much snooping, I had found the truth–stage two cervical cancer.

Treatments were supposed to start soon, and as much as I wanted to confront her and tell her that I knew and I was staying, I knew she wouldn't be pleased. I didn't want to stress her out more than she already was.

She wanted me to follow my dreams–and that meant without me worrying about her.

"It's going to be okay, Ivy," my mother said as she drove toward the airport, "I spoke to your father, and he is going to meet you as soon as you get off the plane."

"That's good, I guess," I replied, staring out the window, unsure of whether or not I really wanted him to be there. To be honest, I would be surprised if he showed up.

Many times, he offered for me to fly out there to see him. Even told me about the magnitude of personal drivers the company had that could take me anywhere I wanted to go. As if that was going to persuade someone like me.

"It isn't going to be that bad, Ivy. I don't know why you feel so negative about the situation. You barely know your father and his family. It will be good for you to go. Trust me." My mother was adamant about me going, and I wasn't sure why.

"My birthday is in a few months, and I won't be able to spend it with you."

"Is that really what you are worried about?" My mother asked as she turned to look at me when she parked the car.

No, it wasn't all I worried about. I worried about her being alone through all of what was going on with her. I worried about something terrible happening and me not being here to take care of her. Most of all, I worried about losing my mother and never getting to say goodbye.

I couldn't help but sigh, "I don't know. I just have a feeling I am making the wrong choice."

"Well, you're not." My mother's tone took me a little by surprise. "You have to do this."

There was no point in arguing with her. She was right, to an extent. I need to stop fighting myself about going to see my father. Spending time with him wouldn't be a bad thing. At least then I could have a reason to hate him if he messed up.

My father was mysterious. He came from nothing and ended up one of the wealthiest people in the country, owning big corporations on the west coast of the states that few knew how he obtained.

Other than that small fact, though, I knew nothing about the man.

As I walked into the airport with my mom, I couldn't help but have a sense of dread wash over me. Something about all of this just didn't feel right, and the more I looked at my mom, I didn't want to go. Tears sprang to my eyes as I thought of leaving her.

"I am going to miss you," I told her softly, causing her to cry as well.

"Aww, baby." She mumbled, wrapping her arms around me. "I am going to miss you as well, but you know what... this is an adventure you will love. I just know it."

Saying goodbye was harder than I thought it was going to be.

As I moved down the terminal and climbed onto the plane, I let my tears fall, and a sense of numbness washed over me. I couldn't show my weakness because if I let it out, then I was more than likely going to run off the plane and refuse to go.

Settling into my seat, I couldn't help but think how much my life had changed. I would no longer have the security of my mother's home and the safety of the town I had grown up in. Instead, I was going to be in a home that I was never welcome in and in a town that was the farthest thing from home I could get.

I was trading warm weather and sunshine for icy breezes and snow.

Groaning to myself, I watched as a bubbly blonde-haired girl strolled to my section, looking at the seat numbers.

"Oh, this is me!" she said excitedly, causing me to groan inwardly. Great, I don't even get to sit by myself.

As she settled in, I raised my brow, watching her maneuver all of her items into her small space. Her long blonde hair was swept into a high ponytail, and her makeup was perfectly on point. She must have been the barbie doll type... a contrast from my dark hair and occasional glasses.

"Hi, there!" she said, her heavy southern accent flowing from her lips as a small twinkle marked the corner of her eye. "Looks like we get to fly together. Where ya headed?"

As she stared at me, I contemplated my choices. One, I could be rude and completely ignore her or two, I could find chatting with her better to preoccupy my mind and pass the time.

Oh, the choices...

"I am headed to Idaho... school." My choice wasn't that hard after all. She looked at me, and her eyes widened.

"Oh my God! Me too!" The joyous expression on her face made my eyes widen.

This girl is also way too excited this early in the morning.

"That's cool. What are you going to school for?" I was curious about her response because there wasn't much you attended the University of Idaho for.

"Oh, agricultural studies. I want to help the planet and all... not really narrowed down to a specific area yet." Her response was interesting, and I knew how she felt. I couldn't pinpoint my specific area either.

"That's cool. I am doing the same."

"Oh, wow!" She squealed. "Maybe we will end up being roommates, too." She chuckled, and I sighed softly, thinking about how I would rather that than stay at my father's home.

"Unfortunately, I wish that were the case... but I am staying at my dad's house. No point in dorms when I can live with him for free, ya know?"

She nodded her head, smiling at me, and I couldn't help but feel at ease around her. She was a pleasant contrast to the bundle of nerves and irritation I had been before.

"Well, regardless, it's going to be a wonderful year. By the way, my name is Kate." Holding her hand out to me, I hesitated before taking it.

"Ivy," I replied flatly before the corner of my lip turned up into a small smile.

I had expected to come to this school and not make any friends at all, and yet here I was, making friends with a girl I would never have considered being friends with before we even left the tarmac.

I was more laid back and closed off. An introvert, if you will, and that was the complete opposite of Kate. She was the girl I would have had issues with through high school. The cheerleader type that cared about how she looked and the social status that surrounded her.

Although, in this case, looks were deceiving. She wasn't that kind of person at all, and for that, I was grateful.

Time passed by quickly as we sat talking, and eventually, the plane made its descent to the ground, stopping at Fountains airport. It was near the school, but my father's home was still 45 minutes away from there. At least it would give me time to catch up with my dad and get through all the uncomfortable silence before meeting the rest of the demons from hell.

"So, who's picking you up again?" Kate asked as we waited for our luggage to arrive. My eyes searched for my father, but not seeing him anywhere.

"My dad supposedly... he must not be here yet," I mumbled before a sigh escaped me.

"Oh my God..." Kate groaned, letting a small sigh escape her, "don't look now, but there are two totally sexy men standing over there to your right."

My brows furrowed in confusion as I followed her line of sight toward the men she was talking about. They seemed to argue with each other, but one of them had a sign with my name on it in their hand, and as I read it, I realized who they were.

"Are you fucking kidding me..." I grumbled, causing Kate to look at me in question.

"What's wrong?"

"Those two are part of the four brothers. Guess my dad didn't have time to come get me after all." If the day couldn't get worse... it just did. "Where is my dad?" I asked firmly as I approached them both, dragging my suitcases behind me. Their dark eyes looking down on me took me by surprise, and I couldn't help but notice how well they looked from the photos I remembered.

They had definitely been working out.

"Ivy?" The taller one with tattoos on his left arm that appeared below his sleeve questioned. His black hair was messy on his head as if he had just gotten out of the shower and couldn't be asked to do anything with himself.

"Yeah. That's me." I retorted, pulling myself from the gaze I was in. He was attractive, I will admit that, but I couldn't let myself get distracted. Even if the current look he was giving me screamed sexual frustration. "My dad?"

The man rolled his eyes, ignoring me, and quickly grabbed my suitcase, dragging it behind him toward the doors. "Sorry, Ivy..." the other said with an apologetic smile. "Damian doesn't say much to anyone. I'm James, by the way."

"Ivy!" Kate squealed from behind me, causing me to glance over my shoulder just in time to see her walking toward where I stood. "I told you I knew the bag was somewhere." She sighed, rolling her eyes. "I'm glad I caught you before I got my cab. I just wanted to say thank you for keeping me company on the plane."

"Oh. It's fine. I enjoyed it." The idea she was taking a cab didn't sit well in my chest. She was a nice girl and had treated me fairly while venturing here. "Look, don't take a cab. I'm sure we can drop you off on campus. Isn't that right, James?"

The look I gave him as I said his name had him speechless. It took him a moment to grasp what was going on, and then he smiled. "Oh yeah, of course. The campus is only, like, ten minutes away. It's no problem at all."

"Awww, well, thank you so much, sugar!" Kate squealed as she threw her arms around me, causing me to stiffen uncomfortably in the hug.

Pulling back, she looked at me, slightly confused. "Not a hugger?"

"Not really," I replied with a chuckle, "but it's okay. Don't worry about it." My eyes shot to James, and a smirk played upon his mouth as if he found my reaction amusing.

"Here, I will take those from you, and we will get on our way," James replied to Kate as his eyes gazed over my body one last time.

Following James outside, the last thing I expected was for Damian to throw a fit about us dropping Kate off. But after my unwavering decision on the matter, he gritted his teeth and agreed. "Get in the fucking car."

His reply irritated me, but Kate and I didn't wait for him to ask us again. As soon as we were loaded up, the car moved toward the campus where we would both be taking classes for the next four years.

The trees and brush passed by on the sides of the road, flying as if they had nothing in the world that could stop them. One thing I had been excited about coming to Idaho was all the nature that would surround me. I had the urge to get lost within it and explore things people never considered seeing.

Growing up, mom and I were considered free spirits and tended to beat to the sound of our own drum. And just because she wasn't with me right now didn't mean I was going to stop. My particular ancestry would be heartbroken if I stopped doing what I was doing just because I moved across the country.

Eventually, turning off the main highway, we moved toward a more symmetrical designed street that held loads of vegetation and historical buildings.

"This is amazing!" Kate whispered, looking out the window.

"Welcome to the University of Idaho." James chuckled, causing Damian to scoff in annoyance.

As soon as we pulled up toward an area that looked like apartments, Damian came to a quick stop, slamming on his brakes, jolting me forward.

"Ouch," I replied in irritation as he turned and looked at me.

"Pay attention next time, then," Damian snapped before jumping out of the vehicle and making his way toward the back, where James was helping Kate pull out her luggage. Groaning in irritation, I hopped out and walked toward Kate. "Do you have it from here?"

"Oh, definitely. Thank you again for the ride," she called out as she waved, "I will see you Monday."

"Sounds great. I will see you at orientation," I called back before Damian yelled to James to hurry and get in the damn vehicle.

I had not even been here that long, and Damian was already proving to be the biggest asshole I had ever met. That would be my luck, though.

"Do you have to be so rude?" I asked as we pulled back out onto the highway, headed toward my dad's home. I wasn't going to allow him to act like this toward me or anyone I associated with. It wasn't needed nor welcome.

I watched as he looked at me from the rearview mirror, his eyes darkening as he glared. Most girls probably would have looked away and shrunk back from him, but me... I would never.

Raising my eyebrow in question, I lifted my hand and gave him the middle finger, causing him to smirk. "You have a lot of fire in you for someone who knows nothing about this place."

A scoff escaped me as I rolled my eyes. "They are all the same in the end. One pathetic excuse of a home after another."

James laughed, shaking his head. "I like her attitude."

"No one fucking asked you," Damian growled, catching me by surprise. His eyes went to mine again as if realizing what he did. "Don't get comfortable here."

Rolling my eyes, I replied. "I wouldn't dream of it. I'm simply passing through."

James seemed welcoming, but Damian definitely wasn't. It made me curious to know what the other two were like.

Were they going to be just as warm and welcoming as the welcome committee that met me at the airport or would they try to devour me like little red riding hood?

After forty minutes of tension and awkward silence, the vehicle finally pulled into a driveway guarded by tall, large, black iron gates. It was clear to see past the gates the land comprised miles and miles of trees until a clearing approached in the distance. It was mesmerizing and definitely more than I had expected.

Multiple houses sat scattered over miles of landscape, while the one Damian was heading for was tall and elegant against the bright blue sky. "This is the house?"

James looked over from the passenger seat and smiled at me, "yeah, haven't you seen it?"

"No." I sighed, "my father was never forthcoming, and he never cared for me, anyway."

James' brows furrowed in confusion at my statement, "huh?"

As Damian parked the car, he didn't bother to wait for me or help, for that matter. He simply climbed out, slammed the door, and ran inside to get as far from me as he could. At least James stayed and waited. He seemed like the only brother who would end up being genuinely nice.

Lucky me... this move was already turning out to be full of surprises. All unwelcome, of course.

Slowly opening the door, I closed it and moved toward the back, where James pulled out my luggage from the hatch. "Thanks."

"For what?" He laughed, slamming the hatch. "All I did was make sure you didn't scratch the truck."

"Wait?! You're not going to help me?" I called out as I watched him turn and walk toward the house. He didn't bother to look over his shoulder at me. Instead, he simply waved and laughed.

"Your dad said to get you to the house alive. He never said once I got here, I had to continue helping you, but I'm sure you'll figure it out."

So much for being nice. He was just as much of an asshole as Damian was.

Groaning, I slung my backpack over my shoulder and snatched the handles on my two large suitcases, attempting to pull them across the graveled driveway. It wasn't going to be easy getting them inside, considering how heavy they were, but I would find a way.

Eventually stepping through the front door, out of breath and irritated, I came face to face with my stepmother. Her brown eyes narrowed at me as she plastered a fake smile onto her face. "Ivy. I was wondering what was taking you so long. We don't waste time in this house. We are all adults here now, and need to remember punctuality is important."

"Sure thing, Alice," I said flatly, watching as she glared at me harder.

"It's Allison." Her gritted tone switched from pleasant to angry faster than a hellcat could shift gears.

Which was amusing, considering how hard she tried to remain proper and elegant at all times.

"Right. Where am I staying?" I asked as I looked around the massive two-story home, curious to think how I would get my bags upstairs.

"Oh, you're not in the main house, Ivy. We made the cottage at the back of the property ready for you. We figured you would like your own space." Allison seemed more than pleased with the notion of keeping me as far from her and my father as possible.

"Sounds perfect... care to point the way?" The fact that her words didn't affect me seemed to irritate her, but instead of arguing with me, she simply turned, and I followed. As we reached the back door, she opened it and pointed to a small brown and white cottage at the far end of the massive property.

It sat delicately next to the wood line, and something about its location made it seem almost magical.

"I know it isn't much, but it's the best we could do on short notice." She sighed, faking her distress over my placement in her home.

She was a joke, and knowing that she was already playing this game made my move here even more entertaining.

Laughing to myself, I shook my head and turned to her with a raised brow. "I'm sure, considering you had four months to plan, and I know there are at least three extra bedrooms upstairs. Not to worry though, I actually love the cottage. It will allow me to stay far away from you and whatever fake company you keep around."

Ignoring Allison further, I let my feet guide me toward the home. My bags no longer felt heavy, and the irritation from my welcome committee quickly left me.

I wasn't sure what about this place seemed like home, but I was pleased that I was going to live my own life here.

Close to nature and far from drama—or so I hoped.

Welcome Home

Pulling my suitcase into the cottage, I looked around at the setup that had been made ready for me. It wasn't as bad as I had imagined it was going to be. In fact, the rustic, cozy feel of the home made me feel like I had walked into something out of a fairytale book.

Small fairy lights and greenery swept the walls, accenting the white drapery that lined the windows and cascaded down upon the floor. The cottage had a small living room with a kitchenette and a bedroom with a bathroom off to the side. With everything here, I wouldn't need to go up to the main house for much.

Which honestly... I preferred.

"Hmm... not bad." I mumbled to myself as I drug my bags into the bedroom quickly laying them upon the bed. If the worse of what I would receive were the conversations that I just had with Allison, and the guys, then this move wouldn't be so bad. That is, just until I began to unpack, and my phone chimed with notifications, causing me to groan.

I had only just arrived at this place, and already I was being blown up.

Pulling my phone from my pocket, I saw my father's text messages and sighed. *'Come inside. I would like to talk to you.'*

Of course he wants to see me now. Yet, he couldn't come to the airport to pick me up?

Fucking, typical.

Sliding back on my flats, I made my trek back up to the main house and entered through the back door. I had no idea where I was supposed to meet him in the big house, but Allison greeted me in the kitchen to ensure I got to where I needed to be.

"There you are. Took you long enough." She sighed, rolling her eyes. "Hurry up, he doesn't have all day."

I could already tell from the way she acted she wasn't going to make staying here easy. Thankfully, I wasn't the same girl I was when I was younger. I didn't let people push me around anymore, and if she thought she could act however she wanted toward me, she would find herself mistaken.

Following behind her, she moved through the house with haste until she came to a large, white wooden door. "Remember, always knock before you enter." She remarked clearly, staring at me with a raised brow as if I was a child who didn't have manners.

"Yeah, got it." Rolling my eyes, I knocked on the door and waited for a response. My father quickly replied to come in, and I made sure to give Allison a smirk of approval before I opened the door.

If she kept it up, I was going to make it my personal objective to do everything I could to piss her off. I may have been an introvert who loved books and nature, but I could be the devil if I needed to be.

My mom can vouch for that as well–I used to have a wicked streak.

Stepping inside his office, I let my eyes take in the dimly lit room until they landed upon a familiar figure standing at the dark brown desk in the center of the room. "Ivy, goodness you have grown!" He said, a smile lighting up his face the moment he saw me.

"It's been two years since I saw you last." I replied with a smile as he came toward me for a hug. The moment was more awkward than I would have liked it, but I hugged him regardless to show that I was trying.

"Yes, it has." He sighed. "I hope that you have found the accommodations to be more than adequate. Allison and I felt that you would like your own space now that you're older. That way, you won't be disturbed by the chaos that seems to float around the main house."

A chuckle left my lips as I nodded. "Yeah, I love the cottage. It's very—"

"You." He replied, finishing my sentence.

"Yes, it's very me." I smiled and watched as he gestured for me to take a seat in the chair across from his desk. "You didn't come meet me at the airport?"

Sighing my father nodded his head, "yes, and I am sorry about that. I am working a deal with a foreign dignitary right now, and I wasn't able to break away. It was important for the deal to go right."

"It's okay. The guys were—" I thought a moment about how to describe them, and watched how my father's face turned concerned with my hesitation, "they were welcoming."

A smile crossed his face as soon as I said what I did. "Well, that's good. Three of them attend the university as well."

Surprise filled me thinking that they were actually attending college. "Really?"

"Yes," my father laughed, "James, Talon, and Hale all attend the college."

It confused me for a moment that only three of them would attend the college, but the oldest one, Damian, didn't. Perhaps his bad boy persona gave him a reason to think he was too good to go to college and get a degree.

"Damian doesn't though?" I was curious about the clarification. If I was going to survive here, I had to know my enemies, and it was clear the guys weren't going to get along with me very well.

"No, Damian actually already finished last year. He works with me in the company, and is helping me to run it. He is a lot smarter than he admits."

I wasn't sure how he was running a business considering it didn't have the most pleasant of attitudes, but then again, looks can be deceiving. Perhaps it was just me that he didn't want to get along with.

"Well, I am glad you have the help." Trying to stay positive with an already awkward conversation was growing harder than I would have liked. A moment of silence fell between us as my father watched my every move. Something about the entire situation was eerie, but I said nothing.

"I have something for you." He finally replied, his smile growing wide. "Come with me."

Standing to his feet, he moved from behind the desk. My eyes following him until I realized he was waiting for me. "Oh–"

Quickly, standing to my feet, he opened the office door, and led me down a hallway through the kitchen toward another door. As he opened it, I noticed the door led toward the garage, and I was slightly curious to know why we were going in there.

"Now, the drive is decent to the University. So I got you something to make sure you could have reliable transportation."

My eyes widened as he stopped in front of a sleek black sedan. Dark tinted windows and chrome accenting decorated the beautiful vehicle, and made me feel breathless.

"You got me a car?" I mumbled, trying to wrap my head around what he was saying. I had been upset about not being able to bring my car from Georgia, but my mom refused to allow me to drive across the country alone. She had assured me I wouldn't need it when I got here, and I had considered it was because I would have a driver.

But man, was I wrong! A brand new fuckin car—- mind blown.

"Yes, Ivy." He chuckled, pulling the key from his pocket. "I got you a car. You are going to change the world, sweetie. I have more faith in you than you know, and I realize I was never there for you before, but now that you are here, that's going to change."

My emotions threatened to expose me for being soft as the tears threatened to rim my eyes. I looked at him and smiled before stepping in and giving him a hug. "Thank you."

I wasn't going to automatically believe that my father had changed from the ways he was, but the least I could do was try to give him a chance to show me that he is different.

"Your welcome, Ivy."

Pulling back, I wiped a stray tear from my eye and looked at him, smiling. "I am looking forward to the next four years here. I hope we will be able to make memories."

"I am sure we will. Now, I know you have a lot of settling in to do before Monday's classes, so I will let you get to it. We are going to have a family dinner this evening at seven. I would like for you to join."

Family dinner... mentally I wanted to slap myself for suggesting making memories because family dinners with the Stepford wife and her arrogant godson's weren't my idea of pleasurable memories. "Of course, that sounds wonderful."

As much as I wasn't pleased with the idea, I suppose I can't just expect them to be the only ones who put in effort. I have to be willing to do the same as well.

I wasn't sure what I was expecting when I came to dinner, but part of me realized that I was widely under-dressed for the most part. It wasn't something super fancy, but it wasn't a jeans and t-shirt thing either.

I could see the disgust in Allison's eyes as I stepped into the dining room wearing black leggings and an oversized band t-shirt. Her lip turned up into a look of disgust before rolling her eyes, and turning away, headed for her seat.

"You can sit in the last chair there." Allison stated, clearly pointing to a chair at the end of the table. One that happens to be right next to a tall, brooding man with rippling muscles and a perfectly styled beard.

I couldn't help but feel hesitant as his eyes looked up to mind, and a smirk crossed his lips. "You must be the famous, Ivy."

Famous... I wouldn't say that, well, at least not yet. "Uh–yeah. That's me."

Moving to my seat, I quickly sat down and watched as servants brought out serving dish after serving dish of food. My eyes widening at the amounts before I was distracted by three other massive bodies entering the dining room.

Damian, James, and another man I had not met entered in all their godliness and took a seat at the table. How was it that one woman had all four of these sexy, sinful men?

God, stop gawking at them! I scolded myself inwardly as I shook my head and focused on the glass of water in front of me, as if it was the most interesting thing in the world.

"Hale, you already met Ivy, I see." Looking toward Damian, I saw the glare on his face. He still wasn't happy with me being here, and I wasn't sure why.

The man who spoke to me before turned to Damian and smiled, "yeah I did. Not much of a talker, though."

"Consider that a good thing." Damian retorted, taking his seat.

As another body sat next to mine across from Hale, I noticed that he and Hale looked almost alike. Doing a double take, I made the mental realization that I was sitting next to two absolutely delicious looking twins.

I slowly let my hand slid under the table, pinching myself to see if I was going to wake up from another one of my erotic dreams. The pain shooting through me made me realize that I, in fact, was actually awake.

"You okay?" The newcomer asked, giving me a perplexed stare.

My eyes widened as a smile crossed my face, "yep... yep. I'm good. Nothing wrong here."

Hale laughed as he shook his head with a smile, looking at the man across from him. "Talon, I think she is shocked we look alike."

"Well, unfortunately, we are twins." The annoyed man stated openly, causing Hale to chuckle. "And I am the normal one."

"Don't let him intimidate you. That's Talon. He is a giant teddy bear, really." Hale said, clearly rolling his eyes at Talon, who shrugged his shoulders and scoffed.

"For some reason, I find that hard to believe." I mumbled, taking a sip of my drink again as I watched my father finally enter the room and take a seat at the head of the table.

The conversation quickly fell into work, and other political aspects as we dug into the food. With having little interest in those kinds of things, I fell into my own thoughts, and tuned out everything they were talking about. I had no interest in getting to know any of them personally and therefore had no reason to hold a conversation.

"What do you think, Ivy?"

The question pulled me out of my internal thoughts, and my eyes looked at them in shock, knowing I was caught not paying attention. "Huh?"

"She isn't' even paying attention. I don't know why you're asking her opinion." Damian snapped quickly at James, causing my father to give Damian a disapproving look.

"She is part of the family, Damian."

"Right." Damian said with a sigh of disapproval while glaring at me.

"I asked what it was you thought about adding a gaming center on the property for the kids that lived here." My father asked again, and I found it odd that he would want to do something like that.

"How many kids live here?" I questioned, my lack of understanding not making me able to give a proper response.

"Well, on the land we own, about 42 of various ages."

I was shocked that many people would live on my father's property. How much land did they actually own?

"See, she knows nothing about the property. There is no point in asking her." Damian grumbled, causing even Hale to look at him as if asking him to shut up.

"Actually, I do have an opinion." I snapped.

"Enlighten us then, Ivy." Allison's voice was laced with sarcasm, and I was getting irritated with the way she kept addressing me. She didn't even know me, and yet was acting like a spoiled bitch.

Smirking, I took a sip of my water, washing down the bite of food I had taken and straightened myself into my seat. "I have a few questions first. How much land do you own and what is the total number of people total on the land?"

My father smiled, "We own about 400 acres of land, and upon that land we have about 150 people total on the property."

"Where are all the education and other resources on the property?"

A look crossed my father's face, and his smile widened. "They attend in the city, forty minutes away."

"Well, there you go. Money shouldn't be spent on something like games, and other mindless things. Try investing in things that will help to educate and change the future. Try getting these children, and their family, into more agriculturally positive activities. Having a library will help to create a better atmosphere for kids, as well as allowing space for tutoring and other things."

Everyone stared at me silently, but my father was the one smiling.

"So you want us to put in a library and waste space with things kids don't use nowadays?" Talon stated, catching me off guard, considering he barely spoke over the entire dinner.

"No, I want you to focus on things that will further the future of the people who live here. Get the youth into things that will make this area prosper. Taking care of our land is how we survive. Building bright minds and futures makes us self sustainable so we're not relying on the surrounding cities."

My words held a lot of weight with my father, and even Allison seemed genuinely impressed. Damian, however, didn't seem happy about what I said. Instead, he stared at me before sliding his chair out and walking away.

I stared at the empty doorway before looking back at the others. "Did I say something wrong?"

"No," James replied with a smile. "He has a lot on his mind. It isn't you."

For some reason, I had a hard time believing that. The look on Allison's face spoke volumes, and as she stood up to follow him, I watched my father look at her and shake his head. I had obviously caused issues, and it wasn't what I was looking to do.

"If you will excuse me. I am going to call it a night."

"Of course, Ivy. Thank you for coming to dinner." My father replied as I stood and moved away from the table, heading toward the back door.

"I told you not to let her come." Damian's voice hissed.

"You know I didn't have a say in the matter, Damian." Allison replied with a groan. I had come too close to a private conversation, but the fact they were talking about me had me stopping in my tracks to listen.

"He is your mate, Allison. You have a lot to say, but you won't." Damian snapped.

Mate? The hell does he mean mate?

"Damian, that's enough. Stop this right now. You will not speak to me how you are."

Damian sighed. "I'm sorry. It's just so hard to focus with her around."

"Well, perhaps make her want to leave. I don't agree with the situation with her, anyway." Allison was getting on my last nerve.

I had done nothing wrong to her, and yet, she always seemed to have it out for me.

Pushing off the wall, I headed toward the back door and stopped once I grabbed the handle, looking toward Damian and Allison, who both stood wide-eyed, staring at me.

"Such a warm welcome." The sarcasm dripped off my tongue as I opened the door and disappeared into the night, back toward the comfort of the cottage at the back of the property.

With the chaos of the day, I was ready to make a hot cup of tea and watch a movie.

I wasn't going to allow them to force me out easily. I had too much riding on my stay here, and if they wanted to play hardball with me, then so be it.

They better know how to play the game, because I wasn't going to fucking lose.

Fantasies and Shopping

Waking up Saturday morning, I had put a plan in motion on how I would approach everything while I was here. Damian and Allison made it clear last night that they didn't want me here. Shit, Allison had made it clear a long time ago that she didn't want anything to do with me.

So, instead of allowing them to bully me or get what they wanted, I was just going to do me. I wasn't going to let them bother me, and minding my own business was the perfect way to do that. I would go into town and get things for my small cottage and stock the fridge. That way, I wouldn't need to go into the house unless it was the garage to get my car.

Slipping on a pair of shorts and a tank top, I grabbed my shoes and purse and quickly head out of the cottage toward the garage. I would get the things I needed to survive without them, and then there wouldn't be a reason for them to try and get rid of me.

As I snuck in through the back door, I noticed how quiet the house was and was grateful for the lack of people moving around. I didn't want anyone to stop and question me about what I was doing.

Moving through the kitchen, I took the route my father had taken me through until I ended up in the garage. My sexy black car sat there by itself, waiting to be driven. As I slid behind the driver's seat, I ran my fingers across the black leather interior. My father had chosen my car perfectly, and thinking about it made me smile.

We may not have had the best of relationships, but he was trying, which was what mattered. Turning the car on, I watched the display come to life. I had read of up on the car last night while lying in bed, and I was glad that it was equipped with GPS. It made things easier for me, considering I had no idea where I was going.

After typing a few things in and saving the routes for later, I put the car in gear and pulled out of the garage and down the road.

My phone immediately began to ring and looking down, I frowned, not recognizing the number. "Hello?"

"Where the fuck are you going?" Damian's voice was laced with anger, and I found amusement in the way he was acting.

"Why the hell do you care? And how did you get my number?"

"Don't change the subject, Ivy. Where are you going? You don't just leave without telling someone where you are going... your father is worried." He replied, trying to guilt trip me.

"That's funny because I sent him a text early this morning telling him I was going to the store today to get a few things. So, do you want to try again?"

There was silence on the other end of the line as I lied, trying to catch him in what he was saying. I hadn't really texted my dad, but I was curious to know what he was going to say in regard to that.

"That's beside the point." I knew he was lying the moment he said it was my dad who was worried. I didn't even know this man, and already he has made me want to pull my hair out since I have been here.

"Look, nice try lying, but I will be back when I get back. Don't call me again."

Hanging up the phone, I didn't bother to hear anything else he had to say. Never had I considered that these four guys would be more trouble than they were worth. I didn't even want anything to do with them, and they acted like complete assholes.

Perhaps it was a male testosterone thing... who knows?

Pulling into town, I found that it was prettier than it had been the day before. I was looking forward to starting school on Monday. I would be kept busy with my schoolwork, and therefor, had no time to worry about the guys, who were hell-bent on making my life shit while I was here.

The grocery store was packed, and it didn't surprise me being so close to the campus. I could almost imagine the college students ransacking the ramen noodles, among other things, making me wish I had come earlier. Ramen was a college kid's life, and even though it wasn't good for you, I enjoyed the salty food, and found it a comfort from home I wouldn't miss out on.

Stepping from my car, I heard my name being called and turned to see Kate walking from the bus stop with a smile on her face. "Oh, hey, Kate!"

"Oh, my God. Is that your car?" She exclaimed, running her fingers over the sleek black paint job as she smiled. "It's gorgeous."

"Yeah, my dad gave it to me yesterday, considering that it's like a forty-minute drive to the campus. Are you grabbing some things too?" I asked her, seeing the large rucksack on her back.

"Yeah, I have to stock up for at least a week." She chuckled, "It's all that fits in this bag."

Kate had been sweet to me the moment that I got on the plane, and thinking about her struggling for the bus to take things back to campus didn't sit well with me. Looping my arm through hers, I smiled. "Don't be crazy. I will take you and your stuff back to the dorms when we are done."

Her eyes widened as she stared at me. "Are you sure? I don't want to impose."

"Of course, I am sure. Besties, remember?" I teased her, causing her to laugh.

"Very true." She said sarcastically as she flipped her hair over her shoulder.

As Kate and I walked inside, we both grabbed our carts and started to shop. I learned Kate had gotten fortunate enough to have a solo dorm room, so she didn't have to share with anyone. Mainly because her mother said that she didn't want her daughter tainted. It still made me laugh with the way Kate explained it. Especially since some of the things Kate told me made me realize her mother didn't know her daughter very well.

"So," Kate said as we turned down an aisle filled with chips and other snacks. "How are things going with those brothers of yours? You didn't seem happy with them yesterday."

I stopped in my tracks, confused by what she was talking about. "Brothers?"

"Uh, yes. The two sexy ripped men who picked you up from the airport." She laughed, causing me to realize what she was talking about.

"Ohhh!" I exclaimed, "dude, they aren't my brothers. They are my stepmother's godsons, and there are four of them. Not the best welcoming committee, to be honest."

"So you're not related to them?! Like even by marriage?" Kate's eyes went wide as an excited look crossed her face. "Oh, my God."

"No, we aren't, and I don't know why you are so excited about this." I chuckled as I pressed onward.

"Ivy, you are literally living every girl's wet dream. Are you kidding me right now?"

My brows furrowed as I tried to understand what she was suggesting. There was no way that I could have a relationship with any of them. Yes, they were incredibly sexy, and my mind had often wandered, but at the same time, it would be weird.

"I don't think so. Plus, they don't like me at all." I reminded her, causing her to sigh.

"Well, I think you should give them a chance. Or perhaps just simply have fun. That's what college is about anyways—having fun and trying new things. Maybe Two or four things at once..." she mumbled, causing me to turn with my mouth open wide as I looked at her in shock.

"Kate!" I squealed. "You can't be serious."

"What?! I am just saying..."

We both burst into laughter as we turned the corner and seemed to run into a wall that didn't want to move. Looking up, I was met with dark sultry eyes and a disapproving glance on Talon's face while Hale held a smile.

"Hale... Talon..." I stuttered in shock as to what they were doing at the store. "What are you doing here?"

"Shopping," Hale replied with a grin as Talon rolled his eyes.

"Who are these people?" Kate whispered as she leaned into me, excitement registering all over her face.

"This is Talon and Hale. The other half of the four..."

"Four!" Kate squealed, causing Hale to laugh. "Holy shit... you mean like one, two, three, four... the number four... four brothers."

Talon groaned, looking at me with irritation. "Why does it matter how many of us there are?"

"Oh, well, because there are these things called a four—" I slapped my hand over her mouth, staring at her in shock as I shook my head no. As much as I tried to muffle what she was about to say, when I looked back at Talon and Hale, they wore shocked expressions.

"We have to be going... have a great day!" I had never pushed a cart so fast in my life. The embarrassment of the situation made my face red as Kate laughed hysterically from behind me. I wasn't mad at her. On the contrary, I was intrigued by the idea she was proposing.

Talon and Hale looked incredible, and more than once, I wanted to reach out and touch them. Shaking my head, I tried to wipe the thought from my mind. I couldn't allow myself to get caught up in those kinds of ideas. There was no way that was right by any means.

They may not have been related to me by blood or marriage, but they still were raised by my stepmother.

I made a point of hurrying myself and Kate through the store, trying to avoid running into Talon or Hale again. Every corner I took, I found myself looking over my shoulder to make sure they weren't right behind me.

"Thank you again for bringing me back here. I had an awesome time this afternoon."

I looked at Kate as I popped the trunk slowly, helping her grab bags out. "I had fun too."

"Hey, let me see your phone. I'll put my number in there so we can keep in contact."

The offer was warm. I hadn't had close friends in a long time. The only person I used to hang out with when I lived in Georgia was Mary, and she moved away overseas our senior year when her father got stationed at a base in Germany.

"That would be cool. Are you sure you don't want help taking this stuff upstairs?" I asked, her watching her fill her rucksack and grab a bunch of bags.

"No, I have it. But I will see you on Monday. Meet me at the small coffee shop in the middle of campus. We can grab coffee before orientation at nine."

By the time Kate and I said goodbye, I was feeling more comfortable with how things went with us. Driving home, I parked the car in the garage and took out the small collapsable wagon I purchased from the trunk. I loaded all of my groceries and a few small appliances I had purchased and made my way toward the cabin.

As soon as I got close, however, I felt like I was being watched. Spinning around, I watched Damian strolling down the path after me, and I quickly turned, making haste to get inside my home before he could say anything to me.

The last thing I wanted was to hear his mouth again. He was doing nothing but getting on my last nerve.

"Ivy!" he yelled at me as I pulled the wagon inside and attempted to close the door.

His hand coming up to stop me, he pushed his way inside, his blue eyes staring down at me with anger. "I know you heard me."

"Yeah, I did. Now get out," I snapped back, trying to get him to leave.

"No, you need to learn that you can't just leave and not tell anyone," he retorted as if I was a child who needed permission to leave.

"Excuse me? I am an adult, and I will do as I please. Now get out of my house."

"Your house? I think you will find that this is all part of my home, and I will come and go as I wish." If I didn't think Damian could be more of an asshole than he was already, I was wrong.

"The last time I checked, this was my father's home. So get the fuck out now before you do something you will regret."

A growl resonated from him and caused me to step back. I could have sworn I saw a glimmer of gold reflect in his eyes for a moment as he stepped closer toward me.

"Watch who you speak to like that. I would hate to have to show you who is in charge around here."

Something about the way he said what he did sent shivers straight to my core. Damian was incredibly sexy, and everything about him drew me in. I wasn't a virgin, but I was not very experienced. The only man I had slept with was at senior prom, and he barely lasted ten minutes before he was sleeping next to me.

"Don't promise something you know you can't follow through with."

My challenge seemed to spark something in him, and quickly he turned and marched out of my small home, slamming the door behind him. I wasn't too sure what his problem was, but at the same time, I wasn't looking to find out any more than I had to.

Damian was dangerous, and men like him were always bad news.

I had four years to spend here, and with everything I had going on, I needed to make sure I didn't ruffle feathers. I didn't want to show signs of weakness and have them thinking they could act however they wanted to with me, but at the same time, I didn't want to cause more problems for myself than need be.

With a sigh, I tried not to think too much about everything and pulled the wagon toward the kitchen, unloading things into the few cabinets and the fridge. I had to make this place feel as much as home as possible because I didn't want to have to go into the main house if I didn't need to.

One thing I found that would help with that was the exterior door to the garage on the side of the house. Which meant no longer did I need to go through the house to get to my car. Damian was making me feel uncomfortable, and I had only been here for two days.

As I made a cup of coffee, I sat on the small sofa, turning on the TV as I pulled out my phone. Kate had texted me, asking how things were going with the brothers again, and her idea of how I could have fun with them sunk in my mind.

They were incredibly sexy, and each of them had unique mannerisms that made me want to know more. If I was going to have a chance of getting close to any though, Hale and James seemed to be a lot more light-hearted than Damian and Talon.

A chime on my phone caused me to look down, thinking that Kate had texted me back. The only problem is that it wasn't her. It was the same number that called me earlier when I left.

'Challenge accepted, little one.'

Damian's text sent shivers through my body. I wasn't stupid. I knew exactly who sent that message, and if he thought he was going to play with me and make me leave...

Well, he would be wrong.

Orientation Day

Monday morning came faster than I expected and waking up early, I dressed in a pair of skinny jeans, a white and navy button-up shirt with my favorite flats. I didn't want to stand out, but I wanted to look nice. Orientation was supposed to take a few hours, and then I would be free for the day. Classes not officially starting till the following week.

Heading toward the school in my car, I managed to think over everything that had happened to me while I had been here. Not only had the guys left me alone since the conversation between Damian and me, but they were also acting weird toward me.

As in, always watching me weirdly.

Pulling into the school, I quickly made my way toward the cafe where I was going to be meeting Kate. I had already had two texts from her asking where I was since I was thirty minutes late.

"Ivy!" Kate called cheerfully, drawing my attention from where I stood just inside the cafe door. I smiled at her, looking at the other two women who were sitting with her, and decided to join them.

"Hey, sorry, I am late. Traffic was bad up the road, and I had to sit behind traffic for four turns before I made it through." I replied with a sigh as I sat down next to Kate.

Slowly, she slid the coffee toward me that she had ordered, and I was more than grateful. I had been dreaming of this moment since the third light rotation in traffic.

"Oh my God, that is so good." I hummed, causing the girls with Kate to giggle.

"Ivy, this is Bree and Mandy. Bree is in her second year, and Mandy is new this year, like us." I smiled, waving to the girls as I wiped the foam from my upper lip.

"It's nice to meet you guys."

"You as well, hunny," Bree replied with a southern accent. "I am from Georgia as well. Kate was telling me you and her are too. That's so neat. We are all from the same state."

"Oh, wow. Yeah, that's crazy," I replied before turning to Mandy. "Where are you from?"

"California." She said with a smile. Her blonde hair contrasted with her green eyes and olive-colored skin. "This place is a huge change from my beaches and sunshine."

The four of us laughed while we shared random memories with each other. Eventually, orientation started, and as it did, we all found ourselves moving in step with the rest of the students as we toured the campus.

"Oh, my God," Mandy replied after a moment, causing us all to stop, "who are those sex machines?"

As my eyes followed the direction of where she was looking, I watched as James, Hale, and Talon climbed out of a large truck, laughing with friends who had come over to join them. A groan left my throat as I watched the girls fawn over them.

"Those right there are Ivy's new roommates." Kate smirked, causing Bree and Mandy to look at me.

"You are messing with the four horsemen?" Bree asked in shock, "how?"

"Horsemen?" I laughed. "They are my stepmother's godsons. They are not as great as one would think. More of a pain in my ass."

"They could be a pain in my ass if they want," Mandy smirked, causing us all to burst into a fit of laughter.

"Oh my God... TMI." I chuckled.

"Don't act like you don't want them." Mady smirked. "They are fucking gorgeous."

I couldn't deny that I hadn't thought about it, but the thing was, I couldn't act on that. Plus, they were not in any way interested in me. "Perhaps, but we all can't stand each other."

"Who can't stand each other?" A sultry, devious voice said from directly behind me. As I looked toward the girls, I watched as their eyes widened, and Bree quickly covered her mouth to stifle her laughter.

Pinching my brow, I sighed before turning around and coming face to face with James and Hale. Hale crossed his arms over his chest, smirking at me as James looked dead, intent on getting the answer to his question.

"We all don't. You, me, and the rest of your crew. Damian made that clear."

James sighed, rolling his eyes as he smiled, "don't believe everything you hear."

"Yeah, sure," I replied with sarcasm as I stepped away from him and gestured for the girls to keep following me. There was no way I was going to allow him to ruin orientation day for me.

Every time I was around them, I was flustered, and they had me thinking things that I shouldn't. I had a career to achieve and work to do. I didn't have time to worry about boys because all they did was agitated me.

"Ivy, you're so—" Kate's voice said before quickly stopping with laughter.

A set of hands wrapped around me, hoisting me up into the air as I found myself hanging upside down over James' shoulder. "Oh, my God! Put me down!" I screamed in shock, trying to register the way I felt as he touched me.

My skin was crawling in pleasure at the feeling of contact with his own skin, and it seemed that I wasn't the only one who was affected. His body tensed, and before I knew it, I found my back pressed against the wall of a building.

His firm grip on my hips had my heart racing. An internal struggle building within him as he began to breathe heavily.

"James..." I whispered, trying to wrap my mind around what was happening.

"James!" Hale yelled as he approached, a low growl emitting from James' throat.

"James, what are you doing..." I tried again, and finally, his eyes cast down toward my own. The gold rings within them glowing brightly and sending shock through to my soul. What was he?

I remembered Damian with the same small tones of gold, and the more I stared at him, the closer his lips got to my own. I anticipated a kiss, but instead, he leaned toward my neck and inhaled deeply behind my ear. "It isn't possible..."

"What isn't—" I asked before he cut me off quickly and pulled away from me. The empty feeling of his body away from my own bringing loss.

"James..." Hale stated again in a warning tone as James stared at me with a confused expression as if he wasn't sure what was going on. His brows narrowed as he shook his head and turned, storming past Hale and headed for the truck.

Hale gave me an apologetic look as he followed after James. Left in shock, my eyes gazed back at the girls who stood nearby. Shock registered on the faces of two of them, but nothing but excitement lay in Kate's eyes.

"Oh, my God. That was fucking hot!" Kate said excitedly as she turned her gaze back toward the guys, watching them.

She was right–it was hot.

"Ivy, are you okay?" Bree finally asked softly as she came to step in front of me, blocking my view from the men.

Shaking my head, I smiled. "Uh–yeah. I'm okay."

"You have to be careful around them. Bad things happen, especially around Damian."

Her statement confused me, and I looked at her for more answers, but she quickly shook it off, walking away from the rest of us and headed back toward the dorms. I wasn't quite sure what her statement meant, but I wanted to know.

The guys were definitely something, but I wouldn't consider them actually dangerous.

Then again, looks could be deceiving, and I didn't have the best track record of making the right choices. It was one of the reasons why I kept to myself back in Georgia. It lessened the risk of me getting into something I couldn't handle.

Even if every part of me wanted to handle him–and the others. Thoughts of how James touched me kept rolling through my mind that night. I couldn't stop thinking about his hard, rippled body against mine and the incredible way he smelt. When I came here, I had planned to keep to myself, and the conflicts I had with the guys upon my arrival made me want to keep my distance even more.

Yet, when James touched me, I felt my body come to life.

A fire ripped through me, and the heat of his touch caressed every edge of my soul as if calling out to it. The more and more I thought about it, the crazier I became, trying to figure out why he acted the way he did.

A sigh left my throat as I stood, pulling my hair up higher into a ponytail before walking toward the kettle and turning it on. The one thing I loved about Idaho so far was the cool evenings that allowed me to open the window, allowing the air to rush through the open space in my living room.

In Georgia, it was hard to do that in the summer months. It was always a constant battle with mosquitos and trying not to be eaten alive. Summers in Idaho were definitely nicer, and the only thing I had to really worry about was when the snow fell in the winter.

Something I wasn't looking forward to.

Standing by the open window, I looked out onto the green lawn that went on for miles. The lights of the main house gleaming in the distance lit the small area around it. To think that for years I had avoided this place because I was worried about my father, and I instead missed out on being closer to nature.

Closer to the way I wanted to live.

As much as I tried to distract my mind from James, I found it hard to do. I hadn't been laid in two years, and the sexual frustration I had built up was taking a toll on me. A glimmering thought traveled into my mind, and a smile played on my face.

Last year as a joke, my mother bought me a vibrating best friend, and at the time, I had been horrified because I couldn't believe she bought it for me. The joke had been that I was too uptight with exams and needed to release some aggression. Thinking back on it, though, I understand what she meant.

It did help to relieve tension.

Pulling the bright purple clitoral stimulator from its pink bag, I stripped down to just my tank top and lay on the bed. I knew it was wrong of me to think of James, but he had gotten me so worked up, and I needed a release.

I needed something.

As the vibrations came to life, I toyed with myself. Soft moans escaped my throat as I moved it. I thought of James touching me and the way his body pressed against me. An image of him kissing me ran through my mind, causing my body to shake as I felt my orgasm build.

"James..." I whispered. "Please..."

As my climax hit, I came undone, and a howling sound echoed through the woods behind me, causing my eyes to open in shock and the toy to be cast aside.

"The hell was that?!" I exclaimed as I quickly pulled my shorts on.

The sound had been close to my cottage, and knowing that I was this close to the woods sent fear through me as I stepped back into the living room. My eyes quickly darted toward the open window, and moving faster than I ever had, I ran to it and shut it quickly.

I could hear the sounds of rustling on the other side of my front door, and with no weapon in sight, I felt myself begin to panic.

"Ivy..." The sound of my name coming from the other side of the door stopped me in my tracks. I knew that voice, but confusion and worry filled me as I wondered what James was doing outside my cottage. "Open the door."

"No..." I replied, "I can't... but you need to get out of here. There is an animal in the woods."

"I know there was..." he replied again, and the sultry sound of him swirled around me, headed straight for my core. He sounded darker than usual, and everything about it made me want more. "Open the door, Ivy... I can smell you."

Smell me?!

Being at my dad's house was beginning to get weirder and weirder with every passing second, and now I questioned whether I should have come here at all. I was happy to be here and hated that I had waited so long to make the trip, but at the same time, these guys were doing a number on my sanity.

"I am not dressed, James."

The small click of the door made my eyes widen in shock as I watched the lock slowly turn and the door open. A surge of adrenaline pushed through me as I stood still, watching him.

"Liar..." The smirk on his face itself was enough for me to get wet, but when he moved closer to me, I felt the anticipation rising and I waited for the moment I was going to wake up from this dream.

"What are you doing here?" I asked breathlessly as he stepped closer to me, his hand raising up to brush down over the side of my face.

"You know, if you leave your windows open, we can hear what goes on inside this little cottage of yours, right?" Realization dawned on me that I hadn't closed it when I was pleasing myself, and my cheeks turned red with embarrassment.

"I don't know what you're talking about, but you need to go," I quickly snapped as I tried to push him out the door.

Instead, my efforts were feeble as I found myself quickly tossed onto the sofa with him between my legs. "Do you really want me to go?" He asked as his fingers trailed over the hem of my shorts.

I hadn't had the time to put my panties back on after my fun in the bedroom. I had been too worried about the animal noise I heard outside and the open window in my living room. Panic and excitement filled me as his fingers slowly brushed down my thigh.

My horny ass moaned softly, causing him to chuckle, "I didn't think so."

"We can't..." I replied as he toyed with the loose shorts that did nothing to conceal my soaking wet core from this point.

James leaned into the area between my legs, his face pressed to the inside part of my shorts as he inhaled deeply. "God, you smell so good," he mumbled before I felt his tongue swipe across my slit.

"Oh, my God," I moaned.

That was all it took before he had yanked off my shorts and buried his face into my soaking wet core, his tongue devouring me as I cried out in pleasure. The more I tried to pull back, the harder he pulled me close, making it to where I couldn't break free from the pleasure he was bringing me.

"James—" I cried out, "oh God, James, please."

"I want all of you," he growled into my core, causing the vibrations to tip me over the edge again.

"Yes–" I moaned, "please."

The moment between James and I had my mind spinning. I wasn't sure what I was asking for, but I didn't care anymore.

My eyes took in the sight of him as stripped before me, releasing the massive erect dick in between his legs. There was no way that it was going to fit inside me. The girth itself was going to rip me open, and suddenly I was second guessing if I wanted to do this.

As he grabbed my hips and pulled me closer to him, I felt the head of his thick cock pressing against my folds, and I cried out as the head slowly slid inside.

However, before he could fully thrust himself in, the door burst open, and Damian stood there in all his fury, a roar echoing through the room before James was completely ripped off of me. "I told you NO!"

I wasn't sure what was going on, but before I knew it, Hale and Talon had entered, both rushing to James to hold him back from completely losing himself to Damian. I curled back onto my sofa, grabbing a blanket and wrapping it around me as I watched in horror at the sight that was unfolding around me.

Damian stood in front of me, partially blocking James' view of my body, and the angry glare James was casting Damian looked like he wanted to kill him. I had no idea what my life was coming to, but I was irritated that Damian added cock blocking to his list of achievements.

This is such fucking bullshit.

Sexual Frustration

Anger soared through me as I watched the scene unfold in front of my eyes. All four of these men were in my home, and three of them were not invited—well, four, but I wasn't complaining about what James was doing to me.

Breaking out of the horror state I was in when Damian ripped James from me, and I stood with the blanket wrapped around me and a scowl across my face.

"Enough!" I screamed at them, seeming to break them from the state they had been in. "What the fuck do you think you're doing breaking into my house like that?!"

"Go to your room," Damian growled at me, causing my core to shake with desire before I shoved it away.

"No." My firm response was enough to make Hale and Talon look at me in shock. I suppose Damian wasn't used to being told no, and the glare he gave me spoke volumes to what was running through his mind.

"Excuse me, princess?" He asked, causing my irritation to flare. Who the fuck did he think he was calling me a princess?

"You heard me. James and I were enjoying ourselves, and you burst in uninvited. Let him go and get the fuck out."

The tension in the room was thick. "Ivy, you don't understand..." Hale tried to explain, causing my attention to snap to him.

"No, you all don't understand. I am not someone you can just put in their place. I am a grown-ass adult, and if I want James to fuck me stupid, then so be it. But you three need to get the fuck out now—actually... take James with you. The mood is over."

James' eyes widened as he looked at me. My demand broke him out of whatever state he had been in.

"Ivy..." he said softly, trying to break from Hale and Talon's grasp.

"No, I am done with this. All of you, please go."

Hale and Talon helped drag James from my cottage as Damian stayed behind, staring at me. His cold eyes looked over me, making me feel all sorts of ways, which was the last thing that I wanted.

"You need to stay away from me and my brothers, Ivy. You won't find what you are looking for with us." His words struck me as if he had slapped me himself before he turned and exited my home, slamming the door.

He had spoken to me as if I was just a whore looking for a quick fuck while I was in town, and that didn't sit well with me. I had never been a person for confrontation, but something about what he said snapped something inside me.

Grabbing my shorts off the floor, I quickly threw them on and ran out my door after them. They had only made a short way, and as soon as I stepped outside, they all stopped in their tracks.

"Listen here, you condescending asshole!" I screamed at him, causing Damian to glare at me. "I am not after whatever the fuck you think I am."

I was not tall by any means. I only stood at five foot three, and at that moment, I felt like I was six feet tall. "Excuse you? I don't think you realize who you are talking to."

Hale stepped forward, trying to block me, and as he did, I pushed against him as his hand came around me to hold me back.

"Ivy—" his voice cut off as I fought to get at Damian.

"I'm tired of you always being a dick!" I yelled at him, "Let me go, Hale. I am tired of his shit!"

Hale froze in his spot and didn't respond to me. I saw Damian's eyes go from me to where Hale's hands were. Recognition shooting through his eyes. "Let her go and go inside all of you."

Hale did as he was told, and before I knew it, only Damian and I were left alone once again. There was nothing but silence between us until he stepped closer to me and sneered across his lips.

"Let me make this clear, since you didn't seem to understand the first time." A tremble ran through me the closer he got, and I had a feeling I wasn't going to like what he had to say.

"Stop," I whispered, taking a step back from him.

"No, you don't speak," he said in a low dark tone, "you will not find yourself with any of my brothers. Do you understand me?"

"Yes–" I whispered, as my eyes cast down, trying to ignore the feeling he created in me due to the proximity we were in.

"You go to school, come home, and stay in your cottage." Before I realized it, I had backed my way to my cottage door, and Damian's hands slammed down on the door on either side of my head. "You will not disobey me, Ivy."

I was breathless to answer him. The only thing I could do was nod my head in agreement and watch as his glare turned into one of uncertainty as he pushed himself off from the door and turned, storming away.

I had never been so scared and aroused in my life.

Every drop of anger I felt when I had marched out of my door drained away and was replaced with the increasing desire to let him ravage me in more ways than one. Letting out a sigh of relief I hadn't realized I had been holding. Tears brimmed in my eyes. The confusion and anger over my behavior caused emotions to roll through. I wasn't prepared for.

Pushing open my door, I slammed it behind me, walked into the living room, and looked around at the mess that had been created. Pillows from the sofa were thrown onto the floor, blankets cast aside, and a chair tipped over.

It looked like a bomb had exploded, and to top everything off, I was more sexually frustrated now than I had been before I got myself off!

"Why me?" Tears threatened to fall down my face, and I wanted more than anything to talk to someone about what had just happened, but the problem was I didn't want to worry my mom, who was the only person I ever spoke to.

As if on cue, my phone began to ring, and through the mess on the floor, I found my phone that had fallen off the sofa. Kate's name flashed across the screen, and I sighed before answering it.

"Hey, girl. What's up?"

"Nothing much. Was just calling to see if you were okay after everything that happened today." I could tell by the way Kate sounded that she was concerned about everything.

Sighing, I flopped down onto my sofa. "Yeah, I don't even know. Shit just happened, and now I am more confused than I was earlier."

"Oh my God... spill it! You can't keep me in suspense."

I couldn't help but chuckle at her reaction. "Well, James came in like a hurricane, and well—"

"Well, what?!" I wasn't even sure how to answer Kate's excitement. Thinking about the whole situation just made me flustered again.

"Well, he devoured me."

"Oh, my God! I knew it. Amazing sex with sinful men." She giggled.

"Dude, we didn't even get that far. Damian busted into my place and snatched James off me before we could even have sex. It was all foreplay, honestly."

I couldn't help grumbling in disapproval, thinking about how Damian looked at me when I tried to confront him. He was a dangerous man, and he made that clear tonight. I wasn't to play around with him, otherwise, I was going to end up getting burnt.

"That fucking asshole! Why would he do something like that?"

"Kate, I don't even know. He told me to stay away from him and his brothers. Whatever that means. He acted like I was some college whore."

"Wow, seriously?!" Kate asked, causing me to sigh again.

"Yeah. I'm so tired of him already, and I haven't even been here a week."

"Well, come out with me this weekend. There is a welcome back party on Friday night, and I think we will all have tons of fun. Mandy and Bree have both agreed to go, and we will pre-drink in my room, then walk toward the frat house."

A fraternity party... what Kate offered did sound fun, but I wasn't the party girl. It just wasn't my scene. Then again, perhaps I could have fun with the night. Damian said I couldn't have fun, and I was starting to like the idea of breaking the rules.

"Count me in. I'll see you then." After a long week of taking care of things on campus, party night came, and I was more than ready for it. All week the guys had been avoiding me like the plague, and James wouldn't even look me in the eye. As much as I tried not to let any of it bother me, I couldn't deny that it did.

Pulling my shopping bag from the trunk, I walked out the back door to the garage and headed for my place. I knew that Kate said I could get ready over at her place, but as great as that sounded, I preferred the comfort of my own home to get ready.

Walking down the cobbled pathway, I stopped in my tracks when I watched James appear against the treeline. Black basketball shorts hung loosely against his hips, and the mouth-watering cut of his V-line was on clear display.

"James..." I called out softly, hoping that he would come say something to me. But as much as I wished that he didn't. A hurt and confused look crossed his face, and it broke me a bit when I watched him turn and disappear into the brush and out of sight.

Of course, this would be how my life was turning out. Rolling my eyes, a sigh left me as I moved forward and disappeared behind the safety of my front door. With the turn of a lock, I flipped on my speakers and plugged in my phone, turning on my playlist.

The loud music coming from the dock screamed sex, alcohol, and drugs. I didn't care anymore about what they were going to say, and as quickly as I had been clothed, I was naked. Stepping into the hot, cascading water of my shower, I let it burn away any feeling of their touch.

Tonight was going to be different. I had come here for a reason, and everything turned disastrous right off the bat. I couldn't allow myself to fall into a rut where I was too worried about a guy and not worried enough about the future I wanted to have. I had to focus on me and me alone. Because only I was able to make my future happen.

Like a horrid eighties ballad, I belted out the lyrics to every song that came on while I cried my eyes out with the frustration I had felt. By the time the water ran cold, I was feeling better about myself and a little more confident than I had been before.

The only problem was making sure that confidence stuck while I continued here for the next four years. If I was lucky, maybe only two, and then I could seek a fellowship while working on campus for my last two years of grad school. Wouldn't that piss them off?

Pulling out all the stops, I dressed myself to impress, applying makeup and curling my hair until the look I saw in the mirror was of a woman on a mission. One that was going to turn heads with every step she made. As I grabbed my purse, I pulled out my car keys and made my way out the door toward the fun.

The black dress I chose at a local boutique hugged my curves in all the right places, and to really highlight the dress, I picked out a pair of red heels as deep as blood and matched them with the perfect shade of lipstick. If seduction and evil had a baby, I would picture it looking like me.

Stepping onto the path, I head toward the back door to the garage, only to be stopped by my father.

"Ivy?" His voice made me feel like a teenager who was sneaking out.

"Yes, Daddy?" I said, putting on a fake good girl smile and looking at him innocently.

"Uh—where are you going and dressed like that?" he asked, his eyes looking me up and down in shock.

"Oh–" I said with hesitation, looking at my outfit, "well, my new friends Kate, Bree, and Mandy are all going to the welcoming party tonight. I don't plan on drinking, but I figured I would go hang out and bond with my new friends. Do I look okay?"

He hesitated, opening and closing his mouth. "Mhmm," he replied, nodding his head. "You look lovely, sweetheart, but if you do drink, please don't drive. Call me, and I will come get you."

"Of course. I won't be too late." I smiled sweetly at him and watched as he walked back into the house. A smirk crossed my face, and as I stepped into the garage, I watched a figure come through the door from the kitchen.

"Ivy—" Hale said, looking me up and down, a lust-filled gaze in his eyes as they darkened over. "Whoa—where are you going?"

A chuckle left my lips as I raised a brow. "Out, Hale."

"Where out?" he asked again as his brows furrowed, obviously not happy with my response.

"To a party, Hale... what's with the twenty questions?"

I didn't have time for whatever games Hale wanted to play. All of them had avoided me since the incident with James, and I couldn't stand that they were acting the way they did. They either wanted to know me, or they didn't, but the hot and cold shit wasn't going to go well with me.

"Are you purposely avoiding giving me a direct answer, Ivy? Damian isn't going to be happy about this."

Laughter erupted from me as I opened my car door. "Does it look like I give a fuck, Hale? Damian made it clear that I was nothing more than a whore, and I was to stay far from all of you. So listen to your brother like the good boy you are, and go fuck yourself."

Shock registered all over Hale's face at what I said, and before he could react, I slipped behind the wheel and closed my door, quickly throwing my car in drive as I took off into the night. Turning up the music, I let the windows down and enjoyed the fresh hair against my skin.

Tonight, I wasn't going to allow them to get to me.

Damian, Hale, Talon, and James—the four horsemen of the apocalypse.

A name that suited their ill-mannered attitudes and fluctuating temperaments. I was a grown-ass woman, and they had absolutely no control over who I was and what I wanted to do. If they wanted me to be a whore like they claimed I was, then maybe I would have some fun tonight.

I'm sure there are some rather sexy college guys out there that wouldn't mind fulfilling the pleasure I wanted. Unlike James and Damian, they tend to start a lot of things they are never able to finish completing.

Tonight was about me and me alone.

Fuck them and their petty bullshit.

If I had to choose—the jokes on them tonight.

Party Time

I never imagined going to a party would be the way it was. I had attended a few in high school, but it wasn't ever my scene. So when I followed Kate into the massive fraternity house, I was in shock. There had to have been a hundred people here, and the smell of sweat and beer lingered in the air.

No wonder I never came.

Scrunching my nose, I moved through the bodies, following Kate toward the back, where drinks lingered and the music blared.

"I am so glad you came out tonight!" Kate exclaimed as she poured us a drink.

"Yeah, me too. I really needed to get away from all the male testosterone at the house. It's become overbearing." I giggled, causing her to laugh. "Where are the girls?"

Kate shrugged her shoulders, looking around. "I don't know. They said they would meet us here."

Looking around, I attempted to search for them but quickly gave up because my eyes landed on a figure I hadn't expected to see—James.

His hands were wrapped around a pretty blonde, and she was giggling at the way he leaned in and kissed her neck. My heart sank at that moment, and the urge to throw up was real. I couldn't believe that he would come on to me the way he did and then turn around and throw me away like I was nothing.

Kate's eyes followed mine, and when she saw what I did, she touched my arm. "Don't, Ivy. He is a complete asshole. Don't let him ruin your night."

"Oh, I'm not," I snarled before downing my drink in one go and pouring myself another.

"Whoa!" Kate laughed. "I thought you said you weren't going to really drink?"

As I looked at him again, I noticed his eyes on me and a look of shock on his face.

"Yeah, well, I guess I changed my mind." Lifting the cup back, I downed it, not breaking eye contact with him, and then held it up in salute before pouring another. "Let's go dance."

Turning, I made my way through the crowd back into the house and into where everyone was grinding and dancing on each other. Kate swayed to the beat with me, and before I knew it, the alcohol took hold of me, and I lost myself in the music.

The warm fuzzy sensation running through my body helped me to forget about why I had been upset in the first place. I no longer cared what anyone had to say or what they thought. At some point, Bree and Mandy had found us, and Kate quickly filled them in on what was wrong with me.

"Don't let him get to you!" Bree yelled over the music, causing me to laugh.

"Oh, I'm not." Grabbing a tall, built body, I pulled it close to me and smiled up at his hazel eyes. I wasn't sure who he was, but he didn't seem to care either, and he held onto me with a firm grip.

He wasn't James or even one of the others, but at that moment, that's what I wanted. Someone to help me forget about the way those four men made me feel.

"Get the fuck off her," someone said as a growl resonated through the living room, causing others to stop and stare at what was going on.

Looking up, I found James' eyes and his disappointed stare at what I was doing. "Is there a problem?" I asked him with irritation and confusion.

"Seriously, Ivy?" His reply was sarcastic. "Let's go. It's time to leave."

"Look, man, she is having fun. Leave her alone," the guys I was dancing with said, causing James to glare at him again and growl.

"Take your hands off her right now, or I will personally beat you within an inch of your life." The guy quickly did as he said and lifted his hands in the air in defense.

"Ain't no bitch worth a beating. Fucking take her, man."

All it took was the guy to call me a bitch, and before I knew it, the guy was lying on the floor with a busted lip. "Disrespect her again!" James yelled, causing me to jump back in shock before his eyes turned back to me.

"Let's go... now."

As I looked toward Kate, her own eyes were wide, and confusion filled me. James, however, wasn't planning on giving me any more time to think about it. He hoisted me over his shoulder once more and carried me out of the frat house and back toward my car.

"James, put me down!" I yelled at him. "You don't get to do this! Go back to that blonde whore you were talking to, and let me have my fun."

James quickly dropped me to my feet, pressing me against the passenger side of my car. "Shut your mouth and get in the damn car, Ivy."

I had never seen this side of James before, and he was beyond furious with me at what happened tonight. The entire drive back to the house was silent, but as soon as the car was parked, I jumped out, slamming the door behind me as I marched myself back toward my cottage in a drunken state.

"Ivy!" James yelled after me as I continued to ignore him.

A night that was supposed to be fun and stress-free turned into a shit show. Opening the door to my cottage, I went to close it and came to face with James, who pushed his way into my place once again. "Would you stop and listen to me?" he asked.

"Why, James? I was having fun, and you just had to ruin it."

"Fun.. with that piece of shit?!" he exclaimed in anger. "He would have used you, then thrown you away like you were nothing!"

"So what! What if I just wanted that one-time release?"

"No." The growl that left him had his eyes turning gold once more. "You will not let another man touch you."

"Are you listening to yourself? You don't have the right to dictate to me what I can and can't do." All the emotions of what was happening let tears build up and slowly stream down my face in frustration.

"There are things I can't explain to you, and trust me, I wish I could. It would make things so much easier..." A sigh left his lips as he ran his fingers through his hair, as if fighting internally with himself on what he was supposed to do.

"Just tell me. What's going on?" I pleaded with him, wanting to understand.

"I can't, Ivy," he mumbled, "I wish I could, but I can't.."

I couldn't understand why they were treating me the way they were. None of it made sense, and the more and more I tried to understand, the worse it made me feel.

"You can't or won't? I know I am nothing but a stupid southern bitch with no sense of life to you and your brothers, but you have no idea how wrong you are."

"Ivy, don't. We don't think that." The concern and confusion on his face sat deep within me.

"Then kiss me...kiss me, James. Or leave."

Hesitation sat between us, and I waited for him to kiss me, but instead, I saw him back up toward the door, and a little piece of me broke. "That's what I thought..."

Shaking my head, I sighed, letting the tears stream down my face. "Fuck it..." His reply caught me off guard, and before I knew it, his lips were on mine.

The heated passion between us blew my mind, and I didn't want it to stop. James made me feel a flow of emotions I didn't know were real, and at that moment, I never wanted them to stop. They say when you meet the person in your life you are destined to be with, they will make you feel like time stops to be with them, and with James, that is exactly what happened. His hands upon my skin set me on fire, and slowly the moans escaped my lips.

As his hands slid down my waist, he grabbed my ass, hoisting me up into the air as I wrapped my legs around his waist. Everything was like second nature, and everything about it made me want to do things that I had only seen in movies.

His lips upon my skin, our fingers ripping the clothing from our bodies...

More and more, I begged and pleaded for him to do things to me I only dreamed of.

"James..." I pleaded as his tongue touched and caressed me. "I can't come again... I need you."

I waited for the moment when we would be interrupted again, but instead, as the head of his thick, erected cock parted my folds, there was no stopping. One sharp thrust had me crying out in pleasure as he moaned. Never had anything filled me to the extent that he did.

"Shit!" I screamed as he began to thrust into me hard and fast. "Oh my God..."

"Fuck, you have no idea how much I have wanted you," he growled as his fist gripped my hair, pulling my head back and allowing him to nip at my neck.

"Yes, please... I want it all." The words slipping from my lips weren't even recognizable. Every thrust seemed fuller and fuller, and the more I moaned, the harder he drove into me. I wasn't sure how I was going to be able to continue with the pace he was setting, but before I could do anything, I felt a sensation I hadn't before.

Swelling... lots of lots of swelling that stretched me out more than I had anticipated.

"James..." I whined, "James, it hurts, but God, it feels so good."

My nails dug into his back as I clawed at him. "Take it, Ivy. Take all of it because it won't go away until I make you mine."

I screamed out in pleasure over and over again; the friction hitting all the right spots.

"Tell me you're mine..." he whispered, hitting harder as he did. "Tell me I can keep you."

"Yes," I cried out, "oh God, yes."

Something about what I said triggered a primal instinct within him because he increased at a speed I wasn't ready for, and as I came, so did he, but at the same time, he threw his head back and came straight down onto my shoulder making me scream out in pain and pleasure.

A swirl of blackness danced through my eyes, and as he pulled back, I could have sworn I had seen blood upon his lips and a golden lustful look in his eyes.

The cool breeze of an open window made my eyes open in surprise. I hadn't anticipated falling asleep with a window open last night, but then again, I could only remember bits and pieces of whatever I had gotten myself into.

Slowly sitting up, I held my head, a headache splitting through my skull like a mini earthquake. "Shit... I drank too much."

"Yeah, you did." James' voice caused me to freeze in my spot. Slowly I looked up toward my door and saw him standing there in nothing but a loose pair of gray sweatpants and no shirt.

Sweet fucking baby Jesus.

The events of sleeping with James flooded my mind, and I couldn't help but think of how delicious he looked this morning. I wonder if he wants to go again because I wouldn't mind breakfast in another way.

'Sounds like a good plan to me.' His voice echoed through my mind, and my eyes widened in shock. The fuck was that!

"Well, I could tell you, but I am sure you will freak out."

My eyes snapped to him, but I wasn't sure if he was referring to my drink or the fact that he had also literally answered the question I had in my head. A chuckle left his lips as he shook his head, watching me.

"Here, take the Tylenol and get dressed. I have coffee and breakfast for you."

I hesitated as he handed me the Tylenol and a water bottle. "We had sex."

His brow quivered, and a smile crossed his lips. "Yeah, we did."

"But Damian said—" Shit! Damian was going to kill me!

"Don't worry about him. One, he is out of town till next week, and two, I don't ever listen to him, so you shouldn't either."

As pleasant as that notion was, I did feel better than Damian was out of town, which meant I could do whatever I wanted, and there was nothing he could do to me.

At least not right now, anyways.

"Well, then..." I said, letting the blanket fall off my naked body and drop to the bed as I slid from it and stood in front of him. "Perhaps, I have something else you can eat for breakfast then."

A smirk crossed his lips, and I watched the hungry gaze return. "Maybe if you're a good girl. But we have company, so unless you want to join the three of us naked, you may want to put clothes on."

"Three?" I asked, confused as I peeked my head out from the bedroom to see Hale and Talon both staring at me. Hale, of course, raised his hand and waved, causing me to give him an awkward wave back.

Shit... are they going to lecture me too?

James laughed again, leaning in and kissing me gently. "No, they aren't. Now hurry up."

Stunned was the only feeling I had at that moment. I wasn't sure why James kept answering all my questions like he could read my mind, but perhaps all the alcohol I had last night had me losing my mind or talking out loud.

Pulling my black silk robe from the closet door, I slid it over my naked body and brushed my teeth before walking out into the living room. Hale and Talon's eyes swept over me, but yet neither of them said anything right away.

"Good morning, guys," I mumbled, trying to find something to say that didn't make it any more awkward than it already was.

"Good morning to you as well, Ivy. It seems you have managed to disregard all of Damian's rules." Hale chuckled.

"Yeah, she did," Talon stated as well, "nothing we can do about it now."

Slowly I turned away from them both, trying to wrap my mind around the fact they were even sitting in my living room to begin with. "So why are you here?" I finally asked, trying to kill the suspense.

"That would be because of me." James replied, giving me a smile, "we need to talk to you."

"You know, historically speaking, sentences that start with 'we need to talk' never end well." My words seemed to bring a humorous moment to the whole situation, and all three men laughed.

"Very true, but this conversation could be very pleasurable to you."

Taking a moment to think about it, I sat on the small armchair and smiled at them. "Well, go ahead and explain. What is it you want?"

"Well..." Hale replied, looking at Talon, who nodded his head before he continued, "to be honest, Ivy, we want you."

The sip of coffee I had been drinking quickly went down the wrong tube, sending me into a fit of coughing as I tried to grasp what they had just said. "I'm sorry—what?"

"I know it may seem like a lot, but Damian, Talon, James, and myself have always been close growing up. We have always done everything together and shared everything together. And now that is what we want with you. To share you between us, and in return, we will only belong to you."

What Hale was saying was like something out of a very expensive porn movie. I couldn't believe that Hale and Talon were sitting in my living room, with James, as they discussed sharing me between the three of them like their personal sex slave.

"So you want a poly relationship?" I questioned, trying to figure out where he was going with everything.

"Kind of," James interrupted with a smile, "we aren't like normal people Ivy, but regardless of that, we all want to share you equally."

I was taken back by what they were asking. When I woke up this morning, I had to only deal with the idea of getting away with sleeping with James, but the twins wanted me too? Never had I ever slept with more than one man at a time, and yet here they wanted to share a moment that most women dreamed of.

"Uh, I don't know what to say."

It was a true revelation. I didn't have the faintest idea what to say in order to make what they wanted work.

Caught by the Twins

My small living space seemed that much smaller with the amount of man that was currently piled within it. James, Hale, and Talon all sat there staring at me as if waiting for me to simply say that it was okay. When I first arrived, they had all treated me less than I should have been.

Yet, here, three of them were sitting, asking me to be in the middle of a massive orgy.

"If I say no..." I was curious to know what their reaction would be if I said no. As I expected, Talon's face contorted into anger, and he stood to his feet, storming toward the door.

"I told you she wouldn't fucking accept us," Talon growled, throwing the door open and storming out of it. My eyes widened in shock as I glanced back at the others. I didn't know what to say or do because I wasn't saying no. I was simply asking what would happen if I did.

A hurt expression crossed Hales's face as he stood to his feet, "No... stay."

My quick reply took him by surprise as I stood, following out the door where Talon had escaped too. The morning sun glared down upon me, causing me to raise my hand above my eyes to shield them from the awful glare.

"Talon?" I called out as I searched around, trying to figure out where he had disappeared to. As I searched near the tree line, I saw a disappearing figure that looked like him. "Talon!" I yelled again, hoping that he would stop so that I could explain.

I didn't like the idea of following him into the woods, but I couldn't let him think that I was telling him no. I had to explain myself and make him understand that I just wanted to know all of my options. Moving quickly through the brush, I entered deep into the thick darkness of the woods.

Every step I took creaked across the foliage as broken leaves ached at the heaviness of my step. "Talon?" I called out again, frustrated that I was out here in nothing but my robe, searching for a man with more anger issues than I knew what to do with.

The sounds of something moving within the forest caused me to halt in my steps. My heartbeat slowly picked up as I spun around in a circle, trying to figure out what it was that was out there. The uneasy feeling of being watched crept through me, and uncertainty settled in.

"This isn't funny!" I screamed out loud as fear swept through me. I wasn't stupid when it came to nature. I knew what could be out there. Bears, mountain lions, wolves... those were just some of the dangerous animals that could be near me at any given time.

The low growl of something sounded from behind me, and I froze. I knew that growl was of a wolf, an animal I had spent time with in a sanctuary in Georgia. Slowly I turned around and came face to face with a wolf more massive than any I had ever seen.

"Oh, shit... shit, shit, shit," I mumbled to myself, "Hey there, little Wolfie—"

The creature snapped in my direction quickly, and I thought I was done, but to my surprise, it seemed to be a warning to watch myself. As a tear slid down my face, I tried to take small baby steps backward, attempting to leave the forest, and get as far away from the creature as I possibly could.

Oh, my God. I'm going to die.

Tears streamed down my face as I heard James yelling my name in the distance. I couldn't call out to him, though, because with every step I took closer to his voice, the wolf took a step closer to me.

"Please don't kill me..." I pleaded with it, not wanting my life to end over something so stupid.

"Ivy!" James yelled again, getting closer. The sounds of multiple footsteps approached until he stopped just short of behind me, holding his hands up to the wolf.

"Enough!" Hale growled, causing the wolf to look at him with uncertainty.

Confusion split through me. With Hales' command, the wolf took a step back as if obeying what he was saying. It was impossible unless this thing was his pet.

"Is this your pet?" I asked, slowly pushing myself behind Hale and James. The mention of it being a pet caused it to snarl at me again.

James, however, found my remark to be amusing. "Yeah... he is our pet," he stated before giving me a smirk.

The feeling that I was safe was comforting, but before I could say anything else, the cracking of bones resonated through the forest, and I watched in shock as the wolf in front of me changed.

"What the fuck are you doing?!" James yelled out in frustration as Hale tried to pull me out of the forest. However, my feet were planted firmly, and my eyes widened in shock as I saw the wolf turn from a wolf to Talon.

"Oh my God—" I whispered.

"She may as well know. What the fuck does it matter if she knows now?" Talon snapped, throwing the statement my way.

James shoved Talon back, who had tried to step closer. "We're supposed to handle this a different way, man. Not like this. She wasn't ready."

Wolves—like fucking werewolves.

No way. Werewolves are real?!

"Whoa, whoa, whoa," I stated, holding my hands up to silence them. "Werewolves are real?"

The three men stood staring at me before Hale smiled and nodded his head. "Yes, we are, as are other creatures from your fairytale books."

It took a moment for what he said to sink in, and slowly I spun around, walking away from them. I wasn't upset that they were werewolves. On the contrary, I was fascinated and excited at the same time. But what I wouldn't tolerate was being lied to.

"See! Look at her fucking leaving like I knew she would!" Talon screamed at Hale and James, causing me to turn around and storm back to him. This time, though, I shoved past Hale and James and walked straight up to Talon, using my hands with all my might to shove him back.

The golden ring was coming to the forefront of his eyes, and James was trying to snatch me away. "No! I am going to say what the fuck I have to say, and this prick is going to listen." I yelled, pointing at Talon.

"What do you honestly have to say? Nothing, I don't already know," he snapped back at me with an agonizing look as if trying to hold himself back.

"Seriously!" Taking my finger, I poked it into his chest while staring at him, "you are a fucking idiot, Talon. All you do is make snide remarks and assume shit, just like Damian."

"Don't you dare talk about my brother like that," Talon growled.

"Oh, what... you don't like me saying that he is an egotistical asshole with no regard except his own happiness? Yeah, that's clearly fucking obvious."

There was no backing down from this argument with Talon. None of them knew the real me. They had never even taken the time to get to know me, and everyone, even James, had done nothing but assumed who I was or what I could handle.

"I'm warning you, human..."

"Ivy, don't do this. He isn't like Hale and me," James warned me, trying to pull me away.

"No, he isn't," I replied, shaking my head in disappointment as the anger slowly slid away and was replaced with hurt. "Just for the record, Talon. I wasn't saying no. I wanted to know more about what you wanted. But obviously, there is a lot I don't know about any of you."

Pulling from James' grasp, I made my way down the path I had gone down before until my feet stepped upon the grass, and the sun once again soaked into me.

"Ivy," James called out, coming up behind me. "Please let me explain."

A sigh left me before I chuckled. "Explain what?" I asked, turning around, "that you didn't think I was able to know the truth about anything because I am a fucking human?"

James was shocked by my response and shook his head. "No, that isn't it."

"Well, obviously, it is. It makes sense now why Damian wanted to keep you guys away from me."

"Ivy, please let me explain," he asked again, gripping my arm gently and trying to pull me toward him. I could have, at that moment, fallen into him and accepted what he was offering, but to be honest, I needed time to adjust to what had just happened.

"No, James. I need time to be left alone."

They say when something traumatic happens in a person's life that, every individual handles it differently. Some cry their eyes out, and some get absolutely drunk. But to me, well, that was a completely different story.

I pretended that none of it even happened.

Pushing in my headphones, I let Fitz blast in my ears, pretending that my life was going to be okay. School had started before I knew it, and I had dropped into my regular routine of going to classes and then coming back and doing schoolwork.

Unfortunately for the guys, I hadn't been very forthcoming. James daily was trying to get me to reason with him and talk to him. He took every chance he could to hold my hand or touch me, and I knew, without a doubt, it was driving him insane with the silent treatment I kept offering.

But I wanted them to realize I wasn't some floozy college girl who would do everything they wanted or said, and while they argued amongst themselves about how to win me over, I researched werewolves.

I was intrigued to learn that such things exist, and I didn't want to rely on them to tell me everything because there was a chance they would hide the truth. At one point, I had considered asking my father, but then at the same time, I wasn't sure if he knew.

My eyes slid over the campus courtyard, and to my surprise, it was packed with students trying to soak up the last bit of sun from the summer before the clouds and cold rolled in, and we were stuck in sweaters, coats, and tons of snow.

"Ivy!" The distant call of my name caused me to turn and smile at Kate before taking one side of my headphones out. "I was wondering how loud you had that thing."

I couldn't help but laugh. "You know me–"

"Super focused," she finished, causing us both to laugh.

With everything that had been going on with me and the guys lately, Kate had become my escape. I, of course, couldn't tell her the guys were werewolves, but I did have to explain the mark on my neck was from kinky bondage sex with James, so she didn't think they were cannibals.

"Are you still not talking to him?" Kate questioned while smirking at me.

"What do you mean? Of course, I talk to him," I mumbled, shifting my stuff in my hands, trying to avoid the conversation. I wanted to climb in his lap and fuck him hard all week, but at the same time, a girl had to have principles.

"Who are you trying to lie to?" She cackled, shaking her head, "look at that poor guy."

Kate pointed behind me, and my eyes followed where she was looking. Talon, Hale, and James all stood by the truck. Talon looked angry about something as usual and was arguing with Hale, but James simply had his eyes on me with a sad, depressing look across his face that broke my heart.

Sighing, I looked back toward Kate and rolled my eyes. "What do you expect me to do?"

"Try giving them a chance to make it right," Kate suggested, causing me to groan. She was right. In a way, I had made them suffer for over a week over what had happened, and instead of being wrapped up within the three of them, I was only making myself suffer.

"Fine." I groaned before grabbing her hand and forcing her to come with me. If I was going to go over there, I wasn't doing it alone. I already knew if the three of them surrounded me, I was going to lose my mind.

James' eyes widened as I approached, and Hale smiled as Talon seemed just as stunned as James. You would have thought that they were watching a miracle happen as I walked toward them.

"Ivy," James said softly, causing them all to straighten up. "Are you okay?"

"Look," I said with a sigh, shaking my head. "I am not saying that I forgive you guys for hiding things from me, but—"

Taking a deep breath, I looked at Kate once more, who gave me 'the look' to continue. It had happened to be the same look my mother was fond of giving me. Looking at James, I considered everything I wanted to do. I wanted to kiss him, and I wanted to be with him and have him make me feel all the things he did, but at the same time, they had to realize I was my own person.

"—But?" he asked as if expecting me to reject him and send him on his way.

"Show me you guys are serious, and I can trust you, and perhaps I will let you guys get close to me."

James' eyes lit up in surprise, and his smile widened even more. "Are you serious?"

I had a feeling that part of me was going to regret agreeing to this, but then, at the same time, I couldn't take being away from James. Every time I closed my eyes, I dreamt of him, and every morning when I woke, I felt an emptiness inside of me from his absence.

"Yes, now I have to go." Turning quickly, I hastened my pace, trying to put distance between us. Just because I had agreed didn't mean I was going to stick around and just start acting like everything was okay.

"Ivy, wait!" James called, forcing me to stop and watch as he jogged to catch up with me. "We have a small problem, and I need to tell you, so you don't think I am hiding things from you."

I didn't like the way James seemed nervous, but I could understand it, considering the fact I had just agreed to give him a chance to show he was serious about me. "What's the problem?"

"Damian is back. He got in an hour ago, and he doesn't know anything yet."

A gut-wrenching feeling filled me at that moment. I knew that I should not have cared, but in a way, I did. I had disobeyed Damian and allowed something to develop with James, even though I wasn't supposed to. Not to mention Hale and Talon both wanted me as well.

"Is there a way we can not tell him anything? At least not right now?"

My question seemed to make James hesitate, and for some reason, I felt bad asking this of him. Damian was his brother, and I had just reprimanded them for keeping things from me, but then I was asking him to keep things from Damian.

"Well, we could try, but the problem is that I don't know how long that will work."

Nodding my head, I smiled. "We will figure it out. Let's talk about it later tonight. It's Friday, and I really want to get this last class over with and go home."

"Ivy—" Hale replied softly with a smile as he sat on my couch, "please understand... Damian is particular."

When I had said that we would figure out a plan with Damian, I hadn't meant that I was going to play prisoner in my cottage all weekend because they were worried about Damian smelling me.

"I don't get it, Hale. What do you mean, I smell different? Last time I checked, I smelt like lavender and roses." If the scowl on my face didn't explain how pissed I was, then my body language definitely would.

"Sweetheart," he attempted to say, but a glare from my direction made him stop. "Okay—Ivy, please understand wolves are different. When we mate with someone, it causes our scent to sort of mingle with theirs. So like for humans, they wouldn't notice it, but Damian would smell James all over you."

I deadpanned as I took in what he was saying, "wait—mate?"

"Yes, mate... That's what you and James did the other night." Hale stated as if confused by my reaction.

"So having sex is mating?" I asked, not understanding what the hell he was getting at. Did that mean the guy who I lost it to had mated with me in a sense? Grossed out by the idea, I shivered, shaking away the image.

"Hmm..." Hale said softly as if hesitant to answer me, "when you and James had sex, he knotted you and bit you, correct?"

Thinking back on the moment, I contemplated what had happened that night. James had asked me to be his, to give myself to him, and in the moment, I did. But I had just assumed it was sexy kink talk that he was doing because it got him off.

"Oh, my god... so he wasn't just talking dirty to me when he asked me to be his!" I exclaimed, covering my mouth with my hand, and causing Hale's eyes to widen in surprise.

"Oh, shit." Scratching the back of his head, he looked out the window toward James, who was walking with Talon back to my home. "Uh—well.."

"James!" I screamed at the top of my lungs, causing him to burst through the door.

"What happened—are you okay–did Hale do something?!" His eyes flared out angrily toward Hales's direction.

"You mated with me," I replied softly, staring at him. It was then that something clicked inside James' mind, and he looked at me as if he had been caught like a kid with his hand in the cookie jar.

"Look, Ivy I can explain–" he replied as I began smacking his arms in anger. "Ouch, will you stop..."

Talon was the one who intervened, wrapping his arms around my waist and pulling me close to his body as he leaned down, inhaling my neck, taking in my scent. "Did he not ask before he did it?" His voice growled, causing my eyes to close as I tried to get hold of myself, pulling my body from his grasp.

"No more touching me... you guys are driving me crazy doing that."

Talon smirked as Hale chuckled as the three men watched me with hungry gazes. "We can smell your arousal as well, Ivy," James replied, causing me to blush.

"Stop trying to change the subject, James. Why didn't you tell me the truth, then?"

A sudden feeling in the air shifted between them, and they quickly gave each other a look of uncertainty before Talon ran out the door. "Look, I will explain later, okay, I promise."

"James, you better," I warned before watching him sprint from the cottage.

I wasn't sure what was going on, but Hale had told me they were supposed to be running in their wolves tonight. Because of this, they wanted me to stay in the cottage and keep the door locked. I wasn't sure why, but Damian being back on the grounds didn't make me feel well about my situation.

As the sky fell into darkness, I opened the window of the cottage and allowed the cool evening air in. I had a mountain of homework to do, and I doubt that Mr. Zebak would allow me an extension on my essay two weeks into the school year. I had to find a way to get the guys to stop distracting me all the time.

Thinking about them distracting me didn't help either, but I had to push through. Pulling my books from my backpack, I took a seat at my desk with my laptop before pulling my hair up into a ponytail and sliding my glasses onto my face.

"The History of Commercial Agriculture..." I mumbled as I typed out the topic for my essay.

"That sounds boring..." a voice called out, causing me to jump as I spotted Hale looking through the open window, a chuckle leaving his lips as he smiled at me. "Did I scare you?"

Rolling my eyes, I smirked, "yes. Now, what are you doing here?"

"Well, I have come to keep watch over you while they run. Unlike the others, I actually do homework and pay attention to school. So I just lied and told them I had to finish an essay. I didn't like the idea of leaving you alone tonight."

The consideration Hale had to make sure I was okay, considering Damian was back, was sweet. Standing to my feet, I gestured for him to come in and quickly walked toward the door, unlocking it.

Hale's tall form was in front of me in a matter of seconds, and I realized just how close I was to him. I hadn't expected him to be more than the man I had first become accustomed to when I moved here, yet he was far different from the others in his own way.

"Umm–you can come in," I whispered, trying to get a bearing on myself as I spun away from him and headed toward the kettle to make some tea and try to clear my mind of the distraction he was creating again.

"I am going to close the windows and blinds–is that okay?" Hale called over to me, causing me to turn and look at him.

"Why?"

"Well, because if Damian does happen to run by here, he will smell you with an open window, and do you really want a peeping tom?" His chuckle caught me off guard and caused me to smirk.

"Oh, you mean like you?" I asked, raising my brow. "Remind me why you went to my window first and not the door?"

"Yeah, yeah," he mocked, rolling his eyes as he moved around the area.

If Hale was going to be here tonight, then that meant I wasn't going to get anything done when it came to homework, and that thought itself was depressing. It was only Friday, but at the same time, I wanted to relax for the rest of the weekend.

"Since you are here, do you think I can pick your brain and ask some questions?"

Hale turned to stare at me, hesitating for a moment as if he wasn't sure, but as I glided over toward him, handing him the hot cup of tea, he smiled. "Sure, why not?"

There was honestly only one question that had been running through my mind since earlier in the day, and that was the subject of mates. I didn't understand it, and one thing made me curious...

"So mating happens with sex and other stuff, or so I am guessing."

"Yes, there is a lot that goes into it," Hale replied with a smile that caused hesitation to fill me as I contemplated how I was going to word my next question.

"Explain to me how I mate with the rest of you."

Time with Hale

Hale

HOURS EARLIER

"Hale, what are you doing?" Damian asked, walking into my room. Looking up from my desk, I gestured to the papers and laptop in front of me.

"Working on my thesis, what does it look like I'm doing?"

A groan left my brother as he rolled his eyes as if me doing homework irritated him. In reality, that wasn't my plan tonight, but in order to do what I wanted, I had to make sure that my staying behind from the run was believable.

"Seriously, Hale? I just got home, and we always run together as a group."

Sighing, I shook my head. "I'm sorry, man. This is important. I have to work on it. Don't worry, though. I will run with you next time."

I watched as Damian stared at me for a moment as if contemplating what I was saying was true, but I had never given him a reason to doubt me before, so why start now?

"Fine," he replied reluctantly, "Hey, what's up with James? He is acting rather off today."

I glanced at him in confusion. Of course, I knew what was up, but at the same time, I couldn't well tell Damian that it was because of Ivy, even though I was jealous myself. I had wanted her from the moment I laid eyes on her, and yet, James was the one that got to take her first.

"Think he is seeing some new chick from campus. Who knows, man, he always has to have his dick wet from someone." Damian chuckled at my response, nodding his head.

"Yeah, well, as long as he is staying away from Ivy, I don't care."

It was still strange how we all were destined for her. On very rare occurrences in history did multiple Alphas share a mate, but to have four Alpha-blooded wolves share one mate—well, it was unheard of.

"Yeah, well, she has been keeping to herself from what I have seen. Stop worrying about her and enjoy your run."

Damian hesitated before sighing. "Yeah, I suppose so. I will catch you later..."

The conversation I had with Damian earlier in the night caused me to think about what Ivy was asking. She was a human who had just been introduced into the world of the supernatural, and she had no idea what she was getting herself into.

The fact that James mated with her without explaining everything had irritated me. Ivy deserved better than that, and it was the exact reason Damian had stopped him the first time he tried it.

James was the youngest of us all, and he didn't stop to think about what he was doing until he had already done it. Sighing, I looked at Ivy and smiled.

"Mating will be different with each one of us."

"Okay, care to explain?" she asked again, and I found myself a little unsure of how the conversation was supposed to go. I was smarter than my brothers, but at the same time, I was the worst at explaining things properly. That job usually fell to Damian since he was the oldest, but he was more complicated when it came to Ivy.

"Each of us likes different things, Ivy. However, because Talon and I are twins, to mate with us means to mate with us both," I said slowly, hoping she understood what I meant.

She was quiet for a moment, and slowly her mouth made an 'O' shape as her eyes widened, "like at the same time!"

A chuckle left my lips as I nodded. "Yes. At the same time. Talon and I like our one-on-one moments, but at the end of the day, we are very close, and sharing you between us at the same time is one of the things we would want."

I could almost see the wheels turning in her head as I spoke, and because of this, I knew that it was going to complicate things if this frightened her. "I see."

"Ivy, don't let that scare you. Sex with us would be on your own terms, and we would never force you to do anything you are not comfortable with."

A smile fell across her lips as she lifted the white cup to her lips and sipped on her drink again. I could see the pink tint to her cheeks and the way she clenched her legs together, trying to hide her arousal. The idea was one that didn't repulse her, but it also made her nervous.

'Hale, where the fuck are you?' James asked through mind link, causing me to hesitate at what I was going to say to Ivy.

'Ahh, little brother. Is the run done already?'

'Yeah, and Damian is looking for you. Please don't tell me you are with Ivy.'

'Perhaps, I am.'

I smiled to myself as I watched Ivy stand from her seat and go to the counter to refill the kettle. She was absolutely beautiful, and the fact that her mind was so extraordinarily bright was something else that turned me on.

'What the fuck are you doing! If he finds you there–'

'Enough, James. I needed stimulating conversation, and Ivy is a stimulating person.'

'Did you two have sex?!'

I could almost feel the anger and jealousy rolling off of him. Because he had already mated her, he was going to be more possessive, but it was really bad right now because Ivy declined him any form of affection right after the bond was complete.

His fault, of course. He should have listened to what I told him to begin with.

'Wouldn't that have been something? But to answer your question, no.'

'You need to get out of there, Hale. Before things escalate.'

'In time, little brother. In time.'

Closing off the mind link to James, I settled my sights back onto the beautiful woman in front of me. She was completely oblivious to the evils in our world, and yet she was so open to the idea that werewolves were real. I would have thought she would have run away repulsed like Damian tried to paint, but instead, she accepted it.

"Why weren't you scared when you saw Talon change?" I finally asked, causing her to stop in her tracks and slowly turn to look at me with a grin on her lips.

"Well, in all honesty, I was shocked. But I worked at a wolf sanctuary in Georgia for two years. So wolves don't frighten me—I mean, they do in a sense, but not in the way you would think. That is why I knew what to do when Talon's wolf first approached me. Had I run, he would have given chase, and there is no telling what would have happened."

Smart woman, and absolutely right.

"You are right, Ivy. I am impressed with the way you handled the situation."

She smiled at me again before coming over to where I was sitting and taking a seat close to me. "Can I tell you a secret, Hale?"

I wanted more than anything for her to share her secrets with me. To confide in me and trust me to help her whenever she needed it. "Of course, Ivy."

"For some reason—" she started before she began to bite the bottom of her lip, the motion making me want to kiss her more than anything as my wolf paced at the back of my mind. "I feel safe around you all, except for Damian—I want to be around him, but it's different. He makes me feel dangerous, and that scares me."

I was happy that she felt safe around the three of us, but to hear what she said about Damian, I felt confused. Damian had always been the one who protected us all and made sure we were doing what needed to be done. He was the Alpha of us all in a way.

"I am glad that I can make you feel safe, but I don't know what to say about Damian. He isn't a bad person, Ivy. He just has been through a lot in life, and you will have to give him time to adjust to you."

Nodding her head, she sighed before her eyes met mine once more. "I understand. You should really go before someone finds you here. I don't want you to get in trouble."

I hated that she was telling me to leave because I wanted to stay here with her forever. "As you wish, Ivy."

Standing to my feet, I set the cup she had given me down and walked toward the door. Before I could reach the doorknob, her voice pulled me back in, "Hale—"

"Yes?" I replied without turning around. I was already fighting to keep my wolf intact, and if I turned back, he wouldn't let me leave.

"Please come back to see me more often. I really enjoyed tonight."

Smiling, I nodded. "Of course, dear Ivy. I will be back again."

And next time, I will have you going to heights of pleasure you didn't know existed.

Ivy

The next few days went by faster than I had expected, and as Wednesday rolled around, I groaned, thinking about the essay I was turning in. Hale had not come back to see me since the night of the run, and the few times James stopped by, he explained that he had to be careful because he didn't want Damian to smell me on him.

I was half tempted to tell Damian I was fucking his brother because the build-up of sexual frustration was causing me to lose focus, and so help me, if I got anything below an 'A' on this essay, I was going to lose my mind.

"Good morning, Ivy," Mr. Zebak said as I walked into his room with a smile. He was young for a professor, but all the girls fawned over how handsome he was.

While most professors were old and balding, Mr. Zebak was tall and well-defined, with gorgeous black hair and beautiful gray eyes. I had to admit that my professor was sexy as hell, but at the same time, he didn't compare to James, Talon, Hale, or even Damian.

"Good Morning, Mr. Zebak. I hope you are doing well today."

Making my way toward my seat, I could almost feel his eyes upon me, and the sensation of him watching me made my heart race.

As class began, I found myself toward the back of the class with prime viewing of the screen. The theater-style seating made it better to get a proper view of the large digital screen he taught from.

I enjoyed my time in Mr. Zebak's class. He had easily become one of my favorite teachers, and when in his class, I was completely focused. At least until images of the guys start to flood my mind, and I find myself drifting from the lesson in front of me.

My phone slowly lit up with a notification and hesitating, I flipped it over. I never answered my phone in class, but since the guys got my number and started texting me, I couldn't help but wait by my phone, expecting to see a message. Just like the one I got now.

My heart swelled when I opened my phone and saw the message was from James. The only problem was when I opened the text, I found it wasn't a normal message, and my face quickly blushed red.

'God, I want to taste you right now. Look how excited you have me.'

My eyes widened even more as I scrolled down, seeing the image of his hard cock.

'Oh, my God! Who the hell sends dirty photos anymore?!'

No matter how much I tried to be turned off by it—I couldn't. Instead, it made the sexual frustration in me even worse. I wanted more than anything to feel him inside me, and the more I thought about it, the more my core ached for him.

'Don't act like texting you like this doesn't turn you on, Ivy.'

James' next message caused me to smile and roll my eyes.

'I am in class, James.'

'Yes, I know. But that's what makes it more fun. So tell me how wet you are for me.'

James was really trying to put me in an uncomfortable position, and I wasn't sure I was ready for that kind of talk with him. James was goofy and fun—not to mention amazing in bed.

But sexting? I wasn't sure if that was my jam.

'I will talk to you later, James. Goodbye.'

I smirked as I sent my message and then put my phone down, trying to focus on Mr. Zebak, whose eyes were solely focused on me before he turned and continued his presentation. I was instantly embarrassed, thinking he saw me not paying attention, and quickly sulked into my seat, trying to remain invisible.

As time carried on, I continued taking notes until my phone signaled another message, and I couldn't stop the urge to groan, wanting to check but not wanting Mr. Zebak to see me doing so again.

With a sigh, I quickly picked up my phone, trying to hide what I was doing behind my laptop, and checked it. I smiled when I saw it wasn't James, but Hale that had messaged me.

'I had fun with you the other night. I would really like to see you again tonight.'

Biting my bottom lip, I thought about what he had said. With James, it was nothing but sexual attraction and fun. With Hale, it was something else completely. I had thought a lot about what he had said about mating with the twins, and I had to admit that more than once, the idea had turned me on.

'How about later tonight? If you are capable of escaping, that is.'

I wasn't one to be a tease, but I loved pointing out at any chance I could how they always wanted to do what Damian said and how worried they were about Damian finding out about me.

In a sense, I was their dirty little secret. As much as I would have thought that would have bothered me—I was surprised when it didn't.

I actually enjoyed sneaking around, but I didn't want to sneak around and not get laid.

The sex had been more than amazing with James, and every night when I closed my eyes, I found myself moaning, thinking about what it would be like with the rest of them.

'Oh, don't you worry about that. I am capable of doing more than you think.'

The playful tone of Hale's message made me blush. *'I look forward to it.'*

A smirk crossed my face as I sent the text to him. I wasn't a girl to text like this, but something about the guys stirred something inside me and made me want to do bad things.

"Ivy? Are you okay?" Mr. Zebak said, looking up at me. Coming back to my surroundings, I realized the class was over, and everyone had left except for my professor and me.

"Oh, I'm sorry. I got so busy with my work I wasn't paying attention." Quickly, I grabbed my belongings and put them in my bag as I stood from my seat.

"Hey–" he said as he hesitated for a moment and cleared his throat. "Don't worry about it, but do me a favor, Ivy—"

"Sure, anything..." I responded happily.

A grin crossed his face at my response, and he smiled. "Please call me Caleb. You are one of my star students, and only my stars get that privilege."

Stunned by his admission, my smile widened. "Thank you, Caleb. I will see you Friday morning."

"Oh, I am looking forward to it, Ivy." The sultry way he said my name sent shivers down my spine, but in a pleasurable way, I hadn't been expecting. Perhaps my lack of sex was starting to make me want to fuck everything with legs.

Exiting the theater, I headed across the courtyard toward the cafe, "Ivy!" Kate's overly excited voice squealed, causing me to turn around and see her, James, Hale, and Talon posted on the courtyard wall with two other guys I didn't recognize. To top it off, one of them had their hands all over Kate.

As I approached, a smirk spread across my face. "Oh, what do we have here?" I taunted, looking at Kate and the man she was with.

"This is Silas–" James replied as he took my books, and Hale took my bag, setting them down on the wall, pulling me in between them. "And the other one not wrapped up in Kate is Jacob."

"Hey," They both said in unison until the one named Jacob spoke up again, "Brandon is somewhere around, but you know him... he is always into someone new every time we turn around."

Laughter settled over the group as I smiled and tried to pay attention to how Hale was running his fingers across the small of my back as James had his arm around my shoulder.

"Well, I need to run back to my dorm, and Silas is going to help me," Kate said with a smirk, causing me to laugh.

"Don't be silly, wrap your willy!" James called out across the courtyard at Silas, causing multiple people to stop and turn to look at us, laughing.

"I really need a coffee," I said softly as I pushed my head against James' shoulder.

"I actually got you one," Talon replied as he came walking back up to our group. I hadn't even realized that he had disappeared, and I found it so touching that Talon had done something like that for me.

"Thank you, Talon. That's so sweet." Gently handing the coffee to me, I smiled and took a sip. It was exactly how I liked it, down to the exact sugar amount, and that blew my mind. "You know exactly how I like my coffee?"

James, Hale, and Jacob all looked at Talon in shock as he stood there trying to look like a badass as he shrugged his shoulders. "Medium roast, cream, two sugars with two pumps of vanilla."

Never had a guy done something as simple as that and been completely romantic. I was the type of girl who was easy to please, and a small sentiment like that went miles with me. Out of all the brothers, Talon: the quiet, angry, and aggressive one, was the one who knew exactly what I liked.

Handing the coffee to James, I stepped from his grip and walked toward Talon. I could see the hesitation in his eyes as I came closer, and his body tensed as if he wasn't too sure what I was about to do. "Come here," I whispered, pressing against him.

Wrapping my arms around him, I rested my head against his chest and hugged him, and it was then that I finally felt him slowly lose the tension, and relax into my embrace. My eyes slowly drifted up to his, and as they did, I wrapped one arm around his neck and pulled his lips to mine.

His eyes widened in shock before I pulled away with a smile.

"Talon—" I whispered as my lips traveled down his neck, stopping underneath his throat. "Thank you for the coffee. That was very sweet."

As I stepped back, he looked at me in shock, and the expression on the other guys' faces as I turned to look at them made me crack a smile. They were all staring at me, shocked, with their mouths parted as if they didn't understand what had happened.

Picking up my belongings, I grabbed my coffee from James and smiled at them.

"You boys have fun. I have to get to class."

Arguments with Damian

Things had become more interesting over the past few weeks than I had expected them to be. I hadn't realized through it all that I was actually finding myself more and more comfortable here every day. The only lingering worry in my mind was that of Damian and why he was acting the way he was toward me.

As I pulled into the garage, close to dark, I had the feeling that someone was watching me, and I wasn't wrong. Shutting the car door, I turned to find Damian standing behind me. The three-piece suit he wore fit him like a glove, and that dark stare in his eye had me curious as to what was on his mind.

"Why are you home late?" He asked, his dark sultry tone swimming around me.

I blinked twice before snapping out of my thoughts and raised a brow in question. I wasn't sure why he was always concerned with where I was going but perhaps it had to do something with this mate thing James and Hale had tried explaining to me.

"I stayed late to study with the girls. Why does it matter?"

He narrowed his eyes at me, "because it matters where you are going. If you're going to be late, you need to let someone know."

A scoff left my throat as I gave a soft chuckle and headed toward the side door of the garage. "I am an adult, Damian. I don't have to tell you anything."

Before my hand could grip the handle, I found myself spun around and pinned against the door. His firm body pressed against my own, and my breath caught in my throat.

"Don't tell me what you will or will not do, Ivy. You will let me know. Do you understand me?" My heart raced at his words as I slowly looked up at him.

"Or what–" I asked breathlessly, "what are you going to do if I don't?"

Damian didn't know that I knew he was a wolf, and I knew very well I was playing with fire when it came to this man. Yet, my mind didn't seem to think straight when it came to speaking to him.

"You don't want to try me, Ivy. I can be a dangerous man if I want to be."

His threat did nothing to me but made my heart race even more. I was rebellious, and at times, I didn't care about anything, but with him, it was far worse. It was as if all my senses completely flew out the door, and a part of me wanted to challenge him.

"I highly doubt that, Damian. So let me go and stop playing games with someone who can play them better than you."

Damian's eyes shot up in surprise, and a wicked grin crossed his face. I couldn't help but notice the look in his eyes as the gold flecks began to peak, and I wondered if he would finally break his streak of acting like he didn't want me.

"You are naïve if you think that you can stand toe to toe with me, girl." Stepping back, Damian let go of me, laughter leaving him as he turned away from me and walked back toward the door he had come through.

I was left shocked as I watched him go. The loss of his touch made something inside me ache as I wanted him back. "Yeah, walk away. That's all you're good at doing, right?"

Rolling my eyes with hurt in my chest, I turned and opened the door, but before I could cross the threshold, he had pulled me back, gripping my neck as he lifted my head and pressed his lips upon my own.

An erotic rush of lust and desire swarmed through me, and instantly, I wanted him to take me. I wanted to be beneath him, begging for him, and the idea of it all made me feel disgusted in myself for being so damn horny for a man who had done nothing but treat me like shit since I had arrived.

As quickly as the kiss came, he tore himself away and looked down at me, sneering. His eyes held hate within them but also confliction. "Get out," he growled, and I didn't understand why he was doing this to me.

"No, stop fighting whatever you are and act on what you want."

Laughing at me again, he shook his head. "Get out of here, Ivy. You aren't worth my time."

His words broke me, but I refused to cry. I wasn't going to be that girl, and I wasn't going to allow him to see how he affected me. "I am not worth your time?" I scoffed.

"You heard me."

A smirk crossed my face as I shook my head. "Try the other way around, Damian. It's okay, though. I don't play games with men like you."

I watched his face contort even more into a disgusted look as if he couldn't understand the words that had left my lips, "men like me?"

"Mhmm... men like you. One's who are incapable of caring about anyone else but themselves." His laughter annoyed me, and the harder he laughed, the more pissed off I got.

"That's good!" he spat out in between his laughter. "I can promise you that none of those little college boys will give two shits about you once they leave."

The cruelty he spat was unnecessary, and the more he continued, the less patient I was getting with him. He was nothing but an egotistical asshole, and if he really wanted to go down the road he was, then I would give him what he wanted.

"Is that so? Because I have had no problem getting more than one man interested in me in all the most amazing ways—screaming in pleasure as they enjoy tasting me has been worth the time I have spent with them."

I wasn't sure where I got the courage to say what I did, but perhaps it was because I was tired of his bullshit and wanted to hurt him in the way he had tried to get to me. I wasn't entirely lying. James had pleasured me in more than one way, but I couldn't tell Damian that—it was still a secret.

An has for Hale, well, perhaps I would take care of that tonight. Who knows?

"You gave yourself away as some common whore!" He screamed at me, and with his words, the door to the house flew open, and James came running out before Damian could step toward me. His eyes looked between us in panic as he grabbed Damian, stopping him.

"The hell is going on?" James asked, looking between us.

"Ivy has been whoring herself out at school. Haven't you?" he seethed in anger as James looked at me wide-eyed, trying to figure out what Damian meant.

"Whoring myself out! That's a bit harsh. Then again, I enjoyed every moment I was screaming one man's name." Saying what I did, James tried to stifle the chuckle in realizing what I was talking about.

However, Damian didn't find any humor in what I was saying.

"Get the fuck out of here!" he yelled at me, and even with the argument, hearing him say that tore a part of me open and caused more pain than I thought it would.

"Ivy, please go," James asked, giving me a heartfelt look as if he knew the pain I was feeling, and perhaps he did. We were mated, supposedly—maybe that was a perk.

"Enjoy your evening," I whispered as I took a deep breath and turned, slamming the door behind me, and headed toward my cottage.

This wasn't how I had wanted my evening to go, but it seemed every time Damian and I were in the same room, we either wanted to fuck each other or kill each other.

My fingers traced over my lips as I thought about the way he kissed me. I hadn't expected it, and when it happened, I wanted way more than what I got. Damian was dangerous, but he also was intoxicating, and that intoxication made me crave more.

"What the hell am I doing?" I sighed. This was all becoming way too much. Stepping into my home, I dropped my bags down on the ground and looked around. I was causing more chaos for myself than was needed. Perhaps what I needed to do was to stop trying to argue with Damian at every turn and just ignore him when he was around.

"Ivy?" Hale's voice caused me to smile as I watched his body exit from my bedroom where he had been.

"What are you doing in my room?" I asked, pushing back the feelings Damian had just caused and forcing happiness to come forth.

"I heard what happened..." His eyes looked to me with concern, and I couldn't help but let my smile falter.

"How? That's so far away. There is no way you heard."

A chuckle left him as he stepped forward, wrapping his arms around me and pulling me in for a hug. "We have really good hearing, Ivy. The window is open."

Looking at the living room window, I saw what he meant. The window was open, and quickly, I pulled away and closed it. If wolves have good hearing, did that mean that people can hear when I have had sex?

"That's not disturbing. I guess that's why Damian caught James' and I the first time."

"No, no. This cottage is actually soundproof. It used to be a music studio years ago. James didn't shut off his link to us before he had sex, and we heard his thoughts clearly." Hale replied with a chuckle, causing me to turn with even more confusion.

"Link?" Wait, does that mean you guys can read thoughts or something?

There was so much about them that I still didn't know, and every time new information came in. I felt like I was so much further behind in trying to understand them.

"Yes, wolves who are linked together can speak telepathically. So, like with you and James... He can hear your thoughts, and from what he said, you project them loudly."

I was in shock. James could read my mind!

"Oh, that isn't an invasion of privacy or anything," I mumbled sarcastically as I went and turned on the kettle.

"Yes, it can be. And with humans, you can't turn it off like we can, but that's actually why I'm here. I brought you something." Turning, I watched Hale pull a small long black box from his pocket and hold it out to me.

With hesitation, I took it, my eyes darting to him as he smiled and gestured for me to open it. As I did, my eyes widened. Within the box was a gold chain with a clear crystal that hung from the end in the shape of a moon.

"Hale," I whispered as I looked at him again, "this is beautiful–"

"It's a moon stone, Ivy," he replied as he took the necklace from the box and helped to set it upon my neck. "It will help to block out the ability for us to read your mind unless you want to reach us."

"Really?" The fact that Hale was respecting my privacy in a way was more than sweet. Every time I spoke to him, he seemed to care more and more about how I felt about things and wanted to help me to understand more about their world.

"There," he replied softly, his body close to mind as his fingers brushed over my collarbone from behind. The touch of him caused me to shiver as I closed my eyes, relishing the way he made me feel. "You are so beautiful, Ivy."

"Hale–" I whispered again as I felt his lips come down on the side of my neck below my ear. "I want you."

"I know you do, Ivy... you smell so damn good," he whispered back, causing a soft moan to escape me.

Hale was completely different from his brothers. He was soft and gentle. Never once did he honestly make me feel unsure of myself. The moment I had met him in the dining room of my father's home, I knew that I could trust him, and yet I wasn't sure why.

"Then why hesitate?" I asked, curious as to why he didn't just take me like James had before.

A soft chuckle came from him, and when it did, I knew that the answer he was going to give was going to surprise me. "Because Ivy," he said softly, "I want to take my time with you and enjoy every moment I am with you."

Turning around in his arms, I looked up into his eyes. Hesitation filled me as I tried to understand what kind of man he really was. With each of them, I felt different as if they each unlocked a part of me that was closed away.

"Then kiss me and show me."

His lips descended upon mine, and as they did, I felt his passion and desire for me growing. His kisses became hungry, and the way he pulled me closer to his body let me know that he was holding back.

I was pulled back toward my bedroom, and quickly the door was closed. I had been thinking of this moment for the longest of times, and now that it was here, I was glad. I didn't want to waste a moment of it with him.

He peeled my clothes off like he was unwrapping a gift. I felt each brush of his skin like a brand. Falling back onto the bed, Hale removed his shirt. I couldn't stop staring at him as I bit my bottom lip. His tone and defined chest cut down to the v-line peaking above his pants. I wanted him like a dehydrated person wanted water in the desert.

"Please, Hale—" I pleaded as his hungry eyes trailed over me, "I need you."

A soft chuckle left his lips as he stared down at me. "Patience, I plan on taking my time with you."

I wasn't sure what he had in mind, but as his lips dipped down to the core between my legs, a gasp left me in realization. The way he devoured me was different from James. Hale tasted me as if I was the last meal he would ever eat, and there was no stopping him.

His hands wrapped around my thighs and held me in place as he made my cries of pleasure increase. I couldn't breathe, couldn't see. Stars flashed over my eyes as he had me coming undone. With every swirl of his tongue and growl of satisfaction, I was tipped over the edge.

"Hale, please—" I whimpered as tears of pleasure slid down my face.

I looked down to see the grin of satisfaction cross him, and slowly he trailed up until he allowed me to taste myself upon his tongue. His long, hard member parted my folds until he thrust deep inside me, a moan leaving both of us as he hilted.

"Oh God, Ivy. You're so wet and tight for me," he murmured next to my ear as he started thrusting slowly in me. The movement was agonizing because I wanted him hard and fast. Every time I thought I was going to come undone, he pulled back and stopped, delaying my orgasm.

Wrapping his arm around my thigh, he lifted my leg upon his shoulder and made deep, slow thrusts inside me. Something about being with Hale was more subtle and romantic. He took care of me, and all he cared about was pleasing me and helping me to feel every inch of him.

As the swelling of his knot began to grow, I cried out in pain as it mixed with the pleasure he was giving me. He was a little thicker than James was, but his agonizing torture of making me wait to cum was beyond anything I had ever experienced.

"I wanna feel you cum," I whispered to him as he kissed me again. My words had some effect on him and his wolf because, with my words, the intensity was suddenly turned on.

His movements became hard and fast, and my fingers gripped at his skin as I screamed in pleasure over and over again, feeling him spill his warm hot seed inside of me. And as he did, he gripped my thigh, sinking his teeth deep into the delicate flesh.

My eyes rolled back in pleasure, and euphoria filled me, and his bite burned through me. I was surprised this time to not pass out from the pleasure he had created like I had with James.

"Fuck," I replied breathlessly as he retracted his teeth from my leg and licked then licked up the blood that had spilled.

"I don't want to pull out of you. It feels so amazing." Hale chuckled as he thrust for fun just a few more times, waiting for his knot to go down. I giggled at his movements as he leaned over, kissing me gently. "You are the most amazing woman I have ever met."

"Mmm–" I moaned with a smile, kissing him again, "I could say the same about you, mate."

Unkept Promises

Laying within Hale's arms after we cleaned ourselves up, I couldn't help but wonder if this is how life would be all the time. Was it possible for four men—to love me forever?

It was an amazing idea, but at the same time, I felt so unsure of it all.

"What's on your mind, Ivy?" Hale whispered from behind me, pulling me closer to him as he wrapped himself around my body.

I didn't want to bother him with my problems, but at the same time, I was conflicted about everything and still worrying about getting my homework done for school. All of the moments I had spent worrying about what I was doing with them had caused me to lose focus on what I wanted.

Yet, even through the chaos that was my life, I couldn't stop my swirling emotions.

"Are you going to hide what you have with me like James does?" I asked softly, curious to know if Hale would be the same way James had been.

"Never. I don't care what Damian has to say, and if I have to move in here with you to show him that, then I will." He chuckled, kissing the back of my neck. His words made me smile, and a giggle escaped me as I rolled over to face him.

"You would move out here with me—"

A smile crossed his lips as he leaned in, kissing me. "I would move mountains for you."

"Hale," a voice called from out in the living room, causing my eyes to widen. I wasn't sure who it was, but it didn't sound like Damian. At least, I didn't think it did. Hale simply smirked at me before sighing and climbing off the bed.

"Talon, you didn't want to join us?"

The teasing sound in Hale's voice made me sigh. He was purposely trying to tease his brother, and Talon didn't seem like the type of man to be enthusiastic about something like that.

I had known for some time that, eventually, I would get to sleep with both of them, but they were going to allow me to decide when I wanted that to happen. That was the wonderful thing about Hale—he wouldn't force me into something.

I watched as Talon stepped into the doorway of the room. His well-defined upper half was on full display due to his lack of a shirt, with glistening beads of sweat dripping down his chest. I was fixed on him, and the sight itself was a turn on.

Laying with a sheet covering half of my body, I smiled at Talon as his eyes fell upon me naked on the bed. "Talon–"

"Go figure," he mumbled, shaking his head and turning away from me. I wasn't sure what had just happened, but my heart broke with the look Talon had given me. Had I honestly done something wrong?

"Dude, what is your problem?" Hale replied, following his brother, my footsteps quickly following behind him as I walked into the living room to spot the two men talking.

"Damian is looking for you. You may want to get back before he comes here."

"Okay," Hale replied as if he didn't care. "What does that have to do with you being rude to Ivy? Go figure?"

Talon's face was void of emotion. "I don't have time for this. Damian needs you and James to take care of an issue with an ally.

You need to go meet him, but I am sure he will smell Ivy all over you, so figure something out."

Hale hesitated for a moment before turning back to face me. I knew that Talon was right, and even though Hale said he wouldn't keep me a secret—it wasn't truthful.

"I have to go," he replied softly as Talon turned and left my home, slamming the door behind him. "I'm sorry, Ivy—"

I hushed him quickly and smiled. "It's okay. I understand."

In all honesty, I didn't understand one bit.

I didn't understand how I could have four amazing men in my life, and yet I was stuck playing dirty little secrets while trying to focus on school. There were a lot of things that I could do to change the outcome of my situation, but honestly, I wasn't sure if I wanted to risk the chance of losing Hale or James.

"I hate that I am having to do this after I promised you I wouldn't."

There was nothing but sincerity in Hale's words, and as I closed the distance between us, I leaned up, planting a soft kiss upon his lips. "Sometimes in life, we have to do things we don't want to, to make sure the ones we care for are safe."

The movie quote made him smile, and with another breathless moment, he stole a kiss from me before turning and quickly leaving. Being alone wasn't something that was new to me. For the longest time, I had been alone even if I wasn't physically alone.

With Hale and James leaving for a while, though, it meant I would be able to focus more on my studies, which was what I needed. I had to learn to control how my life was flowing, and it was hard to do with the two of them lurking around every corner.

"I have to get my life together," I mumbled to myself, letting go of a sigh I hadn't known I had been holding.

Days quickly passed, and with Hale and James gone, I fell into a familiar rhythm with school. I knew very well that with winter approaching, it was going to mean semester exams would quickly follow, and that was something I wasn't ready for.

In fact, I wasn't ready for a lot of things, but I had to keep focused.

"Ivy, did you pick up the notes from Zebak?" Bree asked as we all sat around the table at the University cafe.

I sighed, shaking my head. "No–"

There was a lot I still had to do, and because I had missed Caleb's class a few days ago, I still needed to get the printed notes from the lesson. Caleb had been more than happy to gather the notes together for me, and that was something else that made me feel uneasy.

"Girl–" Kate added, looking at me shocked, "are you sure you're feeling okay? You have been like a space cadet the last few days, and that isn't like you."

"I know, I know." The mumble stumbled out of my mouth as I closed the textbook in front of me and piled all of my belongings into my backpack. "I will stop by there now before I head home."

Kate and Bree looked at each other with concern as I forced a smile upon my face. "Do you want me to come with you?"

"Absolutely not. You have Calculus homework to do," I grinned, causing Kate to groan.

"That she does," Maddy mumbled, causing everyone to laugh but Kate.

It was moments like these that made me remember why I loved the life I had, even if it was more than complicated at times.

"It's not my fault the shit's impossible!" The protest that filled the table caused me to giggle before I waved goodbye and left their heated debate on how math was unnecessary.

I enjoyed the last few days spending every afternoon with the girls studying. I had informed my father the day we decided to do it just in case Damian tried his crap with me again. I didn't want him constantly snooping, and with my father knowing I was going to be late everyday, it seemed to keep Damian away.

"Ivy!" Caleb called out with a smile as he set his glasses on his desk and stood to his feet. "I was wondering when you were going to stop by. Are you feeling better?"

Guilt filled me for lying to him, but I pushed it aside, giving him a smile as I nodded. "Yes, I am much better now, thank you."

I had missed his class because I had claimed to be sick, but the truth was I had been reeling with everything that was going on at home and didn't want to face going to school with my mind a mess.

"That's wonderful. Oh, let's grab those papers."

Caleb turned from me and made his way toward his desk, picking up a yellow packet that had been lying at the corner. I watched him hesitate for a moment before his eyes cast up toward me, and he took the steps to close distance, slowly holding the package out. "I added a few extra things in there for you as well to help with the upcoming exam."

"Oh," I was shocked at how kind he was, and as my eyes lifted to him again, I smiled. "Thank you so much. I really do appreciate this, Caleb."

"You don't have to constantly thank me, Ivy. I don't just consider you a student, but also a friend. If you ever need anything from me, all you have to do is ask."

I felt like there was another meaning behind what he said, and as he stepped even closer to me, I felt a wave of emotions that built up between the gap that still separated us. "Caleb," I whispered. "I appreciate your help."

I had to change the subject and diffuse the situation. There was a chance Caleb was misreading the situation with me, and I couldn't afford to have that happen. Yes, he was incredibly hot, and under any other circumstances, I would have done a lot of naughty things with him, but he wasn't James, Hale, Talon, or Damian.

Those were the only men I wanted.

"I really should be going," I replied softly as the tension between us became almost unbearable. "I need to get home to work on all of this."

Shifting from foot to foot, I turned from Caleb, but not before he grabbed my upper arm, stopping me in my tracks. "Be careful out there, Ivy. A girl like you shouldn't be alone."

Something about the way he said what he had made me feel very vulnerable at that moment. It was like his words were a warning but also something far more dangerous.

"Thank you."

The words left my lips before I had a chance to think about saying anything else. I moved with a speed that surprised even me as I left his class and headed out into the courtyard of the school. My heart raced in my chest, and I wasn't sure why.

As my hand lifted to touch the necklace Hale had given me, I considered taking it off just so I could try to reach out to him or James. I missed our conversations, and since they both had been gone, I hadn't had the chance to speak to either of them.

It was as if they had gone radio silent and were off the grid.

All of which didn't sit well with me, but I wasn't accustomed to the life that they led being werewolves. I didn't know pack traditions or policies, and at times, those facts made me feel like a foreigner in my own home.

Pulling my phone from my back pocket, I quickly checked to see if the messages I had sent to Hale had been read. Disappointment filled me, though, when I saw that they still sat unread as they had two days before.

You would think that because I was their mate, they would be more interested in checking up on me. Sighing, I pushed my phone back into my pocket and pushed forward toward my car to head home.

All I wanted was their comfort, but it seemed like it would be another night of simply studying and going to sleep alone.

Talon and Zane

Talon

My brothers were turning into fools for this girl, and the most annoying part of it all was that Hale expected me to accept her as well. She may have been a lot of things—fiery, smart, and gorgeous to look at with hips that enticed a man. But at the end of the day, she was exactly what Damian had stated: a complication.

"Talon, have you heard from Damian?" Zane asked as he stepped into the doorway of my room, with concern on his face.

Shaking my head, I sighed. "No sir, I have not. He is supposed to be here by now, but you know Damian, he tends to do what he wants."

Zane, Ivy's father, was an aging man with many different complications of his own. He had once been human, but when he mated with Allison, my godmother, it unlocked a dormant werewolf gene that lay within him passed down through generations.

That was one of the reasons why we didn't mate with humans. Our pups had a chance to be more human than wolf, and with repeated mating, the werewolf gene always stayed dormant unless a wolf mated with them and unlocked it.

"I honestly don't understand him. He is supposed to lead this pack once Allison and I step down, and he doesn't seem to act like he wants to do it."

"I know, but with Damian being the oldest of us, it's rightfully his throne," I replied, reminding him that even though we don't all agree Damian should be the next Alpha, we respected him too much to take that position from him.

"Talon," Zane replied, giving me a look that let me know what he was going to talk about. "How are things with Ivy?"

I hesitated in my response. Ivy was a topic Damian didn't want us talking about, and I couldn't tell Zane that Ivy had already mated with James or Hale. If Damian found out, it would and could be disastrous.

"That isn't a conversation to be loosely had," I replied in a very soft and subtle tone to avoid bringing attention to unwanted ears.

Zane looked around the area and nodded before gesturing for me to follow him. It was obvious he wasn't going to let this conversation go. Why would he?

Ivy was his only child. With Allison unable to bear children after an accident with a rogue when she was younger, Ivy was all that they had.

Allison had made it obvious on many occasions that she didn't care for Ivy, and growing up, I remember Zane never having a problem with that—until he learned Ivy was our mate. Then that changed things.

It gave him more power and hold—at least, that was my opinion.

I followed him without question through the house until we were safely behind the closed doors of his office.

"Tell me." His voice was firm and authoritative, and I knew that even though he wasn't of Alpha blood, he was a wise man you didn't want to cross.

"Ivy has mated with both James and Hale."

There it was, the actual truth finally slipping free. Zane's eyes widened in surprise, but a smile crossed his face as he nodded. "Good. What about you?"

"What you are asking for isn't a good idea, Zane," I replied, not wanting to talk about mating with Ivy. "She doesn't deserve to live a life like this."

Zane's face darkened over as an evil glint settled within his gaze. "That isn't for you to decide. The moon goddess selected her for the four of you, and that never happens, Talon. I know that your past is what keeps you from accepting her, but this must be done. Once you join that mate bond, Damian won't be able to say no to her."

Anger filled me as I thought of our previous conversations. The day that Zane found out that Ivy was Damian's mate, he was determined to get his daughter here. He hadn't cared about her before that moment, and in fact, had often discussed how he had messed up earlier in his life by having her.

Now he sat here acting like a caring father, but the thing was, all he cared about was the power he would have with her being our mate. I knew that if Ivy could see how her father was, she would be disgusted by him. But Damian made us promise and swear to never discuss the issue of her father with her.

Eventually, Ivy would see exactly what kind of cold-hearted monster Zane really was.

"We still have time, Zane. I will do what I want on my own time, and that is final."

Zane didn't like what I had to say, but I far outranked him in strength and power. There was nothing that he could do from a wolf's perspective because he didn't amount to what I did. The only reason why I tolerated the man in front of me at all was because of Damian and Allison.

Allison took us in when my parents were killed and raised us as her own. There wasn't any way I was going to hurt her mate after the way she had helped us, but slowly, every day, I was changing my view on that.

"Don't forget what the endgame is, Talon. Our pack was selected by the goddess to hold the power we do, and we have to show unity in order to head all of it. I may be working to make Damian smart in all aspects of business, but each of you has gifts that make you different from others."

Zane's words were like a jab in my heart. We all did have gifts, and I was the one they called upon when it came to war. I was the brother who was more animalistic than reasonable, and it was the biggest reason I kept my distance from Ivy.

"Understood."

There was no point in arguing with Zane, and getting away from him right now was for the best. Zane nodded his head, and I quickly stood to my feet, making my way from his office and slamming the door behind me. If he didn't know I was pissed off before, he surely knew now.

"Talon, I was looking for you," Damian said, coming down the stairs with a curious look on his face. "What were you talking to Zane about?"

Jesus Christ. Can I not get a break with all the questions?

Sighing, I pinched the bridge of my nose and inhaled slowly. "Update from Hale and James. Nothing new. They should be back tomorrow."

Damian stood staring at me, his brow raised in question. I knew he knew I was lying, but I didn't want to continue the conversation with him, and Damian knew when it was a good idea to let it go and not push the issue.

"Very well." His response came slowly, and as I went to pass him, his hand reached out, stopping me. "Have you seen Ivy today?"

"Fucking hell!" I yelled, about fed up with everyone looking at me like I was her babysitter, "no, I haven't fucking seen her. I'm not her keeper! Y'all go out and fucking check yourselves!"

Damian stood with a shocked expression on his face as I pushed past him toward the back door. I needed to run and let off some steam before I did something that was going to be questionable. I didn't want to end up hurting someone, and if I kept on the road I was going down, that is exactly what would happen.

Ivy

"I overslept, Kate."

My mumbled words into the phone expressed how exhausted I was. Never in my life had I overslept for school, and this was a first. My exhaustion, though, was due to the all-nighter I had pulled in order to submit papers on time and also to study for my upcoming final.

"I will get all your work. Don't worry, girl. I was just worried when I didn't see you this morning or in Lani's class. I would advise not missing her class next week. She has been in an evil mood lately, and our exam is coming up."

I groaned in protest, thinking about the exam. Lani's class was the agricultural economics class that I was taking with Kate, and the old woman was a brute when it came to the work she assigned. As much as I wished I didn't have to be in her class. I knew that it was important for my degree.

"Yeah, I know. I will come by this weekend and get everything. Maybe we can get coffee on Sunday or something." Considering I had slept the day away, I had missed all my Friday afternoon classes.

"Sounds good. I will text you Sunday morning."

Hanging up the phone, I stared at my ceiling, wondering once again what James and Hale were doing, considering I had not heard anything from them. It was the start of another long weekend, and even though Damian had been keeping his distance, I could still feel him watching me.

"Ivy," my father's voice called, followed by a knock on my front door.

I wasn't too sure why he was here, but the fact that he came to visit me instead of just texting me to come to the main house didn't make sense. Sliding from bed, I pulled on my robe and walked to the door, opening it.

"Hey. Sorry, I'm just getting up," I replied with a smile as I stepped aside and let him in.

"Are you feeling okay?"

I watched as he moved toward the sofa and took a seat. "Uh, yeah. I'm fine. Is everything okay?"

"Do I need a reason to visit my daughter?" He chuckled as his eyes watched my every movement.

"No, but I just didn't expect you to come here."

Hesitating for a moment, he nodded. "Yes, I can understand why you would think something was wrong then. In all honesty, I just wanted to check on you since I was notified you didn't attend school today."

"Oh!" I replied, shocked, "yeah, I pulled an all-nighter and was exhausted this morning."

There was an uncomfortable silence between the two of us before he stood again. I wasn't sure if his reason for coming was actually truthful, but something about him at that moment seemed off.

"I understand things here are different for you, Ivy. But I want you to remember that no matter how difficult things may seem, you can always come talk to Allison or I about it."

The mention of my stepmother made me scoff, and my father's eyes widened in shock and unhappiness due to my response. "I will not tolerate disrespect toward her."

"I wasn't being disrespectful, but I will have to admit she isn't being very kind in order for me to like her," I replied quickly, crossing my arms over my chest as I watched him.

"Ivy, enough. You will learn to like her one way or another, and I would rather you do it sooner than later. She is your mother."

"No, she isn't!" I snapped back harshly, unable to believe he would say Allison was my mother. "She isn't and will never be anything other than your wife."

I hadn't expected the slap to come, but I should have. The noise echoed through my tiny cottage, and as it did, my hand instinctively went to the side of my face where he had hit me. My eyes wide, staring at my father in shock, and sudden realization filling him.

"Don't you dare ever speak that way of her again! Do you understand me?" he growled, and the silver spark in his eye showed the true nature of my father.

He was one of them.

Before I could say another word, my father stormed from my cottage, leaving the door wide open. I wanted to cry more than anything, but at the same time, I couldn't bring myself to do it. My father had struck me over his mate.

All because I refused to see her as my mother.

"Ivy," Talon's voice called from the front door as he stood panting, staring at me as if he had run all the way here. "Are you okay?"

"I'm fine."

"You don't look fine," he replied, stepping closer to me. "Did he hit you?"

"Does it honestly matter?" I snapped back, "there is nothing that can be done."

"You are our mate—"

Spinning around, I stared at him. "No. I am James and Hale's mate, Talon. You don't even want me, and neither does Damian. I am nothing to either of you."

The moment the words left my throat, I felt guilt over saying it. I didn't mean to lash out at Talon or to make a statement that would make him feel like he was nothing. But in my moment of anger, I did, and the hurt was evident on his face.

"Talon," I replied softly, stepping toward him, "I didn't mean it–"

"Oh, no. You made yourself quite clear, Ivy."

Spinning on his heels, he turned and walked off toward the woods like he always did. Tears threatened to spill, but not because I was sad. But because I was angry and frustrated. I hated how things were becoming, and more than anything, I wanted to be happy with them.

However, that seemed impossible anymore. I could barely get to really know them because I was so caught up in trying to hide things from Damian. Quietly, I stepped toward the door and closed it: a million and one things flowing through my mind.

I need to talk to Hale and James.

As my fingers played with the chain around my neck, I pulled out my phone and tried to text Hale and James again.

'Hale... James... I need you.'

The group text I made with them had me praying that things would work out and they would reply. But as the minutes counted on, I doubted my ability to speak with them.

'Ivy... what's wrong?' Hale finally replied, causing me to let go a sigh of relief.

'Everything. When are you guys coming home?'

'Tomorrow. Did something happen?'

I sighed, thinking of how to tell him what happened, but I didn't know how to begin to explain it because what I said to Talon wasn't fair, and I was in the wrong.

'My dad hit me. We were arguing, and he slapped me.'

No reply came, but a howl in the distance resonated and sent worry through me. I wasn't sure where it had come from, but something inside me was telling me it was nothing good.

Hunter's Prey

Damian

Something was going on around my home, and I was tired of feeling like I was the last to know. My brothers were acting more than suspicious, and I had no doubt that they were trying to get to know Ivy behind my back. It angered me, but then a part of me wanted to be okay with it because my wolf called out for her.

It wanted to be with her, and I was the one preventing it.

'You need to start being the Alpha that's required of you!' Hale's voice yelled through the mind link, causing me to growl at him.

'Watch your tone,' I warned, not sure what he was talking about.

'Watch my tone? Zane just hit our mate on your watch. You may not want her, but you should still protect her.'

A howl of anger left my lips at his words. Ivy had been assaulted on my watch and in my home. I knew that Zane was adamant to press certain issues, but never did I think he was capable of something like that.

My wolf fought against the barrier in my mind, demanding to be set free.

I was going to make Zane pay if he really touched her.

Father or not... I had to make sure she was okay.

Ivy

I wasn't sure what the howl had been, but I didn't want Talon to be mad at me. I felt terrible about how he came to check on me, and the only thing I did was yell at him, which wasn't necessary. Taking a moment to think over things, I put my phone on the table and slid my shoes on, making my way out the front door.

I knew going into the woods wasn't the best of ideas, but I had to fix things with Talon. I had to apologize and explain to him that I didn't mean what I had said. It was just words said in anger, with no meaning behind them.

"Talon!" I called from the edge of the woods as I stood there trying to grasp the courage to go into the forest. James had made it clear that wasn't the best idea, and yet I never seemed to listen to what people told me.

"Damn it, Talon," I grumbled, before pushing forward onto the path in front of me. "If I get killed, I will never forgive you."

The darkness within the woods was far more drastic than I had imagined the first time around, and seeing everything now, I had to admit that it was beautiful in a scary way.

It didn't take long for me to find myself in the place I once had been in when Talon's wolf approached me before, and from behind the brush, it appeared once again. The massive size of the beast caught me off guard, but as it snarled at me—I wasn't scared.

"I am not afraid of you, because I know you will not hurt me."

The confidence in my words was met with a growl and a snap as if he was determined to change that view. For a second my heart lurched in fear, but something within the wolves' eyes made me feel comfort.

"You know it isn't fair that you can understand me, but I can not understand you."

Slowly, I walked toward the wolf and watched as it stared at me with uncertainty. I was just as confused and curious myself, but I tried to act as if my heart wasn't about to jump from within my chest.

Another snarl, and I halted in my pace. "Would you wish me to do as you command?"

Each of them were far different from the next, and I wanted more than anything to have them all, considering I didn't feel right without them near. The wolf seemed to take into consideration what I was asking, and before I knew it, the cracking of bone sounded and the wolf turned back into a man.

"Didn't you learn last time not to come here?" Talon's snarl took me by surprise, but I didn't dare back away from him. There was no need, and I needed him to see how sorry I was for going off on him.

"Talon," I replied slowly, "I am sorry for what I said."

Laughter filled the air following my comment. "Sorry? Why are you apologizing? You made it clear what I was."

"I didn't mean for it to come out as it did, Talon. I'm sorry. Please let me make it up to you."

"Make it up to me? You mean like a whore on her knees... is that what you want? To let me use you like my brothers did?!" His words stabbed deep at my heart, and tears welled in my eyes.

I didn't understand why he was speaking to me that way. I knew that he was angry to an extent, but still, how he was acting was completely baffling.

"That's a bit harsh, don't you think," I replied, feeling hurt and ashamed to even be in front of him for a moment. "I was honestly coming to apologize. Not to sleep with you."

Turning away from him, I shook my head, unsure of why I bothered to even try to explain anything to him. There was no point.

"Stop." His words wrapped around me, and a small grasp of his hand on my arm caused me to stop in my tracks. I had forgotten what it felt like to be touched by him, and as I slowly turned back to face him, I saw a primal hunger lurking beneath his eyes.

"If you want to apologize for what has happened between us... you will run for me."

I didn't understand what he meant when he said I would run for him. The confusion was clear on my face, and as the smile crept across his face, the sound of cracking bones resonated through the air.

I knew what he was asking then.

He wanted to hunt, and I was his prey.

Running.

Never had I expected to run for my life, hunted by a wolf that was sworn to protect me.

My feet moved swiftly across the ground, and as I ran, I knew he was gaining on me. The thought of his breath across my cheek the first time we had met caused my heart to race, and I kept my feet going no matter how much I wanted to stop.

I was the prey running for its freedom, and the wolf behind me was hungry.

Oh God, was he hungry.

The roar of his fury pushed forward, and before I knew it, I found myself unable to continue on. The cuts on my skin seeped with my blood as the branches and sticks cut against me.

The panting of my breath against the cool air of the forest caused my breath to come out in small faint clouds of smoke. I wasn't able to stop long before I caught sight of the massive wolf moving toward me.

He could have caught me many times, and yet he seemed to toy with me.

"Talon..." I whispered as I watched him with wide eyes stalking toward me.

I knew I had no choice. Turning, I tried to run again, but a massive body quickly knocked me to the forest floor and I was pinned beneath the massive wolf that quickly changed into a man.

Talon's hands took my own and pinned them above my head as I lay on my belly. His free hand quickly pulled up my skirt as his breath fanned against my ears. "Mine," he growled, causing wetness to settle between my legs.

"Talon!" The whimper did nothing but arouse him further, and he spread my legs. It didn't take long before his hard, thick erection was forcefully shoved into me from behind.

Most women may not have enjoyed this type of forceful aggression, but I did.

I cried out in pleasure as he pulled me to my hands and knees, wrapping arms around my waist as he hunched over me, thrusting hard and fast. I didn't expect my first time with Talon to be like this, but now I understood this was how he wanted me.

He was more animal than human at times, and as I kissed him over my left shoulder, I saw the gold rims of his eyes shining back at me. He may have been in human form, but this dominant side of lust was all his wolf.

"Mine!" he growled against the vibrations rumbling through me as the thick swelling of his knot took place.

"Yes–" I cried out, "yours... all yours."

His head snapped to something in front of us, and my eyes followed his direction. I saw a massive black wolf breach forth in the forest, growling with eyes staring straight at us. However, there was no stopping what was happening.

Talon's knot had taken hold, and until we were done, it wouldn't release.

Something about the wolf watching felt familiar, but it was Talon who drew me back to his chest, leaning into my ear. "If he insists on watching, then perhaps we should give him a show."

"Talon," I pleaded, crying out again, "we can't..."

His fingers came down and rubbed circles across my clit, making my head fall back as I screamed in pleasure. I rode out the wave of pleasure he was creating in me.

Pushing me forward, he laid on top of me as he stilled, spilling his seed into me. His teeth sank into the back of my neck as I screamed out in a mixture of pain and pleasure.

A howl and growl of displeasure came from the wolf in front of us, and I wasn't sure what was going on. But when the wolf shifted. It was Damian. I knew my secret was up.

Damian

I heard Ivy running, and I wasn't sure why. The last thing I had expected was to see Talon chasing after her. Pushing myself forward, I broke through a small clearing only to see him shift, and pin her to the ground.

I knew what he wanted.

My brothers all had wanted it, and yet she didn't resist him.

She wasn't scared of the fact he was a werewolf, and instead, she welcomed it.

As I stepped through the clearing, I watched as Talon took her, and while he did anger coursed through me. I should have expected this to happen.

Hell, I should have known they wouldn't listen.

But what upset me the most was knowing that she was okay with it, and I didn't get to have her first. I couldn't stop the growl that erupted from me, showing my and my wolf's displeasure.

I could run over there, and yell at them both. Make them fear me for their betrayal, but honestly, what would that accomplish? Spinning on my paws, I ran, anger coursing through my veins back toward the main house.

It made me wonder if Talon had taken his moment with her like the others had as well. It was known that keeping mates apart was hard and that eventually a wolf's lust takes over and makes the mating ritual happen.

It still didn't mean it was fair though—I was the Alpha!

Yet, they keep defying me... my own brothers.

As I let the shift take over, I walked through the back door to the kitchen and just in time to see Hale and James laughing with each other as they came to face me. They were always close when they were younger, and in a way, Hale looked out for James more than I ever had as the eldest.

"Did you both handle things?" I stated flatly causing them both to look at me and nod.

"Yes, it seems that the Silver Crest pack has had the same issue of rogue attacks that we have on the northern side of our territory. It doesn't make any sense though for them to be trying to come here. Something isn't adding up..."

I had been thinking the same thing as Hale for the past few months, and as the attacks grow more frequent, I couldn't help but admit that something seemed more strategic about them. "We have to get to the bottom of this."

As much as I wanted to focus on work, I couldn't stop thinking about Ivy and Talon. That anger was still close to the surface, trying to escape. As the back door opened, I heard the laughter filtering through the opened doorway, and knew that it was Ivy's.

"That's not true..." her voice called out before Talon laughed. "Be quiet... finish the meeting, and then go back... stop it, Talon..."

Her taunting and playful tone made my blood boil.

She was supposed to be like that with me.

As her body moved through the opened door into the kitchen, I could smell Talon all over her. Their scents mixed from their mating, and even though she couldn't smell it, I knew that Talon was well aware of what he was doing.

"Oh," she replied, staring at me with wide doe-like eyes, "I'm sorry... I didn't mean to interrupt. Just going to my dad's office."

Nodding my head, I gritted my teeth as I watched her move slowly through the kitchen. All three of my brothers couldn't keep their eyes off of her, and it was more than obvious that my question on whether they had mated with her or not had been answered.

The way all of them looked at her made my own heart clench.

Hale and James wanted to touch her more than anything, and through our own bond as siblings, I could feel their yearning.

Once her small petite frame had moved from our view, they turned to face me, and my brows narrowed. It was then that Hale's eyes widened in shock having realized that I knew the truth.

"Damian... I can explain."

I was done with their false explanations and lies.

It seemed that there was nothing but betrayal everywhere I turned, and my words as their Alpha meant nothing to them anymore.

Fatherly Admissions

Ivy

Spending time with Talon had been more than amazing, but while the fun was coming to a close, I never expected that my father would text me, asking to speak with me. I was hesitant after everything that had happened, and I wasn't sure if I was ready to face him after he hit me.

"Ivy, it will be okay," Talon stated reassuringly, "I will be close. I won't let him hurt you again."

It was sweet that he was so willing to be protective of me. The moment we completed the mate bond, I could feel everything he did and knew that even though he was more on the aggressive side, he would do anything for me.

What I had not expected when we entered the house through the kitchen was to see Damian standing there with Hale and James. I wanted more than anything to wrap myself in their embrace and welcome them home, but I knew that I couldn't do that because of Damian.

Damian didn't know what I had with them.

Yes, Damian and I fought all the time, but no matter how many times we argued and yelled at each other, I couldn't help but find him attractive.

I couldn't help but want him.

Knocking on my father's office door, I waited.

"Come in." His loud voice boomed across the small space and with nervous hands, I pushed open the door, making my way inside. His rather large and imposing figure sat behind his desk while his eyes barely glanced up at my approaching figure.

"You wanted to see me?" I was hesitant to see him after the argument we had. Our last confrontation ended with him slapping me. Something my father had never done, and I wasn't sure why he had done to begin with.

"Yes," he replied before setting down his pin and looking at me, "I wanted to talk about what happened earlier and apologize for losing my cool. That should never have happened, and I regret what I did."

Shock filled me that my father was apologizing. For him to apologize when he was such a proud man was not something I expected. But then again, he had never tried to hurt me before, so perhaps he really was sorry.

"It's okay. I know it was done in the heat of the moment," I mumbled, taking a seat across from him.

"Indeed." He chuckled, "there are actually some things that I think we need to talk about."

"What would that be?"

"You are mating with the boys, of course," my father said coolly with a smirk that caused my eyes to widen in shock.

How in the heck did he know that?

"I have no idea—"

"Don't try to lie to me like I'm a fool, Ivy," he growled with impatience, shaking his head with a laugh before leaning back in his chair. "It's a good thing, though."

"What's a good thing?" I was hesitant and nervous about where the conversation was going. There was still so much about all of this that I didn't know about. Hale and I had only had a brief conversation about mates and what that meant.

"Did you know that it was much harder to get you here than I expected? But I knew the moment Damian recognized you as his mate when I came back from your graduation... that I had to do what it took to make sure you came here."

My father's riddled words made no sense at all, but I figured it was probably better not to say anything so that I didn't anger him. Instead, I watched how he found joy in the fact that I was miserable in a way but happy at the same time.

"I don't understand."

"Of course not!" he said, "to think you could have been at an Ivy League school, but I pulled some strings. I made sure you were here to fulfill your destiny."

His words were like a dagger to my heart as I tried to understand what he meant. "What do you mean, you pulled some strings?"

"Oh, don't act like that, Ivy," he scolded, "it's for the better. You would never have done well there."

The fact my father did something to prevent me from going where I wanted, and then was telling me I wouldn't have made it there.. It was beyond cruel. He had no idea what I was capable of... they were my dreams.

"You didn't!" I screamed at him, "that was my future!"

"Don't you dare raise your tone with me!" he yelled, causing me to shrink back, but not before the office door flew open and all four of them stood there, eyes glowing gold staring at my father as if he lost his mind.

"You will not speak to her that way," Damian growled, causing my father's eyes to open wide. "You went behind my back and made my brother's mate with her after I said no."

Hale, Talon, and James all looked toward Damian.

Damian had basically just let on to the fact he knew we were all mated, and that wasn't something I had suspected. We were supposed to keep it on the down low and not let him find out.

I was supposed to be their dirty little secret.

"They did as they were commanded, as you should too," Zane bellowed, causing Damian to look at him with fury.

"I am the Alpha, not you!"

I wasn't sure what was going on, but all the testosterone that was floating around was driving me insane. I didn't understand why these men couldn't just let me do what I wanted to do.

I had come to Idaho to get my degree and work toward changing the future. Instead, I came and was made to live this weird love thing that didn't make any sense, and everyone was walking on eggshells around Damian.

"I can't do this," I mumbled, standing to my feet and pushing through the men. I made my way outside of my father's office. My father's tone raised and called out to me as I walked away from him.

"Ivy!" James called out, making his way behind me, "please don't run off. I'm sorry that this is like this. Please just give us–"

"Give you what?" I yelled, spinning around to face him, "time? That's all you guys ask for. You never think about how things make me feel, just think about yourselves."

James stared at me, shocked, as I pulled my car keys from my pocket. I didn't want to keep going down this road with them. Right now, I was more than ready to pack all of my things and book a flight back to Georgia, away from everyone here.

"Where are you going... you can't leave," James' pleaded, grabbing my arm and stopping me from getting into my car.

"James... let me go," I whispered before his lips came down upon mine, taking my breath away. I had missed the way he tasted, but there was no way he could just use the feeling he created in me to change my mind.

Pushing softly against his chest, I leaned my forehead against his and sighed, "I did time, James. I need to wrap my mind around this. You all treat me like a secret, and now I find out my father lied to me. He never cared about me and ruined my chances at the school of my dream just to have me come here and mate with you all..."

"Do you regret it, though?" he asked, looking at me. "Do you regret mating with me?"

"No, but love isn't forced. An isn't just about what one side wants... it's both sides," I said, pulling away from him and sliding into my car, closing the door. I knew that what I said had double meaning behind it, but he was going to have to realize that he couldn't just do what he wanted.

It wasn't just about them... they flipped my life upside down.

And through it all, no one ever asked me what I wanted.

Driving from the main house, I found myself thinking over everything that had happened. Yes, I had created a bond with Talon, and it had been a wonderful moment. But the last thing that I expected when I got called into my father's office was that he was going to explain to me that he had set all of this up.

Tears streamed down my face, realizing that I had been deceived. The only thing that I wanted was to come here and get an education and be able to make a difference in the world. I had thought that I hadn't gotten accepted to those universities because I wasn't good enough. But at the end of the day, it was because my father had made sure I didn't.

He had pulled strings to satisfy his own needs and desires, making sure that I came here to fulfill some destiny that he thought was the right path. No one had explained anything to me, and in fact, no one had even asked my opinion on all of it, or what it was that I had desired.

Instead, they treated me like some child that was incapable of being able to decide what she wanted. I wasn't going to stand for it. If I wasn't finishing up a semester right now, I'd probably pack my bags and leave.

The thought of leaving, though, made a part of my soul ache.

Could I really leave them after everything?

Before I knew it, I found myself outside the cafe that was part of the college campus. Rain poured down outside as if it felt the pain I had within myself. Reaching up, I dried my tears and tried to figure out my next step. More than anything, I didn't want to go home.

At least not right now.

Grabbing my purse, I quickly darted from my car and ran across the sidewalk to the front entrance at the cafe. The bell chimed above the door as I opened and closed it, the delicious aroma hitting me in my face making me feel more at home.

My mother had always said there wasn't a problem that couldn't be fixed with a good cup of coffee or a hot cup of tea. Tonight she was right. I wished more than anything she was here with me right now. I wanted to tell her everything that was going on, but I knew she wasn't in a good state, and burdening her with my problems wasn't the right thing to do. The chattering of individuals could be heard all around me, but it was the soft music that seemed to calm me.

Jazz... a book lover's soulmate... well, at least that was my opinion.

"What can I get for you tonight?" the barista asked as I looked over the menu and quickly ordered a cup of tea with milk and honey.

Paying the woman, I waited patiently for her to complete my order. My eyes scanned the room looking for an empty table and instead fell on Caleb, who was sitting in the far corner going over a bunch of paperwork.

As if sensing I was looking at him, his eyes looked up to meet mine, and a smile crossed his face. There was something about his smile that seemed so familiar to me, and in the chaos of my daydream, I almost didn't hear the barista calling my name. "Ivy!"

"I'm so sorry," I replied sheepishly as I took my drink from her. Her scolding look did nothing for my uneasy soul. Turning back, Caleb gestured for me to come over, and I welcome the idea of casual conversation that didn't involve the current dilemma that was going on at home.

"Caleb, isn't it a little late for you to be out tonight? Shouldn't you be home relaxing?" I stated with a teasing smile as I took my seat across from him.

"I could say the same for you, Ivy," he replied with a deep laugh. "What brings you out tonight? You don't look like you're in a very good position right now."

If only he had known the truth. I was far from being in a good place. In fact, all I wanted to do was lock myself away and be free of all the drama that was going on currently in my life.

"There's just a lot going on at home that doesn't make me feel comfortable being there right now. I wish things were easier, but alas, that is not my life." He nodded as if he knew exactly what I meant, and quickly picked up the coffee that he had in front of him and took a long sip.

"Why don't you explain to me what's going on? Perhaps I can give you some guidance. After all, sometimes an outsider's opinion seems to help people work through their issues."

"Oh, I couldn't possibly do that. I would hate to be a burden on you. I'm sure that you have so much that you need to attend to tonight." He laughed at my statement, shaking his head no.

"Unfortunately, I am a single man who does nothing but work his entire life, so I am more than welcoming when it comes to casual conversation. If you know what I mean."

In fact, I did know what he meant. Sometimes having casual conversation that didn't revolve around the life you currently walked was often a very nice thing to have.

"I completely understand what you mean," I replied with a sigh. "I have some guy issues at home, and I also found out that my father went behind my back and made sure that I didn't get into any of the Ivy League schools that I had applied for, just to be able to make sure that I came here."

His mouth formed an 'O' as his eyes widened in shock at what I had said. "That is definitely something to be upset about. Why on earth would your dad do something like that? Does he not know how wonderful it is to be accepted into a prestigious school?"

"I don't know. My father's and I's relationship has been strained for a long time, and it just seems like he wants things his way and doesn't really take into consideration anything that I want."

Caleb nodded his head, thinking over what I had just said. "I am familiar with the person that your dad is. He is known around the town for being a very aggressive businessman and his godsons, I believe, are not much better than he is."

I was confused by his response and wondered where it came from. I didn't realize that there was a possibility that Caleb could, in fact, know the boys and my father, although it would make sense if he had lived in this town for quite some time.

"Did you grow up here?"

Caleb's smirk crossed his face as he slowly nodded his head. "I did, actually. I went to school with Damian. We ended up graduating a year apart. I graduated ahead of him. But he was definitely known to be a very extreme kind of person while we were in school."

"What do you mean, extreme? I mean, he is a bit of an asshole, but at the same time, I'm sure it's just all the stress that causes him to be that way."

I didn't want to think of the fact that Damian was a complete dick his entire life. Part of me wanted to believe that he could be a soft, sweet, and gentlemanly. That he was simply stressed with all the work and everything else that came with taking over a pack. So they call it. I didn't understand what it all entailed or what his life really was like, but I wanted to find out, eventually.

"Well, they just aren't normal like the rest of us. I guess you could say."

Caleb's statement had me wondering if he knew exactly what they were. I had learned that there were a lot of people in this town who were actually part of the pack Damien controlled. I figured that Caleb more than likely wasn't one of those, but it didn't mean that as a human, he didn't know.

I wanted to ask him, but again, I knew it wasn't for me to mention something like that, and if he didn't know about that, I didn't want him to think that I was crazy. Because honestly, I felt crazy 100% of the time, and I already knew the truth.

"Well, how normal could they actually be? I've learned quite fast when I got here that most of them were as far from normal as possible."

"Oh, so they told you their secret, did they? Well, as much as the majority of humans don't seem to believe in certain things, I think it's pretty obvious that at the end of the day, we are what we are. No matter what DNA says."

Shock filled me. His words were almost as if it was a confession. I wanted to ask him, but I didn't want to intrude. Could the man in front of me be more than what he was? Was he like the rest of them?

"Are you a—" I started but quickly pulled back on my question. I was acting stupid. There was no way that Caleb was a werewolf. He didn't act like the others at all.

"A werewolf?" He finished with a sly grin across his lips, "why yes, Ivy. I am."

Learning the Truth

I couldn't believe what Caleb was saying. He was a werewolf, just like the others!

He was a complete contrast to what I was used to with the guys. Caleb was kind, caring, and compassionate. He had a love for agriculture and literature that I would only dream of finding in somebody, and even though I didn't see him in that way, he'd become quite a good friend to me.

"I've never thought that you were one of them," I admitted shyly.

"It's OK, Ivy. We all have our little secrets, but I want you to know that you don't ever have to be afraid to speak with me. I will be open with you completely about anything you want to know. You simply just have to ask the question."

His smile was warm, and part of me felt overjoyed at the idea he was so willing to help me understand. The truth was that the guys had never really taken the time to explain much to me. Granted, Hale explained a little, but it wasn't what I was hoping for.

I didn't honestly know all that much about them, and that broke my heart.

Caleb cleared his throat, bringing me back from my thoughts and causing me to give him an apologetic look. "I'm sorry..."

"There is no need to apologize. Are you OK?"

"Honestly, I hardly know anymore." My reply was the honest truth. I felt completely off and different from the world floating around me. As much as I wanted to stay on top of the game and be in control, I couldn't find it in myself to be that way.

I felt so defeated, not knowing if I was coming or going.

"It's OK, I understand," he replied with a smile. "Perhaps the best thing for you to do tonight is just to go home and sleep it off and get some rest and be able to recoup tomorrow and figure out what you're going to do next."

Chuckling at his comment, I contemplated sleeping.

Sleeping sounds wonderful, but I definitely couldn't go home—at least not tonight.

I could call the girls and see if I can crash with one of them. The thought was very appealing, but then again, I didn't want to be a burden to anyone.

"Thanks, but I think I'll sit here a little while longer. My plan was to try to call somebody and see about staying at one of their dorms for the night. I just don't feel comfortable going home right now.'

His eyebrows shot up, and he nodded his head. "Well, I know it's a lot, but I do have a three-bedroom house with two spare rooms. If you want, you can crash in my guest room. If you'd like for the night. No strings attached or anything like that. Just trying to give you an option if you don't feel like going home."

I found his offer to be very kind, and I quickly nodded my head. "That would be wonderful, actually... if you don't mind."

"Not at all, Ivy." Caleb chuckled as he quickly slid his chair out, grabbing his bag in his jacket. "Let's get out of here and go get you settled in for the night."

Following him, I wasn't quite sure what was going to happen. I knew that the guys weren't going to be happy about the fact that I wasn't coming home tonight. But at the same time, I didn't care.

I needed the space to clear my mind and comprehend everything I had been learning.

Part of me had hoped that maybe tonight, before I go to bed, I could pick Caleb's mind to learn a little bit more about the life that they were trying to pull me into. They hadn't really discussed and told me anything, and I was supposed to just blindly trust them and follow forward.

I had to learn how to start listening to myself because I was the only one I could trust.

Walking into Caleb's home, I was taken aback by how beautiful it was. He definitely was making good money at the university to be able to afford to live in a place like this. Beautiful wooden floors, granite countertops, lush furnishing. It was a dream come true, and similar to what I hoped I could own—later on in my future.

"Just go ahead and get comfortable. I will take you upstairs in just a minute and show you where your room is."

I stayed quiet but smiled at him before he disappeared around the corner. I wasn't quite sure where he was going, but when he came back empty-handed, and with a T-shirt on and Gray sweatpants, I realized that he had gotten himself a little more comfortable.

"Here, let's go upstairs. I'll show you the room that you're staying in. There should be a change of clothes, some shorts or t-shirts or something in the drawer that my sister left here. You're more than welcome to use them and take a shower if you'd like."

His offer was sweet, but at the same time, I was a little hesitant.

Showering in a house with another man I don't really know in the next room?

"Thank you so much for this," I said from behind him as I followed him up the stairs toward the guest bedroom. "I feel like

I'm being a bother, but you have no idea how much this means to me to be able to get away from it all for a night."

Reaching the top of the stairs, he turned slightly and smiled at me. "You don't even have to say thank you for staying here. My door is always open to you, Ivy."

Taken aback by his offer, I stood speechless, staring at him. Yes, he was my professor, but since I had come to this town, he had slowly become so much more. He had, in fact, become a very good friend. "Thank you, Caleb. You have no idea how much that means to me."

A deep chuckle slipped from his lips as he nodded his head and turned to continue on. The subtle movement of his muscles beneath his shirt drew my eyes in, but a reminder that they weren't one of the guys quickly diminished my thoughts.

I missed them terribly, but at the same time... I was happy to be away.

Walking through the open door, my eyes took in the soft feminine decor of the guest bedroom. I had no doubt that his sister frequented his home because of how it looked. Soft whites, pinks, and yellows littered every inch of the room and brought a smile to my face.

"When you're done, come downstairs, and I'll get us some tea. Perhaps I can answer some of those lingering questions for you." I spun to face him as he slowly closed the door with a grin on his face.

I was shocked that he was able to pick up on the fact I had questions. The chiming of my phone resonated again, and looking down, I saw the fifteen missed calls waiting on my phone.

Each of the men had tried to reach out to me, but I had ignored their advances. Why should I be the one to cave in when they all have done nothing but push me around to get what they wanted... never what I wanted.

All I wanted was my thoughts and opinions taken into account. Was that so much to ask for?

Staring at my phone, I sighed and quickly powered it off. I needed a night that was free from their persistent ways. I wanted a night that was just me, and I had wished more than anything I would have just got a dorm room like the others.

I wasn't sure if there was a way for them to track me down, but with the necklace secured around my neck, I hoped it wouldn't be possible. Thinking back over everything Hale had said to me about what the necklace could do...

I was pretty sure tracking was one thing it prevented—or so I hoped.

Obtaining my privacy felt like a jolt of accomplishment. I was finally able to clear my mind, and also try to gain insight into what I am really getting myself into.

Or at least that is what I hoped would happen.

I cared about them all, but they had been lying and betraying me. In a way, they used me to their advantage. Yes, I enjoyed the moments spent with them. But in the end, I honestly knew nothing of the life they lived.

I was completely ignorant of werewolf life.

Up until a few weeks ago, I didn't even know they existed, but then I came here.

Of course, that's how my life seemed to go.

One thing after another, as if my life wasn't already full of schoolwork.

The hot cascading water felt amazing upon my skin. So much so that I groaned internally when I forced myself to shut it off. The water pressure from the jets was much better in Caleb's guest shower than it was in my small cottage.

Throwing on a pair of shorts and a t-shirt from the draw he had mentioned, I made my way downstairs toward the kitchen.

I wasn't quite sure why a sense of safety filled me around Caleb, but something inside me told me I could trust him.

"Are you feeling refreshed after your shower?" he asked without looking up from the book he had been reading at the kitchen table. His eyes hesitated on the page before finally glancing at me with a smile on his face.

"Yes, I am," I replied, "thank you."

"No need to thank me, Ivy," he replied, closing the book and setting it on the table. "Why don't you take a seat? Go ahead and start on your tea and biscuits, and I will answer any questions that you have."

For a moment, my situation seemed amazing. But then a longing inside of me opened up, wishing it was Hale or someone else that was having this conversation with me.

Taking a deep breath, I moved toward the table and took my place in front of him. The tea was hot and refreshing as I drank it, lost in my thoughts before deciding what question it was I would ask him.

"How does someone become a werewolf? Is it like magic or something?"

A chuckle left his lips as he shook his head. "Uh—I guess you can call it that."

"I'm sorry... I don't even know how to go about asking these questions," I replied shyly, almost embarrassed that I was talking to him about it.

"No, don't feel bad, Ivy. It's completely normal to have these questions when you don't know something." His smile did little to make me feel better, but he quickly stood to his feet and gestured for me to follow him.

Moving from the kitchen, Caleb brought me into a small den within his home and gestured toward an oversized sofa that I willingly accepted getting comfortable on. I had no doubt this conversation was going to belong.

"Alright... Let me see," he replied as his fingers moved over a set of very old books on a large brown bookcase. "Yes, here it is."

Turning toward me, he brought over a large brown book and opened it up to a page before laying it down on the coffee table in front of me. The old written words and photos depicted wolves and humans from what seemed to be another lifetime.

"You see, while being a werewolf is magic related, it's far more complicated than someone just saying a simple spell," Caleb started as he took a seat next to me and flipped through the pages. "We were blessed by the gods and are protected by the moon goddess herself."

"The moon goddess?" I asked with curiosity, "is she like the ultimate mother or something?"

"Uh—yeah, I suppose you could say that, yes. She is our deity."

I was stunned by the recollection of what he was saying. Being a werewolf was definitely a more complex situation. "So she made wolves have mates?"

"Yes, and no... you see, not all wolves get mates. But those of us who do are blessed by her to have a love for eternity with the wolf who completes the other half of our soul. It helps to balance out our wolf."

"That makes sense," I replied, "when I worked at the wolf sanctuary in Georgia, I learned that even they mate for life. A wolf who loses its mate becomes lost and depressed, and if they don't happen to get another, they often die."

"In a sense, yes. See, you may know more than you think," Caleb replied, smiling at me as he turned the page again, "Over centuries, wolves got tired of having to search for their mate for fear that they had died, or perhaps weren't just born yet. So they started taking chosen mates instead. Which, in my opinion, was wrong."

"What? That's horrible."

"Yes, I know, but as time grew on, many stopped believing in her feeling that she had abandoned us so long ago."

Staring at the pages before me, I saw the depicted photo of the moon goddess and couldn't help but run my fingers against the page. "People are far too impatient."

"Yes, there are many of the wolves that also felt that way. But to each their own, I guess you can say." Caleb seemed to be quite quiet as if regarding the information that he had given me.

"Have you not found your mate yet?" When I asked, the look in his eyes spoke volumes about the conflict he felt.

"Uh—well, I did, but unfortunately, she rejected me and claimed another."

"Oh, Caleb. I'm so sorry." My heart broke from him, and before I knew it, I wrapped my arms around him and hugged him.

To be given a mate, and then rejected of their love, must have been horrible. Especially considering the amount of love he obviously had to give.

I wouldn't know how to act if that had happened to me, and I wasn't a wolf.

Swirling thoughts made me take a look at the relationship I had with the guys. I hadn't been with them long, and in all honesty, could I actually say I loved them?

Love was such a strong word.

I cared for them, of course, but I wasn't sure if love reflected how I felt.

"It's okay. It was a long time ago," he replied as I pulled away from him.

"Can I ask something?"

"Of course, Ivy." He chuckled while staring at me. "You can ask me anything."

Awkwardness filled me after he had just told me about his mate, but taking a deep breath, I nodded. "I understand what you mean about the goddess giving each wolf a mate, but then why am I mated to all four of them?"

"All four of them?"

"Yes, James, Hale, Talon, and I have completed the bond. But Damian won't, and he is my mate, too. Honestly, I don't get it and don't even know much about them."

Caleb's eyes widened in shock, his mouth slowly, slowly dropping open. "That's impossible. I mean, I figured it was one of them, but not all four of them. That hasn't happened in hundreds of years. Mates are technically typically one person with another one person or, on rare occasions, two and one."

"Is it bad I am?" I asked, a little taken aback by his outburst. Was it bad to supposedly be mated to this many people? What if it's a bad omen or something?

They had never really explained it when I slept with them, but at the same time, I never stopped them either. When in the act, I welcomed it or almost expected them to take their claim. It was like a powerful urge sweeping over me.

"I just... they never told you anything?" he asked again, looking absolutely dumbfounded.

"No, I mean, Hale explained some things, but not like you have."

"I'm so sorry, Ivy. You've been brought into all of this with people who didn't even take your own thoughts and opinions into consideration. They should have taken it more seriously. At least that's what you typically do, especially with someone who's human." His eyes scanned over me with pity before going back to the book.

"It's okay..." I murmured, finishing off my tea and contemplating going to bed.

"I will try my best to explain some of the stuff that I know to you, but of course, I'm not part of a pack like the others, and I'm what they call a lone wolf, someone who doesn't belong to anybody and primarily keeps to themselves."

Lone wolf was a new term that I hadn't heard before. Of course, I had tried to do a little bit of reading on what I could find about stuff, but it was all fantasy and fiction, nothing that helped me in the real world.

"Anything that you could tell me would be wonderful. I really appreciate your help."

Caleb nodded, his eyes going to the clock on the stove before looking back at me. "Damian is what they consider to be an alpha. The leader of a group of people, almost like a president, would be to a country. But he is the leader of his pack, and his pack happens to be one of the largest on this side of the continent."

I didn't realize that Damian was in charge of so many things. It did make a lot of sense, though. The reason why he was always stressed out and, of course, the reason why Hale and the others had said that he had so many responsibilities.

He was in charge of so many different people.

"That explains a lot, I guess."

An empty pit formed in the pit of my stomach as my mind wandered over to what the guys were probably doing right now. I had turned my phone off so that I could enjoy my peace and had no doubt that I would get nothing but shit from them when I went home in the morning.

"Did you want to continue for tonight?" Caleb asked me as he closed the book and made his way back toward the bookshelf.

Exhaustion filled me as I yawned and shook my head. "No, what you have told me already has my mind spinning. Perhaps we can pick up tomorrow, maybe?"

"Of course, Ivy. Go get some rest, and in the morning, we can continue if you would like."

Taking to my feet, I walked slowly back to my room and closed the door. The softness of the bed was a welcome feeling, and as I lay there, I felt the darkness pulling me closer.

Sleep was overtaking me...

But the thoughts of Damian and their secrets would never stop plaguing my mind.

Words from Mommy Dearest

The last thing I expected when I woke up early in the morning was for the smell of bacon to waft in the air and for my stomach to start growling. I wasn't sure how I felt about everything I had learned the night before. I was angry and had every right to be.

Time to go home.

Groaning, I rolled over and turned on my phone, letting it power up as I made my way toward the ensuite bathroom. As much as I wanted to relax in peace all day, I knew it wasn't possible.

I had to face the guys today, and I needed to find the courage to do so.

Notification after notification, my phone chimed in a chorus of tunes as I brushed my teeth, and by the time I picked it up, I noticed the number of times people had tried to get a hold of me. The guys, my father, Allison... all of them tried to contact me as if something had happened.

Shoving my phone into the back pocket of my jean shorts, I slipped on my shoes and raced downstairs. Caleb's well-toned body stood over the stove as he slaved away to make breakfast.

As much as I wanted to cut out and run, I felt bad about leaving when he worked so hard and decided against it. "Good Morning."

"Oh, well, good morning," he replied with a smile as he looked over his shoulder, "I hope you're hungry."

"Yes, I am. Thank you for this."

"It's no problem. I figured you would have to leave right away this morning, so I decided to make you something to eat before you did leave." Caleb never ceased to amaze me with how sweet he really was.

To think that his mate rejected him broke my heart because it was obvious he had a lot of love to give someone. "You're amazing, Caleb."

"Well, I like to think so," he replied, causing us both to laugh.

As the morning crept on, breakfast finished with laughing and great food, and eventually, I was wishing him goodbye. "Thank you so much for everything."

"No problem. You are welcome here any time."

Nodding my head, I hugged him tight one more time. The feeling of his arms wrapping around me and pulling me in for a tight embrace made me feel like I was hugging a long-lost friend. "I will see you later," I whispered as I pulled away from him. "Time to go walk through the fires of hell."

He chuckled, shaking his head as he watched me. "Give them hell, tiger."

Oh, that's what I plan on doing.

Pulling into the driveway, I should have known there was going to be nothing but chaos, and before I barely made it out of my car, James and Hale were at my door.

"Where have you been!" James yelled, catching me off guard as Hale tried to pull him away, "do you understand how worried we have been about you!"

I figured that Talon or even Damian would yell at me, but for James to yell?

"It's nice to see you as well," I replied with sarcasm, slamming my car door and making my way toward the back door heading for my cottage. If the guys thought I was going to accept them yelling at me then they were sadly mistaken.

I wasn't in the mood for any of it.

"Ivy, please... wait," Hale called after me. "We were just worried."

"Worried?!" I scoffed, spinning to face him, "so worried that you kept me blinded about my commitment to you instead of explaining the truth?"

Fuck y'all. I mentally responded as I spun back on the path and continued to my home. I knew what was expected of me, but at the same time, I wasn't going to play their games. They claimed to care, but they told me nothing.

Caleb had to explain it all to me.

It's all bullshit.

"Ivy, please stop." Hale's words fell on deaf ears as I opened my cottage door and slammed it behind me, making sure to put the locks in place.

I knew I was acting immature, but I had prepared myself on the entire ride over here that I would come home and sit down and talk with them. Then James and Hale had to come out and piss me off. The two out of the four that I figured would never do such a thing.

"Go away, Hale," I responded when I heard him call out to me again, "when you guys learn to talk to me properly, then we discuss more!"

His groan of protest was met with a victory smile on my behalf. I may have been small and weak in some eyes, but I wasn't. I was a strong individual, and I didn't have to take crap from them like I did.

I wish Kate were here to let me vent, but when the semester ended, she took a few weeks to go home, and I was left without someone else to really talk to.

There was one person though I had not spoken to in a few days that I wished was with me more than anything, and that was my mom. Picking up my phone, I lay on my bed and dialed her number.

"Hello?" she said softly through the phone. The sound of her pain was evident in her voice and made me want to come home to take care of her.

"Hey, mama. How are you feeling?" I asked, trying to lighten the subject.

"Oh, my dear. I am doing perfectly. Just tired from work."

I wasn't sure when she was going to stop lying about her situation, but I knew it was because she didn't want me to worry about her while I was at school. She was such a selfless woman in that way, and it killed me because if she died, I would regret forever not being able to be there with her on her last days.

"You need to rest, Mom," I choked out through hidden tears, "how will you ever be ready for a permanent vaca when I get my degree if you're working too hard?"

The ongoing joke made us both laugh as I used the back of my sleeve to wipe away tears.

"So, how are things with those boys? Are they being nice to you?" I had slowly begun to tell my mom about how school was and the new friends I had made, but not about werewolves.

That just wasn't something normal.

"They are okay, I guess. They always like to try and start arguments with me."

"Well, if you remember correctly," she started, and I could hear the smile in her voice, "you were not that easy to live with before."

I feigned hurt at her comment, which caused her to laugh, "I was an angel when I was younger."

"Yes, well, Lucifer was once an angel too."

My mother had a point, and hearing like this warmed my heart. It was almost like how it had been when I was younger. Back before she got diagnosed with cancer. I couldn't imagine my life without her, but a part of me also said that we had to keep up with only the good memories.

"I just wish they wouldn't hide things from me. They like to keep too many secrets," I muttered, trying to figure out how to fix my current situation.

"Well, they are werewolves, Ivy. It's time you accept them as their Luna."

Shock and curiosity filled me with my mother's words.

How in the hell did she know what they were and how they were connected to me?

It was impossible... wasn't it?

"Mom, what are you talking about?"

Never did a thought occur to me that my mother would know about werewolves and hide it from me.

My mother and I never hid anything from each other before.

"Well, I have always known about this sort of thing. In all honesty, I was about your age when I learned the truth." Her soft words weren't comforting this time and instead made the sting of betrayal sink deeper.

She had always been my rock in any situation.

To know she kept it from me broke my heart.

"Why didn't you tell me the truth?" The pain building behind my eyes threatened tears to fall as I tried to comprehend why everyone around me had been lying to me.

"It's complicated, Ivy," she sighed softly, "trust me, my love, I wanted to tell you so many times, and I couldn't. Not to mention your father forbade it, and I was terrified he would make good on his promise and take you from me if I did."

Of course, he would threaten her.

A sneer of disgust crossed my lips as I took in the information she was giving me. I felt horrible that he had treated her that way, but I learned rather quickly the type of man he was.

"It's okay, Mama. I understand."

"Ivy, think of this as a blessing. They chose you to be the mother of the wolves. To help encourage and love those unable to love themselves." My mother's words weren't making much sense, and as I listened, I tried to take in what she was explaining.

Is a Luna like a mother to the pack?

There was a lot that had crossed my mind since my conversation with Caleb, and I found myself curious to know more. But for now, I was going to have to be patient with the way things were.

The guys were not too overly pleased with how I had been acting, and I wasn't too overly pleased with them. I had been considering whether I made the right choice by mating with them, and yet even thinking about leaving broke my heart.

I felt trapped and wasn't sure how to escape.

A knock on my door caused my breath to catch, and as I glanced at it, I froze. "Mama, someone's here. Let me call you back tomorrow, okay?"

"Of course, sweetie. Be safe, I love you."

"I love you too," I whispered as I hung up my phone and moved toward the door.

It didn't take a genius to realize who was on the other side of the door.

Damian.

Taking a deep breath, I stilled my racing heart and slowly opened the door. His cold eyes stared down at me, but something else within them made me question my sanity.

"Damian, what are you doing here?"

"They said you were back, and you looked fine." The sensation of his eyes scanning my body made me shudder in a mixture of fear and delight.

"Then why did you come out here if they told you I was okay?"

"I wanted to come check on you myself," he replied through gritted teeth.

His attitude wasn't what I was used to.

Instead of the cold, arrogant, and angry man I was used to, he had become something else. He was calmer and more maintained as if struggling to hold back from responding as he frequently did.

"Oh, okay. Well..." Reluctance filled me, realizing what I was going to do, "w-would you like to come in?"

Without answering my question, he strode past me into the cottage and glanced around. This wasn't the first time he had been in my home, but it was the first time he had ever willingly come. I wasn't sure why the change.

"I figured you may have some things you want to discuss."

"Discuss?" Caleb had already told me so much, something the guys should have done.

The blank stare on his face was unmoving. "About what you ae, and your situation."

"What I am is human, and I have been destined to be mated with the four of you," I rebutted, moving past him to get a drink of water.

"Who informed you of that?" Damian's comment made my eyes roll. "Was it Hale?"

"Hale only explained that we were all mates and how you form a mate bond. He explained nothing else. I am more than capable though of getting my information from elsewhere." Turning to face him, a smile resting upon my lips, I observed his eyes narrow.

"The only way you would know is if another wolf told you."

Ah, so he is finally putting two and two together.

"Yes, that's correct," I replied weakly as I sat on the sofa.

"Ivy, who have you been talking to?" There was the question I was waiting for.

He was curious.

"Just a friend, Damian. You guys aren't the only wolves in this area, just the largest pack."

A groan of displeasure left him as he pinched the bridge of his nose and glared at me.

"For god's sake, just tell me."

I had accepted for a long time that this was my fate now. That being mated to them was not the worst thing that could happen to me. No, I had thought things would get better.

"No. I won't reveal who I speak with, Damian."

With quick movements, I found him hovering inches over me, with my heart racing.

As much as he angered me, I wanted this. I wanted him. We may fight and argue, but part of me wondered if he accepted me. Would that fighting and arguing turn into intense passion?

"Tell me, Ivy," he growled, the gold swirling specks within his eyes enticing me.

"Make me."

Who knew those two words might change everything between us? Intense fiery passion spread throughout my body as his lips descended upon mine, and his fingers danced along my skin. The moan that escaped from my lips was more intoxicating than anything I experienced with the others.

Pushing and pulling, we fought against each other for control.

Both of us had waited so long for this moment, and now that it was here, neither of us wanted to stop. The scorching touch of his fingers upon my flesh was agonizingly painful—but not in a way that physically hurt.

No, it was because I craved him so much I didn't want to wait.

"Come with me," he growled, hoisting me up over his shoulder and racing toward my room.

A sense of happiness washed over me as I realized that it was finally about to happen.

Damian had been a pain in my ass since I had arrived, but now I would be linked to him eternally.

Mated for life—or so I was advised.

My body bounced upon the mattress as he dropped me. Slowly crawling up as his lips possessed mine again, he trailed down over my jaw. The rough kisses had me begging for more.

That was, until he stopped.

The flicker of confusion in Damian's eyes swam back and forth before settling upon me. With lightning-fast reflexes, he pulled back and put space between us. "Where were you when you left?"

His question was soft and full of confusion. His gorgeous eyes swirled with black and gold as he stared at the navy blue sweater I had worn the night before. I didn't understand why he was acting the way he was. Only a moment ago, we were fine.

Our lips were still swollen from the evidence.

"I went to a friend's house. I met up with them in the cafe on campus. Why?"

"A name, Ivy," Damian demanded with a sterner note.

"Excuse me?" The way he was acting astounded me. "I am not telling you. It isn't my place."

"Tell me who the hell it is, Ivy!" Damian exploded in irritation, causing me to slink back slightly in fear.

"Leave." It was the only reaction he would receive from me.

I refuse to sit here and be treated the way he was treating me.

I wouldn't condone it, and he should realize that by now.

"Not until you tell me where you were."

Disbelief swarmed over me as I shook my head and stood to my feet. "Leave now, or I will take off again."

As soon as he realized I was serious, he moved from the cottage, slamming the door behind him.

My personal life was my own, and they would have to respect that.

Distain of an Alpha

Damian

The moment I smelt Caleb on her sweater, it took everything in me to hold back my wolf. My mate had been around the one man I loathed more than anything in this world. The built-up anger I had for him for years resurfaced in a wave of betrayal.

"She is out of control!" I yelled.

Hale stared at me with utter confusion. "What do you mean?"

"Ivy was with Caleb." My brother's face reflected my own shock and anguish.

Footsteps echoed in the hallway, and James' face quickly appeared. "What the hell is wrong now?"

"Well, supposedly Ivy is hanging out with Caleb," Talon replied coldly.

Just hearing Talon mention what she had done sent me back into a wave of bitter darkness. Just as I was coming around to being mated to her—she did this to me.

How could I be so stupid?

"You are rushing into this in the wrong way," James replied with a stern glare.

Never once in my life had I seen James look the way he did in that moment. He was standing there, with an Alpha's persona of being tall and regal, and not willing to back down from what was being said.

"Explain then," I gritted back, trying to maintain composure.

"Ivy is in one of his classes. He is one of her professors."

"You knew this?!" I yelled, "why didn't you tell me!"

Glancing around the room, I noticed the look from Hale and Talon. They both shared the same indifference to the situation as James. They all were aware Caleb was her professor.

How couldn't they? They all attended school together.

"It didn't seem to really be an issue at the time," Hale finally spoke up. "We all keep an eye on her at school."

An exasperated sigh left my throat as I began to pace around the room. Part of me understood what they were saying, but the other part of me knew that Caleb was up to no good.

My brothers didn't know Caleb as I did.

"Well, now it is a problem." My voice tried to remain calm, but my wolf was on the brink of no return.

"I don't understand what the issue is. We all know that you don't like the guy, but what did he do to upset you?" Hale stated, staring at me with confusion.

I mentally replayed the scene with Ivy in my mind over and over again.

The lookup confusion on her face irritated me. All I wanted was for her to explain herself, and she couldn't even tell me who she had been with.

I already had that answer, though.

I wouldn't mistake Caleb's stench anywhere.

I mentally berated myself for years over what happened to Sophia. It had not been my fault that she didn't understand I would never be with her.

Yet, no matter how many times I had tried to explain that to Caleb, he never listened. Instead, now he was going after my own mate... which was retribution?

"She can't be around him." There was no way around this. "She doesn't know him."

"Damian, are you listening to yourself?!" James exclaimed.

Talon stood to his feet, shaking his head. "For once, I have to agree with James. We only began to fix things with her from the mistakes that were made over the past few weeks. We have a lot to make up for."

"Make up for?" I scoffed. "I did nothing wrong."

Hale and James both burst into a fit of laughter. "Seriously?" James replied, crossing his arms.

"Yeah, you have to drop that act," Hale joined in, "you have been the worst of us all."

What were they talking about? I had done nothing to her but tried to keep my distance.

"You are the ones who didn't listen to me," I replied, rolling my eyes.

They couldn't deny that was true. I explained to them that mating with her was wrong. She should have just taken one of us, and not all. Now she was mated to three of my brothers, and in order for the legend to work, it had to be all of us.

"Stop with the bullshit, Damian," Hale finally said after a moment of silence. "Just because you didn't want to keep her didn't mean we couldn't. She has wanted to complete this bond, and you're the one who is scared."

Did my ears deceive me? My brother thought I was scared. "I am the Alpha!" I yelled.

"Technically, you aren't yet."

Allison's voice piped up from the doorway. The air about her lately spoke nothing but of her hatred for Ivy. Since the day she found out Zane's daughter was our mate, she had done everything in her power to make things difficult for her and for me.

"Watch your mouth," I snapped, "I have had enough of your comments."

"My comments?" Allison snapped, her glare laser-focused on me. "Ever since that little wench came into our lives, you have become a different person."

Rippling anger coursed through my veins at her words. She could say whatever she wanted about me, but I wouldn't allow her to talk about Ivy.

"I said watch your tone, woman!" The snarl that left my lips caused her to shrink back, "I am your Alpha, and she WILL be your Luna. You will not say anything negative about her."

"That's how you are going to treat me after everything I have done for you, all of you?!" She responded in disbelief, her hands clenching together at her side.

"Done for us?!" The laugh that escaped me was a mocking one. "We have showed you gratitude many times. Including letting you, and that mate of yours, to stay in OUR home."

"This is MY house!" she yelled back, causing my wolf to come to edge, "you can't take it from me!"

"Allison, I think it's best you go," James interjected, giving her a sad smile. "This isn't helping things."

"Don't you dare speak to me like that, James Matthew."

Stepping forward, I pushed my brother James gently out of the way, my eyes locking on Allison like a homing beacon. "Start packing your things because the day she becomes Luna... you're gone."

Time would tell what I would have to do, and right now, I was done dealing with a lot of them. Storming past Allison and the others, I headed toward my room. A cold shower seemed more than welcoming after I had just left Ivy the way I did.

Moving up the steps two at a time, the weight of our argument sat heavily upon my shoulders. I shouldn't have acted the way I did toward her. I overreacted as I always did, and the only thing it accomplished was causing more problems.

God! Why can't I get it right with her?

I wanted more than anything to grasp a hold of her luscious boy, and let my fingers dance against the silky curves of her skin. I had her in my grasp earlier tonight, and instead of burying myself inside her and claiming her as my mate– I lost control.

I should have known the situation was too good to be true.

The idea that we could all be one happy family...

"Fucking idiot," I replied, mocking myself.

Now, more than ever, I needed her. I needed to finish the bond and soothe my wolf because, as of late; he had become out of control with the hunger and urge to ravish every inch of her body.

Stepping beneath the silver head of my shower, I let the cold streams of water run over my body. I was hell-bent on driving away my wolf's lust for her tonight. My pack expected me to be strong for them.

To make things work, but at the same time, it was too complicated

Running my hand over my face, I sighed. "Tomorrow is a new day."

Maybe if I actually did what Hale had sggested, and just talked to her, I wouldn't be in the situation I am. Beating my fist against the shower wall, I tried to grasp a handle on myself.

Since the first time I laid eyes on her, I wanted her. But as soon as her innocent eyes looked up at me, I found myself too afraid to admit what I wanted. I knew without a doubt I would end up hurting her.

And then, just like Sophia did to Caleb, she would reject me.

Perhaps that is what Caleb wants. To convince her to reject us and rid herself of the attachment she has to us. Who knows if that is even possible?

The only thing left for me to do was to try tomorrow to convince her of how sorry I was.

To beg her to let me fix things and be the mate I should be.

Ivy

A day had gone by, and without trouble from Damian, I fell back into a normal routine.

Even Hale, Talon, and James apologized and explained their wishes to start over and form a better relationship with me. No way did I hold back on showing them how upset I was. That leaving someone in the dark on what everything meant wasn't acceptable.

Remorse was evident, and even though I was angry, I forgave them.

Perhaps I didn't feel the bond like they did because I was human. But it was no excuse for me not to be forgiven because, for them, the bond is like the air they breathe. When I had cut them off for a short time, it was like I severed an extension of themselves.

Realizing that brought forth guilt I didn't think about—at the time, I only was worried about myself.

"Ivy, did you want to have lunch with us today after classes?" James questioned from my open cottage door as I grabbed the last of my items for school.

Looking over my shoulder, I noticed the hopeful glimmer within. "Uh—yeah, that sounds like a plan. What did you guys have in mind?"

"We like to go to Angelo's, the Italian place in town, the night before the full moon. Carbs are good for our wolf, and he knows what we like."

"What's the full moon do to your wolf?" I replied curiously, to know why they suddenly wanted me to come.

His eyes widened in realization. "Oh... yeah, I forgot you don't know a lot yet. I'm sorry."

"It's okay." I wasn't going to take it personally anymore. "I'd love to know."

His excitement seemed to spread as he looked around. "Full moons are important. Usually, the pack runs together and enjoys in celebrating the moon goddess. It's just a thing we wolves do."

The revelation hadn't even dawned on me before, but considering that they wanted to include me in traditional activities that reflected who they were was warming. "I would love to go."

Accomplishment filled me as I watched the smile of joy cross James' face.

Nodding his head, he quickly took off in a jog toward the house, no doubt to tell the others of my choice. I appreciated the way they were respecting my boundaries.

Eventually, my way of living was going to change.

I would be moved into the main house and then from there be the love of all of their lives.

Or, at least, that was what I assumed.

Would I be able to attend school like I want? Or instead, would I move to online education and private tutors? With everything else I had on my plate, I would also have to begin learning how to be a Luna, as Hale calls it.

Luna... to think I am supposed to be someone important... someone regal.

Shaking off my many thoughts of the future, I grabbed my car keys and headed toward the garage. Classes started early, and I was looking forward to Caleb's lecture today.

The topic was about how reservations are created and maintained by the government and private contractors and the wolves that I was slowly learning, laid claim to a lot of nature reserves. It made sense, honestly. Humans were free to maintain adventuring during the day, and the pack houses that lay on the outskirts of the reservations had access at night.

Talon explained that not all like this concept, but he had seen it before.

"Ivy!" Kate's squeal of excitement as I entered the cafe took me by surprise.

"Oh my goodness, when did you get back?!"

Kate rolled her eyes with a smile. "I know. I'm sorry I didn't text you. I got back last night, but I was so exhausted with everything that I couldn't keep my eyes open. So I figured I would surprise you this morning."

"Surprise indeed!" The laughter that left our lips was welcoming. I missed her terribly when she was gone, and now that she was back, I felt so much better.

Ordering my coffee, I looped my arm through hers and sat down. "You have no idea how much I have missed you."

"Aww, I missed you too. Why does it sound like something bad happened?" More than anything, I wanted to tell her about everything, but at the same time, it was difficult because I couldn't tell her werewolves existed.

She will think I'm clinically insane.

"It's all a little complicated."

My answer wasn't far from the truth. It just didn't make sense to tell her about werewolves.

"A little?" she replied. "Sounds like more than a little."

She wasn't lying.

"It's nothing, really. I will be okay."

Concern filled her eyes as she nodded. "Well, if you change your mind, you only have to say."

The rest of our conversation was filled with light humor about what happened on her trip home and how she wants to bring me back to meet her family sometimes.

The idea of going to visit was not a bad one to have. She didn't live far from my mom, and to be honest, I wished that my mother was with me now.

Walking from the coffee shop, I made my way toward the north of campus to attend my next class. Spending time with

Kate had lightened my spirits, but I was far from being okay with everything.

Perhaps she was right, though. I really needed a vacation.

"Ivy!" Stopping in my tracks, I looked over my shoulder to see Caleb walking toward me.

"Caleb?" I smiled enthusiastically. "Don't you have a class to teach?"

A laugh left his lips as he shook his head, "not for another hour. Are you headed to class?"

"Depends. Are you going to play hall monitor?" I teased.

"Do I need to?" A smirk trod lightly over his lips.

This banter wasn't unfamiliar to me but stopping it was a must. I didn't want Caleb to get the wrong idea about me. I saw him as a friend and nothing more.

"Of course not," I replied, "I am on my way to class, though. Did you need something?"

He rubbed the back of his neck, shaking his head, he smiled at me.

"I just wanted to check on you. I have not heard from you since the other night, and I wanted to make sure you were okay."

My mind blank for a moment, I pondered what he meant. "Oh—yeah. I'm okay, I guess."

"That doesn't sound overly confident." His voice was laced with concern as Kate's was.

I knew that I should speak up about what was on my mind, but the thought of burdening others with my issues wasn't something I really wanted to do.

"I'm–" distant shouting grabbed my attention.

Turning toward the parking lot, I spotted the last person I would expect to see walking across the courtyard, headed straight for me.

Damian.

He held his head high, fists clenched, and a sneer across his lips. There was no doubt in my mind that trouble was brewing.

I was baffled by his approach, but it was quickly quieted as Damian reached me, pulling me behind him and facing Caleb.

"What do you think you are doing?" He snapped, taking me by surprise.

Caleb, however, didn't seem fazed by Damian's attitude. Instead, he crossed his arms over his chest and smiled. "Well, hello to you as well, Damian."

"What's going on?" I asked softly, trying to decipher why there was so much hostility.

Damian turned to me with a cold glare. "Is this the friend you were talking about?"

My eyes widened in shock. "He is my friend, yes. Why does that matter?"

"Is he the friend you stayed with the other night?!" Damian's voice grew a little louder. Catching the attention of people passing by.

"Would you please stop acting like this?" I replied, "you're causing a scene."

"She's right. You're being unreasonable," Caleb retorted.

Damian's anger seemed to flare, and without hesitation, he spun back to Caleb with his teeth bared. "You will stay away from her."

"She doesn't belong to you, Damian." Caleb's statement was only causing more issues.

"Please, both of you, stop it..."

The one thing I hated more than anything was people who caused a scene. It was ridiculous to argue over frivolous things. Not to mention so openly where I attended school.

"She is mine!" Damian roared, the gold swirl of his eyes not going unnoticed by Caleb and me.

If I didn't stop the confrontation going on, there would undoubtedly be a huge problem on campus, and not one I wanted to be part of. Placing myself between Caleb and Damian, I pushed against Damian's chest lightly, trying to draw his attention.

"Please stop this. I promise nothing is happening. He was helping me understand some things."

Damian's cold glare lowered to me, and I wished I had walked away for the first time in a long time.

"He isn't who you think he is, Ivy."

"What?" Looking between the two men, I tried to grasp the turmoil that was running through me.

Yes, I don't know much about their lives or the werewolf kind. But Caleb has been nothing but kind to me.

"That's funny coming from someone who steals other people's mates and then lets them die."

The words coming from Caleb's mouth moved too quickly for me to process.

Frozen in my place, I stared at them both in disbelief.

Did she die?

Secrets of Men

Ivy

Did he take Caleb's mate?

The question swirled like a rollercoaster through my mind. And what did he mean she died?

A dull ache in my head began to grow like a rooted tree that refused to give up. My flight response kicked in and, without waiting another moment, I forced myself to walk away from them.

"If you both want to act like this, then you will do it without me around," I huffed as I stormed off.

If those two wanted to act like a bunch of children, then so be it, but I was not going to wait around to listen to their bickering. Damian and Caleb had both made some wild statements, and out of the two of them, only Caleb had been honest with me so far.

So why would I doubt him? He had never given me a reason not to trust him.

The pounding of feet upon concrete echoed from behind me. Looking over my shoulder, I watched Damian's figure moving quickly to keep up.

"Where are you going?" Damian asked, stopping me in my tracks again.

"Away from the both of you," I retorted, stepping around him.

He was more than persistent as he caught up and kept in step with me. I wasn't sure what he was trying to do, but I had a class to get to and wasn't going to waste another minute on their arguing.

"Will you wait a sec?" His hand reached out, gripping my upper arm, forcing me to stop.

The feeling of his touch against my skin sent sensations to my heart I tried to ignore.

No matter how angry I got with him, I couldn't deny my attraction.

"Wait a second, for what?" I snapped with my brows narrowed. "What do you want?"

"I want to explain myself," he said.

Nodding my head, I smiled. "Okay. Did you take his mate?"

A look of confusion stared back at me. "It wasn't like that."

Wasn't like that? Out of all the answers he could have given me, that was the one he wanted to go with. For a man that was supposed to be a leader or Alpha as they call it, he wasn't the wisest of choices.

"Right... well, you either did, or you didn't."

"You don't understand, Ivy," Damian replied, crossing his arms. "She wasn't a stable person."

"Again, you're not making yourself look better."

Groaning in protest, his eyes darted around before he gripped my hand and began to drag me toward the parking lot. "Where are you taking me! I have class!"

"Just come on. I can't explain things here."

As much as I wanted to get to class, my curiosity got the better of me.

Damn it, hopefully, Mandy can get me those notes.

Kate

I hated lying.

My entire life, I had grown up on the philosophy of not lying if I didn't have to. I mean, what was honestly the point, right?

Yet, here I was, lying to Ivy.

There was so much that I wanted to tell her and had to hold back on. I felt bad for the girl. Everything she had known about her life wasn't what it was supposed to be. Instead, she was fed whatever truth people wanted to give her.

Something that irritated me.

When I went back to Georgia, it wasn't for a family emergency or respite from the semester. No, it was because I had to regroup for my mission. Things were becoming more complicated by the second, and the council demanded action.

It was the reason I was where I was now.

The shadow of the library building concealed me from where I watched. I had always felt that Caleb was up to no good, and as Damian made his way across the courtyard, I knew nothing good was going to come of it.

Caleb might have been a professor on campus, but there was no doubt interest lurking beneath his gaze. I had seen that lust-filled look many times—he gave it every time he looked at Ivy.

"What are you doing?" Mandy replied from behind me, causing me to jump.

"Don't do that!" I exclaimed.

"Sorry," she replied sheepishly. "I had to come to see what you were doing. You're being odd."

"That's because I AM odd," I retorted, rolling my eyes.

"Yeah, that's true. But it's more than usual."

Mandy was a sweet girl, but for some reason, she seemed off to me.

The first day I met her, I could sense she was going to be trouble. Mandy seemed shy and naïve, but as my eyes drifted toward her intriguing figure, curiosity filled me with who she really could be.

The day I met her, Mandy dressed like she was the most high-end girl on campus, but her personality didn't reflect the way she seemed to want to present herself.

"As that may be. I was simply making sure Ivy was okay." Turning away from the corner of the building, my feet carried me toward my car in hopes of being able to get rid of Mandy.

"Can I come with you?" she called out.

Groaning, I spun to face her with a smile. "Sorry. I have some personal stuff I have to do. We can catch up later, though."

Lying again. Letting out an exasperated sigh, I pulled out my phone, checking to see if the message I had been waiting on had come in.

Much to my dismay, it hadn't. Go figure.

Looking back over my shoulder, I watched as Mandy slowly turned and began to walk toward the direction Caleb and Damian had been arguing. It wasn't the wisest of directions to go, but knowing her, she would get in the middle because Ivy was there.

Her funeral.

I didn't trust that girl. She was a snake in tall grass waiting for someone to make a mistake. On more than one occasion had I caught her watching Ivy. Each time she played it off as if she was in the wrong place at the wrong time, but I still didn't trust it.

The bright morning sun beamed off my faded blue four-door sedan as it sat in the parking lot. The sight of the old car brought a smile to my face, and that was because I had missed it terribly.

Yes, I could have flown back from Georgia, but honestly, walking around everywhere sucked.

So my old car was a quick choice.

My mind drifted back to Ivy, contemplating the need to tell her the truth.

If Ivy wasn't careful, she was going to end up in a dangerous predicament, and nothing those guys did would be able to save her from her fate.

"Kate..." The sound of my name being called from my passenger door froze me in my place.

I thanked the gods that my doors were locked once I started the engine because when I faced the newcomer, I saw Caleb's eyes staring back at me.

"Yes, sir?" I questioned, rolling the window down a hair.

"Where are you going? Don't you have class right now?"

Caleb was an inquisitive man, but there was no way he would be able to know my schedule. "No, sir. But I do have an appointment, so I must be going."

"Oh," he replied, thinking, "I could have sworn I saw you in Mrs. Simmon's class the other day."

Now I know he was lying. "I find that hard to believe, Professor. Especially considering the fact I just went back in town last night."

The happy, smiling instructor's act quickly dissipated. "Perhaps, I was mistaken."

Caleb was a man I never was too fond of. "I must be going. Have a wonderful day."

Putting my car into reverse, he stepped back onto the sidewalk, pushing his hands into his pockets. With his brows furrowed, his eyes never left mine. The man was thinking hard about something.

If he was approaching me now, it meant one of two things.

One, he was starting to take an interest in me like he did Ivy, and there could be trouble.

Or two...

He was catching on to what was going on around him—and I was running out of time.

Ivy

Breathing heavily through my nose, I exhaled in annoyance. Damian had brought me to his car in the parking lot and wanted to take me home to explain. All of which I wasn't having.

"You can explain here," I replied, crossing my arms over my chest.

His jaw tightened, and his muscles tensed. For some reason, Damian held himself back from whatever he wanted to do. "Fine." His words spoken through gritted teeth.

Cocking a brow, I leaned against his car and waited patiently. Never before had he been so willing to comply, and that notion on its own made me curious.

"Look–" he stated with a sigh, "I have known Caleb since high school. He is older than me, and when he got his mate before me he was happy. Surprisingly enough, we used to be friends."

It wasn't hard to believe that at one point they had been friends. The way they argued made it seem like they had indeed been close at one point in time. I just never realized that Damian would find it this hard to talk about.

"I figured that," I finally replied. "But what is the deal about this mate?"

"The day Caleb turned eighteen and got his wolf, he found his mate. Her name was Sophia."

Sophia. The same swirled across my tongue, and yet something about her name seemed to light a spark in Damian's eye.

"Did you care for her?"

Shaking his head, he sighed. "Not in the way you think. The three of us had been close friends, but instead of being happy she was mated to Caleb... she rejected him."

"Because she wanted to be with you, right?"

"Yeah," he replied with a sigh, running his hand through his hair, "she was convinced that there had been a mistake and that she and I were supposed to be mates. She was determined she was Luna material, not that of a Gamma's wife."

"Gamma?" The term caught my attention, and I was curious to know what it meant.

There was still a lot about it all that I had not been made aware of.

"Yes, a Gamma is the Alpha's third in command. As I said, it's complicated."

Frowning, I leaned forward off of his car and stared at him. "Perhaps there would be fewer complications had you told me everything from day one. Regardless, it doesn't explain why she rejected him. What would make her want to reject him and go to you?"

"I don't know, Ivy!" he groaned in frustration, "because she wanted to be the Luna? I mean, why do women do half of the things they do?"

His sexiest remark made me roll my eyes in displeasure. "You must have led her on then."

From what the guys had told me, Damian wasn't the man he was now back then. When he was younger, he was a party guy who loved to have fun and sleep with the ladies.

It only made sense that she thought she would have more with him.

"I don't lead people on. That's disgusting."

Disgusting?!

"Seriously?" I questioned, watching as he shrugged his shoulders. "Did you party back then?"

"I don't see how that's relevant."

"Answer the damn question, Damian. Did you party back then?" I asked, getting frustrated with his stubbornness.

"Yes, I did."

"Okay, well, did you hang out with her back then?" I asked, making sure my questions were leading in a particular direction.

"Again, how is that relevant, Ivy?" he replied, shaking his head.

"Please stop making me repeat my questions and just fucking answer them," I snapped, trying to show him that I was done playing his games.

"Yes, we all hung out. What's your next question?" The sarcasm in his words dripped from his lips.

"Did you ever do anything with her before she found out they were mates? Kissing... sex?"

"I'm not answering that question," Damian replied before walking toward the passenger seat of his car and opening the door for me to get in.

"No, answer the damn question. I don't see what's so hard about this."

"It isn't hard, but it isn't any of yours or anyone else's business. Now get in the damn car, Ivy." The growl that left his lips at his words made it clear that he was done playing my game. However, his lack of response to the question made the answer clear.

He had done something with her, and in turn, she thought they could be more.

Poor Caleb.

To think the man had a chance of a mate and lost it because Damian was the center of her attention. In a way, it wasn't entirely his fault. He couldn't have expected them to be mates, or at least, I hoped he didn't continue after he found out.

"Your silence is all the admission I need," I replied after a moment. "I think I will go for a walk and make my own way home."

Damian slammed the car door as I turned around. "Will you stop being so fucking immature and get in the damn car. I don't have time for this shit."

"Just go home, Damian," I countered over my shoulder as I kept my feet moving. No matter what I did, he constantly wanted to argue with me. I may not have known much about mates, but I was sure this wasn't how it was supposed to be.

"Ivy..." With calm collection, Damian grasped my arm once more and turned me to face him. A longing within his eyes gave way to his attempt at trying. "Please, don't do this."

The notion that he was asking for understanding made my heart swell. "No. You can't keep acting like this. I'm tired of arguing with you. Since I got here, all you have done is been cruel to me, and I won't tolerate it anymore."

Pulling away from him, I continued walking across campus. His footsteps never followed me. My chest tightened at the realization that my life was a cruel fluctuation of twists and turns. Constant secrets preventing me from seeing clearly.

Clouded skies gave way to the approaching rain that would soon settle down upon the earth, and with it, winter would begin its approach in just a short time. Never did I realize that love could bring such anguish.

In my own way, I did love each of them—or at least I thought I did.

Staring down at the ground, I thought about what Damian had told me.

My heart broke for them both. I couldn't understand why fate had been cruel to them, but again, there was still so much I didn't know. I was the outsider in the situation.

The foreign entity that came in and changed the game for everyone.

Was Caleb lying to me? Did he have an ulterior motive that he was hiding?

A scream of frustration tore through my throat, bringing the attention of people passing by. I didn't care what they thought. I didn't care what any of them thought.

The only thing I wanted was to have peace in my life.

Peace seemed so far away, though.

"Ivy?" Caleb's voice traveled through the air.

Looking toward the road, I spotted his car with ease. The passenger window rolled down and his face peered through with concern.

"Oh–" I replied. "Hey, Caleb."

"What are you doing standing outside? It's about to start storming," he replied.

A laugh escaped me as I shook my head slightly. "I am trying to figure out why my life is the way it is. I have you acting a certain way, and Caleb telling me something completely different. Through it all... I don't even know what my purpose is."

"Come. Let's get out somewhere warm before it starts storming. I will help you figure this all out." Like always, Caleb's words seemed sincere. But now, with the lingering doubt in my mind placed there by Damian, I didn't know what to believe.

"How do I know you aren't pretending? That this isn't just an act."

I think my question was appropriate, considering what I had seen between them earlier. I didn't even know that Caleb and Damian had known each other till the situation in the courtyard.

Neither man explained that their relationship had been more than acquaintances.

"Have I ever given you a reason to not trust me?" he asked, causing me to hesitate.

He had a point. Never before had he given me a reason not to trust him.

Nodding my head, I climbed into his car and shut the door. "Okay, then."

There was no telling if I was making a mistake, but there was only one way to find out.

Masks of Truth

The wind wailed against the darkening sky, making those around aware of the approaching dangers. It was going to be the most unpleasant of days, but they say one will always find a light through the darkness.

Or something like that.

Caleb's car pushed through the approaching rain toward his home. A sense of unease fell over us on the drive, and an internal debate on whether I had made the right choice made me curious as to what I was currently doing.

Caleb wasn't my mate, and yet, I had so willingly gone with him.

Maybe I'm making a mistake.

Pulling into his drive, I hesitated outside the car. "I think I should just go home."

Caleb spun around, his eyes staring at me with apprehension. "What's wrong?"

"Nothing, I just don't think I should cause more problems."

Caleb slowly nodded his head, pushing his hands into his front pockets. "At least let me make you a cup of tea, and we can get you an Uber if you would like."

Guilt washed over me at his response. Caleb had done nothing but kind to me, and here I was acting as if he was a criminal. It wasn't fair to him. He had done nothing wrong.

"That sounds great." I smiled. "Let's have tea, and then I will call a cab."

A smile crossed his lips as he turned and continued toward the front door.

"I'm sorry about what happened earlier." Caleb's apologetic voice called out as he moved around his kitchen.

"It's okay," I replied softly, "everyone has their issues, and yours and Damian's seem to run deep."

Silence met the air between us as he set the kettle on the stove and prepared our cups.

"Yeah..." he replied after a moment, "it's a shame too because we used to be close."

As the tea was sat in front of me, I picked it up without hesitation and sighed into the delicious taste that filled my mouth. On long days, the best cure is always a cup of tea or, at least, that is what my mother told me growing up.

I remembered sitting around the dining table with her after a rough day at school, and she would make me a cup of tea while we talked about what happened.

Those were memories I cherished.

"Thank you for being so kind and caring," I replied with a smile.

"I am just doing what any caring person would do, Ivy."

Something about the way that Caleb spoke set my nerves on edge. A smirk lay on his face that seemed more off than usual. Nodding my head slowly, I gave a small smile and fiddled my fingers around my cup.

"I appreciate that," I muttered softly, "I think I am going to call that cab now. I'm sure people are beginning to wonder where I am."

Standing to my feet, I stumbled a bit. My eyes blurred slightly, and my head fogged. It wasn't a feeling I had before, and with every step I took, I felt my body become heavier and heavier.

"Are you okay, Ivy?" Caleb's voice replied from behind me. An uneasy feeling settled in my stomach. "Perhaps, you should sit down."

Panic set into my veins as I tried to grasp a handle on myself and found it impossible to do.

"What's wrong with me?" I asked breathlessly.

Unable to stand any longer, my legs finally gave out, and my body collapsed to the floor. A cry of pain left my lips as I tried to understand what was happening to me.

"You don't look good at all," Caleb taunted, his heavy footsteps echoing against the wood floor as he approached me slowly.

"Wha–" I stuttered, my head throbbing with a dull ache, "what did you do to me?"

There was no doubt about it. The situation I was in wasn't normal, and now I was questioning my judgment toward men. Had I misunderstood everything?

Was Caleb really the devil in disguise?

The fluttering of my heart as it raced echoed in my ears, and slowly Caleb's face came into view as he crouched down near my face with a grin spread across his lips.

"Oh, my sweet dear, Ivy," he replied, shaking his head, "I didn't want things to be like this. Honestly, I thought you were warming up to me. Then Damian made the spectacle he did today, and I knew I couldn't waste any more time."

"What?" I cried out in pain and confusion. "Please... I don't understand."

"I know you don't, but don't worry, I will explain everything to you," he replied standing to his feet.

Caleb

For too long, I had endured the idiocy that was Damian. The man wasn't the Alpha his people needed, and instead of being cast aside and one of his other brothers taking over, they accepted him with open arms.

Yet, they didn't know the man like I did.

Growing up in the pack, there was a moral code you went by. A standard that was meant no matter what. It was what was instilled in us since we were pups, and Damian failed at it all. It didn't matter if he and his brothers were orphans– they didn't belong here.

My eyes cast down to Ivy, who lay on the floor, helpless to the drug I had given her. She wanted to know the truth. So who was I to deny her of that?

"Damian never deserved to be Alpha," I stated, "he was a piece of shit when we were kids, and he still is to this day. Always thinking that he was better than everyone else and never taking anything seriously."

I sneered at the memories that tried to resurface.

"What does this have to do with me?" she whispered softly, the medication I gave her working double-time as I hoped.

"It has everything to do with you, Ivy, and in time you will know the details."

Her eyes slowly fluttered until her lashes brushed against her cheek. It was the sign that I had been waiting for. Grabbing the duffel bag from my sofa, I carried it toward my car, quickly preparing to leave for my next location.

The brothers would soon come looking for their mate, and it meant that my time in my home was coming to an end. It wasn't for nothing, though. I had played my part in this town for long enough, and now that I had what I had been waiting for, I was going to move to the next part of my plan.

Constant buzzing from my pocket caused me to groan in irritation. Pulling my phone from my pocket, I watched my the good little wolf's name cross the screen.

"Ah, I was wondering when you would call."

"Yeah, well, I have been busy, as always. Did you get her?" she replied with irritation.

A chuckle left my lips at her tone. "Of course I did. We will be heading that way in just a minute."

"Well, you better hurry," she snapped. "They are up at the school looking for her. Considering your argument with Damian, they will come to your place next. The last thing you need to do is get caught with her in your possession."

The news was unpleasant, and as much as I didn't appreciate how she spoke to me, the girl had a point. I needed to be quick. "Alright. We will see you tomorrow."

Hanging up my phone, I slid it back into my pocket before jogging back inside. Ivy's body lay sleeping on the wooden floor of my living room, her hair sprawled around her like a halo.

"Soon, my dear, things will change in my favor, and I will be able to show you what it's like to be mated to a real wolf."

The thought itself made the bulge in my jeans tighten in excitement. I had wanted this girl since the first day I had seen her. Now that I had her, there was no way I would let her go.

Hale

"Damn it!" I cursed under my breath as I slammed the door of my car. "She isn't on campus."

My eyes scanned the empty campus courtyard, looking for where she could have gone. Rain began to fall from the sky and worry filled me.

If Ivy was out here, it wasn't good. The weather in this part of the country was unpredictable, and with the coming rain, the cold would follow.

I couldn't allow her to get sick or, worse... hurt.

"Ivy!" I yelled again.

"She isn't here, Hale!" James called over a clap of thunder. "Maybe she headed home."

"Without her car?!" I retorted.

When Damian returned home and told me what happened at the school between Caleb and Ivy, I went in search of her. The only problem was Ivy having the damn necklace I gave her made her untraceable.

Regret filled me, realizing what I had done.

Something that was intended to give her privacy now became a hindrance to her safety.

"Where could she be?" James asked as if I would actually be able to answer that question. There was no telling where she could be.

"I don't know. As you may know, our relationship with her hasn't been great," I snapped at him with irritation. All of our wolves could feel the connection with Ivy growing fainter every day. The circle hadn't been fully completed, and now, with her missing, it was a bigger issue.

Moving back toward the car, I slammed the door, my hands hitting the steering wheel over and over again. I had to get her back... even if the bond broke with the harvest moon...

I had to get her back more than anything, but sometimes I worried if she was better off without us. Ivy deserved better than what she was getting.

"What happens if we can't find her before the harvest moon?"

James' question hit me hard. The thought that the bond would sever was unnerving.

Would it mean that we would lose Ivy forever, or was it the possibility she would no longer be able to mate with four but instead just one?

"I don't know, James. Let's just find her."

Silence filled the car as we pulled out from the university and drove around town, looking for her figure with every turn we made. No matter how hard we searched, every angle came up empty-handed.

"What about that guy's house... Caleb? Do you think she went there?"

James, for once, had made a good point. Breaking into a U-turn, I pushed my foot down on the gas and sped toward Caleb's house. I had made a point when Damian had mentioned her hanging out with the guy to discover where he lived, and now it would come in handy.

Pulling onto the concrete drive, James and I were out of the car in a flash. My fist beating upon the door with a sense of urgency. Praying to the goddess, I hoped that Ivy was here because if she wasn't, I didn't know what I was going to do.

"Ivy!" I called out into the air, "Caleb... open up, it's important!"

"Hale... I don't think they are here," James' replied, standing back and looking up at the dark windows of the house.

"She has to be. We have to find her, James."

"I know, but I'm telling you, she isn't here." His reply was firmer this time, and as my eyes met his, I felt it too. She isn't here, and if she had been, she was long gone now.

"Excuse me?" a voice called from behind us, causing us both to turn around.

The gray hair of an older man stood on the other side of a hedge in the neighbor's yard with concern etched on his face.

"Yes?" James replied as we walked closer.

"Are you looking for the young man who lives here?"

"Yes, we are. Do you know if he has been home?" The words left my mouth quickly, hoping for anything that would clue me into whether Ivy had been here.

"Oh, I would say about an hour ago. He and a pretty young girl came home, and then thirty minutes later, they both left."

"Ivy was here..." I mumbled, looking back at the house and wondering where they could have gone.

"Yes, the poor thing looked like she was sick."

Spinning back around, I stared at him in confusion. "Sick?"

Why would she be sick? That made no sense.

"Yes, she could barely walk, and the young man said she fainted, and he was taking her to the hospital."

Tension and suspense filled me as my anxiety skyrocketed. There was no way that she had fainted. None of it made sense, and Caleb knew we were werewolves. He wouldn't have just taken her to a normal hospital.

"Hale..." James' whispered, "we have to tell Damian."

"I know... let's go. I have a feeling Ivy is in trouble."

Ivy

The dull sounds of a motor filled my ears as the fog lifted from my mind. Slowly opening my eyes, the bright light of my surroundings began to fill my vision. I'm moving.

The realization was obvious, but for some reason, my mind couldn't wrap around what was happening. It was as if every fiber of my body protested against what was happening.

"Fuck..." I muttered, sitting up straight and trying to grasp my bearings.

A man's mumbled voice drew my attention, and I could have sworn it was Caleb talking into a phone. His eyes glanced back at me from a mirror over and over again.

"What–" I groaned, my hand trying to move, unable to, "what's going on?"

Focusing my gaze, I took in the brown rope wrapped repeatedly around my wrists. Realization and horror set into my bones as I saw Caleb in the front seat driving.

"Good morning, Ivy," he replied, staring at me from the rearview mirror. "I was wondering when you would wake up."

"Where am I? What is going on!" Pulling against the restraints, my eyes widened.

He kidnapped me.

A man I trusted had taken me against my will and far away from my home.

"Calm down, Ivy. Enjoy the ride. Resisting will only cause you to hurt yourself."

"Your crazy!" I yelled in anger, "let me go right now!"

A growl reverberated from the front seat, causing me to slink back to where I was sitting. "You will watch how you speak to me, Ivy."

This man in front of me was no longer the man I had once known. Instead, he had become something else, and I felt foolish not to had listened to Damian's warning.

Caleb wasn't a good man. He was dangerous, and I walked into his trap.

Tears threatened to spill down my cheeks, and blinking quickly, I tried to push them back.

"Why are you doing this to me? I thought we were friends."

Caleb's deep chuckle made my stomach tighten in fear. "Enjoy the ride. I will explain everything when we arrive."

It was pointless to keep up the emotions I was going through. If I was going to find a way to break free, I was going to have to save my energy.

God knows what this man had planned.

The fluttering of wind from Caleb's open window brushed against the side of my face. The smell of the lake within my nostrils caused me to take in the details outside.

Thick forests in the distance surrounded the water from the lake below. Concrete pillars with spiral tops crested the edges of the bridge against the sky. I wasn't sure where Caleb was taking me, but from the looks of it, it was far from the town I was in.

Perhaps, if I paid attention to my surroundings, I could find a way back.

There was always a chance I could escape.

Hope was the only thing I had to hold on to, because without it, there was no telling where my mind would go. My mother, the guys... they all needed me, and instead of doing what I should have, I decided to ignore them.

I should have stayed home in Georgia and never come to this place.

All I had become was a damsel in my own story, with the big bag wolf ready to devour me.

How do you take your tea?

The car stopped, jolting me forward in my seat. My eyes scanned the darkness of the dense forest around me while I tried to contemplate where I was. This was unfamiliar terrain, though. A cloak of uneasy darkness spread across forests I had never been in.

Yet this is where Caleb brought me.

He drove for hours and refused to stop under any circumstance. My irritation over his behavior and my situation grew by the second.

Just as I thought I couldn't take it anymore, the car stopped, and I was faced with the idea of where our destination was.

Moving quickly from the car, he opened my door, grabbed me by my arm, and roughly pulled me to my feet. The cold fresh air hit my face as I stumbled on the rooted ground. There was no gentle touch from Caleb. Instead, his firm grasp pulled me further and further up a trail toward a small wooden cabin overlooking a bluff.

"You're hurting me." I whimpered as he tugged on me again. His cold eyes darted toward me before looking back on his set target.

"Stop whining. If you listened and moved faster, I wouldn't have to treat you like a child."

Unsure of what awaited me in the cabin, I pushed into him, causing him to stumble, and ripped my arm from his grasp. Moving quickly, I tried to break free, but only managed a few feet before he yanked me back.

"Let me go!" I cried out before I was thrown over his shoulder, kicking and screaming.

"Scream all you want, Ivy. No one is going to hear you out here."

He moved from the dirt path up to the porch, carrying me as if I weighed nothing. The door opened and a cool voice I hadn't expected to flow freely in the air.

"It took you long enough to get here," Mandy said, causing my eyes to widen.

"Mandy?" The gasp that left me caused her to chuckle, and I realized that her friendship to me had been nothing.

"Surprise!" she called out as Caleb dropped me down onto an old worn-out sofa with a grin on his lips. "I have been waiting for this moment for a long time."

"I don't understand. What's going on?"

Her eyes seemed to shimmer in the dim light of the fire as if twinkling with a desire to let me know everything that they held secret. "Give it time, and I will tell you everything you want to know."

"No, you need to tell me now. What the fuck is wrong with you both?!"

The slap across my face was unexpected, but the sting was ever so present. My eyes swirled for a moment as I focused back on what was in front of me.

I had always considered Mandy to be a quiet and sweet girl, but to my surprise, she was a devilish demon in disguise. "Now, look what you made me do."

Her cold words matched her glare before she walked away to the kitchen. My eyes shifted toward Caleb. I tried to search for any part of him that felt remorse, but instead, all I saw was lust in his eyes as he stared at me.

"Caleb, I know you hate Damian, but this isn't how you get revenge. I have done nothing to you."

His lips formed into a thin, straight line at the mention of Damian. "This isn't about him... well, not exactly."

"Then will one of you please tell me what the hell is going on?"

Silence followed the open statement hanging between us. I wanted answers, and I wasn't going to give up. But something told me that with the way they were both acting, I wasn't going to like what they had to say.

"We are saving you, Ivy," Mandy finally replied, stepping back into the living room with a porcelain teapot. "Giving you a chance to change your future."

"Change my future?" Nothing she was saying made sense. "How can you change my future?"

"This is one thing I hate about the four of them. They didn't have the common respect to tell you the truth about who you are and what you will do."

"To be honest, it doesn't seem anyone wants to tell me anything anymore. Including you." I snapped, frustrated with the riddles she was spewing.

Tsk. Tsk. Tsk.

The sound caused my anger to bubble as she stepped closer. "Tell me, Ivy... how do you like your tea?"

Tea! Was she being fucking serious right now?!

"If I tell you, will you start talking?" I replied through gritted teeth.

Perhaps I would have to play their game in order to get questions.

Her eyes cast off for a moment before she looked back toward Caleb, who had taken a seat in the chair across from me. He quickly glanced at her, shrugging his shoulders, causing Mandy to smile.

"Of course. That sounds fair to me."

Rolling my eyes, I sighed. "Two sugars and a splash of milk."

"Wonderful. I will be right back."

Trying to maintain my composure, I leaned back onto the sofa and stared at Caleb. To think that for weeks I spent time getting to know him and helping out in his class.

Even staying the night at his house!

Only to find out he had been playing with me the whole time. That his goal had been this from the beginning, and I fed right into the lies he was creating. I was a fool to trust him.

"Here we go," Mandy replied with a smile as she brought in a pot of tea and a few cups. "Now, why don't we start... Caleb, do you want to tell her or should I?"

"Shut up, Mandy," he snapped quickly with irritation, "stop acting like you're in charge of anything."

Her eyes widened at his temper as did mine, both of us looking at him as if he had lost his mind.

"Excuse me? If it wasn't for me, they would have caught you by now..."

A growl of anger left his throat as his eyes turned black. I had seen Damian get like this a few times, and from what I assumed, it was the beast inside him that was ready to break free.

"It's okay..." I muttered, staring at him, "Please, Caleb... you can tell me."

Mandy glared at me, not pleased with me speaking, but she didn't dare to open her mouth.

"Mandy was right," Caleb finally said after he took a deep breath and leaned forward on his knees. "I am trying to save you, Ivy. Give you a different life."

"A different life?"

"Yes." Sighing, he pinched the bridge of his nose, "you wouldn't have to be mated to them and would be able to choose who you want to love."

Caleb's words weren't words that I was expecting. In fact, I didn't think that there was a way to undo what had already been done. Hale said it was for life, and if it was, then nothing Caleb said was making any sense.

"That isn't possible."

"Oh, no... maybe not for normal wolves, but you are human. Your bond to them isn't complete without Damian." The glint in his eyes caught me off guard.

"You're happy about this?" I stated, making my observation known.

A laugh left him as he before a grin slid across his face. "Yes. Because when the Harvest Moon peaks in two days... the bond will break with the other three, and you will be free to be claimed by another wolf."

The bond will break.

The idea of my attachment to the other guys severing was horrific. Yes, we had our problems, but I didn't want to leave them... did I?

"That doesn't make sense... why would I want another wolf if I let them go?"

"You don't have to want anything, Ivy." Mandy smirked, "but it will be pleasant to watch Damian fall when Caleb claims you for himself."

My chest tightened at her revelation, and everything slowly began to make sense. Caleb wanted revenge on Damian, that was obvious. So, therefore, I became the object he would use to do so.

"But why?"

Standing to his feet, Caleb's eyes met mine, "to make him suffer the loss of a mate, just as I had to endure with him."

A dull ache filled me as my mind tried to wrap around the idea of what Caleb had said. The two of them had completely lost their minds.

How was it that my life had made the turn it did?

All I wanted was peace, and yet I was resorted to participating in a twisted society that deemed holding people hostage as a way to fix their problems.

"Caleb, why?" I asked softly, trying to understand how the sweet man I once met would be so cruel toward me. "This is all ridiculous. You have to let me go."

"I already told you why. What part of that don't you understand?" he snapped, his eyes narrowed in my direction.

"I don't understand, why me...?" I searched for a part of him that could see reason. "I get that you have issues with them, but I never did anything to you."

I watched as he paced around the room. The rigid stance of his body showed the frustration he was feeling. "It isn't about that, Ivy. You mean something to him, and to be honest, I wish it wasn't you. You don't deserve what's coming, but I won't deny the joy I do have in being able to have you as mine. You're special."

Special? This man really had lost his mind. I was nothing special. All I wanted to do was finish school, and make an impact on humanity to help better our planet.

A simple tree hugger, as most would call me.

Sighing in disbelief, my eyes gazed toward the window. Mandy's figure paced back and forth as she talked low on her phone. I wasn't sure who she was speaking to, but when her phone rang earlier, she jumped at the opportunity to step outside and take the call.

"I will never accept you, Caleb," I stated firmly, trying to show him how serious I was.

The one thing Hale had taught me was that mating was about acceptance of both parties. So theoretically, if I didn't accept him, he couldn't claim me, right?

At least, that was the hope.

A deep chuckle echoed from his throat as he stopped and glanced toward me. "It doesn't matter. You don't have to accept me, because when I mark you, it will be too late."

Too late? What does he mean it will be too late?!

"You can't mark me." The statement was meant to be firm, but disbelief laced the words instead.

"Oh, I think you will find that I can do as I want." Caleb laughed before striding toward me, "I know that in time you will love me."

Love was such a strong word to use, and I wasn't sure if I even knew what love was.

"It won't work," I replied, rolling my eyes. "I don't know what delusional world you're living in, but I'm pretty sure love doesn't exist."

"You will change your mind eventually, Ivy." He was confident in his belief that I would love him.

And his arrogance over the matter infuriated me.

"No, I won't!" I yelled, showing him I wouldn't back down, "Damian will come for me, and there is nothing you can do about it."

As the words left my mouth, Caleb gripped my hair and pulled me toward him, his face inches from mine. "Never say his name in front of me again. He is nothing."

A swell of fear rippled through me seeing a new side to Caleb. This was a man who wasn't afraid to get what he wanted, and that wasn't the same man I knew.

"Get your hands off me," I snapped.

No matter how scared I was, I couldn't show him fear. I had to keep myself together and wait for the right moment when I could escape. Who would have thought the sweet and caring professor I once knew would turn out to be a man of insanity?

"Nice try, but I know what's really running through your mind. You say he will come for you, but there is still doubt lurking in the depths of your consciousness." The smirk on his face made my heart sink.

He wasn't wrong. I doubted whether Damian or any of them would come for me. I had done nothing but create problems for them since I had arrived. The conflict of my arrival had torn their happy family apart, and even though they were trying to work through it, I was still a complication.

"Fuck you," I spit, showing emphasis on my reluctance. There was no way I would let him get inside my head. Even if I had doubt, I wouldn't stay Caleb's prisoner. I had to find a way to break free from his hold and get my life back.

Even if that meant running forever. I would do it.

"So feisty." He smirked before firmly tossing me over his shoulder. My eyes widened at what he was doing.

"Put me down!" I screamed as he forced me down into the darkness.

The damp, stale stench of the basement invaded my nose, causing a sputter to escape my lips as I coughed. There was no telling the last time this basement probably had ever seen any kind of attention, and now here I was being locked into it.

"You are going to learn that when I want something, I will have it, Ivy."

A new sense of fear swept through me, my heart racing with every step he took. There was no telling what he was really planning to do, but my mind wandered to what it could entail.

Forced mating. Unwanted desires. Caleb was a man determined to have me and make Damian live in the same pain he had lived in for such a long time.

He quickly threw my body down upon something soft, and as I scrambled to look around, I saw the old tattered bed beneath me.

"The hell are you doing?" I gasped as I watched Caleb reach down and pick up a steel chain from the floor, walking toward me.

"What does it look like?" he retorted, "I can't have you escaping."

"No!" I screamed, my body scrambling backward as I tried to put as much distance between him and me. It was useless, though. Caleb snatched me by the ankle and dragged me toward him before clipping the shackle to my wrist and smiling down at me.

"Only two days left, Ivy. As soon as the moon's high and the bond breaks, you will be mine."

Two days. His words ran through my mind as I watched his figure retreat back up the stairs, leaving me in the darkness.

I didn't see it as I had two days left.

No, I saw it, as I had two days to escape. Reaching up, I grasped the necklace around my neck and yanked it off. The once object of privacy was now my only means of escape.

The thing was, I couldn't let Caleb know I had that over on him.

I had to have the element of surprise. Otherwise, my fate would be sealed with his bite.

Brotherly Arguments

Damian

"How can she be gone?!" I yelled, listening to my brothers explain to me that no matter where they looked, they couldn't find her.

Dread filled me, realizing how badly I had fucked up. I shouldn't have treated her the way I did, and now that I had, the bond was fading. James explained he could barely feel her now, and it made sense since he was the first to have mated with her.

"You know this would never have happened had you not been such a dick," Talon snapped, crossing his arms over his chest as he leaned against the door frame.

"Shut the fuck up, Talon. Don't you think I know that!"

Tensions were high in the mansion, and thankfully, Allison and Zane took a trip for a few days. Otherwise, I would have had to listen to Ivy's father run his mouth as well.

A swirling pit of despair built within my stomach as I played over what could have happened to her. She wasn't the kind of girl to leave... or well; I mean, she was, but not like this.

Fuck, what am I going to do?

"Uh... someone's coming up the driveway and in a hurry," James replied as he stared out the front window.

Moving from the living room, I headed to the front door just in time to see a blonde girl step out of a blue car and come marching straight for me. "Where is she?"

"Excuse me? Where is who?"

"Ivy. Don't play fucking stupid with me. Where is she?" she asked again with her hands on her hips, staring in frustration.

A growl of disapproval left my lips at her tone. "Who the fuck do you think you're talking to?"

"The bitch who is looking out for her pack member," she growled in response, her eyes glowing an amber color as she bared her fangs.

Taken aback in the moment, I found myself speechless at her admission. Pack member? How was Ivy part of her pack?

"The hell are you talking about?"

"Ivy Thorne is part of my pack, and my name is Kate. Now where the fuck are the rest of you? We have a lot to catch up on," she replied, pushing past me and making her way into the house.

Every part of me wanted to put her on her ass for the way she was speaking to me. Yet, I couldn't. I was too curious about what she was talking about to stop her.

Closing the front door, I pushed forward toward the living room where Kate was standing with my brothers, talking over the situation. "You are all idiots," she mumbled.

"Why don't you start telling me why the fuck you're here in my house acting the way you are? You are far from your own territory," I snapped, tired of listening to her bitchy attitude.

Turning around, she narrowed her eyes at me, crossing her arms over her chest. "Excuse me?"

I didn't have time to deal with this woman. I needed to find Ivy.

"You heard me. Now, explain."

Rolling her eyes, she sighed. "When Ivy's father got with her mother, it wasn't just because she was pretty. He knew her family's connection with my pack and my father. He thought by being able to seduce her, he would wiggle his way into our pack to take over."

"So you're saying Zane is a liar?" That was something I already knew.

"He is an egotistical pig that is after money and power. Everything you guys thought you knew about him is a lie. He wants to control this pack. My father knew how much mates meant to wolves, so he didn't want to stop Ivy from coming to you, but he didn't trust Zane."

"What does this have to do with finding her now!" I yelled in frustration.

Yes, this information was important to an extent, but it didn't help me with my current problem.

"As I was saying," she replied, narrowing her eyes, "he wants the bond to complete so he can get rid of you. Once the bonds complete, if Ivy dies, you all do as well, and he can take over this pack. What he didn't account for was your past issues with Caleb."

"Caleb?" James asked, as he glanced at me, raising a brow.

"Yes, Caleb," I retorted, "he may have issues with me, but he isn't that stupid."

Laughter filled the air as Kate shook her head. "That's where you're wrong. He has her, Damian. I have no doubt about that."

A shadow of darkness rose within me, hearing what Kate said. There was no way Caleb would be stupid enough to take Ivy. Regardless of the issues he and I had, I saw the way he looked at her when I confronted him.

He cared for her in some odd way.

"Why would he want her?" Hale replied, staring at me.

Sighing, I pinched the bridge of my nose, trying to let what they were saying process. He would only take her because he wanted to get back at me for what his mate did. It wasn't my fault that she fell in love with me. I had always explained that wasn't what I wanted.

I only would accept my mate.

"Because he blames me for what happened with his mate."

"We have to stop him!" Talon roared, his eyes a swirling black mist of anger. "When the moon rises, he can take her for himself."

Talon was right. As much as I didn't want to believe it, he was right about that.

"I know where he lives. We can go there."

"She isn't there," Hale piped up, "we looked, and the neighbor said that Caleb left with a girl."

"So she willingly went with him?!"

"No, I don't think so.," Hale replied, shaking his head. "She wouldn't..."

His eyes drifted off in a distant look. His mouth partially opened. "Hale, what's wrong?"

"She took off the necklace. I can feel her, but it's faint," he whispered, before rising to his feet. "She is in trouble."

I envied my brothers for having that bond with her. I couldn't reach out to her the way they could, and it killed me. I missed the opportunity to claim her.

I wouldn't allow that to happen again, though.

"She is in a cabin," Talon spoke softly, his eyes searching the ground as if looking for something. "Does Caleb have a cabin?"

"No. As far as I know, he doesn't, but then who knows what he has done over the years."

"Caleb wouldn't be stupid enough to take her to one of his properties," Kate replied, speaking up. "If he had her, he would take her somewhere you wouldn't look."

I was getting sick and tired of this girl. From the moment she had walked into the house, she did nothing but cause more questions and threw her weight around like she was in charge.

"Well," I snapped, "by all means, where the fuck do you think he has her then?"

"You know, you're an asshole." Kate shrugged her shoulders, "no wonder she wanted to go home."

"She wouldn't leave us," James exclaimed, "she loves us."

Kate smirked, shaking her head. "Anyway, I know someone who has a cabin. A girl named Mandy. I had suspected for a while that she was up to something shady, and overheard her on the phone the other day talking to someone about a cabin. I'm guessing it was Caleb."

I wasn't sure why the name Mandy sounded familiar, but if Caleb had someone working with him, it only meant that things were going to be a lot trickier. "Do you know where this place is?"

"No, but I figured Hale could figure it out," she replied, turning to Hale with a smile.

He let a sigh escape him and walked toward the computer on my desk. "On it."

The situation with Ivy had gotten more complicated. First, the issue with Caleb. Then hearing Zane had his own agenda as well. It was a lot to take in.

Ivy had done nothing wrong since she got here, and all I could think about was how horribly I had treated her. My brothers had tried to explain to me that what I was doing was wrong, but I didn't listen.

"Oh, shit... Damian, we have a problem," Hale replied with his eyes widened in shock.

"What's wrong?"

"Mandy is Caleb's dead mate's sister," he replied.

He was right. That was a problem.

Ivy

The dripping sounds of water from the pipes above woke me from my sleep. My mind was a haze from the lack of food and clean air. I had reached out to the guys, trying with all my might to show them or tell them where I was, but my thoughts went unheard.

Was this what I had to look forward to? A life with nothing but false love and attention.

Pulling my weight forward, I sat up and tried to make sense of my surroundings. The cool metal of the shackle at my wrist clanged against the hard wet floor, drawing my attention to the hook on the floor.

If only there was something to undo these bolts.

'Hale,' I called out again in my mind as I pulled at my restraints. 'Please talk to me.'

No matter how many times I tried, my cries went unanswered. "I have to get out of here."

"I'll do what I want!" Caleb's booming voice came from up above.

I wasn't sure what he and Mandy had been up to, but I could only imagine that it wasn't anything good. The sharp pull of a door at the top of the stairs caught my attention. The slow, heavy footsteps on the stairs caused my heart to race.

"Good Morning, my future wife," Caleb taunted as he came into view. "Did you sleep well?"

"Are you seriously asking me that? What kind of man would have his future wife and mate sleeping on a dirty mattress in a cold, damp basement?" The sarcastic retort left my lips with a trail of venom.

There was no way this man was going to be sweet when he had been nothing but toxic since the moment he kidnapped me in his house. Too many times had I fallen for his act, and now that I knew who he was, it would never happen again.

"Be it as it may, the harvest moon is tonight, my dear."

How was that possible?! He said two days. How is it already tonight?

"That's not possible. It was just two days." I whispered, trying to understand.

"Ah, yes." Caleb smiled, walking closer to me. "When you fell asleep, I injected you with a sedative so you couldn't escape."

My eyes widened in shock at what he said. How did I not know that he had done that?

"That's not possible."

"Isn't it?" The smirk that crossed his lips as he walked toward a wooden tool bench set my nerves on edge. This man was more sadistic than I had expected.

"Why would you do that?!" I exclaimed.

Shaking his head, he turned toward the table and started fiddling with the tools on it.

"Tonight, things will change for you, Ivy," he replied slowly. "You will start to see things from a new perspective, and I will give you a life you always dreamed of."

Every ounce of my body screamed to fight and get away, but whatever he had injected into me left me groggy and my body heavy. "Caleb..."

It was no wonder I wasn't able to reach out to Hale or the others. Whatever he had put into my body blocked the link that Hale had told me about before.

"You look a bit stunned, my dear."

Caleb's voice brought me out of the trance I was in, causing my mind to swirl with likely outcomes of what was going to happen. The trouble that was coming was going to make things a lot more complicated.

"Please..." I wasn't sure what I was asking for, but the look in his eyes told me he understood what I wanted, even without words.

"I'm sorry that this is how things are going right now. I never expected things to be this way."

"Then why are you doing this?" Caleb made no sense. He would say apologies, then turn around and act like a man with sadistic intentions.

A howl in the distance stopped our conversation, and Caleb's eyes darkened. A low growl emitted from his lips as he flew to the stairs and took them two at a time.

If he was angry about the howl we heard, that could only mean one thing... Damian was coming.

Kate

I wasn't sure what to expect with these guys, but I had to do what was necessary to get Ivy back. I had been a fool to think I could let her go on not knowing the truth. She was my charge, and I had one task. Protect her and watch her.

Both of which I failed at the moment I let Caleb get the better of me.

It gave him the chance to lure her in and make a drastic move of taking her captive.

"We can't just go in there, guns blazing," I snapped, listening to the plans that they had been running through for the last thirty minutes.

With my help, they were able to narrow down Mandy's cabin. It had belonged to her parents years ago, and when they passed on, it was left to her. I wasn't in the least bit surprised to see how isolated it was, but even though it was a mile off, the view from where we were was perfect.

"Then what do you think we should do?" Damian retorted with disdain.

It didn't take a genius to realize he couldn't stand me, and that was fine because I didn't care for him either. "First of all, we need to make sure that it isn't trapped. I doubt he would rely on just isolation to be enough."

The look in Damian's eyes told me he hadn't considered what I was saying.

Some Alpha.

"Look guys, we don't have time to bicker between each other. We need to figure this shit out, and quickly," Hale replied, shaking his head.

"Perhaps Talon should scout it out. He seems to be the stealthiest of you four," I sneered, rolling my eyes.

"She does have a point," James pointed out, looking at me. "Talon is better suited."

Talon didn't wait for someone to tell him to go. He shifted in front of us, his large dark wolf growling as he took off through the brush toward the cabin. I had no doubt that he would tell us what to expect.

"I don't want anyone to rush in there. The last thing I want is for Ivy to get hurt."

Damian making comments like this pissed me off more than anything. It was his fault that she was in this mess to begin with. He pushed her away and landed her in this riffed situation. "You caring about what happens to her is shocking."

"Will you shut the fuck up and stop being a bitch?" Damian snapped, causing me to laugh.

"I can't wait for this to be over, so I don't have to deal with you anymore."

Damian snorted in disapproval at what I said. "That is a mutual statement."

"Hey, he said it's clear as long as you take the western direction," Hale finally piped up, walking back toward us.

There was a hesitation in his eyes that made me uncomfortable. "What's wrong?"

Hale shook his head and spoke softly to James before turning toward Damian and me. A grave feeling coursed through me that made me uncomfortable.

"There are some things about the place that make Talon uncomfortable. He said that the property is trapped. So he will meet us in a moment, and have us follow him in. It seems there are only the two of them there, but he hasn't seen Ivy."

Taking a moment to let everything sink in, I let a breath escape me.

We were walking into something we weren't prepared for. But I was determined to get my friend back.

"I don't have time for this shit. I want my mate, and I'm going to get her," Damian growled, shifting into his large black wolf.

Its paws dug at the earth as white clouds of heat escaped his muzzle. A determination brewed in his eyes to get his mate. With his determination set, a shifting frenzy as the cracking of bones resonated in the air, and the rest of us followed.

Breaking through the cool wind and into the forest, our destination—Ivy.

Battle for Ivy

Ivy

Darkness. The sound of escalating battle beginning on the earth above caused turmoil to bubble within my soul. I wasn't sure what the situation was, but I had a feeling that before the night ended, I would become a martyr in battle.

"Damn it!" Mandy's voice followed down the stairwell, followed by her footsteps descending the stairs. Cold, dark, swirling eyes greeted me with a malicious smile.

I was in trouble.

"It's time to go," she snarled as she pulled the key from her pocket, snatching at the shackle on my wrist—the movements causing it to dig against my skin in discomfort.

"What are you doing?" I replied, struggling against her as she snatched my arm, trying to drag me across the floor toward the stairs. "Get the fuck off me!"

A blow to the side of my face caused me to reel back to the ground. Mandy stood over me, impatient and unforgiving. "Don't make me kill you because, honestly, I love that idea better."

"Why are you doing this? I thought we were friends."

Laughter escaped her lips as she contemplated what I had said. I should have known from the beginning that this girl wasn't friendly at all. She had always shown such kindness and concern toward me, but it was only after seeing me with Hale and James in the courtyard.

"I was what I needed to be," she retorted before grabbing my hair and dragging me up the stairs with a force I didn't think a woman of her size had.

Werewolf strength. It was undeniable, and every movement sent sharp pains through my back and side with every step she took.

As the door opened toward the main floor, the roar of wolves grew louder. Even though my connection to Hale, James, and Talon was growing weaker, it was slightly stronger now that they were closer. The drugs that Caleb had given me slowly wore off from my system.

"Let me go!" I yelled as I struggled against Mandy again.

I had to get away from her. The further along she dragged me, the closer to the ravenous wolves I was, and that was a place I didn't want to be. I had seen the guys' wolves up close before, but even then, I was scared.

"It's time they realize who has the upper hand!" Mandy yelled, throwing open the front door and dragging me onto the wooden porch.

She pulled me roughly to my feet. Her claws extended on her hand as she brought my back to her chest and held me by my throat.

"Enough!" she roared, causing the wolves to halt in their step.

"What are you doing?" Caleb yelled, quickly shifting back.

The snapping jaws of the black wolf pawing at the earth across from the porch, watching the scene unfold. "I'm done with the childish games of men. The Harvest moon is high, and with time still left, I will handle this as it should be."

"Please..." I cried out in fear as tears ran down my cheeks, "let me go."

"Ivy!" James and Hale called in unison.

My eyes widened upon seeing James and the others. A rush of relief rolled through me, knowing that they had come. I had wondered if everything I had with them had all been for nothing, but deep down, I knew they wouldn't abandon me.

"James!" I cried out, only to have her grip tighten on me. Tears rolled down my cheeks as I watched the wolves stare at the scene in front of them.

"Please don't hurt her..." James begged as his own eyes widened in fear, "she did nothing to you."

"No, she didn't. But Damian did," Mandy retorted with disgust lacing her tone.

I wasn't sure what Damian had done to Mandy, but part of me hoped it was a misunderstanding. Damian may have been a lot of things, but I didn't want to believe he was as bad as they made him out to be.

The breaking of bones echoed in the air as I watched the black wolf shift slowly back into Damian. My heart raced at the sight, having never witnessed it before. His dark swirling eyes caught my attention as they met mine, and an unreadable expression crossed his face.

"Your quarrel is with me, Mandy. Ivy isn't mated to me, so there is no way her death will hurt me. Don't do something stupid."

Laughter left Mandy's lips as she shook her head. "You really are daft, aren't you? Do you think it's her life that actually matters to me?"

Damian's brows furrowed in confusion as he listened to her speak. The more I moved, the deeper her claws dug into my skin, causing a wet sensation to drip down my neck. "What did Damian do to you?"

I had to know what hurt Mandy so much. I was desperate to know what he had done that would cost me my life.

"Oh, he didn't tell you?" Mandy whispered in my ear, "the wolf who killed herself because of him... she was my sister."

Shock rushed through me. Everything made sense.

Mandy lost her sister that day, and for so long, she planned revenge with Caleb to make Damian suffer. However, what she was doing now conflicted with everything Caleb wanted.

"Wait... Caleb wanted to steal me from Damian so he could take Damian's mate. But you?"

The idea ran through my head as I tried to understand her reasoning.

She was doing this for blood... a life for a life.

"No, you can't!" I screamed, trying to get away.

Laughter escaped her as she held me tight to her.

"So you finally understand. At least one of you does," she replied with a smirk.

"What are you talking about?!" Caleb yelled, stepping closer only for Mandy to step back, holding tight to my body.

"Move again, and I'll kill her," she snarled, glaring at the men in front of her.

"She is going to kill me to kill Hale, Talon, and—" The tightening of her grip cut my words off, digging into my throat.

It was true. She was going to kill me to kill them, and even though I didn't want to die, I couldn't allow my death to affect them. They meant more to me than my own life, and I would do anything for them.

Dark spots formed in my vision, and as I was once told growing up, my life flashed before my eyes.

If this was the end, then so be it, but Moon Goddess, if you are out there... spare them and only take me.

Kate

"She is going to kill her to kill your brothers!" I yelled as soon as I shifted.

It made perfect sense—a life for a life.

A vendetta to solve all the problems there once had been. Even with Caleb wanting to take Ivy. Mandy was getting one over on him as well. Ivy had become the center of their attention, and with Ivy gone, they would all lose something.

But Damian would lose the most.

His brothers and his mate–no wolf could go through that much pain.

It would destroy him.

Before another word could leave my lips, Mandy's attention focused on Damian was lost as Caleb charged her and ripped her from Ivy's body. The sweet, petite figure dropped to the floor as the battle between Mandy and Caleb began.

Mandy's lifeless body fell to the floor before us.

As if someone clicked the pause button, the rogues Caleb had with him charged us once more, and I shifted back into my wolf. My teeth snapped and grasped at any wolf I could get hold of.

I wasn't the most powerful of wolves, but I couldn't rely on the brothers to protect me.

I wasn't part of their pack.

The only thing I could do was hope that my efforts weren't wasted and I was able to protect a girl who had become more than just my friend. She had become like a sister to me.

And I would be her protector.

Damian

a few minutes earlier

I fucked up.

It was the only thing I knew for sure, and with every last ounce of breath I had, I would find a way to make it right with Ivy. When Hale found Mandy's cabin, I was the first in the car to save Ivy.

I didn't want anyone else to do this besides me because even though we were all supposed to be her mates, I knew without a doubt that things were worse with her and me. If, for some reason, our bond was broken… I would still try to make it right with her.

I couldn't lose her.

She was perfect in the mess of confusion and clouded thoughts, and even still, I had no way of knowing what I was losing until I had lost it.

Looking up to the sky, I watched as the full moon turned orange and the Harvest peaked in all its glory. I had only an hour to save her. After that, my time would be up, and the bond would be broken.

I couldn't let that happen.

I had to protect the bond. My selfishness was causing us all pain.

As the roar of wolves thundered against the ground, we found ourselves outnumbered, and even though I was an Alpha, there was still only so much I could do.

My brothers at my back, we pressed forward, taking down rogue after rogue.

Hale's human form watched from the porch with a smile on his face before shifting and heading straight for James. James was no match for Hale and snapping a gray wolf's neck, I leaped over two more, running toward my youngest brother.

I had to protect him. To save him from a fate that none of us would get over.

Snarling, my breath came out in white pants of smoke against the cold air. Throwing my body at Caleb, I knocked his wolf out of the way. Growling as I stood protectively in front of James.

No one would mess with my brother but me.

"It's time they realize who has the upper hand!" Mandy yelled, causing us all to stop in our tracks.

Ivy.

Her struggling form was at Mandy's mercy as her claws dug into Ivy's throat. My wolf urged me to press forward and save our mate, but I knew I couldn't be brash. Doing so would only cause Ivy to get killed.

Caleb shifted quickly in front of me. His wolf shedding its skin, leaving a man in its wake. I could kill him right now, but with the situation, it could only make things worse.

"What are you doing!" he yelled as he took two steps toward Mandy. Her body flinched as she watched with a snarl his concern over the girl in his arms.

"Please, let me go," Ivy said, struggling as tears streamed down her face.

The cracking of bones resonated near me as my brothers all shifted in return. "Ivy!"

No one moved. Not even the rogues, as everyone seemed to contemplate what would happen next. If Ivy died, then what would be left? Caleb would have no leverage or purpose in the battle anymore other than to face me himself.

Which was something I knew he had wanted to do for a very long time.

"Please don't hurt her..." James pleaded, his own eyes misted with tears. "She did nothing to you."

He was young and naïve, allowing his emotions to show as they were, but then again, I didn't have the connection with Ivy that they did. Shifting into my human form, I stood waiting for her next move.

Her eyes seemingly calculated what it was I was going to do. "No, she didn't. But Damian did."

Taken aback by what the girl was saying, I found myself baffled.

I stood waiting for her next move. I knew exactly what she was talking about. She blamed me for her sister being dead, just like Caleb did.

"Your quarrel is with me, Mandy. Ivy isn't mated to me, so there is no way her death will hurt me. Don't do something stupid," I replied, watching her.

Laughing, she shook her head, watching me. "You really are daft, aren't you? Do you think it's her life that actually matters to me?"

A growl escaped my lips as I stepped forward. Her grip tightened just a little more.

"What did you do, Damian?" Ivy asked with pleading eyes, trying to understand.

It was the same look she gave me so many times when I disappointed her.

"Oh, he didn't tell you?" Mandy whispered just loud enough for me to hear, "the wolf who killed herself because of him... she was my sister."

It didn't make any sense. The look Mandy gave Caleb was one of hatred, not respect. A rush of confusion ran through me as I tried to understand what Mandy had to gain from acting the way she was.

"Wait... Caleb wanted to steal me from Damian so he could take Damian's mate... But you..." Ivy's face flashed with recognition as if she was processing all the information.

"No, you can't!" Ivy screamed, struggling against Mandy. A wicked laugh left Mandy's lips, causing us all to step forward closer, only to have the rogues on edge, ready to attack.

"So you finally understand," Mandy replied, looking directly at me, "at least one of you does."

"What are you talking about?!" Caleb yelled, stepping closer only for Mandy to step back, holding tighter to Ivy.

"Move again, and I'll kill her," she snapped, baring teeth.

What was I missing?!

'She is going to kill her,' Talon replied through our link. 'He is going to kill her to kill us.'

'No... she can't,' James added, listening in.

'Caleb is going to do something. When he does, we need to rush him and the rogues.'

There was silence among us after my statement, but glancing at Hale, I saw the calculated look he was giving over the situation.

"She is going to kill me to kill Hale, Talon, and—" Ivy's words were quickly cut off as Mandy dug deeper down on her grip. Her body slightly goes lax within her hands.

A mass of movement blurred in the distance as Kate yelled, "She is going to kill her to kill your brothers!"

It all made sense now, though.

With Mandy's attention on me, I watched as Caleb took the opportunity and rushed toward Mandy, ripping her from Ivy's body. The clash of wolves raged once more as I shifted and took them down two at a time.

My brothers battled as well—our goal was to retrieve Ivy, whose body lay unmoving.

Taking down another wolf, I turned to find Caleb standing over the bloodied body of Mandy. His cold, dark, swirling eyes looked toward Ivy before turning on me. He was angry, and the pain fueled that hatred.

Charging at me, he shifted mid-air. His wolf clashed with mine as we ended in a rolling fury of fury and blood. Our teeth snapped at each other in a mixture of anger and frenzy.

I was going to kill him. There was no denying that.

As my teeth bit down upon him, he struggled beneath me. Prey to the bloodthirsty wolf I was, I enjoyed his struggle.

Crack

His neck snapped in my jaw, and with its sound, the rogues that hadn't died stopped in their tracks. Their eyes darted toward me as I let Caleb's wolf slip from my jaws, hitting the ground.

There was no reason for them to fight anymore.

The rogue wolves retreated to the woods in fear as I stepped closer to them. They knew what would become of them if they stayed around. There was no denying my wrath, but at that moment, there was only one person I had my eye on.

Ivy.

Broken Bonds & Sealed Fates

Ivy

Rough hands gripped a hold of my waist, causing my eyes to flutter. Looking up, I watched as Damian's rugged good looks came into view. The steely, fierce force of his gaze upon me as he lifted my body and carried me forward.

"What are you doing?" I whispered in a raspy tone.

"You're injured. We have to get you to the hospital."

The monotone way he spoke to me did nothing but leave me puzzled. Glancing up at the sky, I watched as the red faded from the moon.

The Harvest moon was ending.

"Stop, we have to complete the bond," I moaned softly, trying to move from his grasp. "Put me down."

"No–" he stated softly, "it's over. There is no time."

I was astounded by what he was saying. If we didn't complete the bond, there would be no turning back. The mate bond would be lost forever. "Do you not want me?"

Tears filled my eyes, realizing that I was losing them.

"It isn't that..." His eyes gazed down at me as he stopped in his tracks. "It isn't right for us to keep you from what you want in life. Since you have been here, we have done nothing but cause you problems."

"Put me down," I gasped as I blinked back tears.

"No," he replied before a car door was opened, and I slid into the back seat.

Darkness overtook my thoughts. I tried to keep my eyes open. Drops of crimson stained my shirt as I looked down to my chest.

There was no changing his mind, and just as I had gotten used to it all...

He decided he didn't want me.

As the pull of light drew me back toward reality, I slowly opened my eyes to see the white tile ceiling above me—the sterile smell of cleaning supplies stinging my nose as I looked around my room.

The last thing I remembered was being carried, and then—Damian.

Trying to sit up, I took in Kate's sleeping form sitting in the gray armchair. Her eyes closed, and a white blanket pulled up to her chest.

"Kate," I whispered roughly, jolting her from her sleep.

"Oh, my god!" she exclaimed, scrambling to her feet as she rushed to my bedside. "You're finally awake."

"Finally?" What did she mean, finally? I had only been asleep for a few hours.

Her eyes looked at me questioningly before she slowly nodded her head. "Ivy... you have been in a coma for two weeks."

Two weeks?!

That wasn't possible... the Harvest moon... The guys...

Where were they?!

"No," I mumbled, shaking my head in disbelief. "That's not right."

Kate sighed, looking at me with pity, "I'm sorry, sweetie..."

"Where's James... Hale? Talon?" The fact that I had woken up and they weren't here with me caused a pit of despair to open within my stomach. The betrayal of their absence leaves a sinking hole in my heart.

"Let's not talk about that right now," she muttered softly, "we need to get you better."

"No!" I screamed, the beeping of the heart monitors becoming erratic. "Where's Damian!"

"Ivy, please... Calm down!" Kate yelled, trying to make me see the reason. However, no matter what she said, it fell on deaf ears.

Pulling at the cords that were attached to me, I forced myself from the bed, wanting to progress further. I had to find Damian. I had to know what was going on.

"Damian!" I screamed again, wanting to hear from him about what was going on. "Get me Damian!"

My screams of protest echoed throughout the room until the door opened, and Damian's dark and sultry gaze peered at me from beneath dark lashes.

My heart skipped a beat seeing him, and even though we had so many issues in the past, he was still able to make me feel some sort of way.

"You wanted to see me?" he replied with a thin-lipped expression. His eyes were unreadable, causing an uneasy expression to pass over me.

"What's going on?" I whispered, searching for anything to tell me this wasn't happening. Those things were still okay between us.

"I don't understand what you mean. You were injured and have been in the hospital healing."

"You know what I mean. Why weren't you guys here with me? Where's Hale, James, or Talon... what's going on, Damian?"

Letting out a deep breath, he nodded. "They aren't coming, Ivy."

"What?" I gasped in disbelief, "but they are my mates... why wouldn't they come?"

"Because they aren't your mates anymore. The moon passed, and the bond wasn't completed, so it vanished." Damian replied with a solum stare.

It was true then. The Harvest moon had passed, and I was no longer bonded to the guys.

The men who had captured my attention and made me feel alive and desired for the first time in my existence. "Where are they?"

"Ivy, this is better this way. You have the chance of a normal life. One away from wolves, just like your mother."

My mother? "You know nothing about her," I snapped, the anxiety over the situation rising within me.

"Sweetie," Kate replied softly, "your mother is more than you know. None of that matters, though. Damian is right. Now that you are awake and getting better, it's time we go home to Georgia."

"No!" I screamed, not wanting to accept what she was saying. I wanted to see Hale. I had to see him. Out of the four of them, he was the most logical and could tell me the truth.

Did they really think they were doing this for me?

Or was it because they actually didn't want me?

"You will be leaving," Damian replied formally, "that is final."

"Fuck you, Damian. I understand you never gave a shit about me, but you don't get to speak for your brothers."

I was done dealing with him. Since the moment I got there, he had done nothing but gave me shit. More than once, I had tried to do something to make him happy, and then to top it all off, I was captured by Caleb and Mandy because of him.

Then, to repay me, he wanted to take away people I cared about, calling it 'a normal' life.

Rolling his eyes, he stepped forward with a pained expression, "don't ever think I don't care for you. You have no IDEA, how much I care for you."

"Then why–why are you doing this?" I was desperate at the moment to get him to change his mind. I didn't want him to give up on this. To give up on me.

"It's too late," he whispered softly as he stepped closer and brushed a strand of hair behind my ear. "They have gone their separate ways."

Closing my eyes, I let out the breath I had been holding and allowed the tears to roll down my cheeks. They had left me. Nothing was holding them back now.

"James wouldn't leave me."

As much as I wanted to believe the admission, I knew I couldn't. I couldn't accept what he was saying because deep down, after everything we had gone through, I didn't want to believe they would leave me.

"I'm sorry, Ivy. But you don't deserve a life of chaos. You deserve to be happy with ONE man who can give you everything you need. Not shared between multiple men, never knowing what was going to happen."

Damian's words stirred a determination in me.

I wanted those things, though. I wanted to be with them all, and even though I was confused before, my mind had been changed.

"Do one thing for me. If you still feel the same way afterward, then I will go." I replied softly as my eyes cast up to meet his.

"What's that?" he replied with an edge of concern.

"Kiss me." The demand was clear, and taking a step back, I knew he was hesitant about fulfilling it. "If you still feel the same afterward, I will go."

A quietness flowed over us as he stared at me. Slowly his feet moved, and before I knew it, his lips were upon mine.

Damian had only kissed me once before, and I couldn't understand why I had never taken the initiative to do it more often.

The feel of his lips against mine caused me to moan softly as my heart raced. I could still feel the swarm within my stomach I had once felt with the others, and the emotional rollercoaster tipped me over the edge.

"That isn't possible," he whispered as he pulled away.

"You feel something, don't you?"

The realization that what they thought was real wasn't causing my head to spin. I wanted him at that moment, no matter how I had to get him.

The Moon Goddess hadn't given up on us.

She had only chosen to change the stakes of the game.

I knew the moment that he kissed me, he felt something, and by the look on his face when he pulled away, I knew without a doubt he was confused by what was going on.

Why wouldn't he be?

From what I had learned from Caleb, if the bond had not been completed, then it was stripped from us all, and I was no longer bound to them.

I would have a chance at a new life... or better yet, I could decide my fate.

"Damian," I whispered, "you have to see that what we were told wasn't the truth. What the prophecy said was up for interpretation."

Shaking his head, he cast his glance toward Kate, who looked just as shocked as he was.

"Don't look at me. This is all far beyond my concept of anything. I can call my father, though. Perhaps he may know something."

Kate quickly moved from her chair and made her way from my hospital room. Damian's eyes still stared at the spot where she had once sat, not a word coming from his mouth.

"Please say something," I asked, hoping for the silence to end.

"What am I supposed to say?" He replied as he looked toward me. "This wasn't supposed to happen. We aren't supposed to be mated anymore."

His tone left a sinking feeling in my heart as I tried to understand why he was angry. I thought more than anything he would be pleased with the notion that the bond wasn't gone. That even though my initial marks from the others had disappeared...

We were given another chance.

"Do you not want me?" The question came out before I could stop it. His mouth opened and closed as he thought about what he was going to say. Never had we had a proper conversation about what he wanted with me until this point.

To be honest, I was terrified of what he was going to respond with.

Would he reject me?

"We need to go see someone." He replied, flatly turning on his feet. "I will get you some clothes, and we will leave immediately."

Stunned by his response to the situation, I sat dumbfounded as I watched him leave the room in search of clothing and perhaps a doctor.

An hour later, Damian and I sat in his car flying down the interstate head north toward the northern part of Damian's territory. I wasn't sure what was up there that would cause us to need to venture that far, but whatever it was had Damian determined.

"Will you please tell me what's going on?" I asked softly, my eyes sliding toward the view at the window, tired of his cold persona.

With a deep breath, he sighed, "the woman who told me the prophecy years ago... she lives up here. We are going to go see her and see what happened."

Once again, his wording choice caught me by surprise.

He had to see what happened. As if being mated to me is so horrible.

"Fine," I replied flatly, watching the rush of trees pass by my window until we turned onto a dirt road that led toward a rugged old cabin.

When the car finally came to a stop, Damian quickly exited the cabin and came around to my side of the car. Surprised by his gesture, I took his offered hand when he opened the door and got out.

"Thank you."

He hesitated for a moment before nodding his head and turning toward the cabin. His hand slid through mine as he pulled me with him. The fact that Damian was holding my hand was a surprise on its own. Never had he shown that kind of affection before.

"Priscilla!" Damian called out loudly as he knocked on the door. "We need to have a word."

The door opened slowly, revealing the wrinkled face of a graying elderly woman. Her brows furrowed until her eyes set upon me, and then a smile crested her face.

"Oh, my," she said with a grin, "I see that you have been touched by the goddess."

Touched by the goddess? What the hell does that mean?

"Enough, we need to know what's going on," Damian replied with annoyance.

"Very well. Come in, come in." She retorted as she stepped aside and made her way toward the cabin's small living room. "I suppose you are here to ask how the bond is still there but not as you expected."

"But how–" I gasped, not understanding how she knew.

As her eyes turned toward me, I saw the twinkle in their corner, looking at me with amusement.

"There is no answer to how I know things, child. Just that I do."

"Then explain," Damian snapped, growing impatient. "You told me that the bond would break if we didn't all complete it before the Harvest Moon left the sky. Well, it did. So how is it that I am still bonded to her?"

Laughter left the woman's throat. "You complain like being bonded to this pretty young woman is a bad thing."

"Right..." I snorted. "You would think he was more grateful to have a mate at all."

My remark was meant to be mumbled, but the laughter that left the old woman caused me to look at Damian, who stared at me wide-eyed and in disbelief.

"Seriously?" he snapped with a huff.

"I'm just saying," I shrugged, rolling my eyes again.

The woman leaned forward with a smile, setting her elbows on her knees as she stared between the two of us. "I like this one. She has a spark in her. No wonder the goddess chose her."

"Choose me? Choose me for what?" I asked, not understanding what she meant.

"Well, you asked her for a gift, didn't you?" The woman replied, causing me to think back on what she could be referring to. After a moment, the realization dawned on me and my eyes snapped back to the woman whose smile widened in delight.

"I didn't think she would answer me—"

Damian sat quietly pinching the bridge of his nose with utter annoyance laced in his features as we spoke. "How about someone start explaining what the hell is going on?"

Taking a moment, I sighed, "when I thought I was dying... I prayed to the goddess to take just my life but disconnect me from your brothers so they may live. I knew that losing me you would be able to overcome with their help, but losing us all would destroy you."

Silence filled the air in the living room as Damian sat staring at me with confusion.

"You willingly would have died to save them... To save me?" he mumbled as if he couldn't believe what he was hearing.

"Of course, I would. You may all get on my nerves, but I do care about each of you in a different way," I replied, not knowing how else to explain how I felt about them. They were all so complex, and in a perfect world, things would be easier.

But unfortunately, our world wasn't easy.

Damian's eyes lingered on me for a moment more before turning toward Priscilla.

"So what does this mean, then? Are we all still bound?"

"No, not exactly," she replied, picking up a teacup in front of her taking a sip. "Everything is now in Ivy's court. She can decide to allow the mate bonds to form, or she can decide to have nothing to do with any of you."

The pressure weighed down on me heavily with what she was saying.

No longer could they initiate anything. They wouldn't feel the pull like they did before that drove them to mark and mate with me before. Instead, they would only feel the connection by physical touch if I gave them the chance.

I was the Alpha in charge of this situation, and that notion blew my mind.

"Whoa—" I muttered, leaning back in the chair, letting the information sink in. "Talk about being put on the spot."

"Yes, but you are strong, independent, and fierce. Don't let anyone tell you what to do. You take the initiative of your own life. You don't even have to accept all four of them. In the end, you can pick just one if that's what you want or none at all."

Finishing up our small conversation with Priscilla, we learned more than I had been prepared for. My mind was a rushing rollercoaster of information that would take an eternity to process. Stepping into the car, I sat there in silence with Damian, whose hands gripped the steering wheel.

"I will book your flight to go home tomorrow," he said out of nowhere, catching me off guard.

"What?" I replied with my eyes darting toward him, "what makes you think I want to go home?"

Shaking his head, he looked at me perplexed before putting the car in reverse heading back to his house.

Hours passed, and eventually, the pack house came into view. The towering home shined against the setting sun, and as Damian parked the car, I contemplated what Priscilla had said.

Never once did he bother to address what I had asked, nor did he even acknowledge the other questions I had.

Instead, he was stuck in his own mind playing the silent treatment, acting as if everything that had happened since I got here was nothing.

"Damian!" I yelled, grasping his attention. "Don't fucking walk away from me."

"What do you want?" he snapped, turning to face me, "you're leaving tomorrow. The sooner, the better."

His bitter reply didn't phase me. I realized a while ago when he acts like this, it's deflecting his true feelings because he is scared. Determination set into me as I stormed toward him, gripping his arm and turning him to face me.

"I'm not leaving!" I yelled at him, "stop running away from me you fucking coward."

His eyes widened as he growled, his wolf not appreciating how I spoke to him. "Watch your tone with me, girl."

Narrowing my eyes at him, I scoffed in disgust. I didn't care if he had paid for me to go home tomorrow. I wasn't going, and if I had to chain myself to his front porch, then so be it.

Leaning in close to him, I watched as his eyes stared down at me. He was challenging me, and that thought alone was amusing. If he wanted competition, I could be that girl.

"Go fuck yourself, Damian," I replied softly with a grin on my lips, "I'm not going anywhere, and there isn't a fucking thing you can do about. As Priscilla said before... I control this bond."

Mutual Understanding

Two days passed since I had arrived back at the pack house, and little by little, Damian realized when I said I wasn't doing something–it wasn't going to happen.

He attempted to get me on the plane the day before but I stood firm in my place, and refused to go. There was no talking to me about it... no forcing me to do it. Nothing.

He had my bags packed by the door and even attempted to throw me over his shoulder, but all his methods proved to be useless.

I'm a stubborn woman, and when I say something, I stand my ground.

In the end, he roared in frustration and shut himself in his office with no communication with me for the rest of the day.

Honestly, it was peaceful.

After giving up on the notion of me leaving, Damian had his servants move me into the main house. He claimed he wanted to make sure I wouldn't run away or do something stupid.

As if that would actually happen.

I wanted to know where the others were, and I wouldn't leave until I did.

Determination set into me to find them. To make everything right again, and with that determination, I had found myself so behind in my studies that I struggled to catch up.

Day and night, I went through my textbooks and worked on papers, but no matter how much time I spent working hard to achieve my dream, I always felt a mile away.

"Still studying?" Damian's voice called out as he entered the kitchen.

I had set up a study at the kitchen island while I waited for my pizza to finish a few hours before.

"I don't know–" I said sarcastically, "all my books and my laptop are out. Is that what it looks like?"

He stood there staring at me through narrowed eyes. "You don't have to be a bitch."

"That's rich coming from someone who has been nothing but an asshole toward me since I came to this stupid town.

Sighing dramatically, he turned toward the fridge and opened it. "Are we really going to keep bickering every time we have a conversation, Ivy? Because if that's how it's going to be, you can leave."

Laughter escaped my lips as I shook my head. "You would like that, wouldn't you? The only Alpha in history I hear that wants to get rid of his mate. Some Alpha you are."

"Enough!" He turned to face me. "I'm tired of this shit between us."

"You and I both," I snapped, shaking my head, "I miss the conversations I could have with your brothers. Ones where they actually cared about what I thought and how I felt. Conversations we had that were full of meaning and laughter. So, have you found them yet?"

Hesitation filled his dark, sultry eyes as he crossed his arms over his chest. He didn't acknowledge my question, but there was no doubt that he was hiding something from me.

"You have, haven't you?" I whispered, shaking my head in disbelief. "If you know where they are, we need to go get them."

"Why, Ivy?" He asked with irritation. "Why do you want to bring them back? So you can torture them some more with the fact they lost their bond to you?"

His statement was a cheap shot at my heart. He knew very well that the bond being severed wasn't my fault. He was the one who denied it for so long that by the time he wanted to complete it, it was too late.

"Please, Damian," I whispered, looking down at the book in front of me as I blinked back tears that threatened to fall, "please help me get them back."

I didn't want to argue with him anymore. I didn't want to keep reliving that horrible night in my head every time I closed my eyes.

The only thing I wanted was for them all to be back here and for us to decide together what we would do.

A part of me longed to be back in their arms, but at the same time, a part of me was also scared.

Priscilla said that I had a gift from the goddess of choice.

I was given the choice to accept them all or only the ones of my choosing. No other human or werewolf alive was ever given that choice.

A part of me wondered if that was why Damian was so hesitant because he didn't know if I would choose them and not him.

The very thought had crossed my mind a few times, but I wasn't going to make any decisions until I reconciled with them all and we talked about it.

"Fine," he replied with reluctance. My eyes quickly darted up to him just in time to see him sigh and run his hand through his hair.

"Fine?" I questioned, unsure of what he meant. "You mean... you know where they are?"

As his eyes met mine, I saw a small ounce of defeat in him as he slowly nodded. "Yeah."

I never knew that one simple word could fill me with such joy until that moment. Jumping from my seat, I screamed joyfully before running over and throwing my arms around him.

He stood frozen on the spot, and it took me a moment to realize what I had done. His touch created a feeling in me that my body relished, and as much as I wanted to kiss him in that moment, I couldn't.

As confliction filled me, I stepped back in silence, my eyes looking anywhere but at him. "I'm sorry... I don't know what came over me. I got a little excited."

"Yeah, I can see that," he chuckled as he shook his head. "I will have to see if I can find a way to contact them."

"Contact them?" I gasped quickly, "why don't we go get them?"

"It doesn't seem like you have much time to do anything like that, Ivy," he replied, looking at my belongings littered across the kitchen counter.

He was right. I was busy trying to get school situated that I really didn't have time to do anything else. But at the same time, I didn't want to miss out on the opportunity to find them.

The choice weighed heavily on me, and as it did, a frown crossed my face.

"Well, where are they?" I asked him as I slowly walked back toward the counter and closed my laptop and my books, shoving them back into my bag.

"Not anywhere close, I'm afraid. When the situation with you happened, they took off, and it took a while to get a small idea of the location they were in."

Hearing that they had gone so far just to get away from me tore at my heart, and with that pain, a void in my chest opened. I had to find them, no matter the situation.

They were mine as much as I was there, and mate bond be damned, I wasn't going to lose them. I couldn't lose them. Since the moment they came into my life, they had each found a place that was special to me.

"School can wait, Damian," I replied softly, "we have to get them back. I caused these problems, and I need to fix it."

Letting out a deep breath, I watched as Damian leaned against the countertop and thought over what I was saying. "Your father will be back tomorrow. We can leave then."

Without another wasted moment, Damian quickly turned his back on me and made his way out of the kitchen. Through all the time I had known Damian, he was never the type of person to just willingly agree to do something I wanted.

In fact, most of the time, he acted like he hated me.

It seemed deep down there was a lot about him I didn't know, and perhaps my entire perception of him had been completely wrong.

"Damian, wait," I said as I rushed forward.

"What do you want now, Ivy?" He asked with an exhausted sigh. "It's late, and we both need to get to bed."

"I just wanted to know why you were suddenly okay with helping me find them," I mumbled, shrugging my shoulders as I pushed the strap of my bag further up.

Taking a moment, he slowly turned to face me. A void expression on his face as he seemed to consider his next words, "because you are not the only one at fault for what happened. I am as well, and my brothers don't deserve sorrow because of me."

It was the first statement I had ever heard him say that was genuinely true. He was taking the blame for his mistakes, and in that light, it made me feel differently about him.

I didn't trust him completely, but I found a common ground with him at that moment.

"Well, when we find them, we can fix all of this," I replied, watching as something flickered in his eyes.

As I watched him escape into his office, I couldn't help but wonder if this trip would fix things with us or if it would push us further apart.

Part of me wanted to smother him and make it look like an accident, but then there was another part that wanted to climb him like a tree and ride him into next year.

Both choices weighed heavily on my mind, and with them, I found nothing but conflict.

"Please help me fix this," I whispered, praying to a goddess I had never believed in until I came to Idaho.

If she existed, there was a chance she was the only one who could aid in my venture.

Because even though Damian seemed genuine enough to help me... something inside me made me think otherwise.

Damian

Walking into my office, I felt a surge of anger wash over me that I and my wolf couldn't understand. I wanted more than anything to claim her as mine and make it to where she couldn't leave. But then I would open my mouth and do nothing but push her away.

I was a fucking fool to think that this mate bond or whatever stupid nonsense it was actually held meaning.

Ivy was right about one thing, though. I'm the only Alpha in history that rejects the idea of having a mate, and that was something that most didn't appreciate.

As I approached my liquor cabinet, I didn't stop myself from reaching for the amber-filled bottle, pouring myself a glass to down my sorrows. It had become the only thing I could do lately to dampen my mind from thoughts of her.

Her sweet and gentle nature always pulled me in, and when the fiery spark in her came to life, my wolf and I were automatically turned on.

Just thinking about her in that way made my dick throb with anticipation over the day I would finally get to have her. If she even let me.

Lost in my thoughts, my phone rang to life, and with a groan of irritation, I pulled it from my pocket to see that Allison was calling.

"Hello?" I replied, annoyed by her continuing pestering.

"Damian, I'm just letting you know we will be back late tonight instead of tomorrow."

Rolling my eyes, I sighed, "okay, and why were you calling me to tell me this?"

"Well, because I want to see you when I get there." She replied with amusement, lacing her tone. Disgust filled me, thinking about how many times she tried to hint to me that she and I would be strong together. I was older than the others when we went to live with her, and considering that Allison was nothing but power-driven... I knew her end game.

"I will be in bed, Allison," I stated firmly, "Ivy and I have a lot to do tomorrow before we leave."

"Ivy?!" she shrieked, "I thought you got rid of that little useless bitch, Damian!"

A warning growl left my lips at her words. "Watch how you speak about her. She is still my mate."

Laughter filled the other side of the phone, and I knew her and Zane coming back was going to cause nothing but problems. "Mate? Last time I checked, you and the others lost your mate. It's time you get rid of that little harlot and take a chosen mate, Damian."

I didn't miss the way she emphasized on the words chosen mate.

Deciding to save my battles for another day, I hung up the phone, gripping it tightly in my hand. I had no doubt that when Allison got back with Zane, she was going to cause issues with Ivy.

I only hoped Ivy would be able to stand her ground.

Because if she wants to be Luna one day–she will have to deal with Allison.

Ivy

Waking the next morning, I expected the arrival of my father. Damian had said that he was to arrive sometime today, and as much as normal girls would be excited–I was not.

Fully dressed, I left my room and made my way down to the kitchen to make coffee. The sounds of voices carried toward me, and two of them weren't supposed to be here yet.

As I rounded the corner, I came face to face with Allison and my father. Both of their eyes fell upon me with disgust.

"What the hell are you doing in here?" Allison snapped.

Her words brought my attention back to the present. "I'm sorry, what?"

Narrowing her eyes, she sneered, "I said, what are you doing in here? You have your own place to live, and my house isn't the location."

My father stood there with a smug look on his face that disgusted me. He was really going to allow her to talk to me like that. As if I was the issue.

"I don't know who you think you're talking to like that, but if you have an issue, you need to talk to Damian because the last time I checked, HE is the Alpha, and this is HIS house."

"How dare you speak to her like that!" my father yelled, causing me to flinch at the moment. "You will never speak to her in such disrespect—"

Rage burned through me that he was taking her side on this. All I ever wanted was for my father to actually care about me, and even now, he didn't. He was nothing but a disappointment.

"No!" I scream, slamming my hand against the counter. "Neither of you will speak to me the way you are. You do not have a say in my life, and you will have respect for me."

I wasn't sure where the courage came from to confront them in that way, but before I could do anything, a slap rang through my ears as I realized my father had slapped me.

As soon as it happened, a roar echoed from Damian's office, and I watched as he flew into the kitchen, pinning my father to the wall, seething in anger. "You dare touch her!"

Fear soared through me, seeing Damian this way. He was partially shifted, and the power that dripped off him was enough to bring Allison to her knees.

"Stop!" she cried out. "What are you doing? This girl is nothing! We are your family."

Damian's eyes turned slowly toward Allison with venom dripping from his fangs. "Neither of you are my family. Pack your shit and get out of my house now. You are no longer welcome here."

Throwing my father, I watched as he landed on the floor, and Damian stepped back to stand beside me. "You can't do that!" Allison shrieked. "This is my house!"

"That's where you are wrong, Allison," Damian snapped, "this is my house, and you are lucky that banishment is the only thing you are getting. Attacking a Luna usually means death."

"She is NOT a luna!" my father roared, getting to his feet. "She is not mated to you."

Laughter erupted from Damian as he slowly glanced at me. "Do you want the honor of telling them?"

Taking a moment, I thought over his words and what he meant. He was asking me if I wanted the pleasure of sharing with them that the mate bond wasn't actually gone, and as much as I wanted to rub that in her face, I couldn't.

"No–" I replied calmly with a smile on my face, "they don't deserve that news. Let them find out in a few months when the news spreads."

Never had I stood up to someone like this before. Let alone a parent, and that feeling alone was amazing. For so many years, I dealt with the bullshit sent my way from my father, and for him to break my heart the way he did–he deserved this.

"Come with me. Let's go to my office. We have things to discuss." Damian replied as he took my hand and pulled me from the kitchen.

The touch of his hand upon mine sent sparks through my skin. If you would have asked me a few weeks ago to believe Damian would ever stand up for me, I would have laughed at you.

A few weeks ago, we hated each other and wanted nothing to do with one another.

Now everything was different, and just the touch of his skin upon mine made me second-guess everything I thought I knew.

As my eyes gazed up at the back of his head, I felt the urge to ask him if he cared about me, but at the same time, it felt wrong, and I knew that I couldn't.

Stopping inside his office, he dropped my hand and left me just inside the door. "Sorry about that." He mumbled as he took a seat at his desk, "I didn't want to wake you to tell you they were here."

"When did they get here?" My eyes met his for the briefest of moments, and I watched as an exhausted look crossed his face.

"Last night," he replied, "they got home early."

Nodding, I walked toward the chair across from him and took a seat. I should have known that Allison and my father wouldn't be happy with me being here. Allison had hated me from the moment I entered her home, and I had no idea why.

"Why does she hate me so much?" It was a question that had plagued me for years, and as he stared at me, I got a feeling I wasn't going to like the answer.

"Because she wants to be the Luna of this pack."

"What?!" I exclaimed with disgust. "She raised you like her own children, though. That's disgusting."

"I agree, but in her eyes she feels it's her right. One she will never have, I might add."

At least that was something both of us could agree on. Allison was a twisted individual, and she had shown her true colors for the last time. I was just glad Damian stood by my side through the argument.

Looking down at his desk, I noticed a map and plane tickets. Curiosity filled me as I realized the map was of Mexico. "Where are we going? Are they in Mexico?"

Taking a moment to consider what I said, he chuckled, "I wish it was that easy. One of them is."

"Which one of them?" I asked with an exasperated sigh.

More than anything, I had hoped they would be together, but I knew they weren't.

Everything that had happened had been too much on them, and they went insane trying to kill the pain they were feeling. Pain that I helped to create with the bond being broken.

Had I listened to Damian's warning so long ago, none of this would have happened.

As I waited for his answer, he looked at me with a small smile.

"It's James," he chuckled, "he is living the party boy life in Cancun, Mexico."

Once Upon A Time in Mexico

Taking my seat on the plane, I watched as Damian got himself situated. The swivel of the seats moved as he took his place across from me and continued barking out orders.

"Hey, make sure that Jose meets us at the airport when we land. I need to speak with him about something else," Damian told his Gamma, who nods and quickly exits.

"Whose that?" I asked with curiosity as his gaze turned to mine and the airplane door closed.

"Who, Jose?" Damian questioned as I nodded. "Oh. He is just a friend."

"A friend?" I smirked, "Well, I look forward to meeting this friend."

Things had been different between us since the situation with my father and Allison. Damian didn't seem as hostile toward me as he once had been, and even though I was keeping my guard up, I was curious.

The roar of the engines came to life and before I knew it, the plane was headed down the tarmac. This was putting me one step closer to finding James and the others.

If my life was to get better, then I needed each one of them at my side to make it happen because the way my father and Allison acted toward me had me worried.

Allison didn't seem like the type of person to easily give up on something.

"Are you okay?" Damian's voice pulled me out of my thoughts, and turning to him, I smiled softly.

"Yeah, sorry. I'm just all over the place."

Nodding, he pulled out a file from his briefcase and sorted through the photos inside. Handing them over, I saw who lined them. They were photos of James, Hale, and Talon in their current locations.

Just seeing the photos brought a smile to my face and caused tears to brim my eyes. "Oh wow–"

"I thought you might like to see them," he replied as I chuckled.

"Look at them all." I smiled. "I guess they have changed a lot since being gone."

It had been almost three weeks since the night our bonds were broken, and with the bond breaking, they were torn from my life.

"I promised you I would fix things, Ivy," Damian sighed. "I will make sure that I do."

Regardless of everything that had transpired between us, I wanted to believe him. I wanted to know for sure that he would fix things, but I still felt doubt.

"I know. Maybe I'm just tired. The last few days have been a lot." I mumbled, looking back out the window as I handed him the photos.

Letting a sigh leave his lips, he took the photos. "Why don't you get some sleep then? I will wake you when we land."

Six hours later, a gentle nudge to my shoulder stirred me from my sleep, and as I opened my eyes. I realized that it was Damian at my side. His smiling face looked down at me, I sat up, stretching my arms only to realize the plane had stopped.

"Are we here?" I asked, with hopefulness in my voice. "Are we in Mexico?"

"Yeah," he chuckled. "The plane landed twenty minutes ago. I let you sleep while we finished unloading our luggage. Why don't you come on, and we will head to the villa?"

I wasn't sure exactly where Damian had planned for us to stay, but hearing it was a villa took me by surprise. "A villa? Is that a fancy word here for hotel?"

"Hotel?" he laughed, shaking his head, "oh no. I have a house here, Ivy. On the beach."

It never ceased to amaze me the things I learned about. I kept forgetting that Damian wasn't an ordinary human and had forged a powerful empire as an Alpha.

"Of course you do." I laughed as I descended the stairs of the plane. The warm Mexican sun hit my skin and caused me to smile as my feet eventually touched the ground.

It was more beautiful here than I expected, and as I stepped toward the open car door, I looked forward to what awaited me further in Mexico.

"So I was thinking we could go out and get something to eat later," Damian stated once we were in the car moving. The way he stated what he wanted to do was done with hesitation, and I found the moment sweet.

"That sounds good," I replied with a smirk. "Did you have a place in mind?"

"I did, but it's a surprise." As I looked at him, I watched the subtle smirk cross his face, and with it, I became curious to know what he had in mind for our evening.

Twenty minutes later, we were pulling onto a long driveway that led toward a bungalow sitting on a cliff. The tan clay roofing accented the magnificent structure, welcoming its visitors warmly against the bright sky.

"Wow." As the words escaped me, I heard his chuckle of amusement from beside me.

"I'm glad you like it." He said as he put the car in park, allowing me to step out into the heat and really take everything in properly for the first time.

"Like it... more like love it." As my gaze fell upon him, I was surprised to find him standing there with a small grin on his face, watching me. "What's wrong?"

"Nothing–nothing," he blurted as he walked toward the house with me following him.

To say that the outside had stunned me was really a small comment compared to the astonishment I felt from the inside. Wide-eyed, mouth partially open. I stood staring at the sight before me.

Not a penny had been spared to create this wonderful home, and with the view of the coast in the distance, I enjoyed the salt air kissing my skin as I walked about the large balcony.

"Ivy, if you follow me, I will show you the room you will be staying in. Then we can rest for a bit and go get dinner—if you still want to."

Damian was trying, and the once aggressive, egotistical attitude he had was diminishing every day that I spent with him. I wasn't sure why, but I was happy to know that he was trying.

It was all I ever asked of him. "Sure. Lead the way."

An hour later, I stepped from the shower with a white towel wrapped around my body. Damian said he was going to take me to a local spot he loved, and as much as I wanted to trust his judgment on authentic Mexican food—I was wary.

It was, after all, my FAVORITE food to eat, and I was more than picky when it came to it.

Sliding on my white lace summer dress and sandals, I braided my hair and made my way toward the living room. My mind rattled with the anticipation of what this trip could hold. I wanted more than anything to find the guys, but I also wanted him. Damian.

"Wow, you look beautiful," Damian replied with a grin across his face. His eyes took in the sight before him.

"Thanks." The reply was followed by a heavy red tinting of my cheeks as I blushed. "You clean up well too."

With an outstretched hand, he gestured for me to come near him, and as I did, he quickly took my hand and spun me around slowly. "This dress will be great for dancing."

"Dancing?" I replied, shocked, "we aren't supposed to be having fun. We are supposed to be finding James." I reminded him as he shrugged his shoulders.

"We are, but we can have fun while we do it."

Pulling me behind him, I let him lead me to his unknown destination of choice. I wasn't sure what exactly he had in mind, but I had no doubt that it would be interesting.

Lately, Damian was full of surprises.

Music. Dancing. Tacos, and Tequila.

Who knew that Damian was a man who enjoyed such pleasures?

Round and round, he spun me in circles. The laughter that emitted from me wasn't something I had heard in so long, and every time he pulled me close to him, I couldn't help but wonder who the man before me was.

This wasn't the same Damian I had met so many months before. This Damian was actually fun.

"I can't–" I laughed, holding my side, "I need to sit down."

Pulling away from him, I moved back toward our table, away from the crowd of people who still lined the dance floor. Mexico was more than I expected, and between the music and food, I found myself not wanting to go home.

I could understand why James had come here to get away.

One could really lose themselves within the culture of this place.

"Don't tell me you're already partied out," Damian replied, taking a seat next to me.

"Me?" I scoffed, "never."

As much as I had enjoyed the evening so far, though, I felt wrong. We were there to find James, and instead of doing that, Damian and I were having fun and drinking.

It wasn't right, and a guilty emptiness settled in my stomach.

"We will find him," Damian's voice whispered softly. My thoughts reflected in my facial expressions as I forced a smile and nodded my head.

"I know, but I hate that it's taking so long to do so." I wanted him now. Not eventually.

Taking the bottle of local tequila, Damian poured himself and me another shot, scooting it toward me.

"Drink up," he replied with a smirk, lifting the shot glass into the air. "To finding James."

As much as I didn't think I could manage another shot, I lifted the glass and smirked. "To James."

The smooth taste of the tequila slid down my throat for a sixth time tonight, and between the shots and the margaritas I was drinking, I felt as light as a feather.

No doubt I would regret my decisions in the morning, but for now, I would live in the moment.

"One more dance before we leave."

Looking at Damian, I sighed at his extended hand and nodded. "Just one more."

Sweeping me to the dance floor, he pulled me close to him. The slow tone of the song pulsated around me, and as he glided me across the floor, I couldn't help but take in his intoxicating scent and the way his eyes seemed to peer into my soul.

Unsure of what he was doing, I let myself go in the moment, and with every passing second, the intensity between us grew.

"Damian—" I whispered as he leaned in and kissed softly behind my ear.

"Shhh, just let go for tonight."

There was arguing with the idea as his lips claimed me in a kiss that made the world melt around me.

"Let's get out of here," I urged as a soft growl of excitement left his lips.

I wanted more, and with the ache he was creating between my legs, I had no doubt he planned to sate it. In more ways than one.

The car ride home was faster than I expected, and before I could step toward the door, he had swept me off my feet and closed the front door behind us. It wasn't slow and gentle in the least. Instead, Damian was a mixture of dominance and something far more primal.

Gripping my throat, he pushed me against the wall as he captured my lips. The heat from his body set mine on fire, and as he swept his tongue against mine, I moaned in excitement.

There was nothing more I wanted than for him to ravish me.

To make me explode over and over again till I was begging him to stop.

"What do you want, Ivy?" He whispered in a demanding tone that made me soaking wet already.

"You," I pleaded. "I want you to make me scream."

"I'm not like the others, Ivy," he warned, "I'm not soft and gentle, and when I take you, I will dominate you in every way. Do you understand that?"

Staring up into his dark eyes, I contemplated what he was saying, "you're dominant?"

Slowly, a sinister smirk crossed his lips, giving me his answer. Never had I done anything dark or dangerous like that before, but with the weight of the alcohol and the height of my arousal.

I didn't care. "Fuck it," I replied, claiming his lips once more.

It was the only answer he wanted, and before I knew it, our clothes were shredded from our bodies and scattered from the front door all the way to his bedroom.

"God, you're so wet for me," he muttered as his finger spread against the folds between my legs. The sensation caused me to moan softly as I closed my eyes, relishing in the feeling of his fingers against my core.

"Please."

Pulling away, he smiled down at me. "So impatient."

"Scared?" I muttered with my own smirk that did nothing but caused me to regret my words.

Faster than I expected, he gripped me by my hair and pulled my head back as he wrapped his other arm around my waist. The look in his eyes was sadistic and, when most women would have been terrified, I wasn't.

I was excited, and I wanted whatever he was going to give me.

"I'll show you scared, Ivy," he whispered in my ear, "and you will love every moment of it."

My alcohol-induced thoughts couldn't keep up as he captured my lips once more and tossed me upon the bed. With a forceful grip, he spread my thighs, pulling me to the edge of the mattress as he leaned his head down toward my mound and groaned in satisfaction.

The movements came unexpectedly, but in the moment, I was down for whatever he was going to toss at me. I wanted all of it. ANY way he wanted to give it.

The first swipe of his tongue sent vibrations through my soul with the low growl of approval from his wolf. My back arching in pleasure, he devoured me just like his own personal little Red.

Fingers gripping his thick hair, I moaned in approval. "Fuck, don't stop."

The pleading desire of an expected orgasm pushed me closer and closer to the edge, but every time I expected to be pushed over, he would stop.

He tormented me with his actions, but it only made me grow more needy for his touch.

Needier for the pleasure he would end up giving me.

Gripping my legs, he flipped me onto my stomach, gripping my thighs as he put me on display in front of him. I wasn't sure what was going to come next, but when I felt the cold sensation of leather, I froze. My heart raced as I anticipated his next move.

"Tell me you want it," he demanded, as his fingers gently brushed over my skin. "I promise you will like it."

He wanted to whip me, and that was something I wasn't sure I would like.

Taking a moment, I slowly nodded my head, only to have the swift stinging sensation of the whip brought across my backside. I jolted forward a little but held my position.

It was a painful sensation, but the pleasure was far more great.

"Again," I pleaded.

One after another, he whipped me, and every time had my core tightening for him.

"Enough." He pulled me toward him. The feeling of his thick erected member pushing at my center, craving the release he was bound to give me.

Gripping my hair, he pulled me back as he pushed deep inside me. A cry left my lips as I accepted him. "Don't hold back." I moaned as he feverishly took over every aspect of my body.

The louder I cried out for him, the more I moaned, and as my climax built, he tipped me over the edge countless times before he finally roared in desire, releasing himself deep inside me.

His knot pushed at my walls, making a tear escape down my cheek as I relished in the pleasure it brought.

The excitement, the pain, and the frustration of everything that was Damian had been well worth waiting for. The only problem was that rational me—would never agree to what I just did.

Thank God rational me has checked out for the night.

There was no way I would miss a moment of what he just gave me.

James Appears

Damian

Looking down at Ivy's sleeping form, I took a deep breath, trying to come to grips with what had just happened. I let the tequila and intensity of her body against mine push the evening into a direction I wasn't aiming for.

I didn't expect to get her in my bed tonight, but I damn sure wouldn't object to it.

I had held off for so long because I had a feeling she wouldn't like my taste of sexual desire.

However, I was very wrong.

She embraced it like a champ, and that was only the tip of what I enjoy.

The dim light of my phone lit up in the darkness of my room. Looking down to wear it laid on the nightstand, I watched my private investigator's name cross the screen.

"Hmm..." It was late for him to be calling. "Hello?" I muttered as I quietly shut the bedroom door behind me.

"Damian, sorry to call so late, but we have a lead."

Fantastic, this will make her happy. "What do you have?"

"It seems that he was spotted just outside of a local restaurant tonight near the beach. By the time we got there, he was gone, though."

Pinching the bridge of my nose, I tried to digest the information. "What was the name?"

"Of what, sir?" he asked, testing my patients.

"Of the fucking restaurant," I growled, losing my patience. "What was the name?"

"La Habichuela," Of course, it was. I was drinking, and James had been watching us.

"Shit!" I muttered as I walked toward the windows, peering out of them. "I was there."

There was silence for a moment before he spoke, "you were there?"

"Yes, yes. I was there tonight with Ivy. He was fucking watching us."

It honestly didn't surprise me that he was watching us. It was not surprising that we were in Cancun. Especially when I had been such a big sponsor in helping to renovate the local community to bring them more of a modern touch.

Cancun had a special place in my heart, as did its people.

"What would you like us to do, sir?" the man asked as I shook my head, trying to figure out what exactly I should do. If James was watching us, then it meant he knew what we were doing.

Perhaps it was time I went out looking for him.

"Be here tomorrow late afternoon. We will sit down and discuss things."

Ivy

The bright stream of sunlight cast through the open window of the bedroom. The smell of salt air filled my nose as I stretched within the sheets of the bed, relishing in how amazing they felt beneath my skin.

That was, until I hit something firm and opened my eyes to realize another body was next to me. Not just any body, either. It was Damian.

"Oh–" my heart began to race as the events of the previous night littered my mind.

Lifting the sheet, I looked down at my naked body and gasped.

Holy fuckin' shit. It wasn't a dream.

"Shit. Shit. Shit," I muttered quickly, jumping from the bed, startling Damian, who jumped from the bed as naked as the day he was born, looking around the room for the threat.

"What the fuck?" he muttered when his eyes fell on my naked form wrapped within the white sheets of the bed. "Don't scare me like that."

"Last night–" I muttered wide-eyed, "we...?"

"Fucked," he smirked, crossing his arms over his chest.

Narrowing my eyes, I scoffed, "why do you have to say it like that?"

"Are you regretting your choices?" he chuckled, but the lurking sense of hurt lined his eyes.

With a sigh, I shook my head, trying to wrap my mind around it all.

"No, of course, I don't regret it. It was—" fumbling for the words, I smiled, "amazing."

"So, round two?" he replied with a seductive gleam in his eyes as he stepped forward.

Shock filled me as I stared at him in disbelief. "Noooo!"

Pushing past him, I moved toward the door, only to have him follow me down the hall.

"What the hell's wrong?" he called after me as I opened my bedroom door and turned to stare at him.

"Are you serious right now, Damian?" I asked, trying to understand why he couldn't see how wrong this was. "I loved everything about last night: the food, drinks, and the sex. But we are here to find James... not drink and fuck the week away."

His lips met into a tight, firm line as he stared at me with clenched fists. "So, finding my brother is more important than spending time with me?"

I could tell he was angry. It was of no surprise by his reaction to my comment.

"For you to automatically think that proves how you look at things. I'm going to take a shower, Damian. I think you should do the same so we can start picking up the pieces and get our family back together."

With a sigh of disappointment, I closed the door behind me and left Damian in the hallway. I didn't want to argue with him, but last night shouldn't have happened in this way.

I mean, it should have happened, but not under the circumstances.

I didn't want James to think that we weren't putting him first. Not that he would know.

Frustration filled me as I let the scalding hot water run across my skin, soothing my muscles. The soreness of the night's events was lingering after effect, and my head hurt from the amount of liquor I drank.

Stepping from my room forty-five minutes later, I headed for the kitchen in search of food.

Damian sat at the bar with a plate in front of him and his head on his laptop. Biting my bottom lip, I watched him as guilt flooded my heart. "I'm sorry."

Slowly his eyes looked up at me as he furrowed his brows in confusion. "For what?"

"For acting the way I did," I mumbled as I fidgeted under his gaze.

I wasn't intentionally wrong about how I acted, but at the same time, I could have approached the conversation better. My actions hadn't been fair to him.

"It's okay," he sighed. "You were right."

Taken aback by his admission, a small smile formed across my lips, "I'm sorry... can you repeat that?"

He chuckled, rolling his eyes. "No. I know you heard me. Don't get used to it."

As much as I wanted to hear him say it again, I didn't push the issue. Just knowing that he wasn't upset at me made me happy. At the end of the day, if we wanted to find the guys, we couldn't be fighting with each other.

"Have you got any leads yet?" I asked as I approached him, looking at what he was searching through on his computer. A list of possible tip locations lined a spreadsheet with the guys' names at the top.

The only thing concerning me about this was the fact Talon's column was relatively empty.

"Yeah, I got a tip last night, actually," he replied, "James was at the restaurant."

My fears were accurate, and much as I didn't want James to know what happened, he saw it firsthand. "He was watching us there?"

Nodding, he clenched his jaw. "I know what you're thinking, Ivy. Please don't let that eat at you."

How was he going to tell me not to let it bother me?

James had been there, and I could have been in his arms. Instead, he watched Damian, and I enjoy ourselves while he had been a complete wreck since the bond broke.

"We have to find him, Damian. I don't want him—"

"Ivy, don't. Don't think like that," he pleaded, "I am going out tonight to find him. I promised you that I would, and I intend to keep that promise."

Hope filled me at his words. I wanted more than anything to see James again, and if Damian was going to look for him, hopefully, he would show himself.

Hopefully.

James

Sitting in my darkened hotel room, I mulled over my reality. When I heard that Damian was in town, I contemplated running again. I didn't want him to find me. The moment my bond with Ivy broke, I felt a pain in my chest that was unbearable.

My wolf and I were torn apart—the memory more than I can bear...

***

"James, you have to let her go," Damian had yelled at me in the hospital hallway. "We are nothing but toxic for her. She deserves a normal life!"

Anguish gripped a hold of my soul as my heart raced. "No... I can't... we can't!"

Dropping to my knees, I stared at her hospital door. She was hurt because of me, because of us.

"If you loved her at all, you would let her go. It's too late anyways."

So that's what I did. I let her go.

Snapping back to reality, I launched my beer bottle across the room, watching as it shattered and fell to the ground. I had let her go, but the moment I went to confront Damian at the restaurant, my breath was stolen from me.

She was there. She was with Damian, and they were happy together.

I couldn't understand it. Trying to wrap my head around what I had seen, I stood to my feet and stormed from my hotel room. I need more alcohol. Anything to numb the pain I felt.

"James—" an all too familiar voice called from behind me, stopping me in my tracks.

Damian.

Clenching my fists tightly at my side, I turned to face him. "What the fuck are you doing here?"

He looked the same as he always had. Calm, collected, and here on business.

That was his M.O., after all. "I came to bring you home."

Laughter escaped me as I shook my head. "Are you fucking serious?"

"Don't act like this, James. You have been gone too long, and it's time to come back to reality."

"Reality!" I yelled. "How about the fucking reality that you're here with Ivy, Damian?!"

I watched as he took a deep breath and relaxed his shoulders. There was something about him at the moment that was slightly different, but I wasn't sure what it was.

"She came with me to find you," he finally replied, but the sound of it wasn't as good as I thought. All this time, I had hoped what I had with her, and lost, had just been a dream.

Yet here he was, trying to put it on me as if I was supposed to be excited.

"What happened to letting her go, Damian? What happened to letting her have a normal life!"

Shaking with fury, I wanted nothing more than to beat Damian within an inch of his life. I knew I didn't stand a real chance against him in a fight, but at the same time, I wanted—no, needed anything to relieve the anger I felt.

"Things weren't as we thought, James. The bond wasn't broken, just the terms had been changed."

His riddles meant nothing to me. All he ever did was try to order me and the other around. His lies would not win me over this time, no matter how much I wished they were true.

"Go fuck yourself, Damian," I snapped. "I'm done listening to your bullshit."

Shaking my head in disgust, I turned from him. I couldn't believe he would flaunt her in front of me after everything he did to us and to think she allowed him.

It disgusted me. I loved her—shit, I still love her.

"She came for you, James!" he yelled after me, "if you don't believe me, go see for yourself."

Stopping in my tracks once more, I thought over his words. As much as I didn't want to do that, curiosity filled me to some extent, wondering what he was saying.

"Are you at your villa?" I asked flatly.

"Of course," he replied, chuckling, "I am going to have a few drinks with some friends from the city. I won't be back till the early hours of the morning. Perhaps she shouldn't be left alone all night."

Gritting my teeth, I rolled my eyes, refusing to look at him. I wouldn't give him the pleasure of a response, but as I walked off, I couldn't help but think he was right.

Perhaps she shouldn't be left alone.

Ivy

Hours had passed since Damian left, and with the moon high in the sky, I watched it shimmer across the open ocean. Never had I been curious about the power of the moon, but in that moment, I found solace in its appearance.

"Help Damien find him," I whispered aloud to the moon, wishing the goddess would help us find James. Without him, I couldn't fulfill what my heart wanted.

What I wanted seemed so far off in the reality of things, and yet something told me deep down that I was closer to having it than I realized.

Turning, I made my way into the house. The day had been long with everyone who had been present earlier, and through all the conversations I had sat silently thinking about him.

Wondering if he could still feel me... hear me even.

A longing for the bond we once had. 'James.' I called out through my mind, once again pleading for him to hear me. Pleading for him to come home. 'Please find me.'

Grasping the metal kettle from the stove, I turned on the tap of the sink and filled it—the sound of running water filling the silence around me.

If this is what uncertainty felt like, I didn't like it.

"How?" a breathless voice said to my right, causing me to drop the kettle. Its metal form crashed to the ground as the sound resonated through the air.

Tears filled my eyes at the sight before me, and even though he looked completely different from the man I remembered, I felt the pull to him. The love and anger over his appearance.

"James?" The disbelief in my tone was enough to break him from the trance he was in before he furrowed his brows and looked on in confusion.

"How are you here?" he asked again, "why?"

It wasn't the reunion I had hoped for, but at the same time, I understood his reaction.

"I..." Pausing, I thought over my choice of words, "we came to find you. To bring you home."

"I don't have a home there anymore," he snapped, angry, rolling off him in waves. "If you came to rub your romance in front of me, then you're free to leave. Stop looking for me."

He turned to leave, and with panic coursing through me, I ran to him, gripping his arm. The same electric touch we once had coursed through me, and he turned to me with wide eyes, looking down at my hand.

"Please don't leave, James," I begged him. "It's not broken."

Slowly, his eyes met mine, and as they did, he didn't hesitate. He quickly gripped my head and pressed his lips to mine, devouring my very soul. With every touch we had, our kisses became more demanding. More intense.

I quickly found myself picked up within his arms as he walked toward the sofa, pulling me onto his lap as I straddled him. This wasn't a time for talking. It was a moment to rekindle our feelings for each other, and I was more than okay with that.

Making headway, I reached for his pants, undoing them one by one. "Ivy, we should talk—"

"No," I replied, shaking my head. "We can talk after."

Sliding myself down over his thick shaft, I cried out in pleasure. He was much longer than Damian, and every inch of him forced inside me pressed against my cervix, creating pleasure I had missed.

Slowly, I rode him. My hand on his throat as I bite seductively on his bottom lip. This was about his pleasure over mine. I felt the need to make it up to him with everything he had been through. I wanted him to know that I still wanted him, that I still cared.

"Fuck, Ivy—" he gasped, closing his eyes, his head falling back against the sofa as he gripped my rear end, slamming me down over him harder and harder.

"I want you, James," I whispered, kissing him as I felt his knot fill me. "I want you always."

"You don't know that—" he moaned loudly again as I felt us both close to the edge.

"Yes—" I cried out, "oh fuck... mark me again, James," I begged him.

His eyes met mine with swirling black and gold flecks. His wolf was on edge, and I didn't care.

"Ivy—" he growled, "don't tease me."

My grip on his throat tightened as I pushed my face against his and groaned, "fucking do it."

He didn't hesitate at my command as he pulled my neck to the side and bit down into my shoulder. A cry of pleasure left my lips as I screamed out, coming undone on his shaft.

The feeling of his own release built pressure within me as his knot locked us in place.

A guttural growl of possession filled the room as he released his bite and looked into my eyes. A haze of pleasure washed through me as I smiled at him. "Don't leave me again."

Accepting the Future

Damian

When I walked into the house, I knew it was late. I knew my brother James wouldn't fight the urge to see her. Out of all of us, he cared for her the most in the past.

She was everything to him.

His first real love. His only love.

"You're awake." James turned from the open fridge toward me and nodded. No longer was he unkept and dirty. They must have had fun because he was now freshly shaven and showered in my kitchen. "Where's Ivy?"

"Sleeping," he quickly retorted as he placed a bottle of water on the counter with the sandwich he had obviously made. "Care to explain to me what happened?"

"Are you going to actually listen this time?" I responded with a smirk as I walked toward the counter, taking a seat.

James wasn't impressed by my attitude, but nonetheless, he rolled his eyes and shrugged. "Don't push it, Damian. This was all your fucking fault to begin with."

Pressing back the annoyance I wanted to lash upon him, I squared my shoulders and let a breath escape me. "I understand

I fucked up in the past, James. I can't change the past, but I am trying to fix things now if you will help me."

"Help you?" he snorted. "That's rich."

"I'm serious. We came here to find you first. Next, we are going after Hale."

James stared at me with a blank expression. "He left too?"

Nodding, I sighed. "You all did. She woke up, and I was the only one still there for her."

My revelation made him flinch, but no matter the guilt he may have felt, I knew why he did what he did. I wanted to do the same thing, but one of us had to be there when she woke up.

"How could I not feel the bond before, but as soon as she touched me, I could? That shouldn't be possible, Damian."

"I know." He was right. It shouldn't be possible. "I took her to see the seer. She explained that Ivy is favored by the goddess, and now the bond has been left to her. She can choose a normal life, mating to one of us or a few. Or she can have us all. At the end of the day, though, it's her choice."

"And she didn't run for a normal life..." he murmured with surprise.

"Obviously not if we are here, and from the looks of it, I take it she rekindled her bond with you."

He was silent for a moment before slowly nodding. "I didn't think she was real when I saw her again."

"You mean at the restaurant?" I inquired, knowing full well he was there.

Nodding, he groaned. "I had come to tell you to leave me the fuck alone, but then I saw her. How happy she was, and I couldn't bring myself to do it. Seeing her again was too much."

"I get it. It was a lot for me when I saw her in the hospital awake as well. Even if I didn't have the bond with her like you three did."

Both of us sat there in silence for a moment before he looked up at me again. "Why haven't you bonded with her yet? I smelt you on her, so I know you had sex."

Glancing down at my clasped hands in front of me, I mulled over the idea.

Why hadn't I marked her when I had the chance?

"I suppose, in the moment, it didn't seem right," I responded, looking at him again, "I want you three to reconcile with her first, and then I will have my chance."

"So you could fuck her first but not mark her. That makes a lot of sense," he snapped.

Grinning at his jealous remark, I ran my tongue over my teeth, trying to hold back the cynical comment that was pushing through.

"James, if you remember correctly, you all were fucking her before I did."

Slapping his hand against the counter, I observed the fire swirl within his eyes. "Because you didn't fucking want her. Remember that minor detail?"

"It wasn't because I didn't want her, James. But that is what you want to believe, right?"

"Fuck you, Damian," he snorted. "You didn't want to be tied down. Admit it."

"No," I snapped. "I wanted her to have a normal life, dammit. Was that so hard to ask?"

The anger simmering within James, he leaned back and scoffed. At one point in time, we all wanted her to have a normal life. That's why they all chose to leave.

They could have stayed and refused what I told them to do, but they didn't. They left.

"You didn't have to leave, James. Even if I said to go. You could have stayed."

A growl ripped through him as he clenched his fist. "Fuck you, Damian. You put that shit in our heads and made us feel like we had no choice. We all love her, and you only now see what we lost. How important she is in the long run. She was gifted to us by the goddess herself."

"You're right," I replied with a smirk crossing my arms over my chest. "She was gifted to us."

I knew deep down the moment I had found her as my mate that there would be problems. The idea of one woman being mated to the four of us was just asking for problems.

I had never been one for sharing, and the thought of sharing my mate was disgusting.

At the time, but now I wanted it more than anything. I wanted her.

"How do you even know she truly wants this, Damian? How do you know that she just doesn't feel guilty, and that's what's going on?"

Shrugging my shoulder, a smile crept across my lips. "Ask her yourself."

Confusion flashed through his eyes as I pointed behind him toward Ivy's shadowed figure. I knew very well she had been listening to us, and as he turned, she stepped forth and smiled.

"Sorry, I didn't want to interrupt."

No matter what Ivy did or what she had been through, she was still the most beautiful woman I had ever laid my eyes on. I regretted every moment of not finishing my bond with her, but at last, all I could do was make up for my past mistakes.

"You don't ever have to apologize," James replies, dropping his food on his plate, wrapping his arms around her as he kisses the top of her head. "I'm sorry I left you."

A grin crossed her plump, kissable lips as she pulled away from him, "Damian is right, James. We can't change the past, but we can fix the future."

He seemed to consider her words over mine, and even though the Alpha in me itched to say something about it, I didn't. She would become the luna of our pack, and with her place by our side, she would have the ultimate say.

At least behind closed doors.

"Are you sure this is what you want, Ivy?" he asked with desperation. "You could be free."

Laughter escaped her, though, at his comment. Pulling down the collar of the oversized shirt she wore, she displayed her mate mark. "Too late for that."

"Fuck," James whispered, running his hand through his hair, "I shouldn't—"

Quickly bringing her finger to his lips, she shook her head. "Don't. I have thought about all of this, and this is what I want, James. Damian knows this. My future career can still happen one day, but not without all of you by my side."

The moment she spoke those words, my heart swelled with pride. She truly did care about us, and the look in her eyes when she proclaimed her desire to have us all spoke volumes.

She didn't regret her choice, and she was determined to be with us all.

"Okay, then. Well, what's the plan? Where's Hale?" James asked.

As her eyes met mine, I gestured for her to explain. If she wanted to be the boss, I'd let her.

"Pack your shit. We're heading to Japan." She giggled.

"You know I hate flying overseas," James complained for the tenth time since I told him where Hale was. I found his complaining cute because he looked very distressed about what was going on. He did not like flying. That was obvious.

Damian groaned again as he let out a sigh. He was controlling his temper, and it was taking everything he had to do so. "Once again, you flew to Mexico, James. Why is Japan such a big issue?"

"I took sedatives before flying to Mexico. Unless you have some hiding within your clothing," he sneered, "...or on this plane, you're just going to have to deal with my complaining."

As much as James tried to be okay with what we were doing, I could tell flying was really bothering him. Looking across from me, I watched as his face paled, looking out the window. Leaning forward, I rubbed soothing circles over the back of his hand.

"It's okay." I tried to reassure him as my eyes glanced at Damian, urging him to do something.

"I'll be okay," James murmured, adjusting himself. "I just need to adjust."

Thinking about the situation, a small smile crossed my lips.

"Hey, why don't we play a game or something? Are there cards on this plane?" I asked, looking at Damian, "it will help James take his mind off things."

Damian sat quietly for a moment as he raked his eyes over my body. He had been the one to suggest the blue dress I was wearing, and now I suddenly was unsure of my choice.

"What?" I replied, looking between him and James. "Do I have something on me?"

James' brows furrowed as he glanced at Damian, who gave a slightly raised brow and a smirk.

They were up to something. I just wasn't sure what it was.

Standing to his feet, Damian strolled over to us from where he was sitting.

"Do you really want to help him take his mind off things?" he asked in a sultry way that set my body on fire.

Slowly glancing up at him beneath full lashes, my mouth parted as I nodded. I knew exactly where his mind was going, and the thought of it instantly aroused me.

"On your knees, Ivy," he ordered, causing a smile to fall across my lips as I complied.

"What the hell is going on?" James asked in confusion.

"Don't speak," Damian firmly said as he held up a finger to James, quieting him. "Comply."

Running his hand through my loosely hung hair, I smiled. "Do you know what I want you to do?"

"Yes, sir," I replied, and I felt his body tense at my reply. Never had I addressed him in that way.

Yet, he liked it. "Show me."

Crawling forward on my knees, I slid between James' thighs and slowly moved my fingers over the zipper of his jeans. "What are you doing?" James whispered, looking down at me.

Silence was all he got from me as my hands freed the beast within.

I wasn't overly confident with my actions, but Damian's mind was on the right path.

This would help take James' mind off his fear of flying.

Slowly, I swirled my tongue around the head of his thick erection. A gasp left his gently parted lips as I slipped his length into my mouth.

Up and down, I worked with his shaft, breathing through my nose as I tried to take him deeper into me. The slow movement of his hips and his fingers in my hair let me know that what I was doing was working.

As my eyes looked toward Damian, I almost froze. They swirled with darkness as he watched me. I finally understood why Damian wanted me to please James. He was turned on by what I was doing in general, and I didn't think it mattered who it was to.

He gripped himself through his pants as he stood back and watched.

The outline of his massive erection showed me just how excited he was, and as if on cue, I looked to James, who took note of what I saw.

"Brother, why don't you share her with me? After all, I can't be the only one to have fun."

"Only if you insist," Damian replied as he stood to his feet. He moved behind me, taking a seat in the chair I had once been in. The sound of his zipper opening made me curious, but not once did I stop deep-throating James until Damian's hands gripped my panties, ripping them off.

Reaching down, his fingers brushed across my soaking wet core, causing me to shiver as I moaned with James' cock in my mouth.

"Do you like that?" James asked with a smile, causing me to nod my head.

Pulling his erection from my mouth, he smiled down at my rubbing his thumb over my lip. "God, you're amazing."

Before I could say anything, James pulled me to my feet and backed me toward Damian. Their hands moved over my body as they spread my legs and helped lower me down onto Damian's thick erection.

He filled me to the brink, and as I gasped, James shoved himself back into my mouth.

The intensity of what was happening caused me to cry out in pleasure.

With rapid fire, Damian thrusted up into me. My legs hooked up over the arms of the seat, giving him maximum angle as James gripped my throat, fucking my mouth.

"Oh fuck, Ivy," Damian groaned. "You're so fucking tight and wet for us, aren't you?"

James pulled his cock from my lips with a pop as I cried out, coming undone. "Fuck! Yes–yes!"

Sadistic laughter left them as I found my mouth full once more. Everything about this situation was intoxicating, and never had I done anything like this before.

These men opened me to things I had only read about in books, and I loved it.

No longer was it secrets and hiding amongst the shadows to not let the others know.

They were openly sharing me, well, at least two were.

As the build of another climax began to grow, I felt James' thick member swell in my mouth as he grunted in approval.

"Will you swallow me, Ivy?" he asked, biting his lips. "Do you want it?"

Nodding, with tears streaming down my cheeks in pleasure, I felt the spurting of his orgasm as he erupted. Gagging, I swallowed down as much as I could until it was dripping down my chin.

"Fuck, you're amazing," he whispered as he pulled himself from my lips.

The swell of Damian's knot caused me to gasp as I gripped the arms of the chair. "I can't–"

"I'm going to coat the inside of you, Ivy," Damian grunted, "every inch."

Before I could protest on the verge of exploding, fingers found my clit, and I realized James was going to ensure that I lost my mind with this one.

Sure enough, a scream of pleasure ripped from my throat as Damian held my arms down while James forced me to ride out my orgasm. Even after it went, he kept going.

The sensitivity caused me to come undone a second time as I tightened around Damian, milking every drop of the cum from him that there was. A groan of satisfaction escaped him as he slowed down.

Stars danced before my eyes as I waited for the knot to go down. A smile spread across James' face as he leaned in, kissing me. "That was amazing, Ivy."

"Does this mean I just joined the mile-high club?" I giggled as both men laughed.

Pulling me back, I rested against Damian's chest. "Yeah, you could say that, sweet cheeks."

"I need a nap," I gasped as I slowly closed my eyes.

I didn't worry about the cleanup because both men had done that for me on more than one occasion. In the moment, no matter how dirty and erotic it had been–I felt closer to them.

As if the bond I was told about was growing stronger with every passing moment. Perhaps there was a possibility that this could work with all of them. Even if Damian had once upon a time thought it impossible.

Perhaps there was a way they could share me.
To find out for sure, we had to find Hale and Talon.

Welcome to Toyko

I wasn't too sure what I expected when coming to Japan, but as I gazed out the window of the car, I was taken aback by how pretty it was. Thousands of people lined the streets, moving to get to where they needed to be, and neon lights lined the skies.

I thought once upon a time that New York was the place that was alive all the time, but from the looks of it, this city is more alive than New York.

"It's so pretty here," I mumbled as I took in the sights. "I can't wait to get out and walk around this place."

As much as I wanted to play tourist, I also knew that it wasn't feasible.

"We have things to do here, Ivy. We have to make sure that we are sticking to the plan, and not deviating." The calm, soothing tone of James' voice made my heart melt.

Yet, when I looked toward both men, I saw the dark, grim look Damian was giving me. Something was bothering him, and as much as I wanted to pretend there wasn't, I couldn't.

"Are you okay?" I asked him, watching as his body went rigid and he cleared his throat.

"Yeah, I'm fine." The car's slow stop caught his attention, and before I knew it, he was opening the car door and stepping through it.

From the moment we arrived in Japan, he had been bothered. Part of me didn't want to intrude on his past, but another part of me was curious if something had happened here that made him uncomfortable about coming.

As we stepped into the penthouse apartment Damian had rented for us. My eyes widened at the spectacular sight. Wall-to-wall windows lined the far wall overlooking Tokyo, and with this view, I was able to take in everything.

"Do you like it?" Damian asked from behind me as his arms wrapped around my waist and his chin sat on the top of my head. It was a comforting and romantic notion for him to hold me the way he was.

"It's beautiful." I smiled, admiring the view. "Do you think we will be able to find Hale here, though? The city is so big, and I worry it won't be as easy as Cancun."

Laughter echoed to my right as I turned to see James dropping the rest of our luggage onto the ground. "Hale isn't like I am. He won't be as clouded, and if he wants to be found, he will make himself known."

I wasn't quite sure what he meant, but I could tell that he was being serious.

There were still things I was learning about each of the men, and even though Hale and I had spent so much time together, it was more intellectually than anything else.

"Oh–" I whispered, pulling away from Damian, "well, I guess he will find me then. Like you did."

"Maybe." James shrugged as he grabbed my bags and walked me toward a back room.

Following behind him, I took in the large modernized room and smiled. It was beautiful, but it was just like any other room you would rent. Simply and to the point.

"Why don't you get some rest? We can go out later if you would like," James said as he turned to face me.

"Are you guys not sharing a room with me?"

James' eyes cast behind me, and as I turned, I saw Damian glaring at him with his arms crossed. It didn't make sense for there to be tension between them, but at the same time, Damian was still very much a mystery.

"We won't be sharing a room with you. We will each have our own," Damian replied as he brushed past James and me.

"What's wrong?" My firm, unhappy tone seemed to snap him from whatever funk he was in because his face quickly softened as the corner of his lips turned up.

"Nothing is wrong. This just gives you privacy. I don't want you to feel pressured into anything."

Was Damian being serious right now?

"Right." Clearing my throat, I gripped the door handle and stared at him. "Well, I guess I will see you later then."

Nodding his head, he turned, and I closed the door. Letting a heavy breath escape me, I tried to wrap my mind around his words. It was as if we had landed,, and he became another person, and with that he slowly changed his behavior toward me.

Again.

James

I knew coming to Tokyo was going to be a problem. Damian hadn't come to this place in years, and being back here was going to bring back too many memories.

"You need to tell her," I snapped as I walked into the living room and plopped down on the sofa. "If Shamira does find out you're here and Ivy doesn't know, it's going to cause problems."

"She isn't going to know," he snapped back, glaring at me.

Laughing, I shook my head. "And if she does?"

"She won't, damn it!" he yelled in a whispered tone, trying to prevent Ivy from hearing what he was saying. "We just need to hurry up and find Hale and get the fuck out of here."

"Like that is going to happen," I scoffed. "Hale came here for a reason. I wouldn't doubt he is probably hanging out with Shamira."

There was a swirling amount of contemplation running through Damian's mind, and it was obvious from his concerned yet angry look that he thought that too.

Once again, there were too many hidden secrets, and with how things went the first time–I didn't want the outcome repeated.

"Just call her and stop avoiding things. Then talk to Ivy."

Stopping in his tracks, he looked at me with a dumbfounded look. "Why don't you watch Ivy, and I will try to handle things quietly."

"Sure," I laughed, waving him off. "yYou're the boss. Do what you want."

There was no point in arguing with him. If he wanted to run off and do things his way, then let him. I would stay here and make sure Ivy knew how much I cared for her.

Because if Damian was going to fuck things up again, I didn't want Ivy to leave me. After all, they said she could pick who she wanted, and we didn't need Damian in the end.

"I will," he sneered. "I am going to run somewhere and see if I can find a trace of him. Keep an eye on her, and don't leave until I get back. Do you understand?"

Rolling my eyes, I shooed him off. "I'm not a child."

No matter how much he may have changed for the better when it came to Ivy, he was still the same man she had first met. It killed me that she didn't realize that.

As much as I wanted my brother to be happy, she deserved better than him.

Pulling out my phone, I contemplated calling Shamira myself and asking if Hale was there. She had been a woman who had helped our family many times in the past, and even though she had a more detailed past with Damian, it didn't mean she wouldn't help me.

"James?" Ivy's angelic voice called to me.

Turning, I looked over my shoulder on the sofa just in time to see her step out of the room dressed in a silk nightdress. Her hair tossed, and a sleepy look in her eyes. "Hello, Gorgeous."

Walking toward me, she frowned as her eyes grazed the area. "Where did Damian go?"

Shit.

"Uh–he just stepped out for a moment. He was going to check on a lead while you rested."

"Oh, okay," she smiled sweetly. "Well, goodnight then."

She walked toward me, leaning over and giving me a gentle kiss before turning and walking toward her room. When she acted like this, it made my heart melt.

Guilt filled me, knowing I had just lied to her, but at the same time, I didn't want to be the one to break the news to her about Damian's past. It wasn't my place to do so.

"Sleep well, Ivy," I murmured as I watched her figure disappear from my sight.

Something about today was eating at me, and with my wolf growing restless to get home, I knew that we couldn't be here for too long.

I just hoped Hale would listen to Ivy like I did. He may have been smart, but he and Talon held a grudge like no one I had ever seen.

Twins at their finest.

Ivy

I should have known that they were up to something. I heard bits and pieces of a conversation, but I wasn't sure where Damian had gone. Slipping back into my room, I picked up my phone and began flipping through social media.

A photo of Kate with her boyfriend popped up, and an idea came to mind as I called her.

"Hey, girl!" Kate's warm voice echoed through the phone, causing me to smile.

"Hey, I was wondering if you could do me a favor."

"Oh yeah," she hesitated, "and what might that be?"

"I want you to see what you can find out about someone named Shamira and also what it may have to do with Hale."

There was silence on the phone, and with it, I knew she already knew something. "Ivy–"

"Tell me, Kate," I firmly cut her off before she could say no.

"Well," she hesitated, "from what I know, they spent some time there with the Tokyo pack, and Shamira is the Alpha's daughter. They own a club called Dark Moon."

Hearing the news, I found myself conflicted about what she was saying. Did Damian go to meet her? Did they have something going on with her, the guys, that is?

Too much of it weighed heavily on my mind, but pushing it back, I let a heavy breath leave my lips.

"Okay. Thanks, Kate."

"You're not planning to do something stupid, are you?" she replied with hesitation. At first, I wasn't, but now that she had brought it up, an idea did fill my head.

"Of course not." I grinned, "I'll talk to you later. I'm going to get some sleep."

"Okay–" she sighed, "night, Ivy."

Hanging up the phone, I sat contemplating what she had told me. Damian was hiding something, and it more than likely had to do with where Hale was.

The worry didn't fill me that Damian was doing anything wrong, but to think Hale had gotten with another woman only a few weeks after me.

That idea hurt like hell.

Jumping to my feet, I pulled out a black dress and heels and quickly threw them on. If I were going to get the answers, I would have to do things myself.

"James!" I yelled out. Only to hear him scrambling toward my room, throwing open the door.

"What's wrong?!" he asked frantically as his eyes met mine, and concern filled him.

"Nothing is wrong," I laughed, causing him to sigh. "Get dressed. We're going out."

Pausing in his response, he furrowed his brows in confusion. "What do you mean?"

"I mean, we're going out. Go get ready unless you want to go like that," I shrugged.

"Ivy, no, we're not. Damian said—"

"Since when did you care what Damian thought?" I laughed, shaking my head. "Look, you can either go, or you can stay here, and I'll go by myself."

James carefully considered what I was saying before he reluctantly sighed and nodded his head. "Can I at least know where we are going?"

"Nope... just get your butt ready."

There was no way I was going to tell him we were going to the Dark Moon.

Damian

Coming back to Tokyo hadn't been the best of decisions. Shamira wasn't pleased when I left, and when she found out that I had found my mate, that complicated things further.

They say there is nothing worse than a woman scorned... but they were wrong.

There was nothing worse than a she-wolf with claws scorned.

Shamira was a complicated individual, and she had her eyes set on me for years. So walking into the Dark Moon club, I expected to see things on a difficult level.

The latest music beat through the club as I wound my way through an array of pulsing bodies on the dance floor. My eyes scanned for signs of Hale, hoping that I didn't run into anyone else.

However, I should have known that would be impossible. Especially when I heard a familiar voice behind me.

"Well, well, well. I thought that was you, Damian."

Turning, I forced a smile to my lips as I faced Shamira and two security guards. Her long black hair hung in ringlets over her shoulders as her dark eyes stared at me.

"Shamira. It's a pleasure to see you again."

A cold hard slap came to my face as I pushed against a recoil, trying to reel in my wolf from breaking free. "I suppose I deserved that."

"Yes, you did," she sneered. "You left me and ran off back home to some girl."

The girl she was talking about was Ivy, but at the time, I hadn't even known her yet. The jealousy this woman had was unreal, and the only thing I could think about was finding Hale.

Ivy needed him, and I wanted to grab him and leave without issue.

"Look, that's in the past. I'm here to find my brother."

"Yes, I heard about what happened," she smiled, playfully biting on her nail. "I guess that means you came to see me, too."

Raising a brow, I pondered over what she meant, and like a crashing weight, the realization dawned on me. She heard about the mate bond issue with Ivy, or at least what she thought and thinks that I'm here for her.

"No, you have it—"

"Oh, stop," she laughed as she quickly approached me and placed her lips upon mine in a quick kiss that took me by surprise. "Let's go find Hale. He is in the lounge."

Guilt filled me, having allowed her to kiss me. I was disgusted by her action, but at the same time, I needed her to find my brother. Reigning in my wolf that growled in the back of my mind, I internally tried to calm him.

This is what we had to do to get Hale, then so be it. It's what our mate needed.

I should have known Hale was here, and as much as I wanted to correct Shamira and tell her that I was still with Ivy, I didn't want her to throw me out before I could find my brother.

Following behind Shamira, I let her lead the way down hallways off the side of the club into a private area out on another dance floor. My eyes locked onto Hale, who sat off with another woman in his lap.

"Hale," I said firmly as I approached. "Having fun?"

When he looked at me, he frowned. "What the fuck are you doing here?"

"I could ask you the same thing," I scoffed. "Moving on so quickly?"

Anger laced his eyes as he pushed the girl off of him and stood to his feet. "What the hell do you care? You never cared about her anyways."

"That isn't true–"

"Boys, boys. Let's not talk about her anymore. She isn't here, and I am," Shamira said smugly as she grasped my hand and pulled me onto the sofa.

"I'm afraid I don't really have time for this." I tried to explain as Hales scoffed.

"He never has time for anything," Hale remarked, as he picked up a drink and chased it down.

I knew he was hurting, but as Shamira folded her leg over mine, I couldn't help but feel disgusted by what she was doing.

James

Walking down to the car with Ivy, I had a bad feeling about what was going to happen. She was acting very calm but determined at the same time.

"Where too?" The cab driver asked as we climbed into the back, taking our seats.

"The Dark Moon Lounge, please."

My eyes darted toward hers with shock as the cab lurched forward. "We can't go there."

"Oh, no?" She feigned shock, "why not, James?"

It was obvious that she knew something, and I didn't like the way she was looking at me. If I was right someone had tipped her off because there was no way she would know to go there.

"Who told you?" I asked without hesitation.

Her smile faltered as she raised a brow and turned her attention to the world outside, "I have my sources just as you have yours."

Kate. That was the only person she could have spoken to, and internally, I made a mental note to scold the woman for having told Ivy about this place. If Damian and Hale were there with Shamira, there was no telling what we were going to walk into.

As the cab came to a stop outside of the club, I reluctantly exited with Ivy. Her eyes fell on the building with a disgusted sneer across her face as she moved forward only to be stopped by the guard at the door. "You can't come in here."

"She's with me," I snapped, watching as he bowed his head.

"I'm sorry, sir. You know my orders—" he replied, trying not to argue with James.

"I will handle Shamira. Now move."

Doing as I commanded, he moved aside and let us through. Ivy's eyes glanced at me momentarily as we passed through the main entryway headed for the sea of people.

"Where do you think they are?" she asked softly, "I don't see them."

"If they're here, they aren't out in the main area," I hummed as a nervous feeling flowed through my body.

"Private VIP," she snapped as her eyes narrowed, staring at me. "They went to a private room?"

"Ivy, don't—" I sighed, "don't automatically think the worst. Damian and Hale wouldn't do that to you."

A heavy breath left her lips as she looked away from me as if trying to persuade herself that I was telling the truth. Even if I wasn't so sure.

"Okay," she finally said. "Can we please go get them? I'm ready to find them and go home."

Wrapping my arm around her waist, I pulled her close, kissing the top of her head as we walked forward toward the roped-off VIP section. The guards standing by hesitated for a moment before moving aside for us to pass.

The sound of Hale's voice echoed down the hallway as Shamira's laughter followed. And as we turned the corner, my eyes latched on to the sight before me. Shamira wrapped around Damian as Hale allowed a half-naked woman to cling to his side.

Anger boiled within me as a growl ripped through my throat. I didn't need to see Ivy's face to feel how she felt because I could feel her through our bond. Her heart shattered into pieces seeing the sight before her, but she held herself together the best she could.

Stepping from my grasp, her hands upon her hips, she looked at them all as Damian's face paled. "Seems you both are having fun, aren't you?"

Oh, she was pissed.

Convincing Bar Fights

Ivy

Anger. It coursed through me like a wildfire as I tried to come to terms with what I saw.

"Seems you both are having fun, aren't you?"

"James, it's so lovely to see you." The woman purred as she ran her hand over Damian's chest. His face was unreadable as it paled at the sight of me.

"What are you doing here?" Hale finally asks, as his brows narrow at me. "I figured you would be living your life in Georgia."

The man speaking was not the same Hale I had known before. This man was unrecognizable, and it killed me he was acting the way he was. My heart breaking, I felt James step closer to me, but at the same time, I had to handle this myself.

"Yeah, and I never thought the man I fell in love with would be sitting here with a naked woman, moving on so quickly after everything that had happened. Yet, here we are."

My snarky response caused the woman on Damian to laugh. "Wait, is this the girl?"

Clearing his throat, Damian tried to remove himself from Shamira. Her eyes darted to Damian as he moved before quickly grasping him and pulling him back.

"Interesting," I snapped.

"Oh, she is feisty. Tell me, girl, why are you here?" she asked, putting her gaze on me once more. The look in her eye stirred something inside me that wanted to rip her apart.

"Well, I came to collect what belongs to me, but I see that they have found entertainment where they don't belong. Funny how that works," I grit out as James wraps his arm around my waist, pulling me closer.

"We should go–" he murmurs, causing Hale to look between the two of us before standing to his feet.

"You're mated?" he asks, snapping James' attention, who looks at him with a small nod.

"You have missed a lot, brother, and I thought Damian came here to bring you home, but it looks like that is not the case," James snarled as Damian's eyes flickered, his wolf fighting for control.

Every time Shamira touched Damian, my anger rose a little more. I knew that this wasn't the boys' territory, and even though I was still very new to their world, I had to remain calm. Otherwise, I would do more damage than needed.

"Damian, we need to leave," I said, clearing my throat, deciding to deal with him later.

"Oh, he isn't going anywhere," Shamira laughed. "I don't know why you, as a human, think you have the right to tell him anything. He is mine, and you lost your chance. Plus, humans don't breed strong children where I can."

Her words stung, and as a growl left James, I held my hand up and pulled my hair to the side to show off James' mark. "They are mine, and I am here to collect what rightfully belongs to me, so it's in your best interest to stand down."

Hale's eyes widened as I spoke, and slowly, he stepped near me. "That isn't possible."

"Who the fuck do you think you are to speak to me like that?" The woman shrieked as she stood to her feet, "do you know who I am?"

Laughter left my lips as I shook my head, watching as Damian stood next to her and shook his head for me to stop. But it didn't matter because this was a fight I wouldn't back down from.

"I don't care who you are. I am their rightful Luna, and you will back down now," I said sternly, with more confidence than I thought I had to begin with.

Something about the way I spoke seemed to make the guards step back, and even the woman in front of me to second guess her actions. However, Hale stepped back from me, clenching his fists as he stared at the mark upon my neck.

"I don't understand," he replied, "regardless, this means nothing. What happened, happened?"

The hurt from his words caused pain to shoot to my heart as it crumbled a little more.

"Hale, just come with us and listen to what we have to say. Don't do this," James replied as Damian stepped forward, shrugging Shamira off as she tried to reach for him.

"James is right," Damien replied, staring at me with a lust-filled look that I chose to shrug off. "Ivy, please let me explain. I can see you're upset."

"Upset?" I laughed. "I'm not upset. I don't know what you're talking about."

"Enough of this!" the woman screamed again as she pushed her way toward us and grabbed me, throwing me to the side. "You are a worthless human!"

Growls echoed around me as the three of the guys turned toward her in a menacing way.

"You dare touch what is mine!" James all but roared as I slowly made my way back toward them. His wolf was on the brink of breaking through as I tried to shush him and calm him down.

"Please, let's not do this here," I pleaded with them, "she isn't worth it. Let's just go. Please."

A grip on my hair pulled me back, and I realized quickly that the woman had a hold of me. Turning in her grasp, I lashed out, punching her in her face. Pain radiated through my hand as I realized I had just hit this she-wolf.

"You stupid bitch!" she roared as she tried to lunge at me again, only to be grabbed by an older man with graying hair.

Everyone seemed to freeze at the man's arrival–all but me.

"Enough of this," he replied firmly as he stared at the woman, "you disrespect me with your actions, Shamira."

"Father," she choked out, "she hit me... you have to punish her."

"I saw everything through the camera, Shamira. You started this, and now you will go." Shaking his head, he shoved her toward a security guard who dragged her out of the private lounge. His eyes slowly trailed back toward me.

"I apologize for my daughter's behavior. I have spoiled her too much in life. Are you okay, my dear?" he asked me with nothing but sincerity in his eyes.

"Yes," I replied with a nod before turning to look at James, Damian, and Hale.

They were unmoving and firm in their place as the man's eyes wandered over me before glancing toward them. "I hope that my daughter's actions have not caused ill blood between us."

"She attacked my mate—" James snarled but stopped as I held my hand up.

"There is no ill blood between us, sir. What's done is done, and we will be leaving the city tomorrow. I do apologize for the inconvenience we have caused you."

My response causes a smile to line his face as he clasps his hands in front of him and nods before looking at the guys. "You have a fine, Luna. The goddess has blessed you all with her presence."

"Thank you for your hospitality. We are very blessed to have her," Damian finally said, speaking up as James wrapped his arm around me and pulled me away to let them talk.

I knew full well he was trying to rein his wolf in that wanted blood, but at the same time, we couldn't lash out when we were in someone else's territory. I was glad that he had controlled himself. I didn't want a war caused because of me.

"Are you okay?" Hale's voice said from behind me, causing James and me to stop.

Turning slowly, I looked at him, blinking back tears. "Will you come with us?"

"I don't..." he sighed, trying to find the words I didn't want him to say—questions of whether he had ever actually loved me swirling through my mind.

"I'm sorry." I replied, not waiting another moment to hear him as I pulled away from James and pushed my way through the crowd till I hit the cool air of the night.

My main objective had been to come and get the men I loved, and instead, I was faced with sights I hadn't wanted to see. Damian was in the arms of another woman, and Hale didn't want me.

Hale, a man I loved, didn't want me after everything that had happened.

My mind was fogged over with thoughts as a black sedan pulled up to the curb, and James came out, ushering me inside it. All I wanted to do was to go home. I had hoped finding Hale would have been as it was with James, but I was so wrong.

I had lost him, and that killed me.

As for Damian... could I trust him after what had happened?

I wasn't sure, but part of me wanted to believe he wasn't trying to hurt me.

Walking back into the suite we were staying in, I headed straight for my room. I didn't want to see anyone, and the last thing I wanted to do was talk. My head was a swirling mess of confusion over what had happened.

"Ivy!" Damian's voice called out as the sound of the front door opened. "Ivy?"

"Will you shut the fuck up?" James snapped as the sound of his bedroom door opened.

"Where is she?" Damian replied, and as I sat in my room, I couldn't help but sigh.

I had gone out to find Damian and Hale to bring them both home and instead, I was met with chaos and heartache. Damian and Hale had both been in the arms of other women, and my heart clenched at the fact they didn't seem to care for me.

As tears streamed down my face, I quickly wiped them away only to have my bedroom door thrown open and Damian's dark eyes staring down at me.

"Ivy, please let me explain—"

"No," I snapped, shaking my head. "Your actions spoke louder than words, and I don't think there is anything for you to say to change my mind."

The sobs I fought to hold back tore at me. I had given myself to him and was falling in love with the idea of all of them being mine, and yet he did this to me.

"Stop it," he growled. "You're going to listen to me. That was all an act. I had to make her think things were okay with us so that I could find Hale. Otherwise, we would never have found them."

Stunned by his confession, I couldn't help but feel that there were things he was leaving out.

"Did you kiss her?" I asked him.

"What?" he was taken aback by my question, but at the same time, I had to know.

"Did. You. Kiss. Her?"

Laughter escaped him as he shook his head. "I don't see how that is relevant."

It was clear, though, that the answer to my question was yes. "So you did. Guess you will do anything to stay undercover, then. Especially since you and she have a very close history."

"Who the fuck told you that?" he growled angrily. "Did James tell you that?"

"No, actually, he didn't before you act stupid," I replied, crossing my arms over my chest.

"Then who?" Standing to my feet, I ignored his demand and walked toward my doorway where he stood.

"Get out of my room, Damian," I argued, holding myself together as I tried to close the door. Only to be stopped by his firm grip on the frame and a cold glare in his eyes.

"We're not done talking."

"Damian, perhaps you should listen to her. Tonight has been eventful enough," Hale called out from just out of my sight and pushing past Damian, I stepped into the hallway to see him standing there looking at me.

"You came?" I questioned, trying to understand why he had decided to leave.

Nodding, he sighed before bringing the bottle of whiskey to his lips. "Yep. Call it curiosity."

Watching him, I could tell that the Hale I once knew was gone. No longer was the sexy, happy man I had fallen for in my presence. But instead was a man who had grown cold.

"You don't love me anymore, do you?" I asked softly, staring at him. I wasn't sure what I hoped for, but it wasn't a cold glance and a small laugh as he shook his head slightly as if unsure of how to answer.

"It's hard to love someone who was never really yours, isn't it?"

The answer painfully tore at my heart, and not wanting to let them see me cry, I turned and walked into my room, slamming the door behind me.

How could I have been so foolish to think that things would be different this time?

Damian

Never did I want things to be this way.

The moment she had walked into the club, I knew I fucked up thinking I could have things the way I wanted. Thinking that she wouldn't come seek me out because that was who Ivy was.

She was beautiful. The most beautiful woman in the room, and I broke her heart.

I didn't need the mate bond to tell me I had. What killed me the most was the look she had when she saw Hale. She had waited for days to find him, and her excitement was crushed when he acted as if she was nothing but a problem.

My wolf howled at me to punish him for hurting our mate.

"You fucking idiots," James snapped as I stepped into the living room with Hale beside me.

"Watch your mouth, James," I growled. "You have no idea the problem you caused."

Laughter escaped his lips as he clenched his fists, "I caused? I didn't fucking cheat on her."

"Neither did I!" I sneered. Looking toward Hale, I watched as he took a seat on the sofa, softly laughing to himself. "What's so funny?"

As his eyes met mine, he raised a brow. "The fact you two are fighting over a woman who doesn't belong to us. The bond is broken, and you told us to move on, Damian, so what are we doing here?"

His complete disregard for her angered me. I didn't understand why he was acting the way he was because it was completely out of character for him.

"Because the bond wasn't exactly broken. The bond is still there. She gets to choose whether she wants a normal life or she wants us as her mates. We were given a second chance."

My words seemed to confuse him as he leaned forward on his knees, shaking his head. "What are you talking about? That isn't possible."

"It's true," James finally spoke up. "That's why I was able to mark her."

"Why didn't you mark her then, Damian?" Hale asked me, causing a deep breath to escape my lips as I ran my hand through my hair.

"Because I messed things up the first time, and I wanted all of you to mark her first before I did."

My confession swirled in the air, and as Hale leaned back into the sofa once more, I could see he was contemplating what I told him. As if my words were believable, but then they weren't.

"So after everything that happened, you expect me to forget the pain I went through and act like we are one happy family again?" he questioned while glancing between James and me.

"I don't expect you to do anything for me. I expect you to think of her. She gave up a normal life to be with us and even put off finishing school to come find you all since you took off. She loves you, and she didn't break the bond. That was my fault."

"You're right!" Hale snapped. "It is your fucking fault, Damian."

"I don't need you acting like this. Just fucking go see her," I growled, trying to control myself. I had given my brothers too much leeway over the years to speak to me however they wanted, and I was growing tired of it.

"No," Hale said flatly as he continued to drink. "I don't think I will."

James gasped at Hale's remark, looking at him wide-eyed. "What? Why?"

"Because I don't trust the bond the "goddess" supposedly bestowed upon us. I won't allow myself to be hurt again by some woman. I tried once, and Ivy is everything that I want in a woman, but I won't be a fool again."

Selfish. That was all Hale was.

Turning on my feet, I stormed off toward the front door and slammed it behind me as I exited. I couldn't believe we had come all this way for Hale to act this way.

Talon, I expected it, but Hale... there was no way.

He was so scared and torn up about what had happened before that he couldn't move past it to see the truth. In the end, Ivy was the one who would suffer for it.

The only thing giving me hope was that he would come back to the suite with me. Perhaps there was a chance he could change his perspective being around us. Perhaps there was a chance that he would come back to the states with us.

Only time would tell in the end. For now, I will try to keep my distance from him.

Heated Connections

Hale

Seeing her walk into the club was like a dream.

Too many times in my sleep had I seen her walking back to me, and as much as my heart wanted it to be true, I knew it wasn't possible. She had been torn away from me, and I lived with that pain daily. I just was shocked it hadn't killed me.

"You have to give it a chance, Hale," James said softly as I stared at the front door. Damian had walked through it in a huff, and I was left confused, showing no emotion.

"I don't think that's possible," I said under my breath as I watched James from the corner of my eye shake his head and go toward his room.

My thoughts swirled over the night's events, and memories of Ivy flooded over me.

I could almost taste her on my tongue the first time I ever kissed her. Her pouty pink lips waiting for me in the next room to take once more. Yet, I doubt taking the forefront of any desire I had lingering for her.

With a heavy breath, I laid back on the sofa and closed my eyes. My mind, begging for release.

By the time my eyes opened again, darkness had surrounded us completely. I wasn't sure what time it was but listening carefully, I could tell Damian had come back at some point and he and the others were sound asleep.

Moving to my feet, I walked down the hall toward the bathroom, but as soon as I got to her door, I couldn't help but hesitate. My curiosity begged me to open her door and see her again.

Taking a deep breath, I exhaled and did just that. I pushed the door open and quietly stepped into her darkened room. The smell of her perfume wrapped around me as I pushed forward.

My eyes settled on her petite sleeping form, stirring my wolf.

Slowly, I stepped forward and watched her. How was it that this woman could affect me as much as she did? It was something I would never understand.

She was my biggest weakness, and yet at the same time, my greatest asset.

Ivy

Running. I always seemed to be running, and as I was I could see him. The beautiful wolf I had grown to admire no matter how much he was thought to be dangerous.

"Talon!" I called out, watching as the wolf looked at me with a pained expression and then fought off something that seemed to be trapping him. I didn't understand what was happening, but as I ran through the snow-covered forest I called out to him again. "Talon, please wait!"

It was of no use though. The more I ran and the harder I tried the slower I became.

A heavy weight seemed to fall over me that didn't make any sense, and with it, I felt helpless to the situation. But the sensation I was being watched chilled me to my bones.

Letting my eyes scan the forest I waited for whatever it was to attack. The only problem was I felt myself being pulled, and as I was I realized something—it was only another dream.

The same dream I had been having for the past few nights, only this time, it felt more real.

Something was pulling me back to reality, and I felt him before I opened my eyes.

The smell of his cologne woke me from my slumber as I slowly opened my eyes to see him standing next to my bed, looking down at me.

"Hale?" I whispered, causing him to startle and step backward. "Don't go."

"Why, Ivy?" he asked with more vulnerability in his voice than I had expected.

I was confused by his question, and as I sat up in the bed, I stared at him. "Why what?"

"Why did you come here?"

"Because," I sighed. "I want you with me. The bond... it isn't broken, and I don't want a life without you, Hale. I need you with me."

There was no hesitation in my response. It was all true, and I had to have him realize that no part of me ever wanted to lose him. It wasn't my choice, and despite the opportunity to run from them, I didn't.

"You don't know what you're saying," he replied firmly. "You had the chance to be free, and live a life as a human does. Being with us will take all of that from you."

I was aware of what he was saying, and regardless of all of it, I didn't care.

"I know. Yet, I still came." Standing to my feet, I moved toward him, but as I approached, he recoiled. He didn't want me touching him, and I knew why.

"You shouldn't have come, Ivy," he said, causing me to halt in my steps. My heart, already broken, couldn't take much more, but at the same time, I could see it would be difficult for him to know the truth unless I did one thing...

Before he could move again, I moved forward quickly and wrapped my arms around his waist, holding him tight against me in a hug. The feeling of him in my arms once more warmed me and brought tears to my eyes.

For a moment earlier, I never thought I would feel this again.

Hale was stiff at first, but slowly he melted within my touch. His hands went to my face as he raised my eyes to meet his. Tears lined them as they slowly slid down his cheeks.

"I didn't want to believe they were telling the truth," he sobbed quietly. "How..."

Smiling, my own tears began to fall, and I shook my head. "I don't know, Hale."

It only took a moment for his lips to captivate my own, and with the kiss, I felt my heart swell with love, realizing that in some way I had him back. I had the man who made me swoon, and fall over and over again... back in my life.

"Please don't leave me again," he whispered, leaning his head against my own.

"I won't—" I cried, giving a soft laugh. "I promise, Hale. I won't leave again."

There was a moment of silence between us before the door burst open, and James and Damian stood there staring at us with smiles on their faces.

"Oh, thank fuck for that," James replied, letting out a sigh of relief. "For a moment there, I thought you really were fucking going to blow us off."

Turning in Hale's grasp, I stopped short when he pulled me against him tightly again. His eyes met mine as he shook his head no. I knew that he wasn't ready to let go of me, and I was fine with that. I would do whatever he wanted to make him feel comfortable.

"I'm not saying I understand all of this completely, and that I agree with the prophecy, but I am willing to give it one last try. As you said, Damian, this is for her. Not us."

Damian nodded at Hale, and a bit of uncertainty filled me. I wasn't sure what he meant by that, but I was happy that Hale was at least giving something a chance.

"Good," Damian finally said after a moment, "because we have problems back home and we need to get back."

"We can't yet... we have to find Talon," I gasped, looking at James and Damian with confusion.

"Ivy," Damian replied, shaking his head.

Fear swept through me. I needed them all. "No!" I screamed, "we have to find him. He needs me... I can tell. Talon needs me. I have to find him."

There was nothing but panic in my voice. For too many nights I had dreamt of Talon, and through those dreams, I could tell he was in pain, and the anger he felt was uncontrollable.

Perhaps, they had been dreams, but I couldn't just let that be it. I needed him just as much as I needed the others.

"Ivy," Hale said softly in my ear. "I will make sure we find him, but Damian is right. We have to go home first, and then we can look for him."

James nodded in agreement as he stood with his eyes crossed, looking at me.

It was pointless to argue against all three of them, at the end of the day their word was final.

By the time we had made it back to the states, I was more than worn out. The plane ride hadn't been like the others, and as much as I wished it would have been, I couldn't help but think that was partially my fault.

I wasn't as forthcoming as I was before.

"We're here," Hale whispered softly in my ear as I looked up at him. I was still pressed firmly against him in the back seat of the car as we drove from the airport to the pack house.

"Finally," I replied, "I can't wait to get out of this car and stretch my legs."

There was an eerie silence as the car came to a slow stop. All three of the guys were sitting up straight before looking at each other. "When we stop, Ivy, I want you to stay in the car."

"What?" I asked with confusion. "Why?"

"Just for once, please do as you're told. Please," Damian replied with a sigh as my eyes met Hales, and he nodded in agreement.

"Okay. I'll stay in the car."

Slowly the car moved forward more, but as it stopped, I finally got a glimpse of what was worrying them. Allison and my father stood with a group of older men at the front of the pack house, and a smirk adorned Allison's face.

"What the fuck is she doing here?" I snapped in anger as she stared at the car with amusement.

"I don't know, Ivy," Damian replied, "but just please stay here. We don't want you to get hurt."

Knowing that Allison was here, I couldn't make any promises to him, but one thing was for sure, I would wait and see what happened first.

All three of the guys exited the car and started talking to those present. Voices were raised, and glares were being thrown. However, when Allison slapped Hale in the face, I about lost my shit. Ignoring what they said, I jumped from the car. "Lay your fucking hand on them again, and I'll kill you myself, bitch."

Laughter erupted in the crowd as the group stared at me. "Oh, this little human has jokes, doesn't she?"

James was quickly at my side as he looked down at me, shaking his head. "Why don't you ever listen?" He smirked.

"Hey, I did listen. Until she touches what is mine," I murmured as I watched her say something the guy next to her.

"Why is this human even here?" Allison yelled, "she is nothing to this pack and should be long gone. There is no bond anymore!"

Pushing past James, his arms wrapped around my waist as I glared at her and pulled down the collar of my shirt to expose James' mark. "The bond isn't gone, dumbass. The rules just changed."

Shock ran through the woman, and seeing this sent pleasure through my chest. I had something on her that she wasn't aware of, and I planned to complete the prophecy. Regardless of what Damian and Hale had done... they were both still mine.

"That isn't possible!" she yelled. "It's a trick!"

The men with her didn't seem to be very enthusiastic about how Allison was acting. Her desperate attempts to cause issues were irrelevant. "Allison, enough," one of the men said.

"Ivy, this is the elder council," Damian said in a professional manner.

"Hello," I said softly with a smile. "It's a pleasure to meet you all, but what are you doing here?"

An older graying man stepped toward me, and as he did, James' grip tightened as Hale moved closer. "Calm down. I'm not going to hurt her. I just want to see the mark."

"Oh!" I exclaimed with my cheeks blushing, "of course. Here you go."

Pulling down my collar, I allowed the man to take a closer look, but never once did he touch it. Instead, he stepped back and turned to Damian. "We will be on our way. I do expect to see you all at the next meeting in two months."

Damian nodded his head with a small smile. "Of course, Elder Don. We wouldn't miss it."

Allison and my father still stood speechless as the men gathered into their vehicles and drove away. The pleasure of knowing that whatever she was trying wasn't going to work.

"Ivy?" my father called. "Can we talk?"

"No, we can't," I snapped, "you made it clear what you think about me, and I have nothing to say to you. Both of you need to leave right now!"

I was pissed, but at the same time, I was hurt. I couldn't believe that my own father had done what he did to me and still tried to let his wife hurt me. She was an evil bitch, and I wanted nothing to do with her. At the end of the day, she needed to leave us alone.

"Who do you think you're talking to?" she snapped at me as she took a step closer, only to be stopped by Damian, who stood quickly in front of me.

"If you touch her, Allison, I will kill you," Damian growled in a protective manner as James and Hale stood by, protecting me as well. I didn't need them to protect me, but at the same time, their actions made my heart swell.

"You will regret making this decision, Damian," she warned, "things are not going to end up the way you're hoping."

I wasn't sure what she was hinting at, but I didn't like the sound of her warning. There was a glint in her eyes that made my stomach knot. Yet, Damian said nothing as she and my father turned and got into their car, and left.

How were things supposed to get better for the five of us if we were still having to deal with Allison's issues? Damian sighed as he turned to face me. "Let's get you inside."

Nodding my head, I followed behind him, and Hale with James at the rear. The feeling of having them all around me was comforting, but at the same time, it didn't feel complete yet.

I needed Talon.

"Why don't you freshen up, and we can get some food and hang out for a bit," James whispered in my ear from behind, causing me to blush.

"That sounds wonderful, but... there is a problem," I admitted, watching as all eyes turned to me.

"What's wrong now?" Damian sighed, brushing his hand over his face.

"First off... don't be an ass," I said, rolling my eyes, "I was merely going to ask what room I'm staying in. I don't want to be presumptuous about my accommodations. Unless you want me back in my cottage?"

Hale's eyes widened as he shook his head. "No, no. Come with me, and I will show you where to go while James and Damian sort some things out."

Laughter escaped my lips as Hale gestured toward the stairs, and I caught a glimmer of amusement on James' face. He could sense my emotions, and even though I once found it invasive—I was growing fond of it.

'Perhaps you should have some fun with him,' James replied through the link, causing me to smirk.

'Perhaps I will, but the more, the merrier..."

There was no doubt about what I was hinting at, but I had a feeling the answer would be no.

'As much as I want to, I think you need time alone with Hale,' he replied.

'I know, but he doesn't want that with me right now. He seems scared.' I sighed.

'Then entice his wolf, Ivy.'

The suggestion was one I hadn't thought about before, and perhaps he was right.

Following Hale down the hallway, he stopped outside of the master bedroom and opened the door. "Damian told me he had this fixed for you while you guys were gone. This will be your room."

Confusion filled me at Hale's words, and as I passed the threshold, my eyes widened. A huge bed lay against the far wall, bigger than any king-size bed I have ever seen. White thick blankets on top of it and an abundance of pillows. The entire room had a feminine feel and completely depicted my personality.

My heart swelled with love and appreciation as I gasped, and tears filled my eyes. "He did this for me?"

"Yeah, he isn't as bad as you and others think. Damian just has had a hard time believing in love, but I can already tell that around you, he is changing. He isn't as cold as he used to be."

"I'm beginning to see that," I replied as a heavy breath escaped me, "thank you for coming home, Hale," I said as I turned to face him. "I can't do this without you."

A soft chuckle escaped him as he turned to leave. "I will let you take a shower."

James' comment ran through my mind again as I quickly reached out and grabbed his wrist. "Wait. Don't leave just yet."

"Did you need something else?" he asked with confusion.

I needed him, but I couldn't lead that way. He was still so temperamental, and like James said, I had to entice his wolf if I wanted him to play.

"I uh–just don't want to be left alone. Will you wait in here for me to finish?"

There was evident hesitation in his eyes as he cleared his throat and forced a smile as he nodded.

"Uh, sure. I will just wait on the bed."

Smiling, I tried to get my nerves under control. I wasn't the type of girl to be super outgoing, but I had to learn to be comfortable around them. After all, they were my mates.

Slowly, I began to undress, bit by bit, as his eyes widened slightly, watching me. "Ivy—"

"What is it, Hale?" I feigned innocence as I pulled off my shirt and slowly slid down my shorts until I was just in my bra and panties. "Is something the matter?"

"What are you doing?" he asked, looking slightly uncomfortable.

"Getting undressed for the shower?" I asked, confused, as I raised a brow with a smile. "I can't shower fully dressed.

Reaching around, I unclasped my bra, letting it drop to the floor as his eyes darted to my bare breasts. The gold in his eyes flickered as his wolf slowly fought for the surface.

"I think I should wait downstairs—" he replied with more hesitation as he started to get up.

"Oh, stop," I scoffed with a smile. "I'll go into the bathroom. Never thought you would be one to get all soft around me being naked, Hale. You have seen me naked a few times and even had sex with me."

Shit. I thought that would have worked, but it didn't. Turning toward the bathroom, I moved toward the shower and turned the water on. 'It isn't working. He was going to leave.'

James' laughter echoed through my mind, causing me to groan. 'So, play with yourself and make him stay. His wolf will love it.'

'I'm starting to think this is wrong, James.' I groaned internally. 'It hurts that he doesn't want me.'

'Oh, he does. Trust me on that. He just needs a shove.'

Stepping into the shower, I thought about what he told me to do. 'For some reason, I have a feeling you are going to get me into trouble.'

'Oh, don't worry, babe.' James laughed. 'You are going to like it.'

Secrets of Darkness

'You will enjoy it.'

Those few words that James told me through the link had me hesitating. Yet, as the hot water streamed down over my body, I took the initiative. The bathroom door was open, and I knew without a doubt he had a clear view of me.

Even if he was choosing not to look.

Slowly, I let my hand slide down between my thighs as I cleaned myself. My mind drifted toward the erotic feeling that each of the men gave me. Hale, though, was unlike the others.

The first time he fucked me, I came undone with his teasing and forceful pleasure. Yet, I knew he was holding back. As if back then, he was worried about hurting me.

The more my fingers stroked over my sensitive, swollen clit, the more soft moans began to leave my lips, and as they did, it was when I heard something I wasn't expecting.

A low growl from the bedroom sounded more dangerous than I had expected. I wasn't sure what to expect, but the faster and faster I pleasured myself, the deeper the growl got until Hale finally spoke.

"Stop!" He growled as the shower door was ripped open, and I stood beneath the hot water panting as he stared down at me.

"You have... no idea how hard I am trying to control myself right now."

"Then don't." My comment came out quicker than I expected, and his eyes quickly glossed over as if asking someone to come help him. "They won't help you," I smirked as his gaze came back to me.

"Oh, I don't expect them to." He laughed as he grabbed me roughly by the arm and dragged me from the shower. My heart hammering in my chest as panic slowly crept within me, unsure of what was about to happen.

"Hale," I gasped, "what are you doing?"

Tossing me upon the bed, I landed soaking wet in the center as I watched him exit the room for a moment and come back with James. James' eyes met mine, and they darkened over as a sinister smirk crossed his face. "Are you ready?"

"Ready... for what?!" I exclaimed as Hale gripped my ankle, dragging me toward him as I panicked to get away.

"The more you struggle, the rougher it will be."

The dark sultry reply went straight to my core, and as it did, he inhaled deeply and sighed before catching my eyes. "Do you want to know a secret, Ivy?"

Looking at Hale, I hesitated. "What?"

"We have a special talent rare to most wolves in our area. Something about our bloodline that you would have learned about later, but right now... it's going to happen sooner."

Unzipping the bag, he flipped me over and gestured toward James, who climbed onto the bed and gripped my wrists, holding them down. "James, what are you doing? This isn't funny."

"Do you trust me, Ivy?" He smiled.

"Yes," I replied without hesitation, "of course I do."

Leaning forward, he kissed me slowly before pulling away. "Good, then let what is about to happen. I will warn you; the twins are more attuned with this side of us than Damian or I."

Something cold and hard came in contact with my bare ass, a stinging sensation running through me as I realized that Hale had just whipped me with something. Gripping at the sheets, I struggled against James as it came again.

A cry escaped me as pleasure rushed straight to my core. "Hale—" I moaned.

"Do you want more?" he asked, and James' eyes twinkled, waiting for my response.

Hales's fingers rubbed against the folds of my core driving me crazy for more. "Yes—"

Another smack and my arousal was dripping down my legs. "I knew from the day I met you, you were into the same things I was."

"Is that right?" I smiled, biting my bottom lip, "can I show you something?"

I couldn't see his face, but I felt his hand brushing over the marks he had just created.

"What's that?" Hale asked.

"You have to let me up first, so I can show you..." I taunted with a singsong voice and a soft moan.

'What are you doing?' James asked through the link, causing me to smile.

'Let me go, and you will find out,' I taunted again, watching the confliction in his eyes.

'Don't run... whatever you do... don't run. Hale's wolf isn't like mine or Damian's. He and Talon's wolves are dangerous when they want to be.'

James' words lingered in my mind, and slowly he released me with nothing but gestation as his eyes glazed over. No doubt telling Damian something.

Turning to face Hale, I watched the pitch black of his eyes stare down at me with intrigue as I stepped forward, running my finger over his chest. "I know that you and your wolf share a mindset, Hale. Can I ask his name?"

Narrowing his brows, he slowly raised one with curiosity. "Liekos."

"Liekos," I said softly with a smile, "does your wolf like me?"

"Yes." He said with a heavy breath as he watched me walk around him.

"Ivy," James said again in a tone laced with warning, "tread lightly."

My eyes slowly went to James, who was sitting on the bed, watching me intently. Always the worrier, but right now, I knew he was being serious. I didn't know what the secret was that he was going to tell me, but I wanted to know.

I wanted to know everything about them. "I will make you a deal, Liekos..."

'Stop talking to his wolf, Ivy,' James quickly said through the link. The warning fell on deaf ears as I watched Hale tilt his head to the side.

"What's that?" Hale replied, but for some reason, his voice was much rougher. More animalistic.

Taking a few steps back, I trailed my fingers over hardened erect nipples, "if you can catch me Liekos... you get to have me."

Turning quickly, I bolted from the room naked and ran down the hall. James' screamed "Ivy, no" behind me as a roar erupted from the room that shook me to my core.

'Run!!' James yelled through the link. 'I told you not to do that!'

Fear suddenly escaped through me as I ran toward the stairs, taking them two at a time as the office door flew open, and Damian's panicked face looked at me with shock.

"Ivy, what the fuck did you do?"

"I–I don't know. We were just having fun. I don't understand what's wrong," I said breathlessly.

"We aren't normal wolves, Ivy. We are mixed. It's—fuck, I don't have time to explain. I will hold him off. Run toward the cottage now, and lock the doors."

I didn't waste another moment as I heard the commotion upstairs and took off running toward the back door. My hand ripped it open as I pushed through the door, my bare feet hitting the grass with a fury. I didn't care that I was naked or if anyone could see me.

I had to get away, and I had to hide fast.

Two sets of roars escaped the house as I heard a crash. I knew for a fact one was Damian, but the other—it was otherworldly.

"Oh, shit!" For once in my life, maybe I need to start listening to what people tell me.

Approaching my cottage, I stopped and turned just in time to see Hale burst through the back door. The only problem was he didn't look like the Hale I knew.

Instead, he was taller and almost as if he had partially shifted into his wolf. Long canines over his lips and claws at the end of his fingers. "What in the hell?"

My breathless reply didn't go unnoticed as his eyes landed on mine, and a roar escaped him again. One that rattled through my chest straight to my heart.

Throwing open the cottage door, I darted inside and shut it behind me, locking it in place before escaping into my bedroom and hiding.

I was terrified, but at the same time, something inside me was exhilarated.

This was the secret they were talking about—the one I wasn't supposed to know yet.

I had taunted his wolf, and something else came to play.

Something that wanted to ravage me in a way that aroused me.

"Ivy."

A taunting voice called from outside the cottage, followed by a scratching sound that made me bite my bottom lip. "Why are you hiding from me?"

As much as I wanted to reply, I couldn't. Instead, I remained quiet, and with my silence, I heard the cottage door crash open—his thundering steps echoed over the flooring as he stepped inside.

"Are we playing hide and seek?" he chuckled deeply.

There weren't many places to hide in my cottage. The distant voices of James and Damian echoed outside. "Hale!"

Holding my breath, I watched Hale's shadow from the closet door. He knew where I was, and as the doors flew open. I tried to push past him, only to be snatched by sharp claws and pulled back. A cry escaped my lips as he chuckled. "Why are you running? You said you wanted to play with me."

"Hale, what are you doing?" I whined as I looked up into two dark, swirling eyes. "How are you shifted like this?"

"Because I'm not Hale... well, technically not."

Confusion laced my mind as I tried to come to terms with what he was saying. He was Hale... his human form was present, but small characteristics had changed, and with them, something else came forward.

A more primal side of him took the forefront.

"What do you want?" I asked breathlessly as his tongue slid over my neck before tossing me onto the bed. I was turned on at the moment... To know he and his wolf had a need only I could fulfill, and as he stood over me, I waited.

Waited for him to pounce... waited for him to take me.

The swollen and sensitive mound between my thighs ached, and with every movement, my thighs teased me, begging for a release only he could give me.

"You should have listened to them," he said with a predatory gaze that caused fear to creep in slowly. "You shouldn't have run."

Before I knew it, I was pinned beneath him as his lips met mine. The kiss was not as before, and his touch was not soft at all. Most women would have screamed, but me... I didn't.

I was utterly entranced by what he was doing to me, and as his thick erection parted my folds, impaling me... all I could do was moan in pleasure.

I was his to do as he wanted, and the voices of Damian and James were distant in the fog of pleasure that clouded my mind.

Hale's hand gripped my throat as he fucked me with a force no human man could ever compete with, and cries of pleasure escaped my lips over and over again.

"Oh, shit!" I screamed as he flipped me over and slipped himself back in from behind. The penetration was deep and slightly painful. Yet, it was nothing compared to the sensation of the knot at the base of his cock swelling and pushing against my walls.

"I can't–" I whimpered as he held me down. His lips trailed over my neck as he created more arousal within me.

"You are mine, Ivy. Say it. Say you are mine."

"I'm yours—" I replied breathlessly. "Make me yours." Overloaded to the max, I tried to pull myself together, but his whispered words in my ear stopped me cold.

"Oh, I will. And as I empty myself, you will carry the future." The voice wasn't normal and panicking, I realized it was that of his wolf.

"Wait, what—" Elongated teeth bit down at the base of my neck, and pleasure flooded through me as I screamed, coming undone as I felt the pressure of his release settle deep within my womb.

I didn't care at that moment what he meant anymore. I was willing to surrender to his desires.

Desires that made my heart flutter as darkness slowly crept into my vision. I wasn't sure what the future would hold, but as my eyes began to close, I saw the creature within the darkness—a force unlike anything I could have imagined.

It was a beast waiting to be released. A force of nature that didn't fit with the world we were currently in and none of it made sense.

'Ivy.' It called out in a soothing voice that wrapped around me like velvet. 'I have been waiting for you.'

Fear spiraled through me as my heart began to race. The beast in the darkness stalked toward me slowly as if it owned me. Yet, even though fear was there, I wasn't entirely afraid.

The creature was more familiar to me than I understood, and something deep down inside my soul recognized it. Something deep inside me was calling to it, and as it did, the creature reached for me, plunging me into a dark abyss of constant pleasure and comfort.

Was this the end... or was it simply the beginning of something new?

Something that could potentially destroy us all if we weren't careful.

James

Bursting through the door, I watched as Hale slowly became himself again. His eyes flickered for a moment as he looked at me and then down at Ivy, whose beautiful neck was now lined with another mark next to mine.

His mark... his claim on her.

"You didn't," I gasped, realizing what it meant that he had laid with her in that form. He had claimed her and mated with her in a way that very well could produce a child by the end of a year.

"Oh, fuck–" he said as he realized what I was talking about. "I–I didn't mean to."

Heavy footsteps echoed behind me, and as I turned, I took in Damian's dark glaring eyes assessing the situation. Hale slowly moved as his knot released and grabbed a blanket, laying it over Ivy's now sleeping form.

The mating process took every last bit of energy from her.

"What's done is done," Damian replied firmly through gritted teeth. "She is one with you both now, and it can not be undone as it was before."

"Damian, why haven't you claimed her?" Hale finally asked as I grabbed a pair of shorts from a stash in her closet we had left weeks before and tossed them at him.

"I have given my reasoning before," he sighed. "You all deserve to have her before I make my claim. As should have been done in the past."

"We need to find Talon," I interrupted, causing them both to turn to me before nodding in agreement.

Finding Talon would be a problem. After losing Ivy, he had gone off the radar and stayed to his animalistic side. A side that was hard to reach at times, considering how out-of-control Talon was.

"No matter what we do... you, Hale, can not let that happen again. You have controlled that side of you for years. What the fuck happened up there?"

Damian's scolding question caught Hale by surprise, and I knew I was at fault for what happened, as well as Ivy. I pushed her to do what she did but never did I think that Hale would have lost it.

"It's my fault," I whispered, causing them both to look at me. "Ivy wanted you, Hale, and I could feel how bad it was breaking her to not be with you. To have you so indifferent to her. She expects it from Damian but not from you. So I pushed her to do what she did."

"I knew it!" He yelled as he stormed toward me and shoved me against the wall. "I could have killed her, James!"

"Enough!" Damian roared, causing us both to back down. "I will not tolerate any more of this shit in my pack. We are stronger together, and I will not have us divided. I said what I said, what's done is done."

Damian was more than serious, and I was well aware of what he had to say. "What would you like to do about Ivy?"

His eyes cast down to her as he shook his head, "take her to the room and lay her down. Whatever happens though, from here on out, she can not be a part of retrieving Talon. Especially if the goddess takes pleasure in our situation, and she does become pregnant."

I didn't miss the way his eyes darted to Hale with swirling blackness as he said pregnant.

Yes, she belonged to all of us. However, the Alpha wolf in him wanted to have that right first.

It was about dominance and control. Even if she was shared, his wolf didn't care.

"Of course," I muttered as I walked toward her and lifted her sleeping form in its blanket.

My wolf howled in protest in the back of my mind to the danger lurking around us. I wasn't sure what it was, but the pacing he was doing caused me to grit my teeth as pain radiated through my skull.

'Mate.' It whined as if to try and tell me something was wrong with Ivy.

A feeling of despair slowly grew within the pit of my stomach as nausea swept through me.

"I think something is wrong," I whispered, causing Damian to look at me with concern.

"What do you mean something is wrong?"

Shaking my head, I looked at him with confusion, "I don't know... Just something isn't right."

Our eyes lingered on Ivy's sleeping form in my arms. Her hair swept around her face causing her to seem more delicate than she was. "Isn't the bond the same as before?"

"No," I said softly. "Hale didn't bond with her like he did before. This was different. There is something in Ivy that is different than before, and my wolf is going crazy."

As Damian and my eyes lingered on Hale, he stood speechless. "I can't feel anything."

That isn't good. With the bond solidified between them, he should have been able to feel what I did, and yet, he couldn't.

"Take her to her room and lay her down. We will take turns keeping an eye on her. In the meantime, we need to find Talon. That has to be priority… if we don't, I have a feeling she will turn to drastic measures of trying to find him."

Nodding my head, I made my way back to the house, trying to calm the beast within my mind.

I had no doubt that she would be out for a while. The mating process with anyone was draining, but to mate with the mixed ones… well, that was sure to be more dangerous.

Family Secrets

Ivy

Two days passed since the incident with Hale, and it had become more than awkward around the house. The guys seemed content with whatever project they were working on, but I had no doubt that it had to deal with Talon.

On more than one occasion, I heard his name mentioned and even heard Damian get angry. Walking downstairs, I made my way toward the living room, my eyes landing on James, who sat reclined on the sofa watching television.

"Hey, you." I smiled, watching him turn to me with his own.

"Hey, did you sleep well?" he asked as I slid in between his legs and got comfortable.

"Yeah," I sighed. "has there been any news on Talon yet?"

A heavy breath left him as he pondered over what I was saying. I knew he didn't want to tell me what was going on, but at the same time, it was time they told me something.

"We still aren't sure—"

"Don't give me that," I snapped as I turned my eyes to his. "Don't lie to me. I know you know something. Otherwise, Damian wouldn't be as angry as he is."

"It isn't that, Ivy," he said as he kissed the side of my head. "There are other problems going on, too. Allison is trying everything she can to get you and us removed from our positions. Saying that we are playing with the political aspects of a pack and are no longer capable of leading."

This was something I knew that I hadn't heard before. A few days ago, when we arrived back, I was sure that Allison had been cast aside and was going to leave us alone.

But that would have been too easy.

"Why is she doing this?" I asked, but deep down in my chest, I knew the answer.

She didn't like me, and I was a problem in her eyes.

"Damian already told you about how she has been toward us growing up, Ivy. Everything is more complicated than you think, and he wants you to stay out of it."

"Of course he does," I groaned, rolling my eyes. Damian acted like I was a china doll and didn't want me to be part of anything. He thought he knew best and had since the day I had gotten here. "Can you at least explain to me about Hale?"

James' eyes caught mine again just as footsteps approached the living room. The devil himself appeared, and as his eyes caught mine, I could see his hesitation. "What do you want to know?" Hale asked softly.

"The truth... that's all I ever want. I don't want you lying to me or hiding things from me anymore. We should be past that type of relationship."

I didn't miss the way Hale and James looked at each other as if in some sort of unspoken language. There was more that they were hiding, but if we could start here, I wouldn't push it further.

Hale moved toward an armchair and took a seat across from us. His demeanor had changed since the first moment I saw him, and now something more sinister seemed to lurk beneath the surface.

"Our mother was a full-blooded wolf shifter. She came from this pack, actually, and her family was the original family. Yet, when my mother came of age to find her mate, she found it in the most unlikely of places," Hale said with a sigh, "she found herself mated to darkness."

"Darkness?" I questioned, furrowing my brow, "but I thought it was all about the moon and light."

Soft chuckles left the men as Hale shook his head. "No, Ivy, but that is the dream, isn't it."

"Ivy, things aren't like the stories others have told the world. Shifters are not light and happiness. We are creatures of darkness. Cursed by the moon."

I was beginning to realize that there was still so much I didn't know, and as I let it process, my eyes met Hale's once more. "You aren't darkness, Hale."

A flicker of light in the depths of his eyes seemed to spark for a moment as the corner of his lips turned up. "You always see the light in everything, don't you?"

"Maybe." I smirked, shrugging my shoulders, "continue... I want to hear it all."

Shaking his head, he sighed with a wide grin as he rubbed his hands against the tops of his thighs. "Well... my father was the darkness she found. He was mixed between a wolf shifter and something far more ancient–a Lycan. The race of Lycans died or supposedly had died, but yet something happened where the last of them mixed with wolf shifters to preserve the bloodline."

Something deep inside me understood clearly what he was saying, and my mind raced with dreams that I had had once upon a time. Dreams that were more nightmares and haunted me every time I closed my eyes.

"All of you can look like that?" I finally asked after a moment of hesitation. My eyes glossed over the three of them with curiosity.

"No, Ivy," Damian replied, "just the twins. They took after our father more, where James and I took more after our mother. It's a simple case of inherited genetics. We are stronger than most wolves, though, and our senses are far more heightened than normal shifters."

The sound of gravel outside distracted me from the conversation, and all of our eyes turned toward the front windows of the house. Kate's elegant form stepped from the car with all her badassery, and I couldn't help but smile as I jumped to my feet.

"Kate!" I squealed with excitement as I ran toward the front door. The sound of James laughing echoed behind me as I slung open the door and ran to her. "Kate!"

Pulling me into a hug, our laughter mixed as she squeezed me tight. "Hey, girlie! Oh, my god, it's so good to see you again."

"Likewise," I replied, pulling from her. "What the hell are you doing here? I thought you would have gone home."

"Yeah, well, I did. By the way, your mom looks much better since the pack doctor has taken her under his wing." She grinned, giving me a knowing look.

"MY mother?!" I gasped, "and the pack doctor?"

"Uh, huh?" She nodded as we both laughed. "Turns out that he can't get enough of her, and they have been spending a lot of time together. Her treatments are going really well, and she is doing a lot better. Figured I would let you know since I know she doesn't want you to worry."

Nodding, I smiled. "Thanks, Kate. It means a lot."

"So the party is out here, huh?" James laughed as the three men exited the house. Knowing what I did, I couldn't help but wonder if there were others like them out there. So many questions swirled within the depths of my mind, and I wanted answers.

However, those answers would have to wait for another day. They said it was a secret, and if Kate didn't know, I wouldn't tell her. After all, it wasn't my secret to tell.

As Kate conversed with James, Hale, and I, I couldn't help but notice the other man with her speaking quietly with Damian off to the side. Their hushed words were distractive, and yet I wasn't sure what they were talking about.

Whatever it was, though, Damian's eyes connected with mine for a moment, and the look he gave me was one of worry. His body was rigid, and his hands fidgeting.

Something was definitely off, and I didn't like it.

"Care to share the information with the rest of us?" I asked, placing a hand on my hip. "No secrets, remember?"

The man speaking with Damian quickly closed his mouth and looked between the two of us.

"I'm sorry. I don't think we have been introduced," he quickly replied, stepping toward me and holding his hand out. "My name is Angel. I'm Kate's mate."

"Mate?" I replied, shocked, as my wide eyes looked at a grinning Kate.

"Mhm." She laughed. "We met each other a few weeks ago."

"Oh, my god. I'm so happy for you."

"Thank you." She grinned as he wrapped his arm around her waist. "We are still trying to figure everything out, but with his job and my newfound talent, we will figure a way."

Curiosity piqued my mind as I looked at him with a smile. "Oh, what do you do for a living?"

"Oh, I'm a tracker—" he said before Kate quickly elbowed him in the stomach.

Shaking my head, I looked at Damian and the others with a smirk. "I knew it."

"Ivy–" Damian called out before I held up my hand to silence him.

"If you will excuse me, I will go get some food ready. Kate, I'm sure you both are starving after your trip."

She looked at me with hesitation before nodding. "Let me help you–"

"No, no. No need. You have business to attend to, and afterwards, we can catch up on everything else," I replied before turning on my feet and walking back inside the house.

It was obvious I was the elephant in the room, and with me around, they had to be careful of what they were saying. I didn't understand it, though, and something deep in my stomach clenched at the hidden secrets.

It had to deal with Talon. There was nothing else that they would need to hide from me.

Something was wrong, and they were afraid to tell me.

Deep down, I knew the answer, though—Talon needed me.

Taking the day to clear my mind of all the bodies that have been currently filling the pack house, I made my way into town. The need to escape the madness and find solitude in the only place I knew I could.

My favorite university.

Gripping the steering wheel of my sleek black car, I enjoyed the purring sound it made when I stepped on the gas. I had never had a car like this, and even though it wasn't top-of-the-line like the guys had—it was mine.

Flying past treelines, the car gripped the road without trouble. The silence allowed my mind to go through everything that had happened since the moment I woke up. I wasn't sure where my future would lead, but I knew deep down that what I was doing was right.

It had to be right.

Talon's whereabouts were still unknown, and with him still missing, I couldn't find the closure I so desperately needed. To top it off, James and Damian constantly fighting wasn't doing any good.

James blamed him for everything that happened, and Hale sat quietly like a loose cannon ready to explode. The chaos wasn't healthy for anyone, and if anyone should be blamed, it was me.

I was the one who came here and turned their lives upside down.

I was the one who decided to fix them and give up my chance of being normal.

They were simply following a calling. A beacon of hope that they would have the mate they had always desired, and with it... I brought more chaos.

Tears quietly slid down my cheeks as I let my bottled-up emotions free. The mess I had created broke me bit by bit, and as it did, I had the drive to fix it. I was just terrified that while I was trying to fix it, I would fuck it up even more.

Turning off of the highway, I pulled onto the main streets of town, heading toward the university. Everything in the town was more than normal, and as I spotted some of my classmates walking on campus, I couldn't help but be jealous of them.

That could have been me.

I could have been normal. I could have been so many things, but instead, I felt selfish.

Pushing back my emotions, I pulled into a parking spot on campus and dried my tears. My sole intention of coming on campus was to meet with my academic advisor and go over options to start taking classes again.

Yet, stepping out of my car, I felt weird. The last time I had been here was with Caleb, and his betrayal was a wound that still had not healed. He may have been bad, but he was desperate.

In times of desperation, we all make bad choices, and in the end, must learn to live with them.

Taking a deep breath, I pushed myself forward toward the office.

I had a goal to achieve, and once the five of us were back to normal routine, I wanted to be prepared. I wanted to be able to continue what I had started.

It was about as close as I would get to be normal.

If there was even such a thing as being normal.

Forty-five minutes later, I was given every bit of information I could possibly need to get prepared for online school. The very same type of schooling I had refused to do once before.

It was the best they could do for me, though, considering the circumstances of my immediate withdrawal a few weeks back.

"Ivy!" a voice called as I turned to see Kate smiling and waving at me from across the courtyard.

"What the heck are you doing here?" I called out as she approached me with a grin. "I thought this was just like a cover for you or something?"

Rolling her eyes, a grin lined her face. "No way. I actually like school, contrary to what most people would think and my sexy mate happens to think smart girls are cute. So it's a win-win for me."

"Well, I'm glad he approves." I laughed as I stood there soaking it in. "I have to admit, it's weird to be back here, Kate.",

"Why?" she replied with a concerned look on her face. "You love school, and getting your degree has been a goal forever."

"I know, but so much has changed since the first day I arrived here. My life was practically turned upside down, and I don't know if I'm coming or going anymore."

Pulling me in for a hug, she smiled down at me. "Well, why don't we go get coffee like old times and talk about it."

As we pulled away, I hesitated momentarily and looked toward the campus cafe. It wasn't the reason I had come here, but thinking about it, there was no way I could say no to her.

"Sure, that would be great." Turning, we headed toward the cafe as we had always done before. This time, though, we were down to two people that had usually joined us, and as if she knew what I was thinking, I watched her smile fade.

"It is weird, isn't it?" she said softly as we ordered and took a seat in our favorite booth.

"Yeah, but at least things are slowly getting back to normal—"

"Well, well. If it isn't my lucky day," a snappy voice called to my left, and as I let my eyes gaze over the figure, my blood boiled, and every part of me wanted to lash out.

"Allison," I seethed, "what brings you here to the campus? I didn't realize you were trying to finally better yourself."

All I wanted was normalcy for one day, and as always, fate didn't want to allow me to have that. Instead, I was constantly bombarded by people like Allison.

Furrowing her brows, I watched her jaw clench before a smile lined her lips. "And I didn't think you would be getting back into classes so soon. I had assumed you would have left already to go after your lost mate."

Glancing at Kate, I watched her eyes widen in shock as she stared at Allison. Her lips slightly parted as if she was unsure of what to say. "Allison, don't..."

"Don't?" Allison smirked, placing her well-manicured nails upon her hips. "Don't what?"

"Kate... what is she talking about?"

"Oh, my goddess. You guys haven't told her?" Allison scoffed, "that's pretty sad. To think I thought she was just being a bitch by not going after him. In reality... she doesn't even know."

Staring between the two of them, my heart began to race. They were hiding information from me. Information that led to Talon. "Kate, do you guys know where Talon is?"

Slowly, she nodded her head in defeat. "It's complicated."

"Complicated my ass," Allison exclaimed with disappointment before turning her attention to me. "You think I'm your enemy. You don't have the slightest clue what they are really trying to do. Perhaps you should reevaluate your mates—"

"I fucking get it!" I snapped at her, watching as her eyes widened. "You need to leave."

"What the hell?" Allison gasped as she stumbled over herself, backing away from me. "That isn't possible. It just isn't..."

Allison didn't bother to finish her sentence before her figure disappeared through the front doors of the cafe. Her departure allowed the anger to slowly subside and instead leave a trail of hurt straight to my heart. "Why?"

"Ivy–"

"No, Kate... why are you guys hiding secrets?" I asked more clearly as I turned to her, waiting for an answer. "What just happened? I don't understand."

"Well... a lot just happened," she said, letting out a heavy sigh. "One of them being what you did to her."

Taking a moment to think over what she was talking about, I frowned in confusion. "Huh?"

"Ivy," she whispered, leaning over the table toward me as she looked around, "you just used an Alpha voice on her."

A burst of laughter escaped me as I shook my head. "Don't be ridiculous. One, I'm not a wolf... and two, even if I was... I wouldn't be an Alpha."

"I don't know, man. That was pretty intense."

What she was saying made little sense, and brushing it off, I played it down to Allison overreacting. The woman was beyond irritating, and an enjoyable coffee with Kate had been ruined by the news she gave me.

"So is it true, then? You guys are hiding Talon from me?"

A wave of uneasiness seemed to seep from her before she nodded again. "Ivy, I'm so sorry. Damian said he didn't want to bother you until he knew everything one hundred percent. He didn't want to get your hopes up, and it's way more complicated than we thought before."

"What do you mean? How is it more complicated? I need to understand how finding my mate is complicated, Kate. Getting him back is my top priority."

Slowly standing to her feet, she gestured with her head for me to follow. Unsure of where she was taking me, I didn't bother to question her and instead, fell in step with her out of the cafe and back across campus.

"What are we doing?" I asked her.

"I don't want to discuss this where someone can hear us," she replied as she continued to power walk farther away..

"Uh, why? What's wrong that it's so difficult for you to tell me back there?"

Stopping in her tracks, she turned to me for a moment, and stared as if she wasn't sure she should be saying anything. The hesitation in her eyes hurt, considering how close we had gotten, but I could see her confliction clear as day.

"If I tell you, will you promise me you won't do anything stupid?" She replied with concern laced within the depths of her eyes, "I'm serious, Ivy. Nothing stupid."

Groaning, I rolled my eyes. "Fine. Jesus, just fucking tell me already."

As we walked across the courtyard and headed toward the small park across from the school, I couldn't help but wonder what was so terrible that she was finding difficulty in telling me what was wrong, and Damian, James, and Hale would hide it from me.

"Something's wrong with him, Ivy," Kate finally replied as she stopped in her tracks and looked around before her eyes once more fell on me. "He isn't normal."

I knew it. Deep down, I knew that something was wrong with him from the moment I woke up in the hospital. It was as if I could feel his pain and agony without being connected to him.

I wasn't sure why, but at the same time, I just knew.

"What's wrong with him?"

Shrugging her shoulders, she shook her head slightly with a sad look in her eyes. "We don't know, Ivy. He has become unreachable through the link, and his wolf is acting erratic.

Almost as if he has gone crazy, and his humanity is no longer there."

My heart raced hearing her words. There was no way that was possible. Things like that just didn't happen in this world. He was perfectly fine the last time I had seen him.

Storming away from her, I hurried across the street and bee-lined straight for my car.

"Ivy! What are you doing?" Kate screamed at me as I heard her footsteps quickly approaching from behind me. "You promised me—"

Spinning around, I stopped and stared at her. "I am going to see Damian. It's time they stop hiding things from me as they always do and bring me in on Talon's status. Keeping secrets isn't going to build our relationship, Kate. I'm done with it."

"Shit–" she groaned as she climbed into my passenger side and closed the door, buckling herself in. "Fine, fuck it. Let's go."

"He is going to be pissed, you told me. You know that, right?" I grinned at her. "Sure, you don't want to wait it out?"

"No, just fucking go," she sighed, "you're right. They shouldn't be hiding things from you at all."

Surprised to hear that she agreed with me, a smile crossed my face. The problem was it didn't last long because an ache in my chest grew slowly thinking over Talon.

He was alone wherever he was, and everything that had happened because of me was causing him to lose sight of himself. I needed to find out what Damian knew, and I had to force them somehow to find him.

It had to be done whether they wanted to do it or not.

I need Talon, and I know he needs me.

Bella Donna

Damian

Hearing that Talon was probably too far gone was not the news I wanted breaking to me. I had sent a group of men to the northern woods of Canada to find him, and out of the eight I had sent, only two came back.

Talon had torn them apart, and according to Ralph—he enjoyed it.

He enjoyed it so much that according to Ralph he feasted upon the fallen bodies as if he was dining at the table of the gods. A sight I was glad I didn't have to witness for myself.

No matter what Ralph said... my brother wasn't a monster.

"Damian, we have a problem," Angel stated as he quickly entered my office.

"What kind of problem?"

"The kind where Ivy knows about Talon," he replied as emphasized her name stressing the importance of the situation.

"How the fuck does she know anything?" I snapped, seething with anger as my hand slammed down upon my desk. "I made sure everyone knew not to say anything to or around her. I can't have her upset if things don't turn out right."

"I know," Angel replied looking at me with regret, "unfortunately, it was leaked to her and there is nothing that can be done with it now."

Pinching the bridge of my nose I exhaled deeply trying to wrap my head around the shit show that was about to happen. I had promised her no more secrets, and here I was, lying to her again. "How did you find out?"

"Kate mind linked me and told me they ran into Allison on campus. Allison told Ivy some things, and Kate couldn't lie to her. She hasn't told Ivy everything, but they should be here any moment, and from the sounds of it, Ivy is on a warpath."

Of course, she was. My little vixen was a force to be reckoned with, and everything about her made me proud. I just wished more than anything I could be the man she was expecting me to be.

Until we figure out Talon though I wasn't able to.

Instead, I would have to rely on James and Hale to soothe her. When this was all over though I would make sure to make it up to her. I would get her away from this place properly, and give her the relaxation that she needed.

Show her how mates should be treated. It's what she deserved.

Thinking over Angel's words I tried to understand why Allison was there. For her to be on campus she was solely seeking Ivy out. Which meant that she had inside information on Ivy, and her whereabouts at all times.

That thought alone was uncomfortable. "Angel, when Ivy gets here can I count on you to round up border patrol leaders and tell them to sweep the area and double down on security? I have a feeling we are being watched."

"Of course, Alpha," he replied, bowing his head slightly. "I will see to the task myself."

The sound of gravel beneath tires caught my attention just in time to see Ivy slamming her car door, storming toward the house with a stern gaze in her eyes.

"Shit, she's here," I muttered just as James and Hale walked into my office.

"Why is Ivy pissed?" Hale asked as the sound of someone clearing their voice caught all of our attention.

She stood there with her hands on her hips, tapping her foot with a fuck you look in her eyes. She was beyond upset with us, and I suppose she had every right to be.

"Ivy is pissed because the three of you failed to inform me about Talon. Instead, your bitch of a godmother Allison so delightfully informed me of your failure to explain Talon's dire situation. So which one of you assholes is going to start explaining first?"

Opening and closing my mouth, I tried to figure out where to start. There wasn't much I could say to make things right. "Ivy–"

Holding her figure up, she closed her eyes as she laughed. "Don't even try to deny or push the topic off me. I want you to tell me right now what is going on, Damian. I have a right to know."

"You do have a right to know," Hale interjected as he looked toward me, shaking his head. "We shouldn't keep this from her anymore."

Hale was right. We should be keeping this from her anymore, and I was a fool to think I could.

She was the Luna to this pack and in the end even the Alpha bows to his mate.

Ivy

I hadn't expected Hale to be the one to speak up first. In fact, I had expected it to be James, but for some reason, he seemed so unsure as he passed glances with Damian.

Giving a reluctant sigh, Damian shook his head and took a seat behind his desk. "Okay."

"Okay?" I asked with shock as I raised my brow. "Does that mean you will tell me everything?"

Gritting his teeth, Damian stared at me, unimpressed by my attitude. Not that I gave a shit.

He was the one heading this operation, and he was supposed to be over this kind of thing with me. We had promised each other no more secrets. To be open and honest.

Yet, here we were once again.

"Yes, I will tell you what I know," he sighed, "may I begin?"

Nodding walked toward the sofa and sat down. My legs were shaking from the adrenaline running through my body and if I wasn't careful it was going to take me to the ground.

"We did find Talon," Damian finally admitted causing my heart to swell with anticipated hope of Talon finally coming home. "... but from what we know, he has lost his way. He has taken on his more animalistic side, and with that, he isn't responding to any of us. Even Hale can't get through to him, and they are twins."

"How is that possible?" I asked, looking at Hale, "you guys have always been so close, and connected. Surely he has to be reachable."

Letting out a heavy breath, Hale's shoulders sagged. "We think he has been drugged, Ivy."

"Drugged?" Taking a moment to let what Hale said sink in, I furrowed my brows and tried to understand how a werewolf.. Or shifter, as they called it, was so easily affected by drugs when they heal so fast.

"Yes, drugged," Damian replied, "and he has killed many people in the process of trying to recover him because of this situation."

"That's not possible. You guys heal, though... like stupid fast. How can something small affect you?" Turning to Damian, I watched as a smile spread across his face."What the hell is so funny?"

"Nothing is funny, Ivy. I'm just shocked you have been researching our kind."

"Well, yeah." I shrugged. "If I'm to be your mate and the Luna of this pack, then I think it's important I learn about your kind. I actually found a bunch of books up in the spare room I had been staying in before."

"That's very progressive of you, Ivy," Damian admitted making me feel a lot less angry toward him than I had been before. "I'm impressed."

"Thanks." Even though his compliment made me smile I couldn't allow myself to get distracted. "Please... tell me everything you know. What kind of drugs affect you guys?"

"Well, there are a few, wolfsbane being one..." he replied.

"Don't forget Bella Donna and Hemlock," James added.

My brows furrowed at James' remark. "Bella Donna?"

"Yeah, it's a beautiful flower, but it's also very poisonous," James chuckled. "We don't have any of that here though. It's native to South Africa."

"Do you have a photo of it?" I asked with curiosity trying to see if it was the same flower I had seen before in the house. I knew that it was native to South Africa. I wouldn't be an agricultural student if I didn't, but that wasn't something to point out right now.

Furrowing his brow in confusion, James pulled out his phone and scrolled through it. "I don't understand what this has to do with anything."

"Yeah, Ivy... I thought you wanted to hear what we knew," Damian replied, looking beside himself. There was something about it all, though, that I had to figure out.

Something Talon had told me when I first got here that never once made sense before, but at the same time, nothing like this has ever happened.

"Damian, when I first got here, Talon had called me a Bella Donna. Doesn't that translate to something that has to deal with women?"

"It's Italian. It means pretty woman," Damian reluctantly said. "What does that have to do with anything?"

"Here..." James finally replied as he turned his phone to face me. "Wanna explain why you're acting weird?"

"I'm acting weird?" I scoffed, "you guys really don't pay attention to anything I'm into, do you?"

"Of course we do," Damian snapped. "You are the center of our attention at all times."

Even with his quick reaction, I caught on to the seductive hint he was giving. He was accurate. They did pay attention to everything that had to do with blowing my mind in any position they could get me in.

Deciding to ignore him though I took James' phone and stared at the photo. "Has Talon been to South Africa?"

"What?" Damian replied, "no... why does that matter?"

"It matters because out of all the plants that you guys are affected by, this one would cause a lot of his symptoms, and going crazy is one of them."

"That wouldn't make sense, though," Hale finally said as he stood to his feet from the sofa and began to pace the room. "This doesn't grow around here."

"It doesn't have to be Hale. People import shit like this all the time. I doubt Talon willingly would take this; he was very well verse with nature, and knew a lot about plants."

The room grew quiet as I looked up from the phone and glanced at the three men. Their brows cocked in confusion, and mouths parted open.

"What?" James muttered, staring at me. "The hell are you talking about? Talon didn't care about flowers."

"Seriously—" Letting the shock of their comment roll off of me I took a deep breath. "You know what? We can address that later. Damian, what are the symptoms or characteristics he is showing?"

"From what we could tell, he wasn't able to see quite well. He killed quite a few of our men, and on top of that, he was going crazy. All of which a lot of them do—"

"No," I laughed, shaking my head, "all of them don't. I'm telling you, this is what is hurting him. We need to leave right now and save him before the toxicity ends up killing him. There is a cure—"

Damian slammed his hands upon his desk as he rose to his feet, staring at me. "I didn't tell you so that you could be a part of getting him home, Ivy. Did you not just hear me when I said that he had killed multiple people on this recovery mission?"

"So you're just going to give up?" I gasped, unsure if that was where he was leading. The idea of giving up on Talon wasn't something that I could jump on board with. Talon was the other piece to my puzzle, and I needed him.

I needed him like I needed air to breathe.

"Ivy, my word is final," Damian replied with a glare. "I will not have you part of this."

Turning toward Hale and James, I looked at them for help. Surely, they wouldn't agree with what Damian was saying. "Hale... he's my mate and your twin..."

"I know, Ivy, but he would agree with me in not risking you. If he can't be saved, he wouldn't want me to come after him." Hale tried to keep a straight face. He tried more than anything to hold it in, but I could see right through him.

I could see the tears welling in his eyes that he fought so hard to blink back.

He wanted to save Talon as much as I did. He was just more scared of losing me.

"No," I stated firmly, turning my gaze back to Damian. "I won't stand for this. Where is he?"

Laughter escaped Damian as he watched me. "Do you think I would honestly tell you? I know how you are Ivy, and you're not going anywhere near there, and that's final."

Finality was something that only ordinary people lived by, and I slowly realized I was more than normal. I was a human in a shifter situation, and it was my job to fight for what I wanted whether that be physically or metaphorically.

"No!" I snapped. The words came out of my mouth in a slow and dangerous growl. A growl I had never in my life ever created before. "You will tell me where he is right now."

Damian stared at me in shock, but something inside him stirred, and a dangerous glint crossed his eyes. "You dare speak to me like that—"

"I dare do what I need to get my mate back. With or without your help, Damian."

If this was going to be a battle, then so be it. At the end of the day, though, I was going to find him. No matter the cost, I would have to pay.

Taking Charge

Ivy

The conversation was over. Hoisted over Hales' shoulder, I was carried upstairs toward my room. The swears and curses of my frustration trailed behind us as I made Damian aware of how pissed off I really was.

"I'm sick of your shit, Damian!" I yelled again before my bedroom door was kicked open, and Hale dropped me down on the bed with a bounce.

"Ivy, please. I know you're upset, but we are going to try and figure something out."

Sitting up on my knees, I jabbed him in the chest. "That isn't good enough. Damian's version of trying to figure things out is when he feels like it. If Talon is being poisoned, we have to help him now!"

"I'm sorry, Ivy," Hale replied as he backed away from me. "We can't risk someone else getting killed."

Jumping off my bed, I gave a frustrated groan. "It isn't his fault, Hale. He doesn't know what he is doing."

"I'm aware, but that doesn't excuse what's happening. You can't be involved in this."

"Why?" I scoffed, "because I'm so defenseless and will get killed?"

Hale was silent, and as I paced up and down my room, I couldn't help but take my frustration out on everything around me. Object after object was picked up and thrown across the room. Tears streamed down my face, with the feeling of hopelessness building in my chest.

This had all been my fault, and that was the realization that killed me the most.

"He's your fucking brother, Hale," I replied with defeat as I faced him. "How can you fucking act okay with this? Why aren't you out there yourself fighting the situation and trying to get him home?"

Clear frustration ran through his expression, and I was aware that I wasn't being fair to him. At the same time, though, he and the others were not being fair to Talon. They were acting as if Talon was a lost cause, and he wasn't.

"Ivy, as much as I want to go if for some reason we did... if something happened to you, I would never forgive myself. I would never be able to get over losing you."

There was raw emotion and turmoil running through his voice as he spoke. The way it cracked when he said about losing me made it all the more real.

Hale felt guilty over what he did when I tricked his wolf into claiming me.

He felt guilt for not staying with me when the bond was severed, and now he felt guilt over Talon.

He wasn't the only one, though. I felt the guilt too.

Me coming to this place had changed so much of their life, and even though I hadn't asked for any of it... I wasn't making it better.

Since I had woken up from the incident with Caleb, I had done nothing but fuck things up one thing at a time. My biggest mess-up was not listening to what Damian and the others were telling me.

I couldn't help it, though.

There was a drive inside me that pushed me forward. It made me crave the attention of all of them, and for every moment I spent not wrapped in their arms, it was agony.

Like wildfire, the bond made me crave their touch, their power. It drove me like a burning river to have them all, and I couldn't fight it.

"Sometimes in life, Hale, we have to do things we don't want to do for the greater good. Even though my life means a lot to you, it doesn't matter. Talon is part of us, and without him, we aren't complete."

There was a hidden meaning behind my words that he didn't catch on to. Never had I wanted there to be a division between us, but at the end of the day, Damian had told me he would help me bring them all back.

Even if he wouldn't help me, it wouldn't stop me from getting Talon back. It would simply mean that I would have to do this shit myself.

Hale's eyes watched me in silence as he processed what I was saying. Slowly stepping forward, he wrapped his arms around my waist and pulled me close, letting his lips brush against mine.

"I'm sorry, Ivy. I wish there was more that we could do, but these are waters we are unfamiliar with. Allison was the one who knew about this kind of stuff and, of course, as you know, she wasn't here. Asking for her help would be like giving a child ice cream when she is already jacked up on sugar."

"I will ask her then," I said, letting out a deep breath. "I will plead with her to get him home. He was like a son to her. She won't let him die."

"We were nothing to her but an advantage, Ivy. There is a lot you don't know about the relationship we had with her. She wasn't a kind woman unless it benefited her."

"Then why did you treat her like you did?" I asked, with confusion.

Hale sighed a soft laugh leaving his lips as he looked down at me. "Because we owe her our lives. She saved us when most wanted to kill us. Guaranteed, she wanted us for personal gain, but others saw us as monsters because of our father. The only reason Damian is Alpha is because he doesn't have the gene Talon, and I do. Why do you think I'm not Alpha?"

It all made sense now. Hale had better qualities to be an Alpha than Damian did and he was the second oldest. Damian never wanted to be Alpha, but the thing was no one would accept Talon or Hale because of the Lycan gene in their blood. The ancient wolf of chaos.

"That's not fair!" I gasped.

"Life isn't fair, Ivy. I wish that we could go in guns blazing, but until we know more about Talon's situation, we just can't risk it."

His words weren't the ones I wanted to hear, but with reluctance I nodded as he kissed the top of my head before turning and walking out of the room, shutting the door behind him.

Part of me knew that he was right, but the other part didn't want to listen to what he was saying. I couldn't accept defeat in the situation. I couldn't just allow Talon to go as he was. My heart begged me to go to him, and perhaps that is what I needed to do.

I needed to give Damian a reason to follow through on his promise.

Picking up my phone, I dialed Kate's number. A plan formulated in my mind as she answered on the second ring. "Hello?"

"I need your help, Kate," I said softly.

"With what?" she replied hesitantly as if she had a feeling about what I was going to say.

"With Talon."

There was silence on the other end of the phone before a sigh escaped her. "You're going after him, aren't you?"

"Yes, and you're going to help me," I stated firmly, letting her know that I wasn't backing down from this. I wasn't sure if I would come back alive, but it was Talon. I had to try.

Deep down, I knew that I could be the one who was able to reach him. I just needed to go there, and I had no clue where to look. Kate would know though since her mate Angel was well-informed about what was going on.

He was a skilled tracker, and Damian had called him in for his help.

"This isn't a good idea, Ivy," she replied.

"I know, but if it was Angel, you know you would do the same thing. You wouldn't let someone keep you away from him."

Kate let out a heavy sigh on the other end of the line before groaning. "Okay, fine. What time?"

"Be here at four in the morning. That way, the guys are sleeping."

"Are you kidding me?!" she exclaimed, "that's so fucking early!"

Narrowing my brows, I pinched the bridge of my nose, trying to keep my composure.

"Just do it, Kate, and you better not say shit to anyone else. That's an order man. Hoes before bros and all that shit." I told her as a smile slowly crossed my lips, hearing her laugh.

"Whatever... we are stopping for coffee, though, and your ass is buying."

Hanging up the phone, I smiled to myself, glad that I was able to have Kate as a friend. It was crazy how quickly she and I had bonded, and through everything, she never left my side.

Relief flooded me, but beneath it was a mass of nerves, unsure if what I was planning to do was a good idea. Taking a deep breath, I took in the mess I had created around me. Books were strewn across the floor, and clothing was scattered on the bed and hung from their drawers.

My temper tantrum was unreasonable, but in the heat of the moment, I hadn't considered it. Slowly, I began to pick up the surrounding items. My mind went over the conversation I had with Hale. If Allison could be of some help, perhaps I should trust her, and ask her to help me.

Unless that was the plan, and she really had something to do with this.

My skeptical mind was frustrated with the information and no matter how much I tried to push it away, I couldn't. I knew how to cure Bella Donna. The ingredients we could pick up the way to where we were going and once we got there, I would have to figure out my next step.

"Ivy?" James' voice called softly from my bedroom door.

Lifting my gaze to meet his, I smiled. "Hey, you. What are you doing?"

"I was coming to check on you," he replied with wide eyes as he stepped inside the room and looked around. "I see you did a number on your room."

Blushing, I bit my bottom lip and nodded. "Yeah sorry about that."

"It's okay... it's your room," he chuckled, "I do have to admit, though, for someone as petite as you, you can do some damage."

Chucking a pair of panties at him, he grabbed them mid-air and laughed. "Oh, do I get to keep these?"

"If you want, but I would have thought you would prefer the ones on me."

The seductive nature of how I spoke made him grin. "That's tempting."

"As tempting as it may be, I should probably clean this up first," I replied, gesturing around my room. "It's a mess."

He slowly took steps toward me and pulled me to my feet. A rush of emotions flooded me as my heart began to race. There had always been something about James that excited me, but in a way that I would have been in high school.

Perhaps it was his playful boyish charms that drew me in or the way he smiled. Something about it was comforting, and through it all, he refused to give up on me.

"Who said anything about sleeping?" Kissing the corner of my lips, he ran his hand down my side and cupped my ass, causing me to giggle.

"As much as I would love to do this right now, James, I can't."

The whispered confession wasn't one I knew he wanted to hear, but he nodded regardless and kissed the side of my head. "I'm sorry this is happening."

"So am I."

Pulling me tight against his chest, he hugged me and deeply inhaled my scent. "I know you're planning something, Ivy. I can tell by the emotions rushing through you that you are going to do something, and I'm begging you not to."

I couldn't deny what he was saying, because I knew very well he could tell. However, if I admitted it, I also knew he would stop me.

"Everything I am plotting is to help you guys bring him home. I wouldn't ever do anything without you." It was technically a lie because, at the end of the day, they would come after me once they knew I was gone. Another part of my plan that would be perfectly executed.

Defying Damian

James

A few hours later, and I couldn't stop pacing the living room floor. She was planning something. I wasn't sure what it was, but my gut feeling was hardly ever wrong about things.

"Would you stop pacing?" Damian sighed as he lifted his bourbon glass to his lips and shook his head. "It's giving me a migraine."

Stopping in my tracks, I stared at him with frustration. "She is planning something. I know it."

"She has no idea where to look." Hale reassured, "she wouldn't be able to do anything. Now, if you would like to be helpful, we need to search through these books and find a cure for Bella Donna."

Hale wouldn't get off the issue of Bella Donna being the drug that was affecting Talon. The moment that Ivy had suggested it, he had run with the idea, and he wouldn't allow any other suggestion to be made.

"What makes you so sure it's that?" Damian asked, as if the idea was one he couldn't wrap his mind around. "I don't want us to assume something we aren't sure of."

Laying the book down in his hands, Hale sighed, shaking his head, "Ivy knows a lot more than you give her credit for Damian. We need to start listening to the things she is telling us."

"Do you honestly think I don't?" Damian snapped, "I have been trying to protect her since the moment she got here and every time I turn around you both, or she is going against everything I say."

"We all have fucked up in regards to Ivy, Damian. Not just you, but me, Hale, and Talon have as well. If I could go back in time, I would change things, but what happened made us stronger. She will be the Luna of this pack and even without the ceremony she already is. We need to trust her."

Damian sat staring at us with disbelief. "Is this what you both think?"

Looking at Hale, he nodded in agreement with what I was saying. Ivy needed to be taken more seriously, and we didn't agree with Damian trying to protect her from everything.

"Yes, and to top it off, she is changing."

"Changing?" Damian asked with confusion, "what do you mean?"

"I know you can't tell because you haven't marked her, but something is different about her than it was before. Like something inside her is slowly waking up, and it really started to happen after Hale claimed her again."

Silence fell between us as I took a seat, and Hale went back to his reading. Damian was not the kind of man to look vulnerable, but staring at him now, all I could see was fear in his eyes. He was afraid of what I said, and I wasn't sure why he was afraid.

Damian had always been the strongest of all of us. He had been the one who had taken charge when our parents died. He was also the one who always took a back seat in things to make sure we were put first.

I didn't understand it. In fact, his personality didn't portray a man who would do something like that. Instead, he came off as cold and unlikeable. An Alpha who was ruthless and didn't care for the feelings of others.

It was an act, though. My brothers and I knew the truth without him having to admit it.

Damian was terrified of losing Ivy and even more terrified that she would reject him.

"Maybe we should reconsider the idea of keeping her out of this." Damian said, breaking the surrounding silence. "Maybe it's time I give her a chance to be a part of this instead of always trying to push her away."

A smile lined my face, hearing his words. "I think that is a wise choice, brother. She is sleeping right now, so in the morning I think we should all three surprise her and tell her what we have decided. It will make her happy."

Nodding his head, Damian stood to his feet and put down his empty glass, "I'm going to head to bed. I will see you both in the morning."

"Likewise." I replied as I joined him. "Hale, I take it you're going to stay up for a while?"

Hale was silent as he read, and a nod was the only acknowledgment that I received. No matter how much he was trying to act normal, I could see the truth. He was far from being alright, and that concerned me.

I could only hope that Ivy was able to fix him like she was convinced she could fix Talon.

Ivy

Silence.

The sky outside was still black from the blanket of darkness that had clouded the land. I knew what my objective was, but thinking about it now, I couldn't help the doubt that seeped into my soul.

Was I really making the right choice?

Grabbing my backpack, I quietly moved through the house and down the stairs toward Kate, who had better be waiting just outside. I knew that as soon as I left pack territory, the patrols would wake Damian, but by that point, we would already have a head start.

Dim lighting from the living room had me freezing in my place at the bottom of the stairs. My eyes casting glances toward the open space, searching for a figure that wasn't where I had expected him to be.

Hale sat quietly in his chair with his eyes trained on me. "I had a feeling you were up to something. Especially after James mentioned something about it before he went to bed."

Sighing, I slowly moved forward, stopping in the entryway, and smiled. "I have to do this, Hale."

"I know." He replied, catching me off guard. It wasn't the response I had expected from him, and yet he was okay with me leaving to go after Talon.

"Why are you okay with this? The others would have chained me up to keep me from going."

The corners of his lips turned up into a small smile as he nodded. "Yeah, I know. But I think you're right, Ivy. I think it's Bella Donna poisoning, and I'm starting to wonder if someone close to us did it."

"The guys wouldn't have—"

"No, they wouldn't." He quickly said, cutting me off. "But I think someone else might have. Someone who is trying to cause issues for us, and make sure that you are not able to get to Talon. Someone who would benefit."

His words confused me, and to be honest I wasn't sure who that would be.There were so many people that were close to us, and Allison wouldn't poison Talon.

She needed them.

"Do you think it's Allison?" I asked with hesitation, unsure of how he would respond.

"As much as I don't want to think she would do that, I don't see why she would. We are more useful to her if we are alive. Otherwise, she has no way to get to power. Regardless if Damian is sitting in the Alpha position, we all rule together." He replied as he stroked his chin, staring off into the distance.

"That's not good."

Slowly, his eyes met mine again as he gestured for me to come to him. My feet moved me forward without a second thought until he pulled me onto his lap. "No, it's not, and that is why I need you to be careful. Trust no one, Ivy. Make sure that you watch your back, and when I do come, I want you to be prepared."

Nodding, I pressed my lips to his in a gentle kiss, "I won't let you down."

"You could never let me down, Ivy. Even though I have changed from how I was before, I want you to know it isn't you. I am trying to find the person I was before I lost you. Honestly, I think that I am like this because I don't have Talon."

I didn't know what it was like to have siblings, considering I was an only child, but I could feel the pain of his missing brother through the link. He had opened himself to me emotionally, and the pain of losing Talon was tearing him apart.

"I will bring him back." I said again as I kissed him, "but I have to go now before the others wake up."

Standing to my feet, he patted my back end gently, causing me to look back at him with a grin. I still remembered what he had told me before about twins and needing to mate together, but after everything I had read about their kind—it was mistranslated.

Mating with them together was how I produced an heir.. Not to form the bond.

Something I didn't bother to correct them on, because having children right now was not on the agenda. Although some day it would be nice. The idea itself fills me with pride.

Hale walked with me out to Kate's car, whose eyes bugged out when she saw him coming with me. "Uh—did I miss something?" She stuttered.

"No." I replied with laughter as Hale placed my bag in the car and kissed me one more time.

"Be safe, Ivy." He said, running his hand through my hair. "I expect you in one piece when we get there."

"Funny you say that because I was thinking the same about you, Hale. James and Damian are going to flip out when they find out you let me go."

Shrugging his shoulders, he glanced back at the house, and turned to Kate and I. "You need to go now. James will be up soon."

Wasting not another moment, Kate and I were speeding down the driveway toward the highway. Her lead foot became an asset in our getaway.

"How long until Damian knows you're gone?" She asked, pulling me from my thoughts.

"No long." I smirked just as a roar echoed in the distance, and my phone began to ring repeatedly. "Do you mind if I put this on speaker?"

Opening and closing her mouth, she shook her head with a grin across her face. "Go for it."

Taking a deep breath, I answered the call, "Hello Damian."

"Get your ass back here right now, Ivy!" He yelled into the phone, causing Kate and I both to laugh. We weren't trying to be disrespectful, but it was hard not to laugh at Damian sometimes when he got angry.

A vision of him pacing the living room with his ears turning red from how pissed off he really was taunted my mind and made me smile.

"Now, Damian. This is a team effort, honey." I replied, putting on a fake heavy southern accent. "We all have to work together. Team work makes the dream work."

"Damn it, Ivy. Kate, I swear to god you better turn that fucking car around right now! This isn't a game. Talon is fucking bent and you're both going to get yourselves killed!"

Nervousness seeped off Kate at Damian's words. I knew the complications for myself, but I never took into account the complications for Kate.

Reaching over, I gave her knee a gentle squeeze to help reassure her. My touch seemed to calm her racing mind as I put my attention back to Damian.

"I know what's wrong with him, Damian. The problem isn't with what I'm doing. You need to figure out who is behind it and why. Talon won't hurt me, no matter what you think. Just for once in your life, trust me."

My statement was met with silence as crashing sounds echoed through the background.

"I do trust you, Ivy." He replied exhaustedly. "I just can't lose you."

There was a weakness in his words that he didn't care if even Kate heard. It was fear that forced his choices, and now more than ever, I could see that clearly.

"I promise I will be okay." I sighed, "and I know I will see you soon."

Hanging up the phone, I put it on silent, and leaned back into my seat taking in what I was really doing. Part of me knew I was in way over my head, but there was something else inside me driving me to go to him.

It was a force I couldn't ignore, and I was more than willing to take a leap if need be to save him.

On The Road Again

Two hours.

That's how long Kate and I had been driving, and my ass was sore from our journey. I should have suggested we took my car because Kate's small compact vehicle was not meant for long-distance journeys.

Even if I was short and petite, I had junk in my trunk, and the seat was killing this cushioning.

"Are we there yet?" I asked her again after the hundredth time. Her eyes slowly narrowed as she looked at me with frustration.

"If you ask me that one more time, so help me, I will pull this car over."

Laughter erupted from my lips at her comment. She reminded me so much of my mother growing up when we went on trips. "I'm sorry. Why don't we pull off at the next exit and take a potty break and get coffee?"

The sound of coffee made Kate's eyes perk up, and a grin crossed her lips. "Deal, but this is the last stop, Ivy. We literally have two hours left, and if you keep this up, we will never get there."

"Two hours?" I repeated with confusion. "He's that close?"

Opening and closing her mouth, she tilted her head and sighed, "not exactly."

"You know I hate it when you answer with that. It lets me know that shit's going to get more chaotic for me than just riding in your tiny ass car."

"Hey!" she snapped. "Don't you talk bad about Black Betty. This car is a machine and will outdo yours any day of the week."

She was right. The damn car was a beautiful machine, but at the same time, it wasn't comfortable. "Pain before beauty."

"Damn straight, bitch," she grinned, pulling off on the exit way headed toward a small town with one gas station and a few small diners. There wasn't much here, but food and coffee sounded great.

"I want a last meal before I do." I teased her as she pulled into the gas station to fill up and turned to stare at me.

"Don't say shit like that... you're not dying, Ivy."

Perhaps I wasn't actually going to die... or at least I hoped that wouldn't be the case.

"Regardless, I need food." I smiled at her, watching as she rolled her eyes before getting out to pump gas.

Letting my eyes wander, I took in the area two hours from the pack and admired how lush and green it was. We were high in the countryside, and the size of the small town we were in showed just how secluded life really was here.

We had only just passed through the Canadian border, and from what Damian had said before, Talon was deep within the Canadian wilderness. His animalistic instincts kept him in the forests, and my clothing was not doing anything to control the cold that bit at me.

Furrowing my brow, I pulled myself from my thoughts as Kate got back in the car. My eyes lingered on a figure walking into the gas station I swore I recognized before.

"Kate... that man right there in the black coat with the white ball cap. Doesn't he look familiar?"

Her eyes followed mine as she squinted, taking him in. "I don't think so..."

"No, seriously. I'm telling you, I have seen him somewhere."

Pulling out my phone, I waited until he exited the store, and I snapped a photo, sending it to James. My mind reeled over the idea I had seen that man before somewhere.

It only took a moment, and James' number popped up on the car's Bluetooth.

"Hey, I take it you got the photo."

The sounds in the background let me know they were driving, and a smile crossed my lips, realizing they were indeed right behind us.

"Yeah, that's Bennet. A guy who works on your dad's security team. Where are you guys?"

Looking around, I searched for a sign before looking to Kate for an answer. However, all she did was shrug, unsure where we were.

"We passed the border a little while ago, but not sure of the name of the town. What would this guy be doing here?" I asked as an uneasy feeling grew within my stomach.

"I don't know. We are still an hour behind you, though," James said hesitantly. "Damian wants you to find a place there to lie low until we get there. We're not sure if maybe your dad is involved in this. After all, he wasn't happy about being replaced."

"We don't have time for that, James," I replied, trying to think of what to do. "It looks like he is going into the diner... maybe we can stall him just in case."

"Ivy," Damian finally said through the phone, sending chills down my spine as I smiled.

"Hello, cupcake. How's the drive?"

Kate stifled her laughter as she took a sip of her water.

"It could have been better, but instead, we are chasing after you, as always."

"Well, that's always exciting, isn't it?" I grinned, watching Bennet sit down at a table with a woman I didn't recognize.

"You're not going to listen to me, are you?" Damian finally groaned as Kate, and I began to laugh.

"Nope... probably not. Talk later, though," I said, hanging up the phone. What the hell was this guy doing here, and why do I feel like he is up to no good?

"What are we doing?" Kate finally asked, pulling my attention toward her.

"I don't know," I replied, shrugging my shoulders. "I mean, he could just be like on a date, but it feels too coincidental for my liking. What would you do?"

"Well, I mean, probably slash his tires," she said after a moment of silence. "It would make sure they can't follow you right away or something."

With wide eyes, I turned to her. "I have never slashed someone's tires before."

"Well, you don't want to do it unless you're sure, usually. Otherwise, it could be just a dick move..."

Kate's words trailed off, and through it all, the only thing I focused on was I had never slashed someone's tires before..., and it sounded kind of fun.

"I'm going to do it," I finally said. "I'm going to slash his tires."

"Seriously," Kate said flatly. "You're going to do it?"

Looking at her with a wide, mischievous grin, I shrugged my shoulders. "Fuck it. Why not?"

Kate's eyes lit up with excitement as a grin spread across her face. "Who are you, and what did you do with safe-Ivy?"

"Who said I was safe?" I replied with confidence. "Sometimes a girl has to get dirty in order to protect her assets."

"You mean the four, sex god men that currently like to ravage you? Your Impaler's delight?"

Staring at her dumbfounded, I laughed. "Are you going to sit there all day trying to think of things to call them or move toward that car before the guy decides to leave?"

"Good point,"I replied.

Kate quickly pulled from the gas station toward the diner. As soon as she got close, I jumped out of the car and stabbed the two back tires with the knife, watching as they quickly deflated. The sounds of Bennett running from the diner and yelling at me were amusing, and as I jumped back into Kate's car, she stepped on the gas and took us back onto the highway.

I wasn't sure if the guy was actually following us, but at the same time, I wasn't going to risk it. Why else would my father's security guy be this close to where Talon was, and so convenient when we were on our way there? Something about it didn't seem right, and I wasn't about to allow anyone to hurt Talon or anyone I loved.

Sometimes girls gotta do what a girls gotta do.

Just as she said, two hours later, we pulled up outside of a forest somewhere in the northern part of Canada. I wasn't sure why I would have expected it to be warm. It was later in the year, and there was more snow on the ground here than I had seen back in Idaho.

"Kate, why do you think Bennett was in that town?" I finally asked, breaking the silence between us.

Shaking her head, she looked at me and shrugged. "I don't know. I have been wondering the same thing."

"It's making me wonder if my father and Allison had something to do with all of this. I mean, I don't see why Allison would, but at the same time, I could understand my father wanting to get rid of them."

"Honestly, Ivy, I never liked Allison. I met her years ago at a nationwide pack event, and even then, she flaunted herself as if she was the most important person in the room. I wouldn't put it past her having a hand in this," Kate replied with a sigh. The statement was one I didn't want to hear.

As much as I wanted to give Allison the benefit of the doubt, there was a chance I couldn't. There was a chance that she was trying to kill Talon, and who knows if the guys were targeted next?

Opening the door, I stepped out into the cold Canadian air and froze in my tracks.

"Jesus Christ, it's fucking cold," I complained as Kate and I stepped out of the car.

"Yeah, it's a bit cold," she retorted, grabbing a bag full of gear from the trunk as I slid on my backpack.

"A bit?" I exclaimed. "It's more than a bit cold, Kate. I'm freezing my ass off."

Laughter escaped her as she closed the trunk and walked toward where I was standing. "The best thing about being a shifter... we run hotter than normal. So yeah, it is cold, but it isn't that bad."

Rolling my eyes, I turned toward the forest and contemplated what we were about to do. This was by far the most dangerous thing I had ever done, but at the same time, it was for a good purpose. This would bring Talon home and help to complete our circle.

A circle that should have been completed so long ago.

"No matter what happens, Kate... if Talon charges me, don't interfere," I muttered, watching as her gaze met mine, and shock filled her.

"You can't ask me to do that, Ivy. You're human and can't take him. He could try to kill you."

"He won't, Kate—" I replied before she stopped in her tracks and shook her head.

"But he could!" she exclaimed. "Please don't ask me to do that."

Giving her a pointed look, she slowly caved and nodded her head, biting her bottom lip. Silence fell between us as the sound of snow crunching beneath our boots echoed through the trees. There was no telling what was going to happen, but one thing I knew for sure was I would succeed.

I had to succeed—for Talon.

The sound of crunching snow beneath my boots echoed around me. I wasn't sure what I was expecting, but the surrounding forest was silent except for the noise we made. Kate and I ventured deeper into the forest until a small clearing with a log cabin came into view.

"Is he there?" I asked as we stopped, curious about why a random cabin sat so far within the depths of the forest. It had taken us over an hour to get here on foot, but that was because I couldn't shift to make the process go by faster.

Kate hesitated before slowly nodding, and it became clear that she was nervous about being here, and considering everything the guys had explained to me, I didn't blame her.

Talon was far worse than anyone had thought him to be, and even though I desperately wanted to save him, I knew there was a possibility that I wouldn't be able to.

Taking a deep breath, I stepped forward. The cabin was my target, and if Talon was in there, then I had to see him. I had come too far to turn back now, and there was no way that I would be leaving without him.

"It's okay, Kate. Everything is going to be okay."

My words were meant for comfort, but Kate gave me a look that showed doubt.

"Don't assume that it will be all sunshine and rainbows, Ivy. The Talon you know isn't the same one out here. It's what everyone has been trying to tell you, and if you're not careful, he will kill you."

I knew what she was saying was true, but I also had faith that I could bring him back.

I had faith that he would return to me, and the goddess that loved them would help me do that.

As my feet hit the wooden deck of the cabin's porch, I paused, taking a moment to let everything sink in. There was a chance he was on the other side of this door. There was a chance that with everything I had gone through, I was about to be reunited with him.

The thought alone gave me hope, but as my hand hovered over the doorknob, I couldn't find the strength to open it.

"It's okay, Ivy. Just open it," Kate replied, bumping me with her shoulder and giving me a smile. Nodding, I quickly turned the doorknob and let the door swing open.

I had been hoping and praying that Talon was sitting inside, waiting for me to come to him, but in the end, I was met with nothing but cold emptiness.

"He isn't here," I said as I stepped forth into the cabin, and Kate joined me, shutting the door behind her. "Where is he?"

"Probably in his animal form, Ivy. We aren't sure if he comes back here, but every time he has been seen, he isn't in his human form."

"Why didn't you tell me that before?" I asked, turning to her confused, "you could have said something."

"We have in the past forty-eight hours, you have been told. I'm sorry, Ivy. I wish it was just as easy as us coming here and him waiting for you. It would make all of it so much easier, but unfortunately... we are that fortunate."

Her words weren't comforting, but as my eyes cast around the cabin, I couldn't help but feel like he had been here recently.

The cabin was small and held no bedrooms; instead, it had a very open floor plan that was perfect for the single person. A small bed with a blue quilt sat to the side of one cabin, and a small kitchen sat on the other side. It was perfect enough for someone who was trying to escape his life, but at the same time, it felt lonely.

Tears welled within my eyes, realizing that this was where Talon had escaped to, to escape the pain he felt when my bond with him had severed.

"I have to find him, Kate," I whispered loud enough Kate heard me. "I need to go out there and find him."

"Not tonight, you aren't," Kate replied, catching my wrist, "We will camp here tonight and hope that he either comes back or we can find him in the morning."

"Why?" I asked with confusion. Not understanding why we wouldn't go and find him now. I wanted to find him before the guys got here because I didn't want anyone to get hurt.

Sighing, Kate pointed out the window to the sky. "The sun is setting, Ivy. It's about to get very cold around here, and hungry things come out at night. We can't protect ourselves if we are moving in the dark."

"You can see in the dark, though, right?"

"Yeah, silly. But you can't," she said, stating the obvious. As much as I hated remembering I wasn't one of them, I had to learn to face facts. I was useless in these kinds of situations, and no more than ever, it made sense why they hide things from me.

"So what do we do?" I asked her, letting out a heavy sigh, knowing that there was nothing I could do other than take direction from Kate.

Dropping her bag, she smiled at me, "stop moping. We will figure it out, okay? I'm just trying to keep your sweet little ass alive, Ivy. Now, I will start a fire. Why don't you look for anything useful in the kitchen."

Without another word, I made work of what she told me to do. The entire time, my mind was spinning with the idea that Talon was out there somewhere in the cold. His mind slowly slipped from the poison running through his veins, and time slowly slipped with the chance to save him.

An hour later, we sat near the fire, drinking coffee that I managed to scrounge up in the kitchen. Laughter escaped us as we talked about the escapade we had in the town with my father's man.

It was during time like this I was grateful for Kate because she had the ability to help people forget about their problems just by being herself.

"Do you think he was headed here or was already up here?" I asked her, watching as she shrugged. My thoughts of my dad having his hands in why Talon was sick sent anger to my soul.

"Maybe I wouldn't put it past your dad. He seems like a real piece of work."

Nodding my head, I couldn't deny what she was saying. "Yeah, he isn't the man I was hoping for him to be. Then again, I have been naïve about a lot of things since I came to live with him. I think it's time I start taking responsibility for my actions."

Furrowing her brows, she looked at me confused before setting down her cup.

"It's expected for you to not know much about our lives, Ivy. It was kept from you forever, and no one bothered to properly explain things to you when you did find out."

I could tell she was trying to make me feel better about everything, but at the same time, she couldn't deny that I had made many stupid choices.

"I know," I replied with a heavy sigh. "Still, I have been a bit ridiculous at times."

With hesitations, she nudged me a little and smiled.

"Maybe a little, but you handled the news so well. I was surprised you didn't flip out when you found out I was one, too." She laughed, causing me to crack a smile.

"By the time you told me, I had already grown used to the idea of wolves and whatever else might be out there. Then they drop the whole Lycan thing on me.."

Her eyes widened at my mention of the Lycan situation, and she quickly cleared her throat. "What do you mean—"

Before she could finish her sentence, however, a low growl emitted from within the darkness outside. Both of our eyes darted toward the window on the far side of the cabin as we froze.

Something large outside was slowly circling the cabin, and even though we used the wooden barricade to lock the cabin door—it wouldn't hold back a wolf-like Talon.

"Do you think–" I whispered, only to have Kate glare at me quickly and shake her head no. I wasn't linked with Kate, so communication wasn't possible, but I watched her own eyes glaze over, and I knew right away what she was doing.

She was reaching Angel.

Fear spiraled through me as the hairs on my arms raised with anticipation of Talon finding me. There was a calling between us. Something inside me let me know the monster outside the cabin was him.

As much as part of me wanted to open the door and run to him, I couldn't. I had to think smarter, and I had to be patient. It wasn't just my life out here. It was Kates's as well.

As Kate's eyes cleared, she pulled out her phone and typed out a message showing it to me.

'Angel is with the guys, and he said that they are still forty minutes out. A wreck on the highway has delayed them. They said to stay in the cabin and wait for them to get here.'

Running my hand over my face, I sighed. This wasn't what was supposed to happen.

I came here to save Talon and not sit locked away in a cabin, waiting for the guys to get here to rescue me. Otherwise, why did I come in the first place?

Frustration filled me, realizing that my hands were tied right now. If I went out there, I could get Kate hurt. If I stayed, the guys would be here soon, and there was no way they would let me do anything.

Weighing my choices, I tried to think of a plan, but everything came to a roadblock that only upset me even more.

"No..." I whispered, watching as she stared at me in shock before I broke contact and let my eyes drift toward the front door. "He knows we're here..."

Within moments chaos consumed us as Talons' wolf slammed against the door to the cabin over and over again. The wood holding it together cracked little by little against his massive weight.

I had only met his wolf once or twice before, and both times his wolf hadn't been pleased with my presence, but at the same time, I enticed him.

"Shit!" Kate exclaimed as she grabbed her bag and quickly began to pull out a tranquilizer gun and darts. The realization of what she was planning to do almost broke my heart.

"What–Kate... what are you doing?"

She turned to me with a dumbfounded look as she continued pulling things out. "What the fuck does it look like I'm doing? I'm making sure we stay alive."

"Kate, he won't hurt me," I replied, moving toward the door. "He won't."

She grabbed my arm, pulled me back, and shook her head in disbelief. "Look, I love you dearly, Ivy, so I am going to say this the best I can and I don't want you to take this the wrong way. But have you lost your fucking mind? He isn't the same man you knew before."

The cracking of wood and the biting cold circled us as the door to the cabin gave way to his massive form. His wolf stood before us, spotted with blood from his recent kill, and a murderous look in his eyes.

Slowly, we both backed away from him one step at a time until a low growl echoed from his throat, and he snapped his jaw. "Talon–" I whispered, his gaze quickly locking onto me. "Talon, please, it's time to come home."

As true to their word, Talon, however, didn't recognize me. He didn't know who I was, and the poison from the belladonna or whatever it was coursed through his veins.

Deranging his mind until nothing he once knew made sense.

With his gaze locked on me, Kate took the opportunity to quickly reach for her gun. Only Talon was faster, and he turned swiftly, snapping in her direction. His body blocked her from the only thing that could currently save us.

Thinking quickly, I thought back to what had happened with Hale. When I had enticed his wolf, it was enough that he couldn't keep his focus on me, and even though it could have ended badly... I had to take that chance.

'Hale!' I screamed through my mind, hoping he would feel me and open his link.

The day I could invade his mind like he could do me would be a miracle.

'Ivy?' Hale responded, causing me to sigh as I went between listening to him and focusing on the situation with Talon and Kate.

'What's Talons' wolf's name?' I asked him.

'Ivy, why... What happened?' he asks me with a sense of panic in his voice.

'Hale!' I screamed at him. 'I don't have time for this. Please, he is going to kill Kate unless you tell me.'

'Volaire...his wolf's name is Volaire. Please be safe, Ivy,' he replied with reluctance, giving me everything I needed.

Focusing back on reality, things were getting worse. Talon was only a foot from ripping Kate apart, and losing her would be like losing a piece of my soul.

"Volaire!" I screamed, watching as the wolf's ears flinched at my words. "Volaire, I command you to look at me."

The demanding tone of my voice caused Talon's wolf to look toward me with anger and confliction. A painful whine left his lips as I realized the name I spoke was that of an ancient term, and what happened with Hale could very well happen here.

"Kate, when I get him clear, I want you to shoot him with the antidote. It's in my bag."

"What!" she screamed, "are you fucking insane?!"

Laughing, I backed toward the door while Talon stared at me with amusement. "No matter what, Kate, don't you dare fucking miss!"

Turning on my heels, I did the one thing I was told never do in a situation like this.

I ran... with everything I had, I ran through the snow and toward the trees hoping that Kate was as damn good of a shot as she claimed she was.

Otherwise, there was no telling what was going to happen to me.

Forever Talon

Hale

I should have known that letting Ivy go was going to be problematic. The moment Damian and James found out what I had done, they had a field day with me. They didn't understand, though.

They didn't understand Ivy the way that I did.

Talon was important to our circle, and without him, the union would never be completed. I knew the moment I let the ancient wolf inside me claim her as our mate that there was no going back.

It unlocked something deep inside her that had laid dormant and would have until she awoke the beast within me and released something that I had tried to keep hidden for so long.

Even when I had claimed her the first time, I did it in a way that I was connected but not completely mated. I couldn't release the venom in my body through her. I couldn't allow her to go through the change.

A change that would turn her life upside down more than it already was.

Ivy explained that she gave up her chance at a human life for us because she wanted to be with us, but at the same time, I already voiced to Damian that she didn't know what she was asking for.

Being a shifter came with its challenges, and if she lived the way we did, she wouldn't be able to have the things she wanted. Especially if she became what I am.

Just because Talon and I survived it, it didn't mean that she would, but now all of that was gone. All of that didn't matter because she was in danger, and we were only now just arriving to the shit show that was about to take place.

Bursting from the car, we shifted into our wolves headed for the treeline. Even though as wolves we were fast, it would still take fifteen minutes to get to her, and that was fifteen minutes that she was left defenseless.

Fifteen minutes that could cost her her life if she wasn't able to get through to him.

Pushing myself, I raced toward her and toward my brother, who was slowly falling apart. My heart beat for her, and when this was done, I would spend an eternity making it up.

An eternity making sure that she had a life somewhat normal, whether my brothers agreed to it or not.

'No matter what, Ivy must live.' Damian said through our link with stern intent.

He may not have shown that he cared, but deep down, he did. He was simply scared of losing something he never had—love.

Ivy

"Shit!" I screamed as I stumbled through the forest, tripping over fallen logs and broken branches. Talon was behind me, there was no doubt about that. The thundering of his paws against the fallen snow sent an alarm through to my soul.

I never considered snow could be so loud, but then again, I had never run for my life. Wondering if this was going to be the moment I died.

I didn't want to die, but at the same time, I would sacrifice myself if I had to just to bring him back. I would give anything to make sure the ones I loved lived through all of this.

Love.. it was a thought I hadn't had before, and now that I was, I didn't know if I would be able to survive them, to tell them.

My panting breath came out in clouds before me. The only light I had to show me any way was that of the moon reflecting against the white-breasted snow.

It was beautiful if I thought about it, but quickly those thoughts reflected the blood that would pour from me if I was caught.

A rough shove from behind sent me tumbling through the snow, and as I did, I found myself crying out in pain. Scratches and bruises were sure to line my skin, and as I gasped, I tried to find the will to keep going.

Crawling slowly through the snow that nipped at my skin with painful delight. I found myself quickly pinned, lying beneath the belly of an angry wolf who was breathing down my neck with every intention of killing me.

"Talon, please. It's me." This was a moment of panic, a moment where, for once in my life, I wasn't sure what I was supposed to do.

The realization that, once again, I acted stupidly before thinking about what I was going to do. It was instinct, though, to protect the ones I care about.

Kate had been in danger, and I couldn't allow him to hurt her.

What happened to him was my fault.

Slowly I rolled over beneath the creature, who was standing above me, persistently growling. As scared as I was, though, I couldn't help but be amazed by his enormous beauty.

Every time I saw their wolves, I was terrified but also mesmerized by how beautiful a creature they really were. "Talon, please come back to me. I didn't leave you. The moon played tricks on us both."

As my eyes met that of the deranged wolf staring down at me, I gasped in shock. Blood and saliva dripped from his mouth as reverberations of his growl swept through me.

The only thing that I could do was to keep softly talking to him and hope that Kate was able to catch up or that I was able to break through to him and get him to see that it was me.

"Talon," I whispered, causing him to growl even more. "I know you're in there."

Slowly moving my bare hand, I reached up and brushed my fingers through the mat of fur on his chest. It was a bold move on my part, but I didn't care.

I longed to touch him, even if it was in his animal form.

I should have known, though, that it was a bad move on my part. Talon quickly snapped and growled at me, not knowing who I was anymore—not understanding that I was the woman he was destined for. The woman who loved him unconditionally.

"Shh–" I hushed, "it's okay. Please, come back to me."

It was official... I had lost my fucking mind.

I was trying to get a deranged wolf to understand what I was saying, and it was insane, but he hadn't tried to actually kill me yet... so was he actually gone?

The movements of his eyes and head made me wonder if he battled internally between the feeling I caused within him and his animalistic desires.

"I know you won't hurt me."

Slowly, the wolf's growls began to simmer, and as they did, a soft whimper escaped him as his ears laid back in confusion. It was progress I hadn't expected to make so easily, but nothing in life comes without consequences.

"Ivy!" Kate screamed before the whistling sound of a dart struck Talon, causing a whimper to escape him before his eyes became bloodthirsty, and he turned, launching himself at her.

"Kate, no!" I screamed out, watching as Kate's eyes widened in shock and panic set in. To my amazement, Talon never had the opportunity to get to her though, because a large black mass burst through the trees, colliding with his form, causing them to tumble through the darkness.

Fear swept through us, followed by relief as I watched three more wolves come charging in. One headed straight for Kate. "Don't hurt him!" I screamed at them, only to have James shift and sweep me up into his arms.

"Ivy," he cooed with concern in his eyes, "oh my god. We need to get you to a hospital."

"I'm fine, James." I laughed, my eyes quickly darting toward where Talon and Damian went. "Don't hurt Talon. I think Kate got him."

"Got him?" Hale said as he walked up, completely naked. A blush set over my cheeks as I tried to remind myself this was normal. I still hadn't gotten used to them being so open with nudity, considering I have slept with them many times.

"Yes, Kate had a tranquilizer gun," I replied as James slowly set me to my feet before Kate pushed him out of the way.

"Oh, my god. Are you okay?" she said, looking over at me. "I was so scared he was killing you—"

"I'm fine. Kate, he didn't attack me like that."

"What do you mean?" she asked in confusion.

Sighing, I shook my head. "I don't know. He just didn't. It was like he was fighting something inside him. Trying to make himself remember who I was. I thought he was going to kill me, and he proved me wrong."

"I'm speechless in a sense," Kate replied, trying to process what I said.

"I know, so am I, but I think he knew it was me."

All of them stopped staring at me as rustling from the treeline brought forward the very naked body of Damian. "As much as I would love to continue this, I think we should get out of this cold and back in the cabin. Angel, James... come help me with Talon."

Hearing Talon's name perked my attention as Kate nudged me. "I got him, Ivy. I hit him with the antidote and a tranquilizer."

Tears finally flooded my eyes with pure joy, realizing we were able to contain him. With the antidote, I hoped it would work. That he would be able to slowly get better, but only time would tell if we had the right one.

In the cabin, I watched as James, Damian, and Angel lay Talon down on the small bed. His body was no longer in that of a wolf as peaceful sleep took hold of his body.

I didn't hesitate to move toward his sleeping form and brush my fingers against his hairline, watching as he slept.

"How long do you think he will be out?" I asked, letting my eyes drift toward the others who meandered around the small cabin.

"Depends on how much Kate had in the dart," Damian replied before looking toward Kate. "Kate?"

Kate's mouth opened and closed little by little, like a deer caught in the headlights. I wasn't sure what was wrong with her, but Angel quickly sighed. "Kate, you didn't..."

Shrugging her shoulders, she gave me an apologetic look. "Sorry, I wasn't sure what we were dealing with, so I gave him a lot."

Laughter escaped James and Hale, causing me to glare at them and shake my head.

"We can't stay out here forever," I said softly to Damian, "we need to get him home."

"I know we do, Ivy. At first light, we'll make our way back toward the pack. I'm sure Kate has enough to keep him sedated until we arrive, and then we will have the pack doctor look at him."

His hand lay upon my shoulder in a comforting gesture as I nodded my head. I was thankful on many accounts to have him here. Yes, we fought, and both acted very childish at times, but it's what made us stronger.

It was what connected us.

Each of the guys had their own flaws and weaknesses that made them who they were, and there wasn't a thing I would change about them.

"Alright. Let's get some sleep, then. We leave early."

Leaning forward, I let my body curl up next to Talon's and gently laid a kiss on the side of his face. If we were all staying here, that was fine, but I wasn't going to leave Talon's side again. He needed me.

Three days. It's been three days since we arrived back at the pack, and Talon was still out of it. Damian had the pack doctor long ago pull Talon from sedation, but with the effects of the poisoning, it was hard to bring him back.

Or at least that is what they kept telling me.

Standing beneath the hot, cascading water of my shower, I tried to wash away all of my misery. My heart was shattered upon hearing that we may have been too late to save him. His mind was so far gone that the doctors didn't know if forcing a fix would be good.

I knew what they were telling me was true, but at the same time, I didn't want to hear it. I didn't want to hear them tell me that someone I cared about might never come back to me.

"Ivy?" Damian's voice called softly while knocking on the bathroom door. "Are you okay?"

Laughter escaped me in a maniacal way. "Are you seriously asking me that?" Reaching up, I twisted the shower knobs, turned off the water, and slowly opened the glass shower door. "I'm broken, Damian."

He stared at me with a blank expression, as if he had never had someone explain to him that they were hurt. Damian was a different kind of man, and every day I spent with him, I was reminded that things between him and me were far from normal.

He could be sweet and gentle. There were also moments when he made my heart flutter and he excited me. But most of the time, he was cold and indifferent.

I didn't understand what was going through his mind, but I was sure that one day I would understand. There was just too much to figure out, and only time would be able to tell me everything. Time right now, I didn't have to give to him.

"I'm sorry about Talon," Damian finally said as I pushed past him into my room to get dressed. A hollow pit formed in my chest hearing Talon's name, and once again, tears began to form.

"Did they say what poison it was yet?" I asked, trying to maintain my composure.

"The results of the test should be available today. Hale is there with him now, and James is looking into leads that will tell us who is behind it."

It was comforting to know that everyone was doing something to figure out what happened, but at the same time, I already had a feeling I knew who it was.

"I think it was Allison," I said with a heavy breath. "I think she did this, Damian."

Pulling my shirt over my head, I turned to face him now in a t-shirt and shorts. His eyes lingered over me for a moment, and as much as I would have loved to have him ravish me right now, I couldn't even come to think of doing things like that.

"Kate told me that was your thoughts. However, we can't just accuse her until we have information to peg her with it."

Like that was going to happen. If Allison did have something to do with it, she wouldn't leave a trace behind to track that it was her. It was frustrating, but at the same time, I had to have faith something would bring light to the truth.

"Okay." The soft reply that escaped my lips seemed to surprise him. His brow raised slightly as he stared at me, and quickly I broke the gaze we held.

"Okay?" he asked with curiosity. "You're not going to fight me on this?"

Shaking my head, I chuckled. "No, Damian. You're right... we can't just go around accusing people. We need to make sure that we have solid information against her or whoever did it. I don't want to give them a reason to get away with it."

Voices outside my bedroom door caused Damian and I to halt our conversation before James and Kate entered the room. "James..."

"Oh, sorry, did we interrupt something?" Kate asked, looking between Damian and me with an apologetic glance.

"No, no. He was just filling me in on Talon."

"Oh, good." James smiled, clasping his hands together. "That's why we're here."

Damian gave him a look of question, and James didn't miss a beat when it came to elaborating, "Talon's results are in... and he is awake."

A gasp of relief followed by tears burst from me as I pushed past them all and took off running down the stairs from the pack house. The clinic was only down the hill, and I didn't hesitate to run there as fast as my legs could take me.

This is what I had been waiting for, for days. Talon was awake, and I had to be there.

Pushing through the clinic doors, I ran down the hallways toward his room. Nurses stepped to the side with a gasp as I flew past them and turned the corner, watching as a doctor stepped from his room, and his gaze connected with mine.

"Luna," he said, addressing me by a title I hadn't been called by anyone before. "I was just going to get a few things before you got here."

"He's awake? Did you find out what is hurting him... is it the Bella Donna?"

My words flew from my mouth as I rambled on. My hands trembling, and my heart racing, wanting to know if we were able to save him. If we got to him, in time before, there was any permanent damage.

Nodding, the doctor's eyes softened a little. "Yes, you were right, Luna. It was Bella Donna. However, with the amount in his system and some of the damage, we could already tell had been there... someone had been poisoning him long before the bond broke."

My heart shattered into a million pieces as I fought back the tears that threatened to fall.

"Do we know how long?"

The sounds of echoing footsteps approaching me caught my attention, and without looking, I already knew who it was. James, Hale, and Damian stood at my side, waiting for the same response I was.

"Answer her," Damian said through tight lips as I waited patiently. "How long?"

"Three to four months at least. I honestly don't know how he has been able to fight it this long. It's a miracle, honestly."

Standing dazed, I processed the information. "So around the time I got here, it started."

"If that fits the timeline Luna then yes, but honestly, I think it started before that," he replied with a frown. "I'm going to get his next injection. If you would like to go in, then please feel free. However, do remember he is still restrained."

My eyes shot up, and I quickly turned to look at the guys with shock. "Restrained? Why is Talon restrained?"

"Ivy–" James said with a sad glance that drove anger through me.

"It's for everyone's protection," Damian quickly interjected. "I need to make sure that our people are not hurt if he has another episode."

"Episode? What are you talking about? This is Talon. Your brother and my mate. This isn't right." As much as they may have wanted me to understand, there was no way that I could. Talon... the man I knew would never purposely hurt anyone.

He was lying there sick, and they had him tied up like a criminal seeking blood.

Turning from them, I stormed into Talon's room and shut the door behind me. I didn't want them present right now because my focus couldn't be on anger.

My focus was on Talon and seeing him after so much time away.

Stepping into the dim lighting of the room, my eyes laid upon his still form, covered in white sheets. His wrists and ankles were tied down by thick velcro straps that didn't seem to have any slack. It was a heart-wrenching sight to behold, and as I stepped closer, his head moved, and his eyes connected with mine.

For a moment, his brows furrowed, and as I came closer to the light, they widened in shock. He struggled against his restraints as if scared of me, and I couldn't understand why. "Get out," he snapped, "you're not supposed to be here."

"Talon..." I gasped, trying to hold myself together, "it's me. It's Ivy."

Slowly, the ties around my heart tightened, watching him refuse to even look at me. The rejection broke me further as I moved closer to him.

"I said get out!" he yelled at me, his fangs elongating and his eyes swirling black. "You're not real! You're dead! I'm not playing this game."

Dead. He thinks I'm dead?

"Talon, please." I whispered as the tears fell, "I'm not dead. I'm real."

I wasn't sure what had happened to him while he was out there or why someone would want to hurt him like they did. None of it made sense, and I wanted more than anything to show him that I was right here.

That I was standing before him, and I wasn't going anywhere.

Reaching out, I slowly went to touch him, but the restraint snapped, and a roar echoed from his throat just as Damian and James grabbed me, pulling me away.

"No! Stop!" I shouted at them, "let me go! He doesn't understand!"

Struggling against them was no use. Damian's arms around my waist were like a vise I couldn't shake. All I could do was watch as Hale stepped toward his brother and slowly tried to calm him.

There was an undeniable bond between them, and as I watched Talon, calm tears streamed down his cheeks. "She's dead... it's my fault."

Hale's eyes met mine with the same confusion I had. "What do you mean?"

Shaking his head, Talon refused to speak. Instead, he held his head in his hand and cried. The emotions from him coursing through me in a ghost like way that built a fire of anger in my soul. I had to be there... I had to comfort him.

"Talon, please look at me," I begged him, still fighting against Damian. "Fucking let me go, Damian!"

"No, it's too much, and he isn't ready. You need to go before you get hurt." He snapped as he hauled me out of the room. "You're not doing him any good."

Placed on my feet with Damian blocking the door, I stared at him with anger. I was done with him telling me what I was and wasn't doing. Perhaps he was right, but at the same time Talon is confused and needs to see the truth.

"You have no idea what you're talking about." I snapped back at him, clenching my fists at my side. "Move now."

Laughter escaped him. “You’re really becoming the fiercest Luna I have ever met, Ivy.”

The comment would have usually melted my heart, but right now, it did nothing but anger me more. The fire slowly grew bright as I narrowed my eyes.

“I will not ask you again, wolf. Get the fuck out of my way.”

There have been many times where my words and actions lately seemed to affect the people around me, but with Damian, it was different. It was as if the beast inside him recognized the way I acted, and it reacted.

“Watch who you speak to like that.” He all but growled, stepping toward me. “Mate or not, I will not be disrespected by anyone. I’m trying to protect you.”

Movement behind Damian caught my eye, and I watched as Hale peered over Damian’s shoulder, looking slightly frantic before whispering something in Damian’s ear that seemed to catch his attention before he gazed back at me.

“That’s not possible,” he muttered, crossing his arms over his chest.

“What isn’t possible?”

Another growl echoed from the room as I heard Talon refusing whatever was going on. His pain and his anguish tore at every last thread I had holding me together.

Hale looked at me again with regret in his eyes as he took in the situation. “I agree with Damian, Ivy... you need to go rest.”

Hale’s words caused disbelief to flood through me.

He had been my main supporter when it came to Talon, and now he was siding with his brothers. Choking back my pain, I felt it build—it built until I exploded.

Screaming in fury, I grabbed Damian and, with a strength I didn’t know I had and shoved him to the side as I rushed forward into the room. Hale's arms swung out to catch me, but without a second thought, I ducked past him and right past James, who looked on in confusion.

I had one target in mind, and that was a man staring at me with pitch-black eyes and growing fury I had never seen before.

Leaping onto the bed, he roared in anger. His right hand, now free, gripped my throat, his claws digging into my skin as I touched him. There was no going back for me.

Talon was the reason I was doing this... it wasn't my own selfish desires.

It was always him.

"I'm here," I whispered as I straddled his lap with tears flooding down my cheeks. I felt the sparks of our bond against my skin and the confusion of his internal battle within his eyes.

Forcing myself forward with his death grip on my throat, I tried to ignore the pain, letting my lips brush against his until he finally gave in and claimed them with a desire I never had felt from any of them.

Talon was just as broken as I was, but at the end of the day, our individual sorrows helped us to mend our broken hearts.

"Ivy–" he stuttered as tears flooded his face.

Pulling pack, his eyes fluttered back and forth, staring at me as if I was just an illusion.

"Your–your not..."

Laughing with tear-filled eyes, I smiled, "no... I'm not dead... I'm right here... I'm right here."

I didn't waste another moment as I kissed him again and felt the grip he had on me tighten. No matter the confusion, poison, and hurt he had been through, me being here right now was the only cure he needed.

During our lowest points in life, our minds are our greatest enemies, betraying us to believe that the possible is impossible.

Yet, I couldn't accept that. I couldn't accept losing him or any of them.

I broke them when I came here, and it was my job to fix this.

"I don't understand," he whispered, resting his head against mine.

"Neither do we..." Damian said, pulling us away to the vast amount of bodies within the room. Doctors, nurses, and the guys all sat around wide-eyed, staring at the scene in front of them. "Care to explain why you would act so stupid, Ivy?"

The only thing I could do was smile. "I Love Damian. The love I have for the four of you will never let me give up. I will love you all until my last breath... and even past then."

Legend of Sølvmåne

Talon

Waking up in the hospital was like waking up from a nightmare that never ended. Confusion filled my mind, and pain tore at my heart.

I was numb. So numb that I didn't have the will to live.

Yet, through it all, she was there.

She broke through the darkness and set my soul on fire.

I didn't know how long I had lived in darkness, but I remembered the moment it had swept through me, and that was the night at the cabin. Watching her bleeding, lying lifeless in Damian's arms, I couldn't control myself.

I had failed her.

Every moment of the time it took us to get her to the hospital, my wolf had paced in my mind trying to get out. Trying to get to our mate, and when the moon overhead finally revealed itself, it was like a damn broke.

"She is better without us..." Damian's words replayed in my mind over and over again.

Those words haunted my every thought, and not able to contain myself, I gave my wolf control. I let the darkness swallow me whole and consume me, and after that, I sought the only comfort I had, my beating heart.

It was a blessing and a curse.

Yet, something inside me stirred as my wolf saw her at the cabin with a girl I didn't recognize. It thought the same as I had. She isn't real. Her ghost was haunting us.

A vision of her beauty that never left and taunted our minds with games.

Every broken memory burned me, but letting my eyes flutter open, I realized it wasn't true. She was here with me now, and the moment she kissed me yesterday, I felt my heart slowly mending.

Trying not to wake her, I brushed the loose strands of hair from her face. The same beautiful face I dreamt of so many times. As if realizing that I was awake, her lashes fluttered, and she peered up at me slowly.

"Good morning," she said sleepily, with a small smile across her lips. "I'm sorry. Am I hurting you?"

She was a bit, but there was no way I was going to tell her that. "No, I like having you with me."

Leaning up, she placed her lips against mine. Her tongue pushing for access, I willingly gave in as a soft moan escaped me.

"I will never get used to that," I murmured as she pulled away, blushing.

"Good, because you're not allowed to leave me again." There was seriousness and worry behind her words, and I understood just how she felt.

"I won't," I reassured her. "I promise."

"Wakey wakey, hands off, snakey," a chipper voice called from the door as James peeked his head in and spotted us.

"Seriously?" Ivy laughed, slowly climbing off the bed but not making it far as I reached out and grabbed her hand, not ready for her to leave.

Turning, she smiled at me. "I just have to use the bathroom. I will be right back."

She pointed toward the bathroom door in the room, and reluctantly I nodded and let her go. My eyes, however, never left her sight. Even after the door closed, I panicked internally, waiting for it to open again.

"Talon," Hale said, causing me to peer up at him, not realizing he had even walked into the room.

"You look like shit," I replied with a smile.

He and James both laughed as Hale shook his head. "Says the man currently in the hospital bed."

"Touche."

There was a sense of belonging in the room I had forgotten about. These were my brothers, my best friends, and yet when Ivy had left before, I had forgotten all about them. None of it made sense.

"Okay, now that I'm done with that." Ivy laughed, exiting the bathroom with a smile.

"You can climb back into bed with me," I smirked.

Nodding, she did as I asked and once again rested her head on my chest. "Yes, but I do think we need to move this back to the house, eventually. This bed isn't big enough for the both of us."

"About that..." James piped up. "The doctors aren't too keen on letting that happen anytime soon because of his stability. It seems that the poison in his system has done more damage than they know what to do with, and even though he is getting stronger–"

"Enough," I replied, cutting him off. "I'm not staying here. I want to go back to the house, and if they want to continue my treatment, they will do so there."

"Talon–" Ivy whispered, pulling my eyes to meet hers. "If they think it's best..."

"No, Ivy. I want to go home with you. I won't die here if they think that is what will happen."

There it was. The truth of it all, and at the end of the day, I meant it.

If the poison was killing me, then let it, but let me go home with Ivy and spend what time I had left there.I wouldn't stay in this place and let my mind slowly spiral again.

Hale's hand found its way to my head as he smiled. "If that's what you want, my brother, then that is what will happen."

"Hale, they will refuse–" James whispered but quickly stopped as his eyes came in contact with the door. Turning my focus, I saw Damian standing there with his hands clasped in front of him.

"Is this what you want, Talon? Do you want to go home?" he asked with an expressionless stare.

"Yes."

There was no changing my mind. I wanted to go home with Ivy and my brothers.

"Then it shall be done," he replied quickly, snapping his attention to James, who was about to open his mouth again. "One thing about being Alpha means that they can not refuse a command I give them. If Talon wants treatment at home, then it shall be done."

Without another word, I watched him turn and head out the door. This was a side of Damian I had never seen before, and it was different to see him take charge as he was.

"The hell did you do to him, Ivy?" I asked with a smirk.

She gasped with a partially open mouth and looked between the rest of us.

"I didn't do shit!" She exclaimed as we broke into laughter.

Ivy

Having him back was a breath of fresh air. The moment we fell asleep in each other's arms, I felt peaceful for the first time in a long time. Like nothing could ever harm us.

Damian made good on his word, and after a few rounds with the doctors and a very stern Alpha voice, Talon was moved to the pack house and recovered in his dark, spacious room.

"You know... this room could really use some color," I said to myself as I lay next to him, looking around at everything.

"No." His firm reply was met with an arm around my waist as he pulled me closer. "Don't you dare mess with my room, woman."

There was something about the way he called me–woman–that turned me on, and blushing softly, I leaned forward, kissing him.

"Yes, sir," I replied teasingly.

A low purr of satisfaction left him as he nuzzled his face into the crook of my neck, holding me close. So close that as I drew my fingers across his tattooed skin, I couldn't help but wonder if there was something I could do.

"I wish there was something that I could do to make you better."

He pulled back, meeting my eyes with his own, and smiled. "Being here like this right now makes things better for me."

"I know, but I'm serious. I feel like there is more that I could do. Like something I am supposed to do, and laying here with you now isn't fixing what's wrong with you."

Letting a heavy sigh escape him, he rolled onto his back and stared at the ceiling.

"I wish it was that easy, Ivy, but I won't lie to you... I can feel myself getting weaker, and I don't even know how this happened to me," he replied.

"No one told you?" There was hesitation in my question. I didn't want to be the one to tell him like this, but then again, if I did, maybe there was something he remembered that could help us figure this out.

"Hale told me parts, but Ivy, no one knows for sure. I'm sure you're hoping that I could tell you anything, but my mind is so clouded—"

Pain and confusion clouded his eyes as he gazed at me. "It's okay. We will figure it out together," I assured him as I snuggled in close.

"That we will," he replied with a chuckle. "If I know my brothers like I think I do, they will do anything to save me."

"Yes, they will." I smiled. "You're important to them."

Laughter escaped him before he quickly clutched at his chest, coughing. Sitting up, I stared down with concern. "Are you okay?"

"Yeah. Just thought it was funny, and I got carried away," he replied, clearing his throat.

"I don't know what was so funny." Grabbing his glass of water off the nightstand, I handed it to him, watching as he drank it down.

"Because they are saving me for you..." he said as he handed it back.

"Don't say that, Talon. That's not true."

"Yes, it is." He smiled. "But it's okay because I would do the same thing if it was one of them. Making sure you are happy is what's important to us. That's why we do what we do... even Damian, in his weird-ass ways."

Rolling my eyes, I scoffed with a smile. "I don't know about that. Damian and I do nothing but fight, Talon. Sometimes I think he doesn't want anything to do with me."

A weight of confusion constantly flooded my mind when it came to Damian. The entire time I had known him, he was always hot and cold, and when I thought things were going good... they would go bad.

"It's not that, Ivy. But it isn't my place to explain things to you. When the time is right, he will tell you about his past, but it isn't roses. I can promise you that."

Nodding, I didn't argue with what he was saying. It was something I had already expected when it came to Damian. He was a complex creature, and when the time was right, I would be there waiting.

"Well, since we are talking about secrets–" I smirked. "Why don't you tell me what you and Hale found out about your ancient Lycan history?"

Talon's eyes shot to mine with a haze I had never seen before, and deep inside was nothing but fear. "Who told you about that?"

"Uh–" I hesitated, biting my bottom lip, feeling a little unsure. "It was kind of my accident."

"Ivy, promise me you will never go down that road. Promise me you won't seek that out."

Speechless, my mouth parted as I stared at him. "Talon... I can't–"

"No," he said, shaking his head, "you already have... and with Hale–"

Clenching his fists, his lips tightened into a straight line, and anger grew that was unmistakable. "Talon, please don't be upset. It wasn't his fault. I taunted him, not thinking."

The door quickly opened, and Hale stood in the doorway staring at the both of us. The same look he gave me after he claimed me lingered across his face.

Remorse. Regret. Guilt.

"Did you complete it?" Talon asked, but the question was directed toward me.

"Partially yes," Hale replied flatly, closing the door behind him.

"No, Hale. It will kill her," Talon replied, turning his gaze to his brother.

I instantly felt out of the loop, unsure of what they were talking about, but there was something in Hales' gaze that let me know I was going to find out.

"She's Sølvmåne."

"That's not possible," Talon quickly snapped. "Are you losing your mind? They don't exist."

When Hale's gaze finally left mine, he turned to look at Talon, who was all but almost ready to jump out of his bed and go after Hale for even mentioning such a thing.

"Have you ever known me not to check into things a hundred times before stating facts?" Hale had Talon there. He was a stickler for the details, and even before all this shit happened... he was the smart one who was adamant about education.

Talon quickly quieted down and turned his worried gaze to me. "I can kill you if you try."

"What are you two talking about? What can kill me?"

Silence fell over them at my question.

What was Sølvmåne, and what was going to kill me?

"Sølvmåne, is the lineage that I believe you hail from, Ivy. I knew the moment I met you there was something about you that couldn't possibly be human, and with everything that happened with your father, it didn't fit your situation. Until I looked into your mother."

Hale's words seeped in, and I knew what he was trying to say. But it was impossible.

I wasn't a shifter... I was human. Just human.

"That's... no, there is no way," I replied, shaking my head. "Hale, that's crazy–"

"Is it, though?" Hale replied as he walked closer to me. "I had the doctor your mom was seeing, her new... love interest–send me a sample of her blood. It's currently being processed, and hopefully, I will have the results in a few weeks."

"What does being this mean?" I asked, trying to understand it all. Nothing that he was saying made sense right now because I wasn't sure what this thing meant for me.

Was my life going to change? Was I going to die?

"It means that if you are, you will be one of the most powerful creatures to ever walk this planet because your kind has been extinct for thousands of years. Or so we thought. They are purer of blood, but you and your mother's gene has been watered down over hundreds of years or longer through mixing with humans. Typically, you shouldn't show signs, but for some reason, you have."

"So that's a good thing. Does that mean I can save Talon? Do I get powers or something?"

Talon and Hale both chuckled, shaking their heads. "No, magic is for witches and other creatures of mystery. However, the power in your strong bloodline would be able to cure Talon and help him heal faster. It would give him the one thing he doesn't have right now—time."

Time. It was something I knew for fact that Talon didn't have.

The doctors had made me aware about that before we left the hospital, and no matter the facts they tried to push my way, I refused to believe it. I refused to believe he was dying.

"So, let's do it. How do I save him?"

"No," Talon snapped, shaking his head, "absolutely fucking not. Tell her, Hale, since you want to explain all of these crazy theories. Tell her what will happen if she isn't."

Hale sighed at Talon before looking off, thinking to himself. "We don't have time to wait and make sure you are, in fact, Sølvmåne which is a problem..."

"Tell her, Hale... stop being around the fucking bush."

"Enough," I said with a stern tone looking at Talon, "you can't be stressed like this."

"No, he's right, Ivy," Hale sighed. "I'm fucking this all up."

Moving toward Hale, I wrapped my arms around him and pulled his head toward my chest.

"You're not. Completing this bond to save Talon is important. I mean, what's the worst that could honestly happen if I'm not Sølvmåne or whatever it's called—"

"You'll die, Ivy," Talon replied, causing me to look at him.

Tears filled his eyes, and if I died... it would kill them all.

The situation was suddenly clearer than it had ever been... save Talon, and they could all die.

Save them and not complete the bond, though… and Talon would die.

Mating Damian

Death never seemed so sweet as it did right now.

The choices were clear, and in the end, one choice posed death while the other was only potential. Never in my life had I felt as helpless as I had in that moment.

Yet, something inside me told me not to be afraid. It told me to be strong.

But how could I when there was a chance I was signing someone's death warrant?

"Do the others know?" I asked, staring at the wall ahead of me, trying to judge where everyone's minds were at.

Hale was quiet for a moment, but I knew that was only because he didn't want to admit to me the truth. "Yes, they know."

"What was their verdict?" I asked him, but deep down, I already knew what they were going to say. They would say no because they didn't want me to die.

"Ivy..." Talon sighed, catching my attention. "I'm not worth it."

"Don't ever say that to me again," I snapped angrily. "You are worth everything. All of you are, and I won't have you thinking otherwise. Do you understand me?"

There was no mistaking the choice I would have to make, and even though I didn't want to let them die because of my choice, I knew one of them that would, in fact, live far past us.

Damian.

Standing to my feet, I stormed from the room with Talon and Hale yelling my name.

"Damian!" I screamed as I searched through the house, seeking the tall form that pissed me off more times than I could count. "Damian!"

His dark eyes met mine from behind his desk, and as he looked at me, I could see the haunted thoughts that were crossing his mind. "They told you."

It wasn't a question. His words were a statement, and as I nodded, all he did was sigh and pick up the glass of amber liquid, chasing it down.

"You knew all this time, and you didn't tell me. Why?"

"Why?" He laughed, "seriously, right now, Ivy?"

"Is it because you didn't want to die? Is that why you have waited to mark me so long... because you didn't want to die?!" My thoughts of him not being selfish were slowly diminishing because I couldn't understand why he wouldn't have this told to me much sooner.

"Of course, that's what you would think," he scoffed, "contrary to your belief, I have only known since the day I saved your ass in the woods. We haven't exactly had time to discuss this since then."

Letting out a heavy breath, I sighed. "I'm sorry."

It didn't say anything as he took another sip and raised his brows, letting out a soft laugh. "Yeah, so am I. I already know what you're going to do, and if you want to take that risk, I won't stop you. I just wish that I could join that same quick demise that the rest of you will have."

"Stop being so morbid, Damian. There is no telling if I will die."

Standing to his feet quickly, he slammed his glass against the far wall with a force I had never seen from him. "It's fucking bullshit, Ivy! I have given everything up my entire life, and this is the fucking bullshit that I have to deal with. Fuck that!"

For once, his anger was pouring from him, and I understood. "Then take back what you're afraid of. Join the choice and make death quick if that's what you want."

His eyes hazed over, and moving fast, I found myself pinned against the door of his office, the door cracking under the force of his aggression.

There was no sweet sentiment about what he was doing, and I was fine with that. Our relationship wasn't sunshine and butterflies.

It was raw. Carnal and full of sinful power.

His hands dug at my skin as a possessive growl left his throat. "You're mine, Ivy."

Crashing lips upon mine took my breath away. I wanted this, and I would want this for the rest of my life. Damian gave me something the other didn't. The ability to lose control of myself.

He may not have had the same gene that his brothers had, but he was far more dangerous than they were in all the right ways. He was an uncontrollable beast with a taste for power that took what he wanted without mercy.

And god, I fucking loved it.

"Shit–" I gasped as layer by layer, the clothing that concealed us was torn and tossed to the floor. His lips left a hot trail down my skin that sent pleasure straight to my core.

Pinning me in place, he gripped my thighs and brought me up to his shoulders. His mouth attacked my wet cunt, causing gasps of pleasure to escape me as I let him satisfy his hunger.

Over and over, his tongue evaded me, and when he wasn't evading me, his tongue and lips were sucking on my clit, causing me to gasp out as the knot in my stomach built higher and higher.

"Please, Damian–" I whimpered as an orgasm flooded me. "I need you."

He didn't waste a moment as he dropped me to my feet and spun me around to face the office door. "I won't be gentle," he growled in my ear, causing me to shudder.

"Then don't."

Legs spread, I felt the mass of his erection thrust forcefully inside my tight wet pussy. I cried out at the fullness he brought deep inside me. But as soon as he started to move, I could help but find pleasure in him.

Long deep fast thrust had me teetering on the edge, and the more I cried out in pleasure, the faster and harder he went. My legs were barely able to hold me up as I tightened around him, coming undone.

It wasn't enough, though. He forced me to ride out my orgasm as he continued, and slowly but surely, the thickness of his knot formed inside me, pushing me even further to my limits. I wasn't sure how things would work with the twins, but I knew right now I was on the verge of all I could take.

"Damian, please. I can't." I cried out as the full size of his knot hit its point, and I screamed out, coming again, but this time with a sharp pain straight to my neck as he bit down on me, marking me as his.

A rush of emotions flooded me as he released me from his mouth and roared in satisfaction. The possessive nature of what he had done had blown my mind, but it put me one step closer to saving Talon.

I would do whatever I had to do to save our family, even if that meant succumbing to the darkness that was quickly surrounding me.

Damian

The connection with Ivy was something I never thought I would have. Her body slacked in my arms, and as I peered down at her, I couldn't help but feel the panic slowly rising through me.

"What have I done?" I whispered as my heart raced, and a pale crept across my face.

Naked and holding her in my arms, the door to my office slowly opened, causing me to pull back and sink to the floor with her in my lap.

"Damian?" James said with concern, "what?"

He stopped in his tracks, looking down at Ivy and me. His eyes widened with shock as he quietly stepped in and closed the door.

"Are you okay?" he asked.

"Does it look like I'm okay?" I snapped unintentionally as I held her tighter against me. "She's going to die, and it's all my fault."

"What are you talking about?" James laughed, "she isn't going to die. She is just sleeping from the bond you formed with her. You know this..."

Of course, I knew that, but it wasn't what I was talking about.

Ivy was going to end up dying because I didn't force her to leave and go back to her mothers. I allowed the idea of our bond to control me, and I helped her in bringing us all back together. Now that we know what she is or could be...

It's complicated everything.

"I need to get her upstairs to her room," I muttered as I slowly stood to my feet and lifted her body in my arms. "She needs to rest."

James didn't bother to argue with me but instead opened the door and followed behind me as I carried her up the stairs to her room. As I hit the top of the stairs, I stopped and looked ahead, connecting my eyes with Hale's.

"You accepted her," he said with his arms crossed, staring on in disbelief.

"I can't live without her if that is what is going to happen. Where she goes, I go."

Moving forward, I stepped into her room and laid her upon the soft comfort of her bed, pulling the blankets over her sleeping form. Ivy had no idea what she was doing for us, but at the same time, it was admirable of her to take on such a task.

A woman, more beautiful than anything I could have ever imagined, was determined to show us what love was. I may not have been the first to have her, and I may have put her through hell... but she didn't care.

Instead, through every trial we had undergone, she pushed us to be better than we were. She fought with us to help bring the passion back into our eyes, and all of it was because she cared.

She wanted us to succeed, even when we didn't believe in ourselves.

"Does this mean you're finally going to open up to her?" Hale asked from behind me, pulling me from my thoughts. Staying silent, I moved from her room and down the hall toward my own.

I knew he was following me. I knew that he wasn't going to let this go because deep inside, I had secrets I was hiding that destroyed who I was to an extent.

Secrets I wasn't ready to allow to the surface, and yet now that I was linked with Ivy, there was nothing stopping her from finding out the truth.

"I know what I have to do." I sighed as I pulled on a pair of shorts and turned to stare at Hale and James. "There is a lot we need to discuss."

"I agree," Hale replied as I gestured for them to follow me, and I made my way down the stairs toward my office with my brothers.

Yet, when my feet hit the bottom of the steps, I came face to face with Allison.

"What are you doing in my house?" I asked, crossing my arms over my chest as I glared at her.

"Your house?" She scoffed, "when are you going to get it that this is my house, and we are simply letting you boys play this game–"

"Enough. Get out of my house now," I replied, cutting her off, not wanting to hear any of the bullshit she was trying to spill.

"No. I came to see how Talon's doing," she replied, trying to push her way past me.

"You're not going upstairs near him or Ivy. I want you out of my house now, or I will have you thrown out like the bitch you are," I seethed.

Every part of me felt like she had a part in what happened to Talon, and I was trying my hardest to prove it. I wanted her to burn for her crimes against my brother, and I knew without a doubt that Ivy would feel the same.

The bond between us is already strong and, over time, it would only get stronger.

"I can't believe you have her up there with Talon. What if she is the one poisoning him!"

Allison's ridiculous notions were all but getting on my last nerve. I didn't have time for her, and slowly, as her eyes lingered on me, she frowned.

"Why are there blood spots on your chest?" she asked in confusion.

Looking over my shoulder at James, he didn't waste another second and passed me, gripping Allison's arm, dragging her outside. Her protests were heard all the way in my office, but at the end of the day she wouldn't be allowed to see Talon.

And never again would she be near Ivy alone.

Ignoring the chaos outside, I entered my office and laughed. "It seems that she is never going to give up, is she?"

Turning, I saw Hale's confliction. "We need to talk about this.."

"Talk about what?" I asked him, confused as to what he was referring to.

"Talon doesn't have much longer, Damian. I know what's going through your mind, but at the same time, I don't know if he wants this."

I didn't understand what he was talking about, and yet at the same time, I felt like I did.

"Ivy isn't going to allow him to die, Hale. She did this because she wanted to make the choices together. She wants us to be together."

Nodding slowly, Hale smiled as James quietly came into the office, "I had security take her off pack lands."

"I bet she enjoyed that," Hale replied smugly, causing me to laugh.

"Yeah, she loved it so much that she said she is going to the elder council, and she is going to have us exiled for our crimes against the bloodlines."

This phrase made my blood run cold. It was clear that what she was referring to was the gene we held secret. However, there was no possible way she could know.

There was no way that we had been compromised. It could still cause death to us all.

"Fuck. I'm really getting tired of always possibly dying."

Changing the Future

Ivy

Waking, I thought that everything had been a dream. Everything that Hale had told me made no sense, but then, at the same time, it did.

Slowly, as the days grew on, I felt different, and I had tried to push it off as simply being stressed because of everything that had happened. But that wasn't it.

I should have known that in the crazy world I was living, things wouldn't be this easy.

I should have realized that my place with the guys was more than what I expected it to be, and deep down inside, I should have been curious at some point to know if I had the gene my father did.

Yet, it was never a thought that had crossed my mind.

Placing my hand on my forehead, I slowly sat up and looked down at my naked body.

I was mated with Damian now.

He had been the dam that blocked my bond before, and in desperation, he had allowed me to convince him to complete the bond with me. The only thing I had left to do was save Talon.

Pushing myself from the bed, my legs wobbled beneath me, and I quickly reached out, grabbing the nightstand to support myself. My body felt like it was on fire, and my heart was on the verge of exploding.

I wasn't sure if this was normal when mating with wolves, but I was going to have to get my shit together. If the guys saw me struggling–they would never let me continue.

Slowly I crept to the bathroom and turned on the cold water, letting the icy sting of its drop bead across my skin. A groan of pain escaped my lips as I forced myself to clean up and make myself somewhat presentable.

"Ivy?" Damian's voice came through clearly from my bedroom, and panic swept through me. He was the last person I needed to see me like this.

"Just a moment!" I called out as cheerfully as I could.

"I was just going to see if you were hungry," he replied from the other side of the door.

I hadn't really considered being hungry before, but now that he had mentioned it, I was ravenous. I couldn't remember ever being as hungry as I was right now, and the hunger caused the pain in my body to become more real.

"Yes," I croaked out, "I'm starving. How about putting meat on the grill?"

Sucking in a breath, I gritted my teeth and forced a block on my link so that they wouldn't sense the immense pain I was in.

"Ivy... are you sure you're okay?"

"Yep," I quickly replied, "I'll be down soon."

It took a moment, but then I heard his footsteps turn and head out of the room. With a heavy sigh, I leaned back against the shower wall and closed my eyes.

Whatever was happening to mine was going to have to wait. There were more pressing matters to address, and I had to get my shit together.

Turning off the water, I staggered to the bathroom sink, wrapping a towel around my waist before reaching for a bottle of Tylenol. Hopefully, the medicine would take the edge off, but considering how abnormal I felt, it was only wishful thinking.

I was hungry, and the hunger I felt was overwhelming.

An hour later, and with much debate. I stumbled toward Talon's bedroom door and opened it, peering in to see him sleeping. My heart swelled as I gripped the door frame with a newfound determination.

Today would be the day. I would save him, and when I did, it would change the future.

Even though they thought what I was going to do would kill me—I didn't.

With satisfaction, I slowly closed his door and turned toward the stairs, only to be met with a delicious scent I had never smelt before.

"Oh, fuck..." I groaned as I pushed myself two steps at a time down the stairs and toward the kitchen. "What is that smell?"

James and Hale turned to me with furrowed brows as they continued preparing the food before them. "Uh, steak? Damian just put some on the grill."

Shaking my head, I rolled my eyes. "No, it's not that."

I wasn't sure what the smell was, but as I walked closer toward them, the smell got stronger until I caught sight of the kabobs that James was skewering with brightly colored vegetables.

"Ivy? What's wrong with you?"

His questions and concerns went out the window the moment I reached forward and grabbed a piece of raw steak from the cutting board and brought it to my nose, inhaling deeply with satisfaction.

"Oh, shit," I groaned as I plopped it into my mouth.

"Ivy! What the fuck?" James exclaimed with wide eyes as I snatched the cutting board, disregarding the vegetables and stuffing the raw meat into my mouth.

"This is so good," I mumbled as the hungry feeling within my stomach began to slowly dissipate. "What is this? It's so good."

The French doors opened, and my eyes caught sight of Damian walking in with an empty tray and a pair of tongs. He paused in his steps, looking at all of us with confusion. "Did I miss something?"

"Yeah, you could say that." Hale chuckled, "seems our Ivy has a thing for steak. Just more raw than most."

As I popped the last piece into my mouth, I moaned in satisfaction, licking each one of my fingers slowly. It wasn't until Damian cleared his throat that I really considered what I had just done.

Looking down at the blood on the counter and on the cutting board, my eyes widened.

"Uh, yeah, so I forgot to mention—" I stuttered with a sheepish grin. "There might be something wrong with me."

James burst into laughter as did Hale, while Damian stood shaking his head. "Might? Ivy, you just cleaned the fucking cutting board of meat that wasn't cooked!"

That might have been a problem, but at the same time, he seemed to make more of a big deal about it than needed. Shrugging my shoulders, I rolled my eyes and grabbed a carrot.

"Fine, I'll eat a vegetable."

"I told you, Damian. Sølvmåne." Hale seemed chuffed about his choices, even though he seemed convinced James and Damian were not.

A creek from upstairs made my eyes snap toward it, and before the others could react, I was on my feet and clearing the stairs rushing toward Talon's room.

My heart sank as I saw him lying upon the floor, groaning in pain. Rushing toward him, his eyes met mine, and that was when

I saw it. Black spider-like veins were spreading down the side of his neck and over the right side of his chest.

"Talon–" I cried out softly as he smiled at me. "What are you doing? I have to get you back in bed."

He coughed as he tried to laugh and shook his head no. "I don't want to be up here by myself, Ivy. I want to come down and join all of you."

"Shit–" as James and the others rushed into the room, I stepped back and watched them help Talon back up onto the bed.

"Talon, what were you thinking?" Damian asked, but even though all of their questions were thrown around, I knew what I had to do. There was no more taking time and waiting to be sure.

I had to save him now, and I needed Hale to do it.

"James, Damian, I need you both to get out."

"What?" Damian hissed, casting his glance toward me. "Ivy, no. There still is too much we need to figure out."

"I said to get out," I growled deeply, catching even myself off guard by the action.

James didn't say a word as he stared at me. Moving slowly, he wrapped his arms around me and kissed me. "I love you, Ivy. No matter what you decide."

It was his way of silent approval, and it broke my heart because James had been the kindest out of them all. The way he was with me was free and fun.

"I love you too," I whispered back as he pulled back and turned toward the door.

"It's time, Damian. Let's go finish cooking."

"No!" Damian growled, "I just got you. This isn't going to happen."

There was pain and remorse in his words as I watched him fight back tears. He had kept me at a distance for so long while the others had gotten the chance to know me.

It was his fault, but at the same time, I never gave him a proper chance.

"I will not leave you, Damian. I need you to have faith in me."

With much reluctance, he turned and stormed from the door, but not before I heard the crunch of drywall from the impact of his fist. He was angry and had every right to be.

This wasn't about him, though. It was about Talon, and it was about me.

Selfish, perhaps, but it was something I had to do.

He would have to forgive me later when I fixed our family and brought us closer to our future. Letting out a heavy sigh, I turned to Hale and smiled. "Are you okay?"

"Yes, are you?" He smirked, walking toward me and pulling me close.

"I will be. I just hope that this works and everything we have been through wasn't for nothing."

"I hope the same thing, Ivy. But to be honest, I don't know if Talon has the strength for this in his current state." Hale replied, causing my eyes to look toward Talon, who laid on the bed with his eyes close, and his chest moving rapidly.

If I didn't do this now, there was no way he would make it through the night.

"I know he can't in this way, but there is another way he can."

Turning to Hale, I watched the confusion on his face slowly turn to one of shock as he realized what I meant and began shaking his head no. "You can't. His beast is worse than mine, and I don't know if I can hold him back."

Smiling, I let a soft chuckle escape me as I slowly began to undress. "You won't be holding anything back, Hale."

"What do you mean? Of course, I will. I'm not going to let you be hurt by him."

He didn't understand a single word of what I meant, and as much as Hale had regretted what he did before–it had to be done.

"For the longest time, a voice has rung through my mind as I slept, Hale. I had always thought that it was just my internal voice giving me guidance when I was stressed, but after I mated with you, it slowly became louder..."

"What are you talking about?" he asked, backing away from me with a narrowed glance.

Stepping forward, I let my shorts slip from me, exposing my completely naked body to him. "Do you want to know what it said?" I replied, backing him against the wall.

"What–" he whispered as I gently kissed him.

"Two beasts of the night unlock the goddess in silver light."

Never had I taken much consideration into what it meant. I had always expected that I was slowly losing my mind and that perhaps what was happening to me was a result of my chaotic life.

Yet, the moment I walked into the room and saw Talon on the floor, I knew what it meant.

In order for me to save him, I had to give myself over to their beasts.

After all, they were twins, two parts to a whole that can only be one when brought together by one who completed them. It was rare already that twins shared a mate, but to have two Lycan blood twins share a mate with two other siblings...

Well, it was fucking unimaginable.

As if my words triggered recognition in him, fear struck through his eyes. "Ivy, no... no, no... please, no."

It was too late, though. There was no changing my mind.

"Leikos... oh dear Leikos, won't you come out to play?"

Hale doubled over in pain as he let out a roar of protest. "Ivy, stop!"

"Stop fighting, Hale, let him out," I pleaded with a smile. "I promise it will be okay."

I needed them in their true forms, and the more he resisted, the harder it would be to make this work. "Leikos. I need you to take me."

A flash of gold blew through Hale's eyes as he roared again, but this time the pounding against Talon's bedroom door from Damian caught my attention, followed by James' voice.

I could feel his panic. The fear that was rolling through him at what the twins could do to me. "Damian, please. Go."

I was asking him to do something that went against his nature. For a wolf's mate to be in danger is for the male to protect what's his. However, no one had ever been placed in the situation we were in now.

No one ever expected this to happen because in truth, it had never happened.

"Ivy, stop this! You can't do this!" Damian yelled, "please."

"Do not let him in this room, James!" I yelled, turning my attention to Talon.

I wasn't sure if he was able to make sense of what was going on around him, but I had gotten his beast's attention once before and I needed it now more than ever.

Walking toward the bed, I climbed over to Talon, straddling his waist as I ran one of my hands gently through his hair. "Ivy–no," he mumbled painfully.

"Shhh–" I hushed. "I'm going to make everything better."

He shook his head slowly in protest, "I could kill you. Please, just let me die."

"No." I refused to lose him. I refused to live this life without all of them, and I would give myself for them in a way that no other woman ever would.

Leaning back, I cast a glance toward Hale, who was shifting into the beast I had once seen before. A small smile of satisfaction caught my eyes as his eyes connected with mine.

At one point, I had been terrified, but now... I wasn't.

It was beautiful to watch him change into the creature he truly was, and without hesitation, I whispered, "Volaire—come claim what is yours."

In Talon's weakened form, he was unable to fight against what I was doing, and after a moment, his eyes shot open, and a fierce blue gaze stared back at me.

"Mine." It growled as he began the slow change beneath me. His eyes flashed toward Hale, who stood at my side. The massive size of the creature towered over me like a predator ready to attack its prey.

"Mine," he growled, baring his fangs with a sadistic look in his eyes that made me breathless.

"Yes, I am here for you both," I replied.

"Are you now?" Talon's beast purred, "are you sure?"

"Yes," I gasped as he touched me. "Volaire–Leikos—complete the circle and take what's yours."

Talon didn't hesitate to grip my throat with his sharp claws as he sat up with me still against him. The poison that had been killing Talon did not seem to affect this creature in the way it had Talon's human form.

"What makes you think you're worthy of my claim?" he asked.

Letting my free hand reach up to brush against the side of his cheek, I smiled. I couldn't understand before what my importance was, but with this, I finally knew the reason why the goddess had paired me with them.

A circle of secrets had to come to an end, and with me–it would.

"Because I accept you both for what you are. I bare myself to you both."

His lips crashed against mine with heated frenzy as he kissed me, bringing to light a hunger inside me I had been craving to fill. The moment they both began to touch me, I let myself go falling into whatever pleasure they wanted.

I wasn't sure how they would take me, and how I would survive it, but I didn't care.

I would take whatever they wanted to give.

Pushing me back, Hale stared down at me, and slowly the thick head of his cock was brought to my lips. It was long and thick, and the head curved for intense pleasure.

Like a starved animal, I opened my mouth willingly and let my tongue lick around the head as Talon brought my hips up toward his face.

There wasn't intense, loving foreplay with them. Instead, everything was raw and primal.

It was all about them, and I was completely fine with that.

The moment he latched onto my soaking wet core, I moaned, giving Hale the opportunity to shove the length of his erect cock into my throat.

I gagged on his length, but never did I give up. I let my mouth please him in ways that caused him pleasure. The more grunts Hale made, the faster and deeper Talon's tongue went into my tight pulsating core.

The sensations from them both bring me closer to the peak I sought.

The feeling of pleasuring them both was intense, and it had only just begun.

With a muffled cry, I came undone only to have Hale pull away and grip my hair, pulling me upright to my knees and away from the pleasure Talon had been giving me.

I whimpered at the sudden loss of their touch but quickly reminded myself that this wasn't the usual Hale and Talon. This was far more primal.

"You're going to scream for us," he purred as he nipped at my bottom lip. "I want you to please my brother as I please you."

Casting my gaze toward Talon, I watched him slowly run his hand over his thick cock, and a surge of arousal flooded me. He was large, far larger than I remembered, and with a quick jerk, Hale had my attention.

I moved toward Talon, and as I did, I found myself slowly sliding down upon him. There was no getting used to his size or hesitation. His claws yanked me forward, pressing me against his chest as he drove himself into me repeatedly.

"Shit!" I cried out as his pulsating head pressed against my g-spot, sending sensations straight through to my heart.

"Mine," he growled in my ear, causing me to moan in pleasure.

"Yes, yours. Fucking hell yes, I'm yours."

I wasn't sure what had gotten into me, but I didn't care. I wanted it all. Every last drop of whatever they wanted to fill me with. I would take it all.

Feeling the knot form in my stomach of my rising pleasure, I hadn't expected to feel something unfamiliar. The fanning breath of Hale against my puckered hole as he used his tongue to lick me from my tight core toward an entrance no one had ever ventured.

"What are you–" I cried out, feeling myself about to explode.

"No," Talon growled as he impaled me, going fast one moment and then denying my orgasm as he began to go slow.

It was tortuous, but it was only long-lived when my attention went to Hale's thumb pressing against my backside, slowly slipping in and out.

That sensation tipped me over the edge, and as it did, my pussy tightened as I came undone on Talon. Nails gripped at the sheets as they forced me to ride out a wave of pleasure I hadn't been expecting from the actions Hale was taking.

One by one, his fingers stretched me before I felt his other hand slip into my tight core, pressed against Talon's own erection. They were stretching me, pulling me, and working me out.

I had a feeling about what was going to happen. I would have to take them both into me and let them finish together, or at least that's what I thought until Talon spoke again.

"On your side," Talon ordered as he pulled me to my side to face him. "You are going to take us both, Ivy. Do you understand?"

"Yes," I replied breathlessly. "I understand.

The slow buildup of our interaction tormented me from day one as I had constantly imagined what it would be like to be taken by them both. To have both of them fill me.

I had expected to feel Hale's cock at my puckered entrance, but instead, I felt their heads both press against my tight core. My eyes widened in shock as I stared at him, watching the sinful sadistic gaze he was giving me as they pressed into my tight pussy at the same time.

Once before, I had seen a glimpse of porn that made me question these kinds of things, but participating in them was something I never considered would happen to me.

Taking them both stretched me to painful limits, but as soon as they moved, it was as if I had died and gone to heaven.

Mouths upon my skin and wandering claws, I took both of these beautiful Lycans into me without another thought. I wanted them as much as they wanted me.

"Don't stop!" I cried out over and over again as I bounced against them. My head tilted back, and mouth parted open. I allowed them to use me in whatever they wanted.

Slow and steady were their movements, and eventually, the swell of their knots caused me to cry out as they rubbed me in all the right ways.

Growls of satisfaction left their throats, and as I screamed in pleasure with my body shaking from the heights of their control, I felt the sting of their bites within my skin.

Blinding light filled me as everything suddenly fell silent.

My body on fire, my mind numb. I felt like I was hovering in a place of non-existence.

A place where my life was suspended.

Talon

Waking, I felt brand new. No longer did I feel a painful ache in my body from what had happened to me. Instead, I felt as if someone had struck me with lightning and charged the dying battery within my heart.

My eyes took in the room before landing upon a very pissed off Damian sitting in an armchair in the corner. "Damian?" I asked with confusion. "What are you looking at, perv?"

"Go fuck yourself, Talon," he snapped. "I'm glad to see your sarcastic personality is still intact after everything."

"Fuck are you talking about?" I asked in confusion as I slowly sat up.

Damian didn't say anything, instead he pointed toward the space next to me, and as he did, my eyes laid upon a very naked and sleeping Ivy. Fresh bloodied bite marks on her neck and a slow pulsating aura surrounded her body.

It was then that the memories of what had happened flooded back through my mind, and I realized what she did. "She saved me."

"Yeah, she did," he replied, pinching the bridge of his nose before slowly standing up. It was obvious that Damian was pissed about what had happened, but it shocked me more to notice that on Ivy's neck laid four bite marks, and one that looked over bitten. More than likely, Hale's.

"She is Sølvmåne?" I asked, trying to remember everything Hale had told me before.

Damian didn't say anything, but slowly he nodded his head. Moving from the bed, I stood to my feet and looked in the long mirror by the bathroom at my reflection.

Any trace of the illness was gone, and I looked healthier than I had before.

Bigger, fiercer. "What happened?"

"Well, she provoked yours and Hale's beasts and then proceed to bond with you both in that form, completing the bond Talon."

My eyes shot to his as my eyes searched him, hoping that he was lying.

"She took us both in... did we?" I hesitantly asked, watching as Damian nodded.

"Yes, she took both of your knots at the same time, and as soon as you both marked her, she passed out. She hasn't been up since," he replied with a sad sigh.

"Well, it's only been a few hours, right? She will wake up soon."

I was trying to remain hopeful, but there was sadness in his eyes, and before he could reply, the door opened, and Hale and James walked in.

"Oh, good! You're awake," James said cheerfully. "Welcome back to the land of the living, fuck face."

Rolling my eyes, I flipped him off. "So how long have we been out then?"

"You didn't tell him?" Hale snapped at Damian.

"Tell me what?" I asked again, becoming annoyed with their cryptic conversations.

Hale turned toward me and placed his hand on my shoulder before glancing toward Ivy's sleeping form. "Brother, you both have been asleep for almost a week."

Shock filled me at his revelation. I could understand me being out for a week, but Ivy?

"Why isn't she waking up?" I asked breathlessly.

"We don't know, but there is something else you need to know," Hale replied.

Turning my gaze to him, I furrowed my brows. "What's that?"

"Allison went to the council about our inability to rule, and now we have been summoned." Damian interjected with a steely glare. "An they want Ivy present as well."

Words from a Goddess

Ivy

There was once a time in my life when I considered and aspired to be a princess. A single phrase from a child's book made me feel like anything was possible and that was—Once upon a time.

Who knew those four little words could change so fucking much in my life?

Every young girl dreams of her once upon a time at some point in her life, and when we are young, we never really consider what the complications of our dreams could be. In reality, we aren't given the choice of where our path is going, but instead, how we handle the shit thrown at us.

Some might say that is predetermination, but for me... I call it a miscalculation.

I felt lighter than I ever had before, and when the mist started to clear, I found myself walking from the clouds that surrounded me toward the figure of a woman I had never seen before.

Her golden hair hung around her face in gentle waves while a curious glint held unwavering light in her eyes. "You're finally here," she said as if it was the most obvious thing to happen.

"I'm finally where?" I asked with confusion, watching the amusement flow off of her.

"It isn't about where you are but where you have been," she replied, confusing me even more.

I had been a patient person most of my life, and over the course of the last few months. I would like to think I had been a very patient and understanding individual. So for this woman to stand before me speaking riddles—it was fucking annoying.

"Do you care to elaborate on whatever it is you're talking about since I'm dead and need to like voodoo hoodoo or whatever to the great beyond?" I sighed, not wanting to deal with cryptic messages from this woman.

"Dead?" Laughter escaped her lips. "You're not dead. Do you not know who I am?"

"No," I deadpanned, crossing my arms over my chest. "Am I supposed to?"

A sparkle in her eye caught me off guard as she stepped toward me. Her long white and blue dress flowed behind her like the Greek goddess she seemed to be. There was no telling what would happen to me here, but then again, I have had a lot of peculiar shit happen to me lately.

"I have many names. The wolves, you know, refer to me as the moon goddess. Some even refer to me as Selene. However, the name I preferred for many centuries was the name my husband called me—Frigg.

"Frigg... as in the Norse goddess, Frigg?"

There was no way that was possible, but her smile told me otherwise.

"Ivy, over hundreds of years, people have ordained what they will to find the faith that fits them. The gods and goddesses all have had many names, but there was always one thing that never changed—the love we had for those on earth."

Confusion filled me trying to understand what she meant. If she had loved so many on earth, humans and other creatures alike, then why did they not save those who should have been saved?

It didn't make sense.

"I'm sorry. I'm just not a religious person," I replied, giving her an uninterested look. "So you will have to forgive me when I ask where the fuck you and the others have been for hundreds of years while those on earth have suffered left and right."

"Well," she smiled warmly. "Even though we are what we are, people have to learn to follow their own guidance. It wouldn't be right of us to tell them what to do. How would they grow if we constantly held their hand?"

She had a point. One I couldn't deny.

Evolution was an important aspect of life, and even though we tried to tell ourselves everything happens for a reason and there is always a purpose... it doesn't always make sense.

"I can understand that," I replied. "But what am I doing here?"

Reaching out, she looped her arm through mine and smiled. "Now that is a question I was waiting for you to ask, my child."

The ominous feeling of the place I was in did nothing to ease my mind. I wasn't sure what this woman's intent was, no matter who she claimed to be. Also, if I wasn't dead, then how the hell did I get here?

"Care to elaborate, then?" I asked with a pointed glance.

"Of course, but first... there is someone I want you to meet."

Letting a small sigh escape me, I follow her without complaints. It wasn't like I really had much of a choice anyway because her grip on my arm was like a vise.

"Kara..." Frigg sing-songed as we turned a corner that opened up into a lush garden area with tall white pillars that seemed to disappear into the sky.

My eyes landed on a tall warrior woman with long red hair that cascaded down over the front of her. Her deep sea-green eyes met mine, and as they did, a warm smile crossed her face.

"Is this her?" The woman asked as she took a step closer with a calming aura that ran off her body like a rushing river. Merely being around her made me feel at peace, but I fought against it. I had to stay aware of everything so I could get back to my mates.

I couldn't fall prey to whatever these two women wanted.

Frigg let go of her grip on me and smiled, making her way toward Kara. The sudden feeling of being in the wrong place set a course through me I wasn't sure of.

"Yes, it is. Our very own Eternal." Frigg turned to stare at me, tilting her head. "Never had I thought the Eternal would be as beautiful as she is."

"Eternal?" I questioned. "Will one of you please fucking tell me what's going on because honestly, if I'm not dead and supposed to be here, I would love to go back to where I was."

Both women began to cackle at my response as Kara took the initiative to come closer to me. "You were never told anything about your history?"

"No, up until I went to live with—" pausing, I realized the one thing I hadn't even thought about before. "I need to go back. They're waiting for me. Please tell me how I get back to them. Are they okay?"

My heart clenched, thinking how they would react to me not being there if I wasn't dead. They barely had made it without me before and Talon.

"Oh god, is Talon okay?"

"Shhh—" Frigg hushed as she appeared at my side. "Your mates are okay. They think you're sleeping, child. Don't worry."

"But Talon... did it work?" I asked, fighting back the tears that threatened to fall.

"Talon?" she questioned, looking off while she was thinking. "Oh! You mean the angry ancient? Yes, he is still alive."

"Angry ancient?" I replied with hesitation. "Why do you call him the "angry" ancient?"

"Because he is," Kara snickered. "Volaire was angry in the beginning, and even though he was recreated in his new form, he will continue to be angry. Such a grumpy creature. I don't understand why..."

Running my hands over my face with furrowed brows, I tried to understand what the hell they were talking about. "You mean that he was alive before Talon? I'm so confused right now. You guys are literally talking in circles around me."

"Everything runs in circles, Ivy. Life grows, lives, and dies. When you die, your spirit is cast-off to be reborn again. Typically, within the same family generation, you lived before and without any memory of your prior life." Kara explained as she picked up a flower and watched it wilt in her hand.

"Well, there is an exception to that..." Frigg chuckled, looking at Kara, who rolled her eyes and nodded.

"Yes, because your sister loves to play funny jokes, Frigg."

Both women continued going back and forth about some family dilemma as I stood trying to process everything they were telling me. Talon and Hale were not just as they were by accident.

They were reborn with the spirit and bloodline of another creature?

"Look, will you both stop? You're confusing the shit out of me," I finally snapped, catching their attention. "So, you're telling me that someone else is inside them?"

"No," Kara replied with a raised brow. "They are reborn into new lives, but the gene in which they care is descendent from the original."

"Why don't Damian and James have it? They don't have the gene?" I replied, trying to catch them up on whatever webs they were spinning.

Instead, though, their faces fell, and sorrow took over them. "They have the gene, Ivy. James has not unlocked his, and Damian... well, his was destroyed when he was a child."

There were so many questions racing through my mind at her words, but I felt the metaphorical stab of a large blade through my heart.

"What do you mean Damian's was destroyed? What happened to him?"

With a heavy sigh, Frigg shook her head. "That isn't our story to tell Ivy. You will have to wait until he is ready to tell you."

Damian will never be what his brothers are, and James... he hadn't unlocked the side of him that he was so thankful he wouldn't have.

"Can you tell me why you said I'm Eternal?" I whispered before I let my eyes lift to meet their gazes.

"Ivy, you are the one we have waited for, for so many generations. You defied the odds and broke your father's family curse. You were not recreated, but the heavens created you. You're not one of them."

Frigg seemed almost speechless at what she was trying to explain, and slowly the pieces started to fit, and I felt myself understanding.

"I'm like you?" I asked, watching as tears filled her eyes.

"Yes. You're one of us, but you are the celestial of earth. You derive from an eternal bloodline that was extinct, or at least, that was what we thought."

All of this... It was more overwhelming than I expected. I knew when I completed the circle with the guys, things were going to change, but with all the answers they gave, there was still so much context that was missing.

Everything was a mystery I felt in the end, only I could figure out.

"So what does this mean for our future?"

Kara stood firm as she thought over my question.

"There will be a large hurdle in your future, Ivy," Kara finally spoke up. "You will be challenged, but no matter how hard it gets, you need to listen to yourself. We won't be able to help you in the future... you will be on your own."

Of course, I would be. I groaned internally.

"Alrighty then. Well, as much as this has been fun, I need to go. So, can one of you show me how to get home?"

"Ivy, this is serious..." Kara tried to explain, but holding up my hand, I cut her off.

"No, I am quite aware of how serious this is. Like you said, though, you can't help me. I have to figure this out on my own. Right now, though, I need to go home."

Kara stepped forward but was quickly stopped by Frigg, who gave her a stern glare and shook her head.

As her eyes turned to lie upon me once more, the corners of her lips turned up into a smile. "You're right. We shouldn't keep you away."

As she spoke, a tingling sensation rose over my skin, and the white light that had blinded me once before slowly began to grow. There was more I had wanted to know, but there was no time for me to consider them now.

I needed to get home to the guys. I needed to make sure they were okay because with things the way they were before I completed the circle, there was no telling how Damian would be acting.

"Ivy!" Frigg called out one last time as the white began to close. "Control your hunger. Don't let it control you."

Her words were the last thing I heard before I was once again plunged into a blinding light with no escape. My heart grew warm and my fists clenched, I felt a jolt of pain through my system like that of a bolt of lightning.

The pain caused a scream to tear through my throat as I found myself jolted from my sleep with wide eyes looking around at the white walls of my room from a different perspective.

"Holy fuck."

Placing my hand on my head, I groaned at the slowly forming headache at the base of my skull. I wanted to believe everything had been a dream, but I knew better. My life was far more complicated than that.

I was shocked though, that none of the guys were here to greet me as I awoke. As I took the opportunity to look around again,

I took note I was freshly washed and changed into a clean pair of clothes.

However, that wasn't what intrigued me the most. It was, instead, how brightly colored everything seemed to be. It was as if someone had completely enhanced the color and view of every object around me as I slept.

My senses overloaded as I let it all soak in.

"This is different," I mumbled as I slipped from the bed and padded my way into the bathroom. Looking in the mirror, I caught a glimpse of myself. Long reddish-brown hair hung down to my waist, healthy and shining.

The sight almost caught me off guard, but what caused my heart to quicken was the color of my eyes.

An iridescent sheen of blue stared back at me. The various shades illuminated against the white of my eyes. It was shocking to remember looking one way, and then suddenly waking up to see you have completely changed.

"Holy shit. What the fuck is this?!" I exclaimed, looking in the mirror. "My eyes look like the aura lights. The hell... Oh, they really do have a sense of humor, don't they?"

Pinching the bridge of my nose, I looked up toward the ceiling as if speaking to the sky itself. "Very fucking funny, Frigg. How the hell am I supposed to walk around looking like this? Damn it? This is what I meant by wanting to get back to my normal life!"

Frustration filled me but was quickly cut off as the sound of strained voices floated toward my ears. Damian was pissed off and arguing with someone below. I wasn't sure why I could hear things this clearly but wasting no time, I moved quickly from my room, and to my surprise, I was at the stairs faster than I expected.

Mental note: address that shit later.

I stared down at the foyer below. None of them noticed me as they stood on edge with three men I did not recognize standing before them. Two looked to be police or guards of some sort, and the other was an elderly man with an eerie disposition.

"This is bullshit!" Damian roared. "Things came up, and we weren't able to be there."

"It doesn't matter, Damian. We have to take you into custody for failure to appear. You're lucky we aren't taking you all," the man snapped, not wanting to see reason.

I wasn't sure what was going on, but I wasn't going to let them take Damian anywhere. In a flash, I was down the stairs and standing next to Damian, staring up at the man in front of him with curiosity.

"My apologies. I'm Ivy. I don't believe we have met before."

They all looked at me, shocked, as the man looked toward the stairs, confused as to how I just appeared at Damian's side. "You–where did you just come from?"

Frowning, I bit my inner lip and shrugged, "I don't understand what you mean. I have always been here. Now, what seems to be the problem?"

"Ivy–" Damian said softly as I quickly held up a finger, shushing him. It was more subtle than me telling him to shut the fuck up in front of these men.

"You were all summoned to the council and refused to come. Therefore, we have to take him into custody–"

"Oh, please. I can explain that." I smiled cheerfully, watching as the man's eyes darted to the teeth. I hadn't gotten a proper look at them, being as distracted as I was, but as I ran my tongue over them, I could feel how sharp they were.

"Uh–I'm sorry, but this is pack business, and I don't know," he replied, narrowing his brows as if to show he was better than I was.

Shoving my hand into his for a handshake, I smiled, not giving him a choice but to shake my hand. "I'm Ivy Thorne. Their mate and the Luna of this pack. I do hope you will honor my place within this government."

Laughter from James caught my ear, causing me to smirk, but never once did I let my eyes fall from the man in front of me.

"Unfortunately, I can't verify that, so you need—"

Gripping the man by the throat, I pulled him close and inhaled his scent deeply. "As I was saying... I don't tolerate disrespect, sir. I have warmly introduced myself and have been willing to explain what's wrong."

"Get your hands off me!" he groaned, gripping my hand as if getting me to release him was a difficult task. "I'll listen... I'll listen..."

Thrusting him backward, his guards looked ready to shit themselves over how terrified they were. "Would you boys like some iced tea? Coffee, perhaps." I cheerfully said collect myself. "I'm sure we can come to an agreement."

"No, no," the man coughed, rubbing his throat. "I see that you were simply sick before... Is that right?"

My smile brightened even more, hearing his words. "Yes, of course, council elder. It was simply I was sick, and being a new mate, I have been trying to adjust. I'm sure you understand how that can be."

"Yes..." he muttered. "Could we perhaps reschedule for three days from now?"

"Of course. That would be lovely, and the men and I will all be present at the meeting. I am sure we can clear up whatever issues there may be."

Giving a single nod, he turned to his men, and the three of them scrambled from the front door that I quietly closed behind them. A felt powerful and alive, having handled them. I wasn't sure what the meeting was for or whatever, but I was chuffed.

"That went well," I laughed as I turned to face the four men who had changed my life forever. Damian's eyes were wide, and his mouth parted slightly, as was James'.

However, Hale and Talon stood in the background with their arms crossed over their chest and proud smiles on their lips.

"Hey, gorgeous," Talon smiled as I took him in and almost cried.

"Talon…" Pushing past the others, I ran to him, throwing my arms around his neck as he wrapped me in his embrace, holding me tight against him.

"I take it you missed me, then. I always knew I would be the favorite."

Pulling away, I smacked him playfully, causing him to laugh. "I don't have favorites. I love you all equally."

"How are you here?" Damian asked softly behind me. Turning my eyes met his, and shaking my head, I shrugged.

"Fairy dust," I smirked. "Are you and James going to stand there and stare at me, or are you going to give me a hug?"

Damian didn't bother waiting for James as he cleared the space between us and wrapped his arm around my waist, crashing his lips against mine. His tongue parted the space between them as he swiped the inside of my mouth, causing me to moan.

The sensations he brought within me were different from before. This time I felt every little thing they did, and as he pulled away, I could feel how scared he was that he thought he lost me.

"You thought I was dying?" I asked him, watching as he went speechless.

"We all did, Ivy," James replied as I pulled away from Damian and hugged him. "It's been almost two weeks."

"Two weeks? What are you talking about? It's been a few hours, or maybe a day," I gasped, staring at them. There was no way I had been out that long.

It was clear looking at them they were being sincere. I had barely had a moment to breathe, and yet, I was being thrown into chaos once more.

"Ivy, maybe we should go sit down," Damian suggested. "Are you hungry?"

I was hungry, ravenous, actually, but for the time being, I needed to figure out more important things.

"It can wait," I replied as I stepped toward the living room, knowing very well they were following me.

Hale and Talon didn't give me a chance to sit before I was swiped away by the both of them, and forced to sit upon their laps as they shared in the comfort of having me close.

"You smell divine," Hale whispered in one ear as Talon inhaled deeply at my other side.

"Seriously, guys..." James groaned. "How come I don't get to sit with her too?"

Talon didn't bother answering James as his growl said enough as it was.

"Talon, enough," I whispered as I kissed him. "Let's pay attention."

My gaze fell upon Damian once more as I grinned. "So care to fill me in on everything I have missed?"

"It's complicated," Damian sighed as he took a seat across from me. "When you guys completed the circle, it seems Allison was starting shit with the council. They are trying to prove we are unfit to run the largest pack in North America. She is trying to have us replaced."

"Excuse me?" I snapped. "Replaced by who?"

"Your father and Allison," he sighed, gritting his teeth.

Anger coursed through me hearing this. There was no way that Allison could persuade those people to do something like that. She wasn't even of Alpha blood, and my father–my father was a piss poor man with negative ambitions.

"That's fucking bullshit," I growled. "What the hell makes her think she has the right to do that? They can't just take your place from you. She isn't even an Alpha!"

"We know this, Ivy," Hale said, my eyes turning to him, seeing the defeated look in his expression. "Unfortunately, she has a lot of those men blinded."

"How is that even possible?" I asked, turning back to Damian, completely confused. They had known Damian and the others since they were small. They had even known their parents, and these men questioned everything about them.

"We aren't sure yet. However, us not going to the first meeting poses a problem."

"Well, we will go to the next." I shrugged, trying to think positively.

"Yeah, but after what happened with the elder who came here, that is a worrying thought," James said, looking at his brothers, who all sat quietly.

I didn't understand why they would find it worrying. I was polite and sweet. I was acting like a Luna... or at least what I read before about how a Luna was supposed to act.

"I didn't do anything wrong, though. I thought I handled myself rather well."

Damian and the guys broke out into soft laughter as they nodded.

"Yeah, you did, but he only agreed because he thought you were going to kill him," Damian chuckled. "Hell, we all thought you were about to kill him. The aura radiating off you was nothing I had ever seen before."

"What are you talking about?"

I was being my normal self, and the fact they were saying I was something else didn't make sense. Taking a moment, I reflected and realized it must have been my eyes.

"Oh! Was it because my eyes are freaky looking?" I asked, turning to them but watching confusion flood James and Damian's faces.

"What are you talking about? There is nothing wrong with your eyes. They look as they always have," Damian stated, furrowing his brows.

"Wait... you two don't see it?" Talon asked, looking at Hale, who was just as dumbfounded.

"See what?" James questioned as he stood and walked toward me. "They look normal to me."

"Holy shit," Talon broke out into laughter. "It's because she is cloaking it. We can only see it normally because of—"

"Enough!" I roared, my shoulders heaving as I closed my eyes and took a deep breath. "I would appreciate it if everyone would simply be fucking clear when they speak. I'm sick and tired of all these fucking riddles all the damn time."

Opening my eyes, I stared at them all, and that was when I saw the shock on James and Damians' faces. "Oh, well, there ya go," Hale snipped out with a grin as he crossed his arms, getting comfortable.

Sighing, I shook my head, only to catch a glimpse in a decorative mirror of what they were seeing. My eyes were once again the iridescent color they had been before, but this time they were glowing.

"Great... so now when I'm pissed, they glow. That's fucking brilliant."

Insatiable Hunger

Hale

It's been two days since Ivy woke up, and every moment she was awake was a blessing. However, I couldn't help but be concerned that the changes in her were something to be worried about.

"I don't understand why you're worrying," Talon replied for the third time today as we sat listening to Ivy shower in the next room with James. Her moans of pleasure echoed from behind closed doors as he took her again for the second time in two days.

"Do you hear that?" I said, looking at Talon with wide eyes as a carnal roar traveled down the hall. "She is no longer the sweet girl we once knew. She has become something else."

Rolling his eyes, Talon continued stuffing his face. My brother's appetite was larger than I remembered it being before. I knew I should just be happy we were finally all together, but things just didn't add up.

"Sounds like they are going at it again," Damian said as he entered the kitchen.

"Yeah, you could say that. She has literally taken us all on since she woke up, and yet, her appetite for sex doesn't seem to be dying down."

"You act like that's a bad thing," Talon mumbled through a mouth full of food. "Don't fucking overthink this shit and ruin it. I waited too long to have her... we all have."

I didn't miss the glance Damian gave me as well. Both of them wanted me to let it go, but I couldn't. Something was far more different from what we could see, and perhaps it was time I had a talk with her.

"We are leaving early," Damian finally said, sighing as he lifted a glass of tea to his lips. "I'm not sure what's going to happen tomorrow, but I'm really worried about what Allison is going to try and pull."

"As am I," I pointed out firmly. "Why do you think I'm so concerned about this new version of her? If she is transitioning, then we need to be prepared, because she hasn't shifted yet... at least not completely. There is no telling what could happen if Allison pisses her off."

"Hale, you should give me more credit than that." A soft voice I knew all too well said from the doorway behind me.

Both Talon and Damian smirked at her comment, and slowly I turned to face her. She was still dripping wet from the shower, and James seemed almost exhausted behind her. "The fuck happened to you?" Talon laughed.

James side glanced looking at Ivy, and then his eyes widened as he shook his head, not saying anything. Through it all, though, she didn't keep her eyes off me. Instead, she seemed to look at me with a carnal hunger I wasn't expecting.

"Ivy... I hope you're feeling refreshed," I said, clearing my throat.

"I am... for now," she smirked as she walked closer to me. "Perhaps you can make sure I'm satisfied again later."

There it was again. The same hunger that should have been quenched from James and the others showed itself full force.

"Actually, before we talk about that, I wanted to see if we could clear a few things up."

Sighing, her iridescent eyes twinkled as she nodded her head and made her way toward the fridge. "Go ahead, Hale. Ask your questions."

"We don't have to do this right now," Damian interjected. "You have to be tired."

Laughter escaped her as she pulled out a few containers from the fridge and turned, placing them on the counter. "No, actually I'm not. So let's not be rude. If Hale wants to ask a few things, then why not?"

Watching her open the containers and stuffing food in her mouth should have been disgusting, but instead, it was a turn-on. Everything she did was tantalizing, and I wanted right then to fuck her till she screamed my name.

Clearing my throat again, I shook my head and tried to focus.

"So, as we know, you're changing into something else. Transitioning into—"

"Stop right there," she said, cutting me off with a smile.

"Stop what?" I asked, with confusion.

Shaking her head, she shook her finger and smirked, "I'm not changing..."

"What?" Damian and I said at the same time.

"Of course you are," James laughed. "You're definitely not the same girl you were before. Now you're a kinky sex deviant looking to devour my soul."

Talon and Ivy both burst into laughter at James' admission. He seemed so defeated by what they had done upstairs and being a wolf shifter, we are stronger than usual, but still, he was worn out.

"You weren't complaining in the shower." She smirked.

"Well... yeah, but that was because your sinful love taco was sucking my soul out of my dick. Fucking addictive ass pussy—" he mumbled, laying his head on the counter.

"Perhaps that's why she was given four mates," Damian questioned silently.

"I sure as hell hope so," James scoffed. "It's bomb ass pussy, don't get me wrong, Ivy. You're a fucking goddess in every way, but fuck me... I'm not that good."

I couldn't help but notice how Ivy sat silent as she watched the guys carry on with amusement in her eyes as if she was expecting this. James was right about her being different, almost godly.

"What are you?" I finally asked, watching her gaze snap to mine.

"I thought you would never ask, Hale," she said sweetly as she put her fork down and downed a bottle of water as if she was dying of thirst.

Waiting patiently, she let a sigh escape her lips, and slowly her smile fell. I wasn't sure what had happened to her when she was out, but she seemed to think everything over slowly, contemplating what she was going to say before she spoke.

"I'm not entirely sure what I am, and there is a lot I still have to learn. What I do know, though, is I'm not like any of you. Not exactly. You four are called the Ancients, whatever that means, but me... I'm Eternal."

There was silence amongst us while we took in what she said. Talon and I looked at each other with confusion as we turned to look at Damian and James.

'She said the four of us, but only you and I have the gene, right?' Talon asked me through the link.

'Yeah. Something is different with her. I know she is still Ivy, but what if the thing inside her is controlling her?' I replied, only to have Ivy pull us from our thoughts with a huff.

"Or perhaps the two of you will stop talking about me in the link being rude, and voice your thoughts on how you think this "thing" inside me is controlling me."

Shock filled me as I stared at her. "How did you–"

"There are no more secrets, Hale. I guess my new form of self has gifts, too."

Speechless, I didn't know what else to say. Every question I had I wanted to ask her flew out the window at that moment. She had abilities that shouldn't be normal. She was becoming something more… something different.

It terrified me in a way because if the elder council saw this, she would be a target.

The elder council would eliminate any threat they couldn't control.

Perhaps that was the whole reason Allison was bringing us there.

To get rid of Ivy.

Ivy

I didn't understand why Hale was so adamant to find fault in me as if I was unstable. I felt a million times better than I ever have, and after a long talk with my mom early in the day, I was feeling even better.

I hadn't told her about the changes, but she was happy to know the bond was complete and promised to come visit me in two months once she was one hundred percent better.

"Guys look. I know I'm different. I know that you're all concerned, but I promise you we will just have to figure it out one day at a time. I will be fine tomorrow. I will make sure before I leave to satisfy my needs and then take the meeting like a champ."

My eyes drifted to Talon and Damian with a smirk on my face.

"Oh thank fuck, Ivy. I need like two days to recover," James replied as he stood to his feet and came over, kissing me gently. "Can I go lay down and hibernate till we leave?"

Laughter escaped me at his dramatics. "I don't care. I will leave you be… for now."

The "for now" made his eyes fill with lust, but I knew he was tired.

Watching him leave, I turned my attention back to Hale. "All I know is that I'm Eternal. That I am supposed to be here for a reason, but I don't know what else."

It wasn't entirely true, but I figured I would tell them the truth when we got back tomorrow. I didn't want them worrying more about me going to the council because of certain... things.

"Fine," Hale finally said with reluctance. "I will go look into what it means to be Eternal."

The air quotations he used caused me to smile as he stood to his feet and made his way from the kitchen. Being left alone with Damian and Talon was tempting.

Both of them were known to be dangerous apart, but I couldn't help but wonder how they were together.

"I think I am going to go enjoy some fresh air," I said with a smile as I stood to my feet and walked toward the back door. Without even saying anything to them, I knew they would eventually follow.

The slowly setting sun brought forth the cold, and even though there was a chill outside, I myself wasn't cold at all. "Interesting..." I mumbled as I continued to press forward.

It wasn't until I stood at the edge of the treeline I felt I was meant to be there. An insatiable hunger coursed through me begging to be released. Closing my eyes, I inhaled deeply, catching the sweet scent of something in the distance.

"Ivy, don't," Talon quickly said, appearing at my side with Damian.

However, as I glanced at them, I felt something inside me snap. I took off running through the forest as fast as my feet would carry me. Branches and shrubs scratched against my bare skin as I picked upon the scent again.

Stopping at the bank of a creek, I spotted the large elk standing on the other side. His head bent grazing upon the grass without a clue he was in danger.

That wasn't what I wanted, though. I wanted to chase... I wanted its fear.

"Aren't you beautiful?" I said softly, watching as the elk's eyes darted up to me before bolting through the forest. The chase was on, and with a laugh, I almost didn't recognize, I pursued the creature, pushing myself faster and faster.

I was no longer thinking clearly. Instead, I was driven by an animalistic nature to feed. The hunger within me overtook any normal rationale, and as I lunged at the animal, it had no way of escaping me.

Blood drenched the front of me as I gorged, and when I came back to my senses, I looked up to see the eyes of Damian and Talon staring down at me.

There was worry within their gaze, but there was something else.

Lust and my hunger weren't yet satisfied.

Standing, I pulled my shirt over my head and stripped off my shorts. Their eyes never left mine as I quickly grabbed Damian and kissed him before placing my lips on Talon. "Don't be gentle," I purred, watching them almost break at my words.

There was no hesitation as Talon's eyes flashed with dark amusement as he shoved me to my knees. My mouth greedily sought their thick cocks as they stripped their clothing.

Two at a time, I rotated between sucking on their heads and then letting them fuck my mouth. "Fuck, your such a good little slut for us aren't you, Ivy," Damian all but groaned as he lay on the ground. "Get your ass over here and sit on my face while you suck his cock."

I didn't bother to argue. I did exactly as he said and lost myself in the pleasure as his tongue took hold of me.

Mouth parted over, Talon didn't hesitate to shove his full length inside me, fucking my mouth until I couldn't breathe and then letting me up to do it all over again.

The build-up was more than it had been before. Coated in blood, and being devoured by them brought something else out of me. Something almost primal, and as I screamed out in pleasure, I came undone.

It didn't last long though, as Talon picked me up, a thigh over each of his arms as he pressed me against a nearby tree and thrust inside me. He didn't seem to care for sharing with Damian, and as I looked over his shoulder, I saw Damian watching.

"Don't worry, I have another hole you can fill if you want..."

The invitation caught Damian by surprise, but as my gaze turned to Talon, he knew exactly what I meant. "You want to share?" the beast within him almost growled.

"I want to be filled, and Hale is inside. He is mine as well."

Talon's beast didn't argue, and spinning me around, I found my back against Damian's chest. Slowly, his finger probed at my puckered hole before his thick erection met with Talon's, and they both took me.

"Shit!" I screamed out, feeling Damian fill my backside, pressing against Talon's erection from my tight wet cunt. The movements caused my head to fall back as they simultaneously brought me to new erotic heights.

As Talon's knot slowly formed, I felt Damian still inside me before pulling out, allowing Talon to take me further until I was buried at his hilt. The orgasm he forced me to ride out had my claws dug deep into his skin as his lips took my own.

The touch and caresses between them both was something I never wanted to end.

The Idea of taking all four of them caused my mind to wander.

Perhaps being coated from head to toe in their cum would be an experience worth trying. For tonight, though, I had Damian and Talon to satisfy me.

Tomorrow, the council, and then from there the future.

Sanctum of Elders

Being new to the shifter lifestyle, I had never been to the Sanctum before. The home of the elder council, and the place of governing reign for the shifter community. I expected it to be something like the pentagon or even the white house.

Instead, though, it looked like a castle in the middle of nowhere that needed severe renovations, and something bright to take away from its gothic appeal.

I was all for the gothic looks, but this… seemed more run down.

"Are they poor or something?" I asked no one in particular as I looked out the window.

The guys all laughed as I turned my gaze to James, who was smiling.

"No, the outside looks like this for a reason. So no one comes in and they can carry on as they please," Hale replied, casting glances at Damian in the front seat.

"Ivy, when we get in here, I want you to stay close to one of us at all times," Damian said softly as he glanced at me through the rear-view mirror. "Please."

"Okay, okay. No wandering off. I got it." I chuckled as the car moved down the driveway and came to a slow stop.

Security was high in this place, and it took six security guards surrounding the car before we were able to get out and move toward entering the building.

"This is a little much," I said under my breath, causing Damian to give me a side glance that spoke volumes to how much I needed to stop talking. With a smirk though, I looked back at the twins, who were trying to contain their laughter as we walked up the steps toward the main door.

The doors swung open by two more guards as we entered through to a very elegant main foyer. I finally understood what they said before because the outside did not depict at all what the inside would look like. "Whoa..."

"Do you like it?" A voice called from the distance as I took note of a brunette walking toward us in an elegant pants suit. "I do love to see newcomers' reactions."

I wasn't sure who this woman was, but something about her didn't sit well with me. Perhaps it was her professional appearance or the fact she was wearing hot pink heels with a leopard print suit, but she wasn't someone I would confide in.

"It's definitely lovely. Thank you for having us," I replied, putting on my best Luna voice as I admired her choice of clothing. She must have gotten dressed in the dark.

"Yes, you must be Ivy. I have heard so much about you," she said with a smirk as she turned her attention to the guys at my side. Her smirk grew as she took them in.

Laughing to myself, I stepped forward, catching her attention with a smirk of my own.

"Yes, I am. And they're all mine. I was blessed with four mates."

The girl's smile slowly fell as she ran her tongue against her teeth, grinning. "Well, aren't you lucky? Right this way."

The clicking of her tacky heels against the tile floor was grating on my last nerve, but thankfully we didn't go far before we stopped outside large double doors where two older men stood in black robes, with three security guards.

I felt the confusion run through the men as they took in the sight before them, but gently touching Damian's arm, I was able to calm down the one who was stressed the most.

"Welcome, all," one of the men said firmly, with no expression on his face. "Thank you for being able to make it. I was sad to hear that you missed our last meeting due to a sick mate."

"Yes, well, I'm sure you know how hard it can be for new mates sometimes," I replied sweetly. "I'm feeling much better now, and I'm happy to help however you might need it."

It was a lie. I didn't trust these men, and even though he was looking at me with intrigue, I wasn't going to show him I actually was picking up on his behavior.

I had a feeling something was off, but it wasn't until the woman addressed me again that I realized they were really up to something.

"If you will follow me this way, Ivy. I'll show you to our waiting room while the men discuss business."

"Excuse me?" Talon snapped, looking toward the woman as he pulled me closer to him.

"Now, now," the older man replied. "It's okay, but we just can't have her in there for private meetings. It's for Lunas and Alphas only."

"She is our Luna," Damian replied. "What game are you playing at, Ralph?"

So that was his name. Talon's grip on my arm was tight and turning to him, I shook my head before slowly letting him kiss me.

"Yes," Ralph replied slyly. "She may be your mate, but she hasn't officially been made your Luna."

The growls from the men shook the room, and it was clear that the disrespect this man was trying to throw around wasn't going to go over well if he continued. It was obvious though he was doing this on purpose.

He was trying to get a rise out of the guys, and that was something I couldn't let happen. 'Enough.' I said through the link.

Their eyes turned toward me, and slowly I shook my head again. 'Do as they say.'

'Ivy, no.' Damian and Hale responded at the same time.

'Don't argue with me,' I replied, before turning my attention back to Ralph.

"Goodness, these men just don't like to let me out of their sight." I laughed, causing the others to let go of their tension and laugh as well.

"Of course, of course," Ralph replied. "She will be just waiting down the hall in the lounge area. There is nothing to worry about. It shouldn't take long."

Kissing each of them, I smiled, and they reluctantly let me go. I knew they were watching me, but I didn't want to look back. If I did, there was a chance I wouldn't be able to continue.

Because even though I was keeping myself together for show. I was slightly afraid. I was afraid that if something happened, I wouldn't get there in time, and I wouldn't know what to do if something happened to one of the guys.

Even thinking about that now made my heart race and my palms sweaty.

"Right in here, please," The woman replied, gesturing toward the open door.

"Thank you."

"Of course." She laughed. "Someone will be with you shortly."

As the door closed, I took in the surrounding room. There wasn't anything special about it, but it did have a flare to it that spoke volumes about whatever "woman" decorated the room.

The only reason why I said that is because the room literally said for the ladies of the packs and had a very feminine virtue to it.

However, I could be wrong. One of my best guy friends back in Georgia was gay, and he had better style than any woman or man I knew.

Thinking about him at that moment made me make a mental note to call him when I got home. He should have been getting ready to start his new job in Miami soon, and I couldn't wait to hear how it was going.

Walking around, I stared at the photos on the wall until a knock came on the door and I turned to see the one person I wasn't expecting to see—Priscilla, the seer.

"Priscilla?" I gasped with confusion. "What are you doing here?"

A twinkle of mischief in her eye caught my attention as she closed the door behind her. "Well, the same thing Kara is doing here, of course."

"Hello, Ivy," a voice said, causing me to spin around to see Kara standing behind me.

"How the fuck did you get here, and why is Priscilla here?"

I was more than confused. I was spooked out.

I hadn't been what I was for very long, and I was still getting used to everything, so to have Kara popping up like that was unexpected. Yet, watching them both take a seat, I felt that whatever they were here to say was important.

"We don't have much time dear, please sit down." Priscilla gestured toward the seat across from her.

I didn't bother to have her ask me a second time as I straightened out my dress, and sat down across from her, waiting for them to explain what they were doing here.

"You are growing just as beautiful as I expected you would." Priscilla smiled as Kara watched on. "I was hoping that things wouldn't go as they are now with the council, but it is still falling in line with prior visions."

"I don't understand what you mean," I replied, shaking my head. "You knew that I was going to do this?"

"Of course I did." She laughed. "But before I get to me, you need to listen to what Kara tells you. There has been something to happen you will need to be careful of."

"She is right," Kara replied with a sad smile. "There has been an issue to occur, and unfortunately one of our own is down here causing issues."

"Issues?" I asked blankly. "Can't you guys like... do something about it? I don't know why you're telling me—"

"Well, I'm telling you because you're going to be affected," Kara replied. Her eyes displayed more emotions than I had seen before and shaking my head, I tried to wrap my head around how she was even here.

"How the hell did you get in here?" I asked, looking around for a secret door.

"I'm a celestial, Ivy. I can go where I want."

"So, I can pop in and out too?" I asked with excitement, thinking of all the places I would go with that kind of power.

"No. You're not. You may be a celestial descendent, but you are different. It's complicated," she replied with amusement.

"That sucks." Something like that really could have come in handy.

"Ivy, I came to warn you to be careful. This person isn't to be trusted, and if he gets his way, there could be drastic changes for the future of you and your mates."

Looking at Kara and Priscilla, I couldn't help but feel that something was wrong. How was I supposed to protect people I cared about if I had no idea what I was up against?

Before either of them could say another thing, I felt something come over me that didn't seem right. A wave of uneasiness that seemed to start out slowly, and slowly begin to grow. "Something's wrong..."

"Yes, you need to go to them, Ivy," Priscilla said softly, catching my attention. She was a strange individual with an aura around her that was familiar, yet made me question the faith I could put in her.

"Will I be able to take on what's coming?" I asked her, wanting some kind of verification that my future with the guys would be okay. Hoping that I wasn't going to lose them when I only just got them.

"I can't tell you what will happen that far. There is no use in changing fate, only you will be able to determine how your future goes. However, I will tell you to listen to the voice inside you. It will guide you in the direction you need to go."

Once again, a cryptic message that gave me no answer. At the same time, though, I was well aware that I was more than just some human girl who didn't know how to protect herself. Completely the bond with the guys gave me an edge.

Moving toward the door, I hesitated for a moment, looking back at them once again. Only this time Kara was gone, and Priscilla stared at me with a content smile.

"Thank you for everything." I whispered, watching her nod her head.

Something was wrong with the guys, and my mood quickly changed when I left the room. I would go on a warpath for them, and it was the last thing any of them wanted me to do.

Rise of a Luna

Damian

I should have known that coming here was going to be a problem. The fact that they were so adamant on us bringing Ivy it should have thrown a red flag, and I should have resisted. She was still in a fragile place, and far more unpredictable than I liked.

So the moment she walked off down the hall, I couldn't take my eyes off her, and neither could my brothers. What if this was the last time we saw her?

'I will kill them all if they touch her.' Talon says to the rest of us through our link.

'Ditto,' Hale and James replied.

I knew they would keep to their word as well. They would rip everyone apart, and the twins losing themselves wouldn't be good. No one knew what they were. Not even Allison knew the exact truth.

It was something we tried to hide as much as we could. No matter how much she tried to pry into our personal lives.

'Just keep a level head. She will be fine.'

My reply to them was forced. I wasn't sure she would be alright at all. However, as the doors to the council room opened, it was clear that this meeting was anything but nice.

Walking in with my brothers at my side, I watched the elder men sitting ahead of us in their high-placed brown seats. Guards lined the walls in the room, and a sense of hostility floated through the air.

I should have been worried, but staring at the elder who came to my house, I wasn't.

"Afternoon, gentleman. Shall we begin?" My response to them was one an Alpha would give. I found the best approach was to remain stoic, but through it all, I wasn't sure if they would react well.

"Damian. You and your brothers are brought before this court because you are accused of not properly running your back, and bringing light to humans about our kind. On top of that, it's known that there are rumors of false claims to the Luna position by someone who isn't even your mate, but instead, a human falsely claimed."

Shock and anger flowed through me at his words. Was this really what Allison was telling them? "That's all false."

The main elder Sir Edgar looked up at me from his papers and raised a brow. "Is it?"

"Yes, it is. I'm not sure who is telling you these things, but all of it is lies," I replied, seething. I could feel my brothers also in anger, but they knew better than to say anything. I needed to address the problems, considering I was Alpha.

"Bring forth the witnesses," Edgar replied as a side door opened, bringing forth Ivy's father, Zane, and Allison, my godmother.

"What the hell are they doing here?" I asked Edgar, with confusion. This meeting was supposed to be about private matters, and to have Allison and Zane here in a private meeting was not protocol.

"They are witnesses for the trial. They have a place here," Edgar replied with a smirk.

"Trial?!" I exclaimed as my brothers growled. "What trial? This is supposed to be a private meeting to discuss issues, not a trial."

"Unfortunately, you were told wrong. You're on trial, Damian, and if you and your brothers don't get yourselves together, you will be put down."

The way he said 'put down' sounded like he was addressing a dog at the pound. Even though this could be the equivalent. "This is bullshit, Ed. I did nothing wrong."

Edgar sighed in a dismissive manner as he turned his attention to Allison and Zane.

"Did you not give a written statement to us that they took a human against her will and forced her to mate with them even though there was no bond?"

Allison stared at me with a fake sorrowful glance and nodded. "Yes, her name was Ivy. The poor girl didn't stand a chance against them, but please... go easy. They are still suffering from the loss of their mother."

"Are you fucking kidding me!" Hale yelled as he and Talon grew angrier. "She is fucking lying! She hates Ivy, and she tried to kill her!"

"Enough!" Edgar yelled, his voice booming against the walls. "I will have order in my courtroom!"

The four of us grew silent as we heaved with anger, trying to figure out what was going to happen next. I wanted to scream and yell, but knowing that Ivy was down the hall alone and unprotected forced me to follow Edgar's rules.

"Zane," Edgar finally said, letting out a heavy breath as his glance slid from me to Zane. "Can you please state who you are for the courtroom?"

"Yes, I am Zane Thorne. Ivy Thorne's father," he said softly.

"Very good, and Zane. Can you tell us what happened to your daughter?" Edgar asked, looking over papers and glancing back up at Zane.

"Yes. After my daughter graduated, Damian caught a glimpse of her scent and saw a photo of her. He wanted her more than anything, but I told him I wouldn't allow it. When she came to stay with me for school, he roped his brother into forcefully taking her. This way he would have control over me and steal my company."

The fucking bastard! I groaned internally. I was going to kill this fucking bastard once I got a hold of him. He was more a liar than Allison, and the fact these elders actually believed the shit was a bigger problem.

'We are going to have to get out of here.' James said through our link, panicking.

'Just calm down. Everything will be okay. No one does anything.' I told them not wanting them to make a break and make themselves look guilty.

We had done nothing wrong. Allison and Zane were only showing their true colors, and I was going to make them pay for their lies.

"If I may say something," I called out, watching all eyes turn to me. "They—"

"You may not speak, Damian," The elder snapped, cutting me off. "We have heard enough from you and your brothers. Guards, take them into custody."

Shock filled me as the guards came toward us. My brothers fought against the restraints they put upon us. Silver and chaos clouded the area, and roars of defiance spread through the room.

There was no way we were going to go down and leave Ivy.

"Get off me!" I growled, throwing a man to the side as silver chains were wrapped around my neck and arms, slowly pulling me to the ground.

"I have every right to kill this one," Zane said through clenched teeth as he stepped in front of me, his eyes glaring down at my form knelt upon the tile flooring.

"Yes, well, I suppose that would only be fair," Edgar replied, causing my eyes to open wide as Zane raised his hand to kill me.

The only problem was the blow never came.

Ivy

Bursting through the doors, I felt the chaos consuming my mates. I couldn't believe my eyes. My father stood there with Allison, and even though I didn't know what was going on, I saw my father about to strike Damian, and my blood ran cold.

With a rush I never felt before, I charged forward and plunged my hand into his chest, watching as his eyes met mine with shock I had never seen in him.

"You broke my heart the day you betrayed me. Let me repay the favor."

In one swift motion, I tore his heart from his chest and watched his body drop to the floor. My eyes stared down at him, but no remorse filled me.

Instead, I enjoyed watching the blood seep from his body as the life left his eyes. I wasn't sure if this new feeling in me was good, but at the same time, I felt victorious.

The same hunger that filled me rose, and as my eyes darted toward the elder council, I tilted my head and let a sadistic grin cross my face.

"Let them go unless you want the same fate as my father."

"What is this!" one of the men yelled, standing to his feet. "Murderer! Cease her!"

Two guards rushed at me with silver chains, and before they could get close, I had killed them both. "If you men know what's good for you, you will unhand my mates and step back. I will not hesitate to kill you all."

Allison's screams echoed around me as she stared at my father's lifeless body. Her pain filled me with joy as my eyes turned toward her. I had killed her mate, and at the end of the day, I considered it a paid debt for what she did to Talon.

"You fucking bitch! I should have killed you when I had the chance!" she roared, charging at me only to be met with my claws at her throat.

"You did try to kill me, Allison. After you tried to kill Talon, consider this us being even."

She struggled beneath me as I looked toward the guards standing to the side with shock on their faces. None of them knew what to do, but at the same time, none of them had seen someone like me.

"Take her into custody now," I ordered them. Without hesitation, they complied and grabbed her, holding her in chains as I turned my attention to the council. "I am not sure what they have told you, but I want to know what right you have to take my mates."

"Who are you?" another man asked with confusion as hushed murmurs of agreement echoed around them.

"My apologies," I replied, looking down at myself and quickly wiping my hands. "I'm Ivy Thorne. You are already familiar with my father."

Gesturing at my father's dead body, I saw a look on the men's faces that was one of confusion. "You're supposed to be human."

"Ah, yes." I laughed. "Please let go of my mates now, and I will gladly explain. It seems that some of your guards aren't too sure who to listen to, and I promise you that adhering to my demands would be wise."

There was hesitation between them all, but eventually, the man at the head of the elder table nodded at the guards behind me. Turning, I watched them remove the chains of silver and slowly back away from where the guys were on the floor.

"Please continue," The man exclaimed with anger, causing my attention to turn back to where they sat. Staring at him, I was curious to know whether he had been a part of this conspiracy to attack my mates.

It didn't make sense why there was this sudden harsh treatment unless it had been planned. "I'm not human. Even though I will admit I thought I was for a long time."

"So, what are you?"

The questions the men were asking didn't feel right. Something inside me told me not to tell them, and with a smile, I remembered what Priscilla said and decided against it.

"I'm a shifter, just like them," I said softly. "I'm simply newer than most, and my father lying to you all and causing my mates to be hurt caught me off guard."

"What do you mean, he lied to us?" a woman asked, who had been quiet the entire time the commotion had been going on. "Please explain everything."

"Of course, I would love to."

"Don't listen to this scandalous bitch!" Allison screamed as she struggled against the men holding her. "She is a liar!"

"Shame on you, Allison. It isn't very ladylike to act the way you are." I taunted with a smile. "Honestly, council... Allison is a very sick woman. She has delusions that have been plaguing her. However, she did try to commit murder by giving Talon BellaDonna for the past few months. This can be confirmed by our pack doctors."

"Bella Donna?" They gasped. "How are you sure it was her?"

"Because if she killed one of them, then they couldn't complete the circle with me, and he was the only one that wasn't of value to her." I smirked, watching the admission rise in her eyes.

She knew exactly what I was talking about, and watching her realize that brought me great pleasure. She wouldn't win this war with me.

Yes, I could easily kill her right now. However, making an example out of her seemed so much sweeter. "Your honors, I ask that you reprimand her for execution. An attack on an Alpha or Luna demands payment by blood."

"Who are you to order that?" The main elder asks with a scoff. His attitude toward the situation wasn't surprising. I was, in a way, taunting his power and forcing him to do something he obviously didn't want to comply with.

"If you don't, then others will think they can do whatever they want without you having any power. Wouldn't it seem better to make an example out of her so that the elder council isn't questioned?"

Hesitation again filled the room, and as the elders stared at me, I could almost see the clocks ticking in their heads.

"What about you then? You made a spectacle here. What makes us believe you aren't going to do something to overthrow us?"

Laughter escaped me as I felt the guys come to stand around me protectively.

"Your honor, if I wanted to overthrow you... I would have done it by now."

Starting a New Adventure

They say that when you die, there are no second chances. That no matter what life has thrown at you, the end is the end. That fate was supposed to be predetermined, and no matter how hard people work, it won't matter if the gods decided for you.

I refused to believe that, though.

There was no way I was going to let anyone determine who I was going to be, even if I was something that no one had ever seen before.

The elder council sat before with confusion on their face and fear in their eyes. They feared me, as most of those in the room were scared of me.

"All those in favor of letting Luna and her mates go. Raise your hand."

It was a unanimous vote amongst the terrified people in front of me that made my heart swell. They were more than happy to let us go, but glancing at Damian, I couldn't ignore the worried look in his eyes.

"Thank you." As I let my eyes drift toward the council again, I said with confidence, "I hope for nothing but peace between us. I simply want to live my life with my mates."

"Then go." The elder in the front spoke up. "Go live with your mates as the shifter you have become. The rest will be dealt with accordingly."

I wasn't sure what he meant by that, but Hale and Talon gently nudged me toward the double doors of the room to live.

It wasn't until we made it outside and safely back into the car that Damian spoke up. "We have a problem."

"Damian, not now," Hale interjected, trying to change the subject. I hated how they constantly tried not to speak about business around me. There were things I needed to know if I was going to be their Luna, and one of those was if there was to be an issue.

"Do you think they are going to come after me?"

They all recognized my whispered response, and with a heavy sigh, Damian nodded. "Perhaps. You didn't shift like before, but you showed them you were gifted far more than regular shifters.

"I was trying to control myself," I mumbled, slouching into the seat as the car sped from the driveway and headed back toward the pack house.

All of this was hard for me. I wasn't meant for this kind of life, and on more than one occasion, I should have shut up and listened to what was being said to me.

"Do you think I went too far?" The question was one that brought silence throughout the car, and with the silence, I had my answer.

There was a way for me to act, and there was a way for me not to.

All of which was shit I still had to learn, and it was what would help me grow to be who I was supposed to be. I just wish I didn't have to wait so long for that to happen.

"In time, things will get easier, Ivy." James smiled from the front seat. "When we get home, we can relax, and then we need to figure things out. That is only going to work if you're completely honest with us.

Honesty.

The idea of telling the guys everything that has been going on made me feel crazy. How was I supposed to tell them about goddesses, and the heavens, or anything like that?

How was I supposed to admit even though I seemed calm and collected, I was terrified of what was happening to me?

There were so many questions and not enough time to find out the truth.

At least not enough time, in my opinion.

By the time we arrived back at the house, we were all exhausted from everything that had happened. The guys, now healed from their wounds, trudged through the front door and made their way upstairs.

All but Damian.

Instead, he lingered toward his office and, biting my bottom lip, I followed him. I didn't know what to say about everything, but I felt in that moment I disappointed him.

"I'm sorry, Damian."

His eyes met mine briefly, and shaking his head, he turned his attention away again. "There is no need to apologize, Ivy. You were following your instincts."

"I was, but I also wasn't," I replied, watching as he furrowed his brows and stared at me again.

"What do you mean?" he asked.

Letting out a heavy breath, I sighed. "I wasn't just protecting you. I was trying to strike fear in the others. I didn't want them to think they could hurt us and get away with it."

Damian stared at me blankly for a moment before a smile crossed his face.

"More and more every day, you impress me, Ivy. I'm sorry that I don't show you enough how amazing you are. You deserve better than what I have given you."

I was shocked at his admission because he had never really said anything to me like that before. "Thank you," I whispered, watching him with curiosity.

"No, thanks are needed. I mean it when I say you deserve better," he replied.

"Well, fate has paired me with you and the boys, so here is where I will spend the rest of my life, and you know what?" I said with a smile.

"What's that?" he asked, stepping closer to me.

"I don't regret a thing." I smirked as he wrapped his arms around my waist, "except maybe I should have smacked you around in the beginning and made you realize how silly you were acting."

A deep chuckle left his throat as he leaned down and kissed me gently. "You know what there is left to do now, right?"

"What's that, Damian?" I smirked, thinking that the situation was going to head toward a more sexually natured situation.

"You need to have your Luna ceremony."

The words that left his lips took me by surprise. I had read about what a Luna ceremony was but never had I considered having my own. Things had been so chaotic lately that a Luna's ceremony never even crossed my mind.

"I can have one of those?" I asked, not thinking about what I was saying. My question caused him to laugh as he nodded.

"Yes, of course, you can. James has actually been talking about it for a while, and he wanted to help plan it out for you. Not sure why, but he does have a better smile than anyone else I know."

"Are you talking about me again?" James groaned, fresh from the shower as he plopped down on the seat in Damian's office.

"He said you want to plan my Luna Ceremony..." I replied, looking at James with a smile who blushed at the statement.

"I mean... if you want me to. Of course, I'm sure you know what you want–"

"James, stop." I laughed before pulling away from Damian and crawling onto James' lap. "I would love for you to plan it. I honestly know nothing about it, and it would seem so much more special if you put your heart and soul into making it special for me."

Leaning down, I kissed him gently, making him smile.

"You're amazing, Ivy," he whispered against my lips, "I'm so proud of you for what you did at the sanctum. How did you know?"

Staring at him for a moment, I shrugged my shoulders, "I felt you. Your pain and your fear. I felt all of you."

Damian and James looked at each other with furrowed brows before turning their gaze back to me. I wasn't sure why it was weird considering we already established I was like them, or at least was sort of like them.

"Is that bad?" I asked, breaking the silence.

"No, not at all. It's just we still don't know much about you and what you can do. So until we figure it out, we will just be surprised." Damian replied, easing my worry.

"So, when do we do this ceremony?" I asked, changing the subject. "Do we have to wait for a special time or something?"

James' chuckled, kissing the side of my face. "Don't you worry about that. I will take care of everything."

Two weeks passed without any issues. I was surprised at how easily we fell into step with each other, and how normal it felt. Normal wasn't something that I thought I would ever feel again, and yet here I was, having the most normal relationship I had ever experienced.

"Are you sure about this?" I asked Kate as I stared at myself in the mirror.

My hair was curled to perfection and hung in loose curls over my shoulders. My iridescent eyes were highlighted in a smoky styled makeup and, to accent the look, Kate insisted on the deep blood-red lipstick I had stashed away for seductive situations.

I wasn't sure that this was what a Luna would wear to her Luna ceremony, but Kate assured me I wasn't any kind of Luna.

The tight white corset top dress was seen through and held left nothing to the imagination. Even the high slit that went up to my hip made everything about my appearance scream sex, and in the end, that was what I was hoping for.

To be ravished by four men all at once and fall into absolute bliss.

"Are you nervous? Kate asked, breaking me from my dirty thoughts and back toward the present where the clock was ticking closer to the hour I would be crowned.

"Surprisingly, no. I thought I would be nervous, but in all honesty, I'm not. I feel empowered, and I'm not sure if that's because of what's going to happen or the full moon rising in the sky. Either way, I'm ready."

Kate smirked as she stepped toward me with a black velvet box with a red bow. "Speaking on crowns... here. An early gift."

Looking down at the box, I shook my head, "Kate, you didn't have to."

"Oh, it's not from me. It's actually from your mother."

"My mother?" I asked hesitantly as I opened the box and peeled back the tissue paper to reveal the most beautiful piece of jewelry I had ever laid my eyes on. "Oh, wow."

"No kidding," Kate exclaimed as I pulled it out, admiring the crown.

It was as silver as the moon, with crystal teardrop jewels hanging against the metal that moved gently. Within the middle of the crown, though, was a round stone that shimmered in the light. I had never seen a stone like it in my life, and when I touched it, I felt something.

"What kind of stone is this?" I asked Kate, her eyes furrowing before she shrugged her shoulders.

"Who knows, but let's get it on because we have to get going soon."

Nodding my head, I shook the thought of the stone from my mind and turned back to the mirror, watching Kate place it upon my head. "It's beautiful."

"It is... but time is up. We have to get going." She laughed as she walked toward the door, and I let out a deep breath of excitement.

Step after step, I walked down the flower trail James had made for me. Candles lined the dark walkway as the moon shone brightly in the sky. Every pack member was present, and even some who weren't a part of our pack.

Kate had explained to me that when the blood bond was completed in ritual with my mates, I would be linked to the rest of the pack. I wasn't sure what that meant, but I did know that I would be able to mind link them all.

As exciting as that sounded, I was worried. Would they also be linked to me in other ways? If they were, would that affect them? I wasn't a normal shifter, after all.

"Welcome, everyone!" Damian said loudly, his voice echoing through the night as I stepped before the stage that had been built. "Tonight, we bring in a new era. One with the Luna of this pack, who is the goddess proclaimed fated mate to me and my brothers. Would you please join us, Ivy?"

Four sets of eyes looked down at me, and with a smile, I took his outstretched hand and walked up the steps. Their eyes looked at me with lust, and as I turned to face the pack members that scattered about in the hundreds, I felt pride in this moment.

I would be a proclaimed mother to them all, and with it came great honor.

Even if I was still new to this and had a lot to learn.

A high priest stepped forward without hesitation, holding a silver blade dripping with blue and yellow jewels. Gesturing for my hand, I held it out, and in a swift motion, he cut my palm and those of my mates.

"With the blood, we combine the souls of the mates with the souls of the pack."

His words were a blur as we dropped our blood into a chalice and then were instructed to drink from it. Each of the guys went first, and as the chalice was handed to me, I hesitated.

It was now or never. Lifting it to my lips, I drained the rest of the contents, and a flicker of power surged through me, causing my eyes to shoot open and the cup to drop from my hands.

Every wolf in front of me howled out as if in pain. My heart raced as I looked at the guy who was just as confused. The only problem was there was no sign of pain upon their faces but instead one of adrenaline.

"What's going on?" I asked softly, staring at the pack members who celebrated the event—their howls of delight and glee for their new luna echoing through the air.

"It seems that whatever power you possess, Luna has energized that of your pack." The priest said softly, causing me to look at my mates again.

"Is this a bad thing?"

The guys laughed as Talon pulled me close and kissed the side of my head.

"Only for anyone who tries to go against us. It seems sealing you as our Luna has made us more powerful than anyone could have imagined."

"He's right," a voice called from below where I stood.

Looking down, I spotted Priscilla, whose smile spread across her face in delight.

"Priscilla... what are you doing here?" I didn't understand how she kept popping up at the oddest of times, but I was thankful to see her. There were still so many questions I wanted to ask.

"I came because you need me, my dear." She smiled as I stepped down from the stage and took her hand.

"I'm ready to listen to what they have to say. I should have before—"

"Now, now. There is no need for that." She chuckled, looking at the men who followed behind me. "There is plenty of time to learn what you must. That is why I'm here. The gods have shown me a path, and over the next year, my guidance will be everything."

"What's going to happen?" I asked curiously, trying to understand the never-ending riddles that this woman constantly spewed.

"Well, for one–" she said, casting her gaze down at my stomach. "Would you like to know why you're always hungry?"

Furrowing my brows, I tried to understand what she meant, but Hale beat me to it.

"Oh, shit," he gasped. Turning to face him, I saw his wide-eyed expression as his gaze traveled to my stomach. "It makes so much more sense now."

"What does?" I asked curiously, "What makes sense?"

"Ivy, you're pregnant," Hale replied, causing the others to go silent.

Spinning to face Priscilla, I laughed, shaking my head. "No, I'm not. That's not—I mean we—"

Thinking over it, I could formulate words to come up with a reason for the way I had been acting. The uncontrollable hunger. The immense sexual urges. My personality flips at the drop of a dime, and I'm always crying.

"Oh, fuck me..." I murmured. "I'm fucking pregnant."

There was no telling where our future would go, but this was definitely a new adventure. One that I was happy to take as long as I had my mates by my side. Anything was possible with them, and no matter what the future threw at us, I had confidence we could beat it all.

I, Ivy Thorne, may have started out as a simple college girl from Georgia. But now, I was a Luna, descendant from an ancient pack that hailed from the celestials. A goddess among men and a protector of my people.

Fate be damned, I would show the world who I was to protect the ones I love.

The end.

Prequel to Book Two

Three months after the claim

Ivy

Three months. That's all it had been, and yet life couldn't get any better. Sure, things were different now, but that was to be expected, right? Wrong. God, how stupid could I be to think everything was normal?

One moment I'm a normal college student expecting to go to a new place and finish my degree. The next, I'm some fucking goddess shifter thingy, and my life is being turned upside down by four men who are amazing, but also very fucking annoying.

"Damn it, James!" I screamed from the kitchen as I stood with the refrigerator door opened, searching for the Snickers I knew I had hid in there. "Did you eat my fucking candy bar?"

Laughter erupted from the living room, and I had no doubt it was the twins finding my hormonal cravings to be the center of their amusement.

Did I find it funny, though? Of course I didn't and if one of them didn't produce a fucking Snickers bar in the next five seconds, someone was going to get their ass beat.

"Calm down," James sighed, rushing into the kitchen with a smile on his face. "I just put it in a safe place so it didn't get lost behind all the groceries I went and got."

Watching, he reached into the fridge and pulled out a small pink container with the words 'Ivy's shit' on the top of it. The small sentiment was enough to bring tears to my eyes James quickly hugged me for.

"Please don't cry," he whispered, not wanting to get yelled at by Damian again for bringing me to tears.

Since I found out I was pregnant, I had started going through weird changes. One minute I was happy, and the next, I was crying. You would think it was only me that would be going through these changes, right? Wrong again.

It seemed my mates were each having their own version of sympathy pregnancy symptoms, and on more than one occasion, Damian had to feel the wrath of my sadness.

Which in turn made him start crying, and we all know... Damian isn't that kind of man.

"It's just sweet," I said, forcing back the tears as he opened the container and handed me the Snickers. "Just next time, tell me."

"Of course, sweetie. How are you feeling today?" he asked, and a sigh escaped me.

"Like a freakish monster carrying children who could potentially destroy the world."

Rolling his eyes, he shook his head, "I don't know why you keep saying that."

"Uh–maybe because that's what everyone thinks." I shrugged my shoulders.

"Not everyone thinks that," he groaned. "All that was said is we have no idea what traits will be passed down."

"Uh–and that you're worried about what could happen. Come on now, I'm not stupid and I can read between the lines, James."

He couldn't argue with me there. The more and more they tried to sugar coat shit with me, the more annoyed I became. I just wanted the truth when it came to shit and over the past few months, they had gotten better at telling me things.

Yet, part of me still couldn't help but wonder if what I was doing was right.

I was the Luna of the pack. The matriarch and mother to all... or so I was told.

Yet, everyone seemed afraid of me in a way and I couldn't understand why. I had never given them a reason to fear me and with everything that was going on now with the pregnancy, I didn't want to be looked at differently.

"Look, you just have to give things time. I mean, look at Rosa. She was a little unsure of you at first, but now you guys are like BFFs." He said, crossing his arms over his chest.

"James, she is the midwife. Of course, we fucking get a long." I turned from the kitchen and made my way towards the living room.

I knew he was just trying to be helpful, but in all honest—he fucking wasn't.

I had to face facts. I'm a freak with unknown supposed powers, and every day I sit here, I find myself to the point of losing my mind. "I need a hobby."

"You have one, gorgeous," Hale commented, putting down his book as he made room for me next to him on the sofa.

"Oh yeah, what's that?" I said in a flat tone while stuffing into the delicious chocolate treat I had been craving for the past few days.

"Us, of course."

Smacking him on the leg, he, James, and Talon broke out into a fit of laughter. "Just because my sex drive is through the roof doesn't mean it's a hobby."

"True, but it's a great way to stay in shape." Talon pointed out as he scrolled through his phone. "I mean, look at me... I haven't been in better shape in a long time."

"I'm being serious guys," I groaned in frustration. "I think I want to start going back to school. I need something to focus on, and I can't just sit around here forever."

All three of them fell silent at my statement. Damian and I had spoken about it before, but every time we did, he always shot it down.

Not long after I went to enroll again, people started asking questions about Caleb. The guys had formulated something that made it look like he just moved out of town, but the friends he left behind questioned it all.

They were humans, and it wasn't like we could tell them what really happened. Humans weren't supposed to know our kind existed.

"You know what Damian said," Hale sighed, shaking his head. "He isn't going to allow it... at least not right now."

"That isn't fair, Hale. I want something to do, and there is only so much learning I can take with Priscilla. I love her to death, but if I have to sit through one more meditation session with her, I'm going to scream."

"What's going to make you scream?" Damian said as his voice drifted in from the front door.

Jumping from my seat, I skipped towards him and wrapped my arms around his neck. He had been gone for the past week, and I was glad to see him home.

Business overseas hadn't been going the way he liked and now that the drama was over, he had taken his roll back within the company on a more serious note.

"You're back," I smiled, kissing him gently. "Welcome home."

He smiled down at me, pulling me into his arms before letting his hand rub against my stomach. Things between Damian and I had gotten entirely better since my Luna ceremony and finding out that I was pregnant.

Instead of the cold, demanding and asshole-ish person who he was—he became an Alpha everyone respected.

We had all agreed after the ceremony he was still going to be Alpha. With him taking that position, Talon and James took over training, and making sure the borders were protected.

Hale, on the other hand, worked more with me. He helped out tremendously in the pack hospital and on more than one occasion; I had told him he should have become a doctor. It just wasn't what he wanted to do, though.

Instead, he managed the pack hospital and oversaw the pack school.

There was an intelligence about him that stumped even me, and with everything else going on, I was glad to know I had them close.

"I want to go back to school, Damian," I whispered softly. "The guys even agree.. don't you?" The glare I gave them had their eyes wide and their mouths parted.

"I mean—"

"Uh—well..."

"I didn't say shit," Talon finally piped up as a gasp left my lips.

"Talon, seriously?" I asked in disbelief.

Standing to his feet, he shook his head, "look, honestly, I don't think it's safe. Especially considering you're pregnant. Outside of the pack territory, I can't keep you protected like I can when you're in it. Your pregnancy isn't a secret anymore, and everyone now knows about what happened at Sanctum. Who knows who wants you..."

I knew he was right, but I couldn't believe he would be so against it. It was like even though my life had become amazing. I was a prisoner.

Fear enveloped those who didn't understand something, and with me, there was so much people didn't understand. Every day, though, I tried to help people see I was normal.

It just wasn't always possible.

"I will be safe," I begged, looking at Damian with the biggest puppy dog eyes I could put on. "Please let me... I mean, technically

I don't have to ask permission, but I'm trying to have you agree and be supportive."

"Look," Damian sighed. "I will agree that you can go back to school, but I would prefer it be after the baby is born. Can you at least agree with that?"

It wasn't the answer I was hoping for, but understanding his concerns, I smiled.

"Okay, deal." I replied, leaning up to kiss him.

In the end, I won the situation somewhat. Now the only thing left to happen was to get through the rest of this pregnancy in one piece, and pray nothing crazy happens with my pregnancy.

The last thing I wanted was to turn into a Godzilla wife, because honestly, that would be my luck. I would have something insane happen, and then watch... the world would literally depend on something completely bizarre.

Like the last piece of pizza that always seemed to disappear when I try to save it.

Life wasn't easy, that was for sure, but as long as I had my guys, anything was possible.

"Ivy!" Priscilla called from the front door as she walked in behind Damian. "Oh, Damian, you're back!"

"Yes, it's lovely to see you again, Priscilla. I hope those classes for Ivy are coming along well?"

"Yes, they are, but she still has a long way to go." She turned her gaze to me and smiled. "Are you ready?"

"Yeah, as long as this baby lets me actually get some peace." I giggled, rubbing my hand over my small protruding bump.

"Don't you mean babies?" Priscilla said with a grin, causing my eyes to widen.

"You're fucking joking..."

"Twins!" Hale laughed. "I fucking knew it!"

"You don't know shit, Hale." I scolded as I watched James and Talon fork money from their wallets and handing it to Hale. "I haven't even gotten the ultrasound done yet. Don't count your chickens yet."

I knew what Priscilla said was true. Over the past month, I wondered if it was two, and something inside me told me it was. I just had been avoiding the ultrasound for this particular reason.

How the hell was I going to deal with Twins?

Oh, wait.. I have two grown ass one's standing in the living room. Goddess, help me.

Lightning Source UK Ltd.
Milton Keynes UK
UKHW020744270123
416054UK00013B/1528

"Sometimes being bad is a good thing."

"You don't belong here."

"Perhaps to you I don't, but I'm not going anywhere," I replied, unwilling to let him scare me.

A deep chuckle left his throat as he stepped closer. "I can do terrible things to you."

The sultry sound of his voice wrapped around me and pulled me in. I knew I was playing with fire, but this was a life I couldn't just run from. Damian and his brothers were a mysterious sort, and every moment with them, they had me begging for pleasure.

~~~~~~~

When Ivy Thorne got accepted to one of the best Universities for Agriculture, she refused to miss the opportunity. The only problem she never expected was the four shifters who lived in her father's home would gradually turn her world upside down.

Dangerous things don't live just in the wild. Often, they lurked closer to home and if she wasn't careful, she would find herself the center of their hunger.

Little Red thrown into a world of wolves.

ISBN 979-8-88796-754-7
9 798887 967547

Parental Guidance Advised.
18+ Mature Guidance Only
~~~~~~~